# Dramatis
# Sourcebook

## 1995–96 EDITION

# Dramatists Sourcebook

### 1995-96 Edition

Complete opportunities for
playwrights, translators, composers,
lyricists and librettists

**EDITED BY**
**Linda MacColl**
**Kathy Sova**
**Wendy Weiner**

**Theatre Communications Group • New York**

Published by Theatre Communications Group, Inc.
355 Lexington Ave., New York, NY 10017-0217

Manufactured in the United States of America

ISSN 0733-1606
ISBN 1-55936-111-5

---

Theatre Communications Group gratefully acknowledges the support of
The Andrew W. Mellon Foundation for this edition of *Dramatists Sourcebook*.
Additional funding is provided by the National Endowment for the Arts
and New York State Council on the Arts.

---

# Contents

Preface                                                                    vii

**Prologue**                                                                ix
A Simple Working Guide for Playwrights
*by Tony Kushner*


**1: Script Opportunities**                                                 1

Production                                                                   3

Prizes                                                                      69

Publication                                                               112

Development                                                               130

**2: Career Opportunities**       **157**

Agents       159

Fellowships and Grants       164

Emergency Funds       183

State Arts Agencies       185

Colonies and Residencies       192

Membership and Service Organizations       206

**Epilogue**       **243**

Useful Publications       245

Submission Calendar       250

Special Interests       260

Index       276

# Preface

A year ago in these pages we waxed hopeful about an improving economic and political climate for the arts. Unfortunately, recent federal elections do not augur well for government arts funding. Nevertheless, *Dramatists Sourcebook* once again demonstrates the remarkable range of support available to foster and encourage playwrights and playwriting. The 1995–96 *Sourcebook* includes more than 850 opportunities for playwrights, from production and publication to development, funding and professional support. This year we added sixty-three new entries to our pages.

The *Sourcebook* represents one of Theatre Communications Group's most important projects for playwrights, and we work very hard to ensure that the guide is up-to-date, precise and accurate. Each year, most entries are modified in some way, so we encourage you always to work with the most recent *Sourcebook*. Study the book closely; use the Special Interests Index to help you identify the best production, development, publication and funding programs for you and your work. It is far better to send your work to five carefully chosen projects than to scatter your script to hundreds of organizations.

Once you've found the entries that interest you, plan ahead. Use the Submission Calendar as an aide-mémoire and checklist. Most important, remember that despite our painstaking updating process, deadlines and guidelines may change after this book has gone to press. Plan ahead and give yourself plenty of leeway for any delays you may encounter along the way. When instructed to "write for guidelines," do so. When a program requires an application form, send for it early. Get accustomed to writing the kind of brief synopses often required on application forms or in lieu of a script. Boiling a masterpiece down to three sentences can be a daunting task even for the finest playwright, but don't put off the challenge—it's a necessary and important part of the process.

Read the *Sourcebook* carefully. You should know that throughout this book, "full-length play" means just that—a full-length, original work for adult audiences, without a score or libretto. One-acts, musicals, adaptations, translations, plays for young audiences and screenplays are listed separately. Don't mistake notification dates for deadline dates. Always assume the deadline dates in this book refer to the day materials should arrive, not the postmark date. Don't send a script to a theatre if its submission procedure asks for a synopsis and letter of inquiry. (Take a look at the prologue by Pulitzer Prize-winning playwright Tony Kushner for further advice on script preparation.) Always send a photocopy of your work, never the original. And always, always include a self-addressed stamped envelope for the return of your script, unless the organization states that materials will not be returned. If you don't provide an SASE or explicit instructions for the disposal of your script, the organization is under no obligation to consider your submission, let alone return it.

We've made a few changes in the *Sourcebook* this year in hopes of creating a more user-friendly book. Entries are alphabetized by first word (excluding "the") even if the title starts with a proper name. So, for instance, you'll find the Mark Taper Forum under M. In the index, you will also find this theatre cross-listed under T. (You should note, however, that regardless of the way "theatre" is spelled in an organization's title, we still alphabetize it as if it were spelled "re," not "er.") We have also expanded the Prizes section to include full listings of biennial prizes whose next deadline falls after the dates of this *Sourcebook* (after August 1996). In the Membership and Service Organizations chapter we've begun listing Fax numbers and E-mail addresses.

Finally, I am pleased to have the opportunity to thank my co-editors on this project. Unless you've worked on a reference title like this one, you cannot imagine the energy, dedication and care required to contact hundreds of organizations, double-check dates and guidelines, and write brief and accurate entries in the elusive "DSB style." Kathy Sova, TCG's new managing editor, dove into the project with gusto and edited the majority of entries in this edition. Wendy Weiner, who assisted on last year's *Sourcebook*, proved a superbly deft and knowing editor this year. Their deep regard for playwrights and playwriting is evidenced by their fine work on this volume.

Linda MacColl
June 1995

# Prologue

## A Simple Working Guide for Playwrights
by Tony Kushner

A) *Format:* Most playwrights use a format in which character headings are placed centered above the line and capitalized:

LIONEL

I don't possess a mansion, a car, or a string of polo ponies...

Lines should be one-and-a-half spaced. Stage directions should be indented and single-spaced. If a character's line is interrupted at the end of the page, its continuance on the following page should be marked as such:

LIONEL (cont'd)

or a string of polo ponies...

There are denser, and thus more economical, formats; since Xeroxing is expensive, and heavy scripts cost more to ship, you may be tempted to use these, but a generously spaced format is much easier to read, and in these matters it doesn't pay to be parsimonious.

B) *Typing and reproducing:* Scripts should be typed neatly and reproduced clearly. Remember that everyone who reads your script will be reading many others additionally, and it will work to your serious disadvantage if the copy's sloppy, faded, or otherwise unappealing. If you use a computer printer, eschew old-fashioned dot-matrix and other robotic kinds of print. Also, I think it's best to avoid using incredibly fancy word-processing printing programs with eight different typefaces and decorative borders. Simple typescript, carefully done, is best. Check for typos. A playwright's punctuation may be idiosyncratic for purposes of expressiveness, but not too idiosyncratic, and spelling should be correct.

C) *Sending the script:*

1) The script should have a title page with the title, your name, address and phone number, or that of your agent or representative. Scripts are now automatically copyrighted at the moment of creation, but simply writing © and the date on the title page can serve as a kind of scarecrow for thievish magpies.

2) Never, never send an unbound script. Loose pages held together by a rubber band don't qualify as bound, nor do pages clamped together with a mega-paperclip. A heavy paper cover will protect the script as it passes from hand to hand.

3) Always, always enclose a self-addressed stamped envelope (SASE) or you will never see your script again. You may enclose a note telling the theatre to dispose of the copy instead of returning it; but you must have the ultimate fate of the script planned for in the eventuality of its not being selected for production. Don't leave this up to the theatre! If you want receipt of the script acknowledged, include a self-addressed, stamped postcard (SASP).

D) *Letter of inquiry and synopsis:* If a theatre states, in its entry in the *Sourcebook*, that it does not accept unsolicited scripts, believe it. Don't call and ask if there are exceptions; there aren't. A well-written and concise letter of inquiry, however, accompanied by a synopsis possessed of similar virtues *can* get you an invitation to submit your play. It's prudent, then, to spend time on both letter and synopsis. It is, admittedly, very hard for a writer to sum up his or her work in less than a page, but this kind of boiling-down can be of value beyond its necessity as a tool for marketing; use it to help clarify for yourself what's central and essential about your play. A good synopsis should *briefly* summarize the basic features of the plot without going into excessive detail; it should evoke both the style and the thematic substance of the play without recourse to clichéd description ("This play is about what happens when people lose their dreams..."); and it should convey essential information, such as cast size, gender breakdown, period, location, or anything else a literary manager deciding whether to send for the play might want to know. Make reference to other productions in your letter, but don't send thick packets of reviews and photos. And don't offer your opinion of the play's worth, which will be inferred as being positive from the fact that you are its parent.

E)　*Waiting:*　Theatres almost always take a long time to respond to playwrights about a specific play, frequently far in excess of the time given in their listings in the *Sourcebook*. This is due neither to spite nor indolence. Literary departments are usually understaffed and their workload is fearsome. Then, too, the process of selection invariably involves a host of people and considerations of all kinds. In my opinion you do yourself no good by repeatedly calling after the status of your script; you will become identified as a pest. It's terribly expensive to copy and mail scripts, but you must be prepared to shoulder the expense and keep making copies if they don't get returned. If, after a certain length of time past the deadline, you haven't heard from a theatre, send a letter inquiring politely about the play, reminding the appropriate people that you'd sent an SASE with the script; and then forget about it. In most cases, you will get a response and the script returned eventually.

One way to cut down on the expenses involved is to be selective about venues for submission. Reading *Sourcebook* entries and scrutinizing a copy of *Theatre Profiles* (see Useful Publications) will help you select the theatres most compatible with your work. If you've written a musical celebration of the life of Phyllis Schlafly, for example, you won't want to send it to theatres with an interest in radical feminist dramas. Or you won't necessarily want to send your play about the history of Western imperialism to a theatre that produces an annual season of musical comedy.

F)　*Produce yourself!*　In *Endgame,* Clov asks Hamm, "Do you believe in the life to come?" and Hamm responds, "Mine was always that." The condition of endless deferment is one that modern American playwrights share with Beckett's characters and other denizens of the postmodern world. Don't spend your life waiting. You may not be an actor, but that doesn't mean that action is forbidden you. Playwrights can, with very little expense, mount readings of their work; they can band together with other playwrights for readings and discussions; and they can, if they want to, produce their work themselves. Growth as a writer for the stage depends on seeing your work on stage, and if no one else will put it there, the job is up to you. At the very least, and above all else, while waiting, waiting, waiting for responses and offers, keep reading, thinking and writing.

Tony Kushner's plays include *Angels in America; A Bright Room Called Day; The Illusion*, his adaptation of Corneille's *L'Illusion Comique*, and *Slavs! (Thinking About the Longstanding Problems of Virtue and Happiness)*. His work has been produced by Mark Taper Forum, the New York Shakespeare Festival, New York Theatre Workshop, Hartford Stage Company, Berkeley Repertory Theatre and Los Angeles Theatre Center, as well as other theatres around the country and abroad.

*Angels in America, Part One: Millennium Approaches* and *Part Two: Perestroika*, which are currently on national tour, were commissioned by the Eureka Theatre Company and also received productions at Mark Taper Forum, the Royal National Theatre in London, and numerous other productions throughout the U.S. and the world. Among their many awards, *Millennium Approaches* and *Perestroika* each won a Tony Award for best play, and *Millennium* received the 1993 Pulitzer Prize for Drama.

# Script Opportunities

- **Production**
- **Prizes**
- **Publication**
- **Development**

# Production

## What theatres are included in this section?

The overwhelming majority of the nonprofit professional theatres throughout the United States are represented here. In order to be included, a theatre must be a TCG member. (A handful of TCG theatres asked not to be listed, in most cases because they don't do new work or they create all of their own material.) To be eligible for TCG membership, a theatre must have been operating for at least two years and must meet professional standards of staffing, programming and budget. *Commercial and amateur producers are not included.*

## How should I go about deciding where to submit my play?

Don't send it out indiscriminately. Take time to study the listings and select those theatres most likely to be receptive to your material. Find out all you can about each of the theatres you select. Look to TCG's *Theatre Profiles 11* for information on most of these theatres, including seasonal lists of plays each performed from 1991–93. Read *American Theatre* to see what plays the theatres are currently presenting and what their other activities are. (See Useful Publications for more information.) Whenever possible, go to see the theatre's work.

**When I submit my play, what can I do to maximize its chances?**

First, read carefully the Simple Working Guide for Playwrights in the Prologue of this *Sourcebook* for good advice on script submission. Then follow each theatre's guidelines meticulously. Pay particular attention to the Special Interests section: If a theatre specifies "gay and lesbian themes only," do not send them your heterosexual romantic comedy, however witty and well-written it is. Also, bear in mind the following points about the various submission procedures:

1) "Accepts unsolicited scripts": Don't waste the theatre's time and yours by writing to ask permission to submit your play—just send it. If you want an acknowledgment of receipt, say so and enclose a self-addressed stamped postcard (SASP) for this purpose. *Always* enclose a self-addressed stamped envelope (SASE) for the return of the script. Note that you may not receive any response to your work if you don't include this SASE. Many theatres enclose their response letter with the script when returning it.

2) "Synopsis and letter of inquiry": An increasing number of theatres require a synopsis rather than the script itself. Never send an unsolicited script to these theatres. Prepare a clear, cogent and *brief* synopsis of your play and send it along with any other materials requested in the listing. The letter of inquiry is a cover note asking for permission to submit the script; if there is something about your play or about yourself as a writer that you think may spark the theatre's interest, by all means mention it, but keep the letter brief. Unless the theatre specifies that it only responds if it wants to see the script, always enclose an SASP for the theatre's response.

3) "Professional recommendation": Send a script (not a letter of inquiry) accompanied by a letter of recommendation from a theatre professional. Wait until you can obtain such a letter before approaching these theatres.

4) "Agent submission": If you do not have an agent yet, do not submit to these theatres. Wait until you have had a production or two and have acquired a representative who can submit your script for you.

5) "Direct solicitation to playwright or agent": Do not submit to these theatres. If they are interested in your work you will hear from them!

Note that we've persuaded theatres requiring letters and synopses to give us two response times—one for letters and one for scripts they ask to see. All response times are average and approximate. Even if it takes the theatres longer to respond than they say it will, don't pester them; practice patience, and get on with your life and your art.

## A Contemporary Theatre

100 West Roy St; Seattle, WA 98119-3824; (206) 285-3220
Peggy Shannon, *Artistic Director*

**Submission procedure:** no unsolicited scripts; agent submission; will accept synopsis, 10 pages of dialogue and letter of inquiry from Northwest playwrights only. **Types of material:** full-length plays, translations, adaptations, musicals. **Special interests:** contemporary social and political issues; plays innovative in form and perspective; not keen on "kitchen-sink" realism. **Facilities:** A Contemporary Theatre, 450 seats, thrust stage. **Best submission time:** Sep–Apr. **Response time:** 1 month letter; 3 months script. **Special programs:** new play development workshops. First Act: play commissions and workshops for local playwrights. Young ACT Company: tours WA schools annually.

## A. D. Players

2710 West Alabama St; Houston, TX 77098; (713) 526-2721
*Literary Manager*

**Submission procedure:** no unsolicited scripts; synopsis, resume and letter of inquiry. **Types of material:** full-length plays, one-acts, adaptations, plays for young audiences, musicals. **Special interests:** works that "state or affirm the centrality of God's love and power in the issue of life." **Facilities:** Grace Theater, 212 seats, proscenium stage. **Production considerations:** cast limit of 12, prefers less than 10; no more than 2 sets, maximum height 11' 6"; no fly space, minimal lighting. **Best submission time:** year-round. **Response time:** 2 months letter; 12 months script. **Special programs:** staged reading series. Theater Arts Academy: includes playwriting classes; contact theatre for information.

## Academy Theatre

501 Means St NW; Atlanta, GA 30318; (404) 525-4111
Frank Wittow, *Artistic Director*

**Submission procedure:** no unsolicited scripts; synopsis, bio and letter of inquiry with SASE for response. **Types of material:** full-length plays, one-acts. **Special interests:** plays completed within last 2 years or plays-in-process, primarily by metro-Atlanta or Southeast-region playwrights. **Facilities:** Studio, 60 seats, black box. **Best submission time:** year-round. **Response time:** 3 months letter. **Special programs:** New Play Series: rehearsed readings followed by audience discussion. Three Plays in May: annual staged readings of 3 plays-in-process followed by audience discussion. Theatre for Youth Touring Company. Academy Theatre New Play Development Program (see Development).

## ACTheater

Box 1454; Anniston, AL 36202; (205) 236-8342
Josephine E. Ayers, *Producing Artistic Director*

**Submission procedure:** no unsolicited scripts; synopsis and letter of inquiry. **Types of material:** full-length plays, adaptations. **Special interests:** southern writers;

sociopolitical issues. **Facilities:** ACTheater, 100 seats, thrust stage. **Production considerations:** prefers cast limit of 10, minimal changes of location. **Best submission time:** year-round. **Response time:** 10 days letter; 2 months script.

## THE ACTING COMPANY

Box 898, Times Square Station; New York, NY 10108; (212) 564-3510
Margot Harley, *Producing Director*
Pegge Logefeil, *Managing Director*

**Submission procedure:** no unsolicited scripts; recommendation from professional familiar with company's work and goals. **Types of material:** full-length plays, one-acts, translations, adaptations, musicals. **Special interests:** mainly classical repertory but occasionally produces new works suited to acting ensemble of approximately 10 men, 4 women, age range 24–45; prefers works with poetic dimension and heightened language. **Facilities:** no permanent facility; touring company which plays in New York City for 1 or 2 weeks a year. **Production considerations:** productions tour in repertory; simple, transportable proscenium-stage set. **Best submission time:** Nov–Jan. **Response time:** 12 months.

## THE ACTOR'S EXPRESS

King Plow Arts Center, J-107; 887 West Marietta St NW; Atlanta, GA 30318;
    (404) 875-1606
Rob Nixon, *Literary Manager*

**Submission procedure:** no unsolicited scripts; synopsis and letter of inquiry, accompanied by professional recommendation if possible. **Types of material:** full-length plays, translations, adaptations, musicals. **Special interests:** socially relevant material; minority and gay themes; works with poetic dimension. **Facilities:** Actor's Express, 200 seats, black box. **Production considerations:** no fly space. **Best submission time:** Nov–Jan. **Response time:** 1 month letter; 4–6 months script.

## ACTORS THEATRE OF LOUISVILLE

316 West Main St; Louisville, KY 40202-4218; (502) 584-1265
Michael Bigelow Dixon, *Literary Manager*
Michele Volansky, *Assistant Literary Manager*

**Submission procedure:** accepts unsolicited 10-page one-acts for contest only (see below); professional recommendation for all other plays. **Types of material:** full-length plays, one-acts, translations, adaptations. **Special interests:** plays of ideas; language-oriented plays; passion, humor and experimentation. **Facilities:** Pamela Brown Auditorium, 637 seats, thrust stage; Bingham Theatre, 340 seats, arena stage; Victor Jory Theatre, 159 seats, 3/4-arena stage. **Best submission time:** year-round. **Response time:** 6–9 months (most scripts returned in fall). **Special programs:** National Ten-Minute Play Contest (see Prizes).

## ALABAMA SHAKESPEARE FESTIVAL
1 Festival Dr; Montgomery, AL 36117-4605; (334) 271-5300
Kent Thompson, *Artistic Director*
Eric Schmiedl, *Literary Associate*

**Submission procedure:** accepts unsolicited scripts with letter of inquiry for Southern Writers' Project only (see below); agent submission for all other plays. **Types of material:** full-length plays, adaptations, plays for young audiences. **Special interests:** new plays with southern or African-American themes, especially plays dealing with the Civil Rights movement; plays for young audiences. **Facilities:** Festival Stage, 750 seats, modified thrust stage; Octagon, 225 seats, flexible space. **Best submission time:** year-round. **Response time:** 8 weeks letter; 6–8 months script. **Special programs:** Southern Writers' Project: project to commission and develop plays based on southern and/or African-American issues; address submissions to Southern Writers' Project.

## ALICE B. THEATRE
1634 11th Ave; Seattle, WA 98122; (206) 322-5723
Andrew J. Mellen, *Artistic Director*

**Submission procedure:** no unsolicited scripts; synopsis, 10-page sample and letter of inquiry with SASP for response. **Types of material:** full-length plays, one-acts, translations, adaptations, musicals, performance art. **Special interests:** only works with gay/lesbian characters or themes; works addressing racism, sexism, ageism and/or homophobia; site-specific works. **Facilities:** Broadway Performance Hall, 350 seats, proscenium stage; Theater Off Jackson, 150 seats, corner stage; New City Theatre, 125 seats, proscenium stage; also uses other spaces. **Production considerations:** prefers small cast, simple sets. **Best submission time:** year-round. **Response time:** 4–6 weeks letter; 3–6 months script.

## ALLEY THEATRE
615 Texas Ave; Houston, TX 77002; (713) 228-9341
Gregory Boyd, *Artistic Director*

**Submission procedure:** no unsolicited scripts; professional recommendation. **Types of material:** full-length plays, translations, adaptations, musicals. **Facilities:** Main Stage, 800 seats, thrust stage; Arena Stage, 300 seats, arena stage. **Best submission time:** year-round. **Response time:** 2–6 months.

## ALLIANCE THEATRE COMPANY
1280 Peachtree St NE; Atlanta, GA 30309; (404) 733-4650
*Literary Department*

**Submission procedure:** no unsolicited scripts; synopsis, dialogue sample if possible, and letter of inquiry. **Types of material:** full-length plays, musicals. **Special interests:** new musicals; southern themes; works that deal with moral and/or spiritual questions of life in multicultural America. **Facilities:** Alliance Theatre,

864 seats, proscenium stage; Studio Theatre, 200 seats, flexible stage. **Best submission time:** Mar–Sep. **Response time:** 2–4 weeks letter; 6 months script.

## AMERICAN CONSERVATORY THEATER

30 Grant Ave, 6th Floor; San Francisco, CA 94108-5800; (415) 834-3200
*Literary Manager*

**Submission procedure:** no unsolicited scripts; agents and theatre professionals only may send synopsis, maximum 10 pages of dialogue and letter of inquiry. **Types of material:** full-length plays, translations, adaptations. **Special interests:** theatre plans to work with selected playwrights on company projects and adaptations. **Facilities:** Marines Memorial Theatre, 640 seats, proscenium stage; Stage Door Theatre, 550 seats, partial thrust stage; Geary Theater, 100 seats, proscenium stage (reopens Jan 1996). **Best submission time:** year-round. **Response time:** 1–2 months letter; 3 months script.

## AMERICAN MUSIC THEATER FESTIVAL

123 South Broad St, 25th Floor; Philadelphia, PA 19109; (215) 893-1570
Carol Bixler, *Associate Producer*

**Submission procedure:** no unsolicited scripts; direct solicitation to playwright or agent. **Types of material:** music-theatre works including musical comedy, music drama, opera and experimental works. **Special interests:** works by minority writers; contemporary music works using popular forms and styles, e.g., country and western, jazz, Cuban rhythms. **Facilities:** Walnut Street Theatre, 1050 seats, proscenium stage; Annenberg Center's Zellerbach Theatre, 900 seats, thrust stage; Plays and Players Theatre, 300 seats, proscenium stage.

## AMERICAN REPERTORY THEATRE

64 Brattle St; Cambridge, MA 02138; (617) 495-2668
Steven Maler, *Artistic Associate*

**Submission procedure:** no unsolicited scripts; agent submission. **Types of material:** full-length plays, translations, adaptations, musicals, cabaret/revues. **Special interests:** prefers plays "which lend themselves to poetic use of the stage." **Facilities:** Loeb Drama Center, 556 seats, flexible stage; 12 Holyoke Street, 350 seats, proscenium stage; 0 Church Street, 200 seats, black box. **Production considerations:** cast limit of 15.

## AMERICAN STAGE FESTIVAL

Box 225; Milford, NH 03055-0225
Attn: New Scripts, EARLY STAGES

**Submission procedure:** no unsolicited scripts; synopsis, 10 pages of dialogue and letter of inquiry with SASE for response; include cassette of 2–3 songs for musicals. **Types of material:** full-length plays, musicals. **Special interests:** material with strong emotional content that tells a compelling story; material that encourages new theatrical techniques and a new sense of theatrical reality.

**Facilities:** American Stage Festival, 497 seats, proscenium stage. **Production considerations:** cast limit of 10 for plays, 15 plus 5 musicians for musicals. **Best submission time:** Sep–Dec. **Response time:** 2–3 months letter; 4–6 months script.

## APPLE TREE THEATRE

595 Elm Pl, Suite 210; Highland Park, IL 60035; (708) 432-8223
Mark Lococo, *Literary Manager*

**Submission procedure:** no unsolicited scripts; will accept synopsis and letter of inquiry; include cassette for musicals. **Types of material:** full-length plays, adaptations, plays for young audiences, musicals. **Facilities:** Apple Tree Theatre, 171 seats, modified thrust stage. **Production considerations:** cast limit of 9, unit set. **Best submission time:** year-round. **Response time:** 1 month letter; 4 months script. **Special programs:** staged readings.

## ARDEN THEATRE COMPANY

Box 779; Philadelphia, PA 19105; (215) 829-8900
Terrence J. Nolen, *Producing Artistic Director*
Aaron Posner, *Artistic Director*

**Submission procedure:** no unsolicited scripts; synopsis and letter of inquiry. **Types of material:** full-length plays, translations, adaptations, musicals. **Special interests:** new adaptations of literary works. **Facilities:** Mainstage, 150–175 seats, flexible stage. **Best submission time:** year-round. **Response time:** 3 months letter; 6 months script.

## ARENA STAGE

6th and Maine Ave SW; Washington, DC 20024; (202) 554-9066
Cathy Madison, *Literary Manager*

**Submission procedure:** no unsolicited scripts; synopsis, 10 pages of dialogue and letter of inquiry. **Types of material:** full-length plays, translations, adaptations, musicals. **Special interests:** unproduced works only; plays for a multicultural company; plays by women and writers of color. **Facilities:** Fichandler Stage, 827 seats, arena stage; The Kreeger Theater, 514 seats, modified thrust stage; The Old Vat Room, 110 seats, cabaret stage. **Best submission time:** late summer/early fall. **Response time:** 1 day letter; 6 months script. **Special programs:** New Voices for a New America (see Development).

## ARIZONA THEATRE COMPANY

Box 1631; Tucson, AZ 85702; (602) 884-8210
Matthew Wiener, *Associate Artistic Director*

**Submission procedure:** accepts unsolicited scripts from Southwest playwrights only. **Types of material:** full-length plays, translations, adaptations, musicals. **Facilities:** Temple of Music and Art (in Tucson), 600 seats, proscenium stage; Herberger Theater Center (in Phoenix), 800 seats, proscenium stage. **Best submission time:** spring–summer. **Response time:** 6–12 months. **Special programs:**

New Play Reading Series: rehearsed readings followed by discussion with audience. National Hispanic Playwriting Contest (see Prizes).

## ARKANSAS REPERTORY THEATRE
Box 110; Little Rock, AR 72203-0110; (501) 378-0445
Brad Mooy, *Literary Manager*

**Submission procedure:** no unsolicited scripts; synopsis and letter of inquiry. **Types of material:** full-length plays, musicals, cabaret/revues. **Facilities:** Arkansas Repertory Theatre, 354 seats, proscenium stage; Second Stage, 99 seats, black box. **Production considerations:** prefers small cast. **Best submission time:** year-round. **Response time:** 3 months letter; 3 months script. **Special programs:** New Playreading Series.

## ARROW ROCK LYCEUM THEATRE
High St; Arrow Rock, MO 65320; (816) 837-3311
Michael Bollinger, *Artistic Producing Director*

**Submission procedure:** no unsolicited scripts; direct solicitation to playwright or agent. **Types of material:** full-length plays, translations, adaptations, musicals. **Facilities:** Arrow Rock Lyceum Theatre, 410 seats, semithrust stage.

## ARTISTS REPERTORY THEATRE
1111 Southwest 10th Ave; Portland, OR 97205; (503) 294-7373
Allen Nause, *Artistic Director*

**Submission procedure:** accepts unsolicited scripts. **Types of material:** full-length plays, adaptations. **Facilities:** Wilson Center for the Performing Arts, 110 seats, thrust stage; Winningstadt Theatre, 275 seats, flexible space. **Production considerations:** cast limit of 10, 1 set or unit set. **Best submission time:** year-round. **Response time:** 6 months. **Special programs:** Play Lab: staged reading series.

## ArtREACH TOURING THEATRE
3074 Madison Rd; Cincinnati, OH 45209; (513) 871-2300
Kathryn Schultz Miller, *Artistic Director*

**Submission procedure:** accepts unsolicited scripts. **Types of material:** plays for young audiences. **Special interests:** intelligent, well-plotted plays; subjects not usually explored in children's theatre, e.g., Vietnam, Hiroshima. **Facilities:** touring company. **Production considerations:** cast limit of 3; plays must be 50–60 minutes in length and easy to tour. **Best submission time:** Jan–Mar. **Response time:** 3 months.

## Asolo Theatre Company
Asolo Center for the Performing Arts; 5555 North Tamiami Trail;
    Sarasota, FL 34243; (813) 351-9010
Bruce E. Rodgers, *Associate Artistic Director*

**Submission procedure:** no unsolicited scripts; 1-page synopsis and letter of inquiry with SASE for response. **Types of material:** full-length plays, translations, adaptations. **Facilities:** The Mertz Theatre, 499 seats, proscenium stage; The Conservatory Theatre, 161 seats, proscenium stage. **Best submission time:** Jun–Aug. **Response time:** 2 months letter; 6 months script.

## Bailiwick Repertory
1229 West Belmont; Chicago, IL 60657-3205; (312) 883-1090
David Zak, *Executive Director*
Cecilie D. Keenan, *Artistic Director*

**Submission procedure:** send SASE for manuscript submission guidelines. **Types of material:** full-length plays, translations, adaptations, musicals. **Special interests:** translations and adaptations; theatrically inventive and/or politically intriguing works; plays by women for Women's Work series. **Facilities:** Bailiwick Arts Center: mainstage, 160 seats, flexible/thrust stage; cabaret/studio, 100 seats, flexible stage. **Best submission time:** year-round. **Response time:** 4 months. **Special programs:** note: all playwrights submitting to these programs must first send SASE for manuscript submission guidelines. Pride Performance Series: year-round exploration of works of interest to the lesbian and gay communities, culminating in summer festival. New Directions Series: fully staged performances of works that experiment boldly with form and content. Director's Festival: annual directors' showcase of 48 plays, 10–50 minutes long, staged in black-box setting; *deadline:* 1 Jul 1996. Studio series to include workshops and readings of plays, performance pieces and musicals to be instituted during 1995–96.

## Barksdale Theatre
Box 7; Hanover, VA 23069; (804) 559-4804
John Glenn, *Artistic Director*

**Submission procedure:** no unsolicited scripts; synopsis and letter of inquiry. **Types of material:** full-length plays, one-acts, translations, adaptations, plays for young audiences, musicals, cabaret/revues. **Facilities:** Hanover Tavern, 199 seats, thrust stage. **Production considerations:** small cast, minimal production demands; no fly or wing space. **Best submission time:** summer. **Response time:** 2 months letter; 6 months script.

## Barter Theatre
Box 867; Abingdon, VA 24210-0867; (703) 628-2281
Richard Rose, *Producing Artistic Director*

**Submission procedure:** no unsolicited scripts; synopsis, dialogue sample and letter of inquiry. **Types of material:** full-length plays, translations, adaptations, plays for young audiences. **Special interests:** social issues and current events; works that expand theatrical form. **Facilities:** Barter Theatre, 406 seats, proscenium stage; Barter's Stage II, 150 seats, flexible stage. **Production considerations:** cast of 4–12. **Best submission time:** Mar, Sep. **Response time:** 6 months letter; 9 months script. **Special programs:** Barter's Early Stages: script development program.

## BAY STREET THEATRE
Box 810; Sag Harbor, NY 11963; (516) 725-0818
Mia Grosjean, *Literary Manager*

**Submission procedure:** no unsolicited scripts; agent submission. **Types of material:** full-length plays, musicals. **Special interests:** plays that challenge as well as entertain; plays that "address the heart of our community and champion the human spirit"; small-scale musicals only. **Facilities:** Mainstage, 299 seats, thrust stage. **Production considerations:** cast limit of 10–12; prefers unit set; no fly or wing space. **Best submission time:** year-round. **Response time:** 3–6 months. **Special programs:** Reading series: readings of 2 new plays each fall and spring; playwright receives $50 honorarium and travel from New York City; scripts for special programs selected through theatre's normal submission procedure.

## BERKELEY REPERTORY THEATRE
2025 Addison St; Berkeley, CA 94704; (510) 204-8901
Tony Kelly, *Literary Manager*

**Submission procedure:** no unsolicited scripts; agent submission. **Types of material:** full-length plays, translations, adaptations. **Facilities:** Mark Taper Mainstage, 400 seats, thrust stage. **Best submission time:** Sep–May. **Response time:** 6–8 months. **Special programs:** Parallel Season: productions of 2–3 new plays each season. Commissioning program. In-house readings.

## BERKSHIRE THEATRE FESTIVAL
Box 797; Stockbridge, MA 01262; (413) 298-5536
Arthur Storch, *Artistic Director*

**Submission procedure:** no unsolicited scripts; agent submission. **Types of material:** full-length plays, one-acts, musicals. **Special interests:** thought-provoking vacation entertainment; theatre on the "cutting edge." **Facilities:** Playhouse, 413 seats, proscenium stage; Unicorn Theatre, 99 seats, thrust stage. **Production considerations:** cast limit of 8 for plays; small orchestra for musicals; prefers simple set. **Best submission time:** Nov–Dec. **Response time:** 3 months. **Special programs:** staged reading series.

## BILINGUAL FOUNDATION OF THE ARTS
421 North Ave 19; Los Angeles, CA 90031; (213) 225-4044
Guillermo Reyes, *Dramaturg/Literary Manager*

**Submission procedure:** accepts unsolicited scripts. **Types of material:** full-length plays, translations, adaptations, plays for young audiences. **Special interests:** plays with Hispanic themes or by Hispanic playwrights only. **Facilities:** BFA's Little Theatre, 99 seats, thrust stage; uses theatres at Los Angeles Center for the Arts for some mainstage productions. **Production considerations:** cast limit of 10, simple set. **Best submission time:** year-round. **Response time:** 3–6 months.

## BIRMINGHAM CHILDREN'S THEATRE
Box 1362; Birmingham, AL 35201; (205) 324-0470
Joe Zellner, *Production Coordinator*

**Submission procedure:** no unsolicited scripts; synopsis and letter of inquiry. **Types of material:** plays for young audiences. **Special interests:** interactive plays for preschool–grade 2. **Facilities:** Birmingham-Jefferson Civic Center Theatre, 1073 seats, thrust stage; Studio Theatre, up to 250 seats, lab space. **Production considerations:** prefers cast of 5–10. **Best submission time:** Sep–Dec. **Response time:** 2 weeks letter; several months script.

## BLOOMSBURG THEATRE ENSEMBLE
Box 66; Bloomsburg, PA 17815; (717) 784-5530
Tom Byrn, *Play Selection Chair*

**Submission procedure:** no unsolicited scripts; synopsis, dialogue sample, letter of recommendation from theatre professional and letter of inquiry. **Types of material:** full-length plays, translations, adaptations. **Special interests:** new translations of classics; plays suitable for 9-member acting ensemble. **Facilities:** Alvina Krause Theatre, 369 seats, proscenium stage. **Production considerations:** small to mid-sized cast, 1 set or unit set. **Best submission time:** year-round. **Response time:** 3 months letter; 6 months script.

## BOARSHEAD: MICHIGAN PUBLIC THEATER
425 South Grand Ave; Lansing, MI 48933; (517) 484-7800
John Peakes, *Artistic Director*

**Submission procedure:** no unsolicited scripts; synopsis, character breakdown, 10 pages of dialogue and letter of inquiry with SASP for response. **Types of material:** full-length plays, plays for young audiences. **Special interests:** plays that make use of theatrical conventions or create new ones; social issues; comedies. **Facilities:** Center for the Arts, 249 seats, thrust stage. **Best submission time:** year-round. **Response time:** 1 month letter; 3–6 months script. **Special programs:** staged readings of 5 new plays a year.

## BORDERLANDS THEATER
Box 2791; Tucson, AZ 85702; (602) 882-8607

**Submission procedure:** accepts unsolicited scripts. **Types of material:** full-length plays, translations, adaptations. **Special interests:** cultural diversity; race relations; "border" issues, including concerns of the geographical border region as well as the metaphorical borders of gender, class and race. **Facilities:** Pima Community College Center for the Arts: 1st theatre, 400 seats, proscenium stage; 2nd theatre,

160 seats, black box. **Production considerations:** cast limit of 12, minimal set. **Best submission time:** year-round. **Response time:** 3–6 months. **Special programs:** Border Playwrights Project (see Development).

## BRAVE NEW WORKSHOP & INSTANT THEATRE COMPANY
2605 Hennepin Ave S; Minneapolis, MN 55408-1150; (612) 377-8445
Dudley Riggs, *Producing Director*
Linda Jacobs, *Associate Producer*

**Submission procedure:** accepts unsolicited scripts with synopsis and reviews (if any). **Types of material:** one-acts, revues. **Special interests:** presents only satirical revues (and occasionally one-acts) based on current events. **Facilities:** Dudley Riggs Theatre, 230 seats, modified thrust stage. **Production considerations:** cast limit of 10; minimal production requirements; small stage. **Best submission time:** year-round. **Response time:** 1 month. **Special programs:** playwright-in-residence program; participation by invitation only.

## CALIFORNIA THEATRE CENTER
Box 2007; Sunnyvale, CA 94087; (408) 245-2979
Will Huddleston, *Resident Director*

**Submission procedure:** accepts unsolicited scripts; prefers synopsis and letter of inquiry. **Types of material:** plays for young audiences. **Special interests:** classics adapted for young audiences; comedies; historical material. **Facilities:** company primarily tours to 1500-plus–seat, proscenium-stage theatres; home base: Sunnyvale Performing Arts Center, 200 seats, proscenium stage. **Production considerations:** cast limit of 12 for professional touring productions; minimum cast of 15 for conservatory productions; modest production demands. **Best submission time:** year-round. **Response time:** 4–6 months.

## CAPITAL REPERTORY COMPANY
Box 399; Albany, NY 12201-0399; (518) 462-4531

**Submission procedure:** no unsolicited scripts; synopsis, first 15 pages of text and letter of inquiry. **Types of material:** full-length plays, translations, adaptations, music-theatre works. **Facilities:** Market Theatre, 299 seats, thrust stage. **Production considerations:** cast limit of 10, simple set; modest musical requirements. **Best submission time:** late spring. **Response time:** 4–6 months letter; 6–8 months script.

## CENTER STAGE
700 North Calvert St; Baltimore, MD 21202-3686; (410) 685-3200
James Magruder, *Resident Dramaturg*

**Submission procedure:** no unsolicited scripts; synopsis, sample pages and letter of inquiry. **Types of material:** full-length plays, translations, adaptations, music-theatre works. **Facilities:** Pearlstone Theater, 541 seats, modified thrust stage;

Head Theater, 100–400 seats, flexible space. **Best submission time:** year-round. **Response time:** 5–7 weeks letter; 3–5 months script.

## CENTER THEATER

1346 West Devon Ave; Chicago, IL 60660; (312) 508-0200
Dale Calandra, *Literary Manager*

**Submission procedure:** no unsolicited scripts; synopsis, resume and letter of inquiry with SASE for response. **Types of material:** full-length plays, translations, adaptations, musicals. **Special interests:** comedies; plays creating a heightened reality; language-oriented plays; dramas of substance; original musicals only. **Facilities:** Mainstage, 75 seats, modified thrust stage; Studio, 35 seats, black box. **Production considerations:** cast limit of approximately 12; limited wing space, no fly loft. **Best submission time:** year-round. **Response time:** 3 months letter; 3 months script. **Special programs:** Playwrights Workshop Series: participation by invitation only. Actor/Director/Playwright Unit: participants meet monthly to work on scripts; some scripts given staged reading, possibly leading to 2-week developmental workshop and performances and/or full production; participants selected through personal interview; Chicago-area playwrights contact Dale Calandra, Workshop Coordinator, for appointment. Center Theater International Playwrighting Contest (see Prizes).

## CHELTENHAM CENTER FOR THE ARTS

439 Ashbourne Rd; Cheltenham, PA 19012; (215) 379-4660

**Submission procedure:** no unsolicited scripts; synopsis/description of play and letter of inquiry. **Types of material:** full-length plays, translations, adaptations. **Facilities:** Bernard H. Berger Theater, 140 seats, proscenium stage. **Production considerations:** cast limit of 10. **Best submission time:** Jul–Feb. **Response time:** 1 month letter; 6 months script.

## CHICAGO DRAMATISTS WORKSHOP

See Membership and Service Organizations.

## THE CHILDREN'S THEATRE COMPANY

2400 Third Ave S; Minneapolis, MN 55404; (612) 874-0500
Gary Gisselman, *Associate Artistic Director*

**Submission procedure:** no unsolicited scripts; synopsis, resume and letter of inquiry. **Types of material:** full-length plays, one-acts, translations, adaptations, plays for young audiences, musicals. **Special interests:** adaptations or original plays for young audiences. **Facilities:** Children's Theatre Company, 745 seats, proscenium stage; Studio Theatre, 80–100 seats, black box. **Best submission time:** Oct–Apr. **Response time:** 2 weeks letter; 5 months script.

## CHILDSPLAY
Box 517; Tempe, AZ 85280; (602) 350-8101
David Saar, *Artistic Director*

**Submission procedure:** no unsolicited scripts; synopsis and letter of inquiry. **Types of material:** plays for young audiences, including full-length plays, adaptations, musicals, performance pieces. **Special interests:** nontraditional plays; material that entertains and challenges both performers and audiences; new work; 2nd and 3rd productions prior to publication. **Facilities:** Tempe Performing Arts Center, 250 seats, black box; Scottsdale Center for the Arts, 800 seats, proscenium stage; Herberger Theater Center: Center Stage, 800 seats, proscenium stage; Stage West, 350 seats, proscenium stage; also performs in Tucson (no permanent space). **Production considerations:** some van-sized touring productions. **Best submission time:** Jun–Oct. **Response time:** 1 month letter; 3 months script. **Special programs:** 1–3 works commissioned each season; each receives minimum 2 years of development.

## CINCINNATI PLAYHOUSE IN THE PARK
Box 6537; Cincinnati, OH 45206-0537; (513) 345-2242
Edward Stern, *Producing Artistic Director*

**Submission procedure:** no unsolicited scripts; maximum 2-page abstract including synopsis, character breakdown and playwright's bio, 5 pages of dialogue and letter of inquiry, submitted by playwright or agent. **Types of material:** full-length plays, translations, adaptations, musicals. **Facilities:** Robert S. Marx Theatre, 629 seats, thrust stage; Thompson Shelterhouse, 220 seats, thrust stage. **Best submission time:** year-round. **Response time:** 2 months letter; 8 months script. **Special programs:** Lois and Richard Rosenthal New Play Prize (see Prizes).

## CIRCLE REPERTORY COMPANY
632 Broadway, 6th Floor; New York, NY 10012-2614; (212) 505-6010
Lynn M. Thomson, *Dramaturg/Literary Manager*

**Submission procedure:** no unsolicited scripts; professional recommendation. **Types of material:** full-length plays. **Facilities:** Circle Repertory, 162 seats, flexible stage. **Best submission time:** year-round. **Response time:** 4–6 months. **Special programs:** Projects-in-Progress: staged readings with 2 weeks of rehearsal. Playwrights Project: participation by invitation only.

## CITIARTS THEATRE
1975 Diamond Blvd, Suite A-20; Concord, CA 94520; (510) 798-1300
Richard H. Elliott, *Artistic Director*

**Submission procedure:** accepts unsolicited scripts. **Types of material:** full-length plays, translations, adaptations, musicals. **Special interests:** small-scale plays, musicals and revues with an edge that will appeal to both urban and suburban audiences. **Facilities:** Willows Theatre, 203 seats, proscenium stage; Maggie Crum Theatre, 154 seats, thrust stage. **Production considerations:** cast of 2–15; limit of

8 musicians for musical works; prefers simple set, unit set or environmental staging which uses theatre space as setting. **Best submission time:** 1 Jul–1 Oct. **Response time:** 3 months. **Special programs:** staged readings and workshop productions.

## CITY THEATRE COMPANY
57 South 13th St; Pittsburgh, PA 15203; (412) 431-4400
Marc Masterson, *Producing Director*
Gwen Orel, *Literary Manager*

**Submission procedure:** no unsolicited scripts; synopsis, dialogue sample and letter of inquiry. **Types of material:** full-length plays, translations, adaptations, chamber musicals. **Special interests:** comedies of substance; plays with strong storyline; American themes. **Facilities:** mainstage, 250 seats, proscenium-thrust stage; laboratory theatre, 99 seats, black box. **Best submission time:** year-round. **Response time:** 2 months letter; 3 months script. **Special programs:** staged readings.

## CLARENCE BROWN THEATRE COMPANY
206 McClung Tower; Knoxville, TN 37996; (615) 974-6011
Thomas P. Cooke, *Producing Artistic Director*

**Submission procedure:** no unsolicited scripts; synopsis, character breakdown, 1–2 pages of dialogue and letter of inquiry. **Types of material:** full-length plays. **Special interests:** contemporary American plays. **Facilities:** Clarence Brown Theatre, 600 seats, proscenium stage; Carousel Theatre, 400 seats, arena stage.

## CLASSIC STAGE COMPANY (CSC)
136 East 13th St; New York, NY 10003; (212) 677-4210
Lenora Champagne, *Artistic Associate*

**Submission procedure:** no unsolicited scripts; synopsis, dialogue sample and letter of inquiry. **Types of material:** translations, adaptations. **Special interests:** translations and adaptations of classic plays; adaptations of major nondramatic classics; prefers highly theatrical work. **Facilities:** CSC, 180 seats, flexible stage. **Production considerations:** cast limit of 8. **Best submission time:** year-round. **Response time:** 1 month letter; 3 months script. **Special programs:** developmental program of rehearsed readings.

## THE CLEVELAND PLAY HOUSE
8500 Euclid Ave; Cleveland, OH 44106-0189; (216) 795-7010
Scott Kanoff, *Director-Playwrights Unit/Resident Dramaturg*
Coleen Hubbard, *Director of New Play Development*

**Submission procedure:** no unsolicited scripts; dialogue sample and letter of inquiry. **Types of material:** full-length plays, adaptations, musicals. **Facilities:** Kenyon C. Bolton Theatre, 612 seats, proscenium stage; Francis E. Drury Theatre, 501 seats, proscenium stage. **Best submission time:** 1 Sep–1 Mar, 1 Apr–30 Jun.

**Response time:** 6–8 weeks letter; 1–3 months script. **Special programs:** Next Stage (see Development).

## CLEVELAND PUBLIC THEATRE
6415 Detroit Ave; Cleveland, OH 44102-3011; (216) 631-2727
James A. Levin, *Artistic Director*

**Submission procedure:** no unsolicited scripts except for New Plays Festival (see below); synopsis and letter of inquiry. **Types of material:** full-length plays, one-acts. **Special interests:** experimental, alternative, poetic, political works; voices not heard in the mainstream (people of color, women, gays and lesbians); "no sitcoms or made-for-TV movies." **Facilities:** Cleveland Public Theatre, 150–175 seats, adaptable stage (arena/proscenium). **Production considerations:** simple set. **Best submission time:** year-round; New Plays Festival, 1 Mar–1 Sep. **Response time:** 6 weeks letter; 9 months script. **Special programs:** Katherine and Lee Chilcote Award (see Prizes). New Plays Festival: staged readings of 10–12 full-length and one-act plays; submit script and $10 reading fee to Terence Cranendonk, Director, New Plays Festival; *deadline:* 1 Sep 1995; *notification:* Dec 1995; *dates:* Jan 1996.

## THE COLONY STUDIO THEATRE
1944 Riverside Dr; Los Angeles, CA 90039
Judith Goldstein, *New Play Selection Committee*

**Submission procedure:** no unsolicited scripts; send SASE for submission guidelines. **Types of material:** full-length plays, adaptations. **Facilities:** Studio Theatre, 99 seats, thrust stage. **Production considerations:** cast of 2–10; plays cast from resident company. **Best submission time:** year-round. **Response time:** 3–6 months.

## COMPANY ONE THEATER
233 Pearl St, 3rd Floor; Hartford, CT 06103; (203) 233-4588
Maxine Kern, *Artistic Director*

**Submission procedure:** no unsolicited scripts; synopsis, 10-page sample, resume and letter of inquiry. **Types of material:** full-length plays. **Special interests:** highly theatrical plays that take formal risks; plays featuring multicultural and women's themes and aesthetics. **Facilities:** The Cathedral Theater, 100 seats, proscenium stage. **Best submission time:** Jan–May. **Response time:** 6 months letter; 6 months script. **Special programs:** Script Teas: 4 rehearsed readings a year in Atheneum cafe; playwright receives remuneration; scripts selected through theatre's normal submission procedure.

## CONEY ISLAND, USA
Boardwalk at West 12th St; Coney Island, NY 11224; (718) 372-5159
Dick D. Zigun, *Artistic Director*

**Submission procedure:** no unsolicited scripts; synopsis, resume, reviews of prior work and letter of inquiry. **Types of material:** company books in already existing productions of plays and performance art. **Special interests:** new and old vaudeville; pop music; pop culture; Americana bizarro. **Facilities:** Sideshows by the Seashore, 150 seats, arena stage; also open-air performances on streets, boardwalk, beach. **Best submission time:** year-round. **Response time:** 1 month letter; 6 months script.

## CONTEMPORARY AMERICAN THEATER FESTIVAL
Box 429; Shepherdstown, WV 25443; (304) 876-3473
Ed Herendeen, *Producing Director*

**Submission procedure:** no unsolicited scripts; synopsis and letter of inquiry. **Types of material:** full-length plays. **Special interests:** new American plays; contemporary issues. **Facilities:** Main Stage, 350 seats, proscenium stage; Studio Theater, 99 seats, black box. **Best submission time:** fall. **Response time:** 1 month letter; 2 months script. **Special programs:** staged readings each Tuesday night during summer season.

## CORNERSTONE THEATER COMPANY
1653 18th St, #6; Santa Monica, CA 90404; (310) 449-1700
Alison Carey, *Founding Director*

**Submission procedure:** no unsolicited scripts; letter of inquiry only. **Types of material:** full-length plays, adaptations, musicals. **Special interests:** company primarily interested in collaborating with playwrights to develop new works or contemporary adaptations of classics, focusing on specific communities. **Facilities:** no permanent facility. **Best submission time:** year-round. **Response time:** 2 months.

## THE COTERIE THEATRE
2450 Grand Ave; Kansas City, MO 64108-2520; (816) 474-6785
Jeff Church, *Producing Artistic Director*

**Submission procedure:** accepts unsolicited scripts from established playwrights in youth-theatre field; others send brief synopsis, dialogue sample, resume and letter of inquiry. **Types of material:** works for young and family audiences, including adaptations and musicals. **Special interests:** ground-breaking works only; plays with culturally diverse casts or themes; social issues; adaptations of classic or contemporary literature; musicals. **Facilities:** The Coterie Theatre, 240 seats, flexible stage. **Production considerations:** cast limit of 12, prefers 5–7; no fly or wing space. **Best submission time:** year-round. **Response time:** 4 months letter; 8 months script.

## CROSSROADS THEATRE COMPANY
7 Livingston Ave; New Brunswick, NJ 08901; (908) 249-5581
Pamela Faith Jackson, *Literary Manager*

**Submission procedure:** no unsolicited scripts; synopsis and letter of inquiry. **Types of material:** full-length plays, one-acts, translations, adaptations, musicals, cabaret/revues. **Special interests:** African-American, African and West Indian issue-oriented, experimental plays that examine the complexity of the human experience. **Facilities:** Crossroads Theatre, 264 seats, thrust stage. **Best submission time:** year-round. **Response time:** 1 month letter; 12 months script. **Special programs:** The Genesis Festival: A Celebration of New Voices in African American Theatre: spring series of public readings and special events for the purpose of developing new plays; scripts selected through theatre's normal submission procedure.

## CUMBERLAND COUNTY PLAYHOUSE
Box 830; Crossville, TN 38557; (615) 484-4324
Jim Crabtree, *Producing Director*

**Submission procedure:** no unsolicited scripts; synopsis and letter of inquiry. **Types of material:** full-length plays, adaptations, plays for young audiences, musicals. **Special interests:** works for family audiences; works with southern or rural background; works about Tennessee history or culture. **Facilities:** Cumberland County Playhouse, 478 seats, proscenium stage; Theater-in-the-Woods, 200 seats, outdoor arena; Adventure Theater, 180–220 seats, flexible black box. **Best submission time:** Aug–Dec. **Response time:** 2 weeks letter (if interested); 6–12 months script.

## DALLAS THEATER CENTER
3636 Turtle Creek Blvd; Dallas, TX 75219-5598; (214) 526-8210
Rich Whittington, *Artistic Administrator*

**Submission procedure:** no unsolicited scripts; professional recommendation. **Types of material:** full-length plays, adaptations, translations. **Special interests:** plays that explore language or form; African-American or Hispanic material. **Facilities:** Kalita Humphreys Theater, 466 seats, thrust stage; Arts District Theater, 530 seats, flexible stage. **Best submission time:** year-round. **Response time:** 6–9 months.

## DELAWARE THEATRE COMPANY
200 Water St; Wilmington, DE 19801-5030; (302) 594-1104
Cleveland Morris, *Artistic Director*

**Submission procedure:** accepts unsolicited scripts. **Types of material:** full-length plays, translations, adaptations. **Facilities:** Delaware Theatre Company, 300 seats, thrust stage. **Production considerations:** cast limit of 10. **Best submission time:** Feb–May. **Response time:** 6 months. **Special programs:** Connections (see Prizes).

## DELL'ARTE PLAYERS COMPANY
Box 816; Blue Lake, CA 95525; (707) 668-5663
Michael Fields, *Managing Artistic Director*

**Submission procedure:** no unsolicited scripts; synopsis and letter of inquiry (company customarily creates its own original works but may from time to time produce plays by or collaborate with other writers). **Types of material:** full-length plays, translations, adaptations, plays for young audiences. **Special interests:** comedies; issue-oriented works in commedia dell'arte style; Christmas plays for young audiences. **Facilities:** Dell'Arte Players, 100 seats, flexible stage. **Production considerations:** company of 3–4 actors; production demands adaptable to touring. **Best submission time:** Jan–Mar. **Response time:** 3 weeks letter; 6 weeks script.

## DENVER CENTER THEATRE COMPANY

1050 13th St; Denver, CO 80204; (303) 893-4000
Tom Szentgyorgyi, *Associate Artistic Director/New Play Development*

**Submission procedure:** accepts unsolicited scripts from Rocky Mountain region playwrights only; others send synopsis, 10 pages of dialogue, resume of writing experience and letter of inquiry. **Types of material:** full-length plays. **Facilities:** The Stage, 642 seats, thrust stage; The Space, 450 seats, arena stage; The Ricketson, 196 seats, proscenium stage; The Source, 155 seats, thrust stage. **Best submission time:** year-round. **Response time:** 4–6 weeks letter; 2–3 months script. **Special programs:** Denver Center Theatre Company U S WEST Workshops (see Development).

## DETROIT REPERTORY THEATRE

13103 Woodrow Wilson Ave; Detroit, MI 48238; (313) 868-1347
Barbara Busby, *Literary Manager*

**Submission procedure:** accepts unsolicited scripts. **Types of material:** full-length plays. **Special interests:** issue-oriented plays. **Facilities:** Detroit Repertory Theatre, 194 seats, proscenium stage. **Production considerations:** prefers cast limit of 8–10. **Best submission time:** Sep–Feb. **Response time:** 3–6 months.

## DIAMOND HEAD THEATRE

See Diamond Head Theatre Development Programs in Development.

## DOBAMA THEATRE

1846 Coventry Rd; Cleveland Heights, OH 44118; (216) 932-6838
Jan Bruml, *Literary Manager*

**Submission procedure:** accepts unsolicited scripts with synopsis. **Types of material:** full-length plays. **Special interests:** plays with opportunities for ethnically diverse casting; plays that make a statement about contemporary life. **Facilities:** Dobama Theatre, 200 seats, thrust stage. **Production considerations:** prefers cast limit of 9; limited production demands; no fly space. **Best submission time:** year-round. **Response time:** 9 months. **Special programs:** Owen Kelly Adopt-a-Playwright Program: 2 full-length plays by northeast OH residents each given 2 weeks of developmental work with director, dramaturg and cast, culminating in workshop production; playwright must be available to participate; to apply, submit script to the attention of the program; *deadline:* 1 Feb 1996; *notification:* 15 May 1996; *dates:* Jul 1996. Marilyn Bianchi Kids' Playwriting Festival: annual short-play competition open to students attending Cuyahoga County schools, grades 1–12; several winners may receive savings bonds, publication and/or full production; write for application in Sep 1995; *deadline:* Feb 1996; exact date TBA.

## EAST WEST PLAYERS

4424 Santa Monica Blvd; Los Angeles, CA 90029; (213) 660-0366
Ken Narasaki, *Literary Manager*

**Submission procedure:** accepts unsolicited scripts with SASE for response. **Types of material:** full-length plays, translations, adaptations, plays for young audiences, musicals. **Special interests:** plays by or about Asian-Pacific–Americans. **Facilities:** East West Players, 99 seats, thrust stage. **Production considerations:** minimal production demands. **Best submission time:** year-round. **Response time:** 3–8 months.

## EL TEATRO CAMPESINO

Box 1240; San Juan Bautista, CA 95045; (408) 623-2444
*Literary Manager*

**Submission procedure:** no unsolicited scripts; synopsis, character breakdown, resume and letter of inquiry. **Types of material:** full-length plays, one-acts, translations, adaptations, plays for young audiences, musicals, cabaret/revues. **Special interests:** socially relevant works; works that reflect a multiethnic world; contemporary adaptations of classics. **Facilities:** El Teatro Campesino Playhouse, 150 seats, flexible stage. **Best submission time:** Jan–Apr. **Response time:** 6 months letter; 12 months script.

## THE EMELIN THEATRE FOR THE PERFORMING ARTS

Library Lane; Mamaroneck, NY 10543; (914) 698-3045
David G. Watson, *Executive Director*

**Submission procedure:** no unsolicited scripts; professional recommendation. **Types of material:** full-length plays, one-acts, translations, adaptations, musicals, cabaret/revues, stand-up comedy, performance art. **Facilities:** The Emelin Theatre, 280 seats, proscenium stage. **Production considerations:** small cast; no fly space. **Best submission time:** year-round. **Response time:** 2 months.

## THE EMPTY SPACE THEATRE

3509 Fremont Ave N; Seattle, WA 98103-8813; (206) 547-7633
Eddie Levi Lee, *Artistic Director*

**Submission procedure:** accepts unsolicited scripts from regional playwrights (AK, ID, MT, OR, WA, WY and BC); others send synopsis and letter of inquiry. **Types of material:** full-length plays, one-acts, translations, adaptations, musicals. **Facilities:** The Empty Space Theatre at the Fremont Palace, 150 seats, endstage. **Production considerations:** prefers small casts. **Best submission time:** year-round. **Response time:** 3–4 weeks letter; 4–6 months script.

## EN GARDE ARTS
225 Rector Pl, Suite 3A; New York, NY 10280; (212) 941-9793
Carol Bixler, *Managing Director*

**Submission procedure:** professional recommendation. **Types of material:** full-length plays, translations, adaptations, musicals, performance art. **Special interests:** site-specific works only. **Facilities:** no permanent facility; various sites in and outside of New York City, e.g., Central Park Lake, Chelsea Hotel, Victory Theatre, meatpacking district. **Best submission time:** Jun. **Response time:** 6–8 months.

## THE ENSEMBLE THEATRE
3535 Main St; Houston, TX 77002-9529; (713) 520-0055
Eileen J. Morris, *Artistic Director*

**Submission procedure:** accepts unsolicited scripts. **Types of material:** full-length plays, adaptations, plays for young audiences, musicals. **Special interests:** works reflecting the African-American experience. **Facilities:** Hawkins Stage, 109 seats, proscenium stage; Arena Stage, 75 seats, black box. **Production considerations:** cast limit of 10, maximum 2 sets. **Best submission time:** Oct–Apr. **Response time:** 2–3 months.

## ENSEMBLE THEATRE OF CINCINNATI
1127 Vine St; Cincinnati, OH 45210; (513) 421-3555
David A. White III, *Artistic Director*

**Submission procedure:** no unsolicited scripts; synopsis, dialogue sample, resume and letter of inquiry. **Types of material:** full-length plays, adaptations, plays for young audiences. **Special interests:** issues that awaken audience's social conscience. **Facilities:** Ensemble Theatre of Cincinnati, 202 seats, 3/4-arena stage. **Production considerations:** cast limit of 6, simple set. **Best submission time:** Sep. **Response time:** 2 weeks letter; 2 months script.

## EUREKA THEATRE COMPANY
330 Townsend St, Suite 210; San Francisco, CA 94107; (415) 243-9899
David Parr, *Artistic Director*

**Submission procedure:** accepts unsolicited scripts with resume. **Types of material:** full-length plays, one-acts, translations, adaptations. **Special interests:** contemporary plays responsive to social, political and cultural forces affecting our world. **Facilities:** no permanent facility. **Best submission time:** year-round. **Response time:** 6 months. **Special programs:** Discovery Series: regularly scheduled rehearsed readings of new plays presented for public and followed by audience discussion.

## FIRST STAGE MILWAUKEE
929 North Water St; Milwaukee, WI 53202; (414) 273-7121
Rob Goodman, *Producer/Artistic Director*

**Submission procedure:** no unsolicited scripts; synopsis, resume and letter of inquiry. **Types of material:** works for young audiences, including translations, adaptations and musicals. **Facilities:** The Performing Arts Center's Todd Wehr Theater, 500 seats, thrust stage. **Best submission time:** spring–summer. **Response time:** 1 month letter; 3 months script.

## FLORIDA STUDIO THEATRE
1241 North Palm Ave; Sarasota, FL 34236; (813) 366-9017
Chris Angermann, *Associate Director*

**Submission procedure:** no unsolicited scripts; synopsis and letter of inquiry. **Types of material:** full-length plays, one-acts, translations, adaptations, musicals, cabaret/revues. **Facilities:** Florida Studio Theatre, 170 seats, semi-thrust stage; The Cabaret Club, 100 seats, cabaret space. **Best submission time:** Apr–Nov. **Response time:** 1–2 weeks letter; 6 months script. **Special programs:** Sarasota Festival of New Plays: 3-tier May festival includes Young Playwrights Festival: workshop productions of plays by playwrights grades 2–12; *deadline:* 15 Mar 1996; Florida Playwrights Festival: workshops, seminars, staged readings and cabaret performances in conjunction with workshop productions of 3 plays by FL playwrights; scripts selected through theatre's normal submission procedure; National Playwrights Festival: workshop productions of 3 new plays; playwright receives stipend, travel, housing; scripts selected through theatre's normal submission procedure. Fall and summer reading series. American Shorts Contest (see Prizes).

## THE FOOTHILL THEATRE COMPANY
Box 1812; Nevada City, CA 95959; (916) 265-9320
Philip Charles Sneed, *Artistic Director*

**Submission procedure:** accepts unsolicited scripts. **Types of material:** full-length plays, one-acts, translations, adaptations, plays for young audiences. **Special interests:** plays dealing with history of northern CA and/or the western U.S. **Facilities:** The Nevada Theatre, 246 seats, proscenium stage; also rents small spaces with 50–100 seats. **Production considerations:** very limited fly and wing space. **Best submission time:** year-round. **Response time:** 3–6 months.

## FREE STREET PROGRAMS
1419 West Blackhawk St; Chicago, IL 60622; (312) 772-7248
David Schein, *Artistic Director*

**Submission procedure:** no unsolicited scripts; letter from writer with "a concept for a show or a brilliant idea for a new theatre program." **Types of material:** plays and performance pieces, including shows to be performed in public places or out of doors. **Special interests:** inner-city kids/teenagers; cultural empowerment of new populations; developing works with communities; enhancing literacy through the arts; new work by Chicago-area artists. **Facilities:** touring company; mobile outdoor stage. **Production considerations:** no expensive production demands. **Response time:** 2 months.

## FULTON THEATRE COMPANY
Box 1865; Lancaster, PA 17603-1865; (717) 394-7133
Kathleen A. Collins, *Artistic Director*

**Submission procedure:** no unsolicited scripts; accepts synopsis and letter of inquiry; prefers professional recommendation. **Types of material:** full-length plays, musicals. **Special interests:** contemporary themes. **Facilities:** Fulton Opera House, 684 seats, proscenium stage. **Production considerations:** cast limit of 10, unit set. **Best submission time:** year-round. **Response time:** 3 weeks letter; 4 months script.

## GALA HISPANIC THEATRE
Box 43209; Washington, DC 20010; (202) 234-7174
Hugo J. Medrano, *Producing/Artistic Director*

**Submission procedure:** accepts unsolicited scripts; prefers synopsis/description of play and letter of inquiry. **Types of material:** full-length plays. **Special interests:** plays by Spanish, Latino or Hispanic-American writers in Spanish or English only; prefers Spanish-language works with accompanying English translation; works that reflect sociocultural realities of Hispanics in Latin America, the Caribbean or Spain, as well as the Hispanic-American experience. **Facilities:** GALA Hispanic Theatre, 200 seats, proscenium stage. **Production considerations:** cast of 6–8. **Best submission time:** Apr–May. **Response time:** 2 weeks letter; 1 month script. **Special programs:** poetry onstage.

## GEORGE STREET PLAYHOUSE
9 Livingston Ave; New Brunswick, NJ 08901; (908) 846-2895
Wendy Liscow, *Associate Artistic Director*
Tricia Roche, *Literary Manager*

**Submission procedure:** no unsolicited scripts; professional recommendation. **Types of material:** full-length plays, one-acts for young audiences, musicals. **Special interests:** comedies and dramas that present a fresh perspective on our society and challenge our expectations of theatre; voices not traditionally heard on America's main stages; social-issue one-acts suitable for touring to schools (not seeking any other type of one-act for young audiences). **Facilities:** Mainstage, 367 seats, proscenium-thrust stage. **Production considerations:** prefers cast limit of 6 for plays, 10 for musicals. **Best submission time:** year-round. **Response time:** 6–8 months. **Special programs:** staged reading series.

## GERMINAL STAGE DENVER
2450 West 44th Ave; Denver, CO 80211; (303) 455-7108
Edward Baierlein, *Director/Manager*

**Submission procedure:** no unsolicited scripts; synopsis, 5 pages of dialogue and letter of inquiry with SASP for response. **Types of material:** full-length plays, translations, adaptations. **Special interests:** adaptations that use both dialogue and narration. **Facilities:** Germinal Stage Denver, 100 seats, thrust stage. **Production considerations:** cast limit of 10, minimal production requirements. **Best submission time:** year-round. **Response time:** 2 weeks letter; up to 6 months script.

## GEVA THEATRE
75 Woodbury Blvd; Rochester, NY 14607-1717; (716) 232-1366
Jean Ryon, *New Plays Coordinator*

**Submission procedure:** no unsolicited scripts; synopsis and letter of inquiry. **Types of material:** full-length plays, translations, adaptations, musicals. **Facilities:** GeVa Theatre, 557 seats, modified thrust stage. **Best submission time:** year-round. **Response time:** 1 week letter; up to 6 months script.

## GOODMAN THEATRE
200 South Columbus Dr; Chicago, IL 60603-6491; (312) 443-3811
Susan V. Booth, *Literary Manager*

**Submission procedure:** no unsolicited scripts; synopsis, professional recommendation and letter of inquiry. **Types of material:** full-length plays, translations, musicals. **Special interests:** social or political themes. **Facilities:** Goodman Mainstage, 683 seats, proscenium stage; Goodman Studio, 135 seats, proscenium stage. **Best submission time:** year-round. **Response time:** 2–3 months letter; 6–8 months script.

## GOODSPEED OPERA HOUSE
Box A; East Haddam, CT 06423; (203) 873-8664
Sue Frost, *Associate Producer*

**Submission procedure:** no unsolicited scripts; synopsis and letter of inquiry. **Types of material:** original musicals only. **Facilities:** Goodspeed Opera House, 400 seats, proscenium stage; Goodspeed-at-Chester, 200 seats, adaptable proscenium stage. **Best submission time:** Jan–Mar. **Response time:** 3 months letter; 12 months script.

## GREAT AMERICAN HISTORY THEATRE
30 East Tenth St; St. Paul, MN 55101; (612) 292-4323
Ron Peluso, *Interim Artistic Director*

**Submission procedure:** no unsolicited scripts; synopsis and letter of inquiry. **Types of material:** full-length plays, adaptations, musicals. **Special interests:** works involving people, events, issues, ideas and places in history; nonrealistic works preferred; no pageants; small musicals only. **Facilities:** Crawford Livingston Theatre, 597 seats, thrust stage. **Production considerations:** cast limit of 10, moderate production demands. **Best submission time:** winter–spring. **Response time:** 1 month letter; at least 2–6 months script.

## GRETNA THEATRE
Box 578; Mt. Gretna, PA 17064; (717) 964-3322

**Submission procedure:** no unsolicited scripts; synopsis, 5 pages of dialogue, character list with descriptions, production history and letter of inquiry; no cassettes for musicals. **Types of material:** full-length plays, plays for young audiences, musicals. **Special interests:** plays suitable for conservative community; prefers comedies; small-cast musicals only. **Facilities:** Mt. Gretna Playhouse, 700 seats, proscenium stage. **Production considerations:** open-air facility; 14' ceiling over stage. **Best submission time:** Aug–Apr. **Response time:** 1 month letter; 3 months script.

## THE GROUP: SEATTLE'S MULTICULTURAL THEATRE
305 Harrison St; Seattle, WA 98109; (206) 441-9480
Talvin Wilks, *Literary Manager*

**Submission procedure:** no unsolicited scripts; synopsis, 10–15 pages of dialogue, resume and letter of inquiry with SASE for response. **Types of material:** full-length plays, translations, adaptations, plays for young audiences, musicals. **Special interests:** plays suitable for multiethnic casts; serious plays on social/cultural issues; satires, musicals or comedies with bite. **Facilities:** Seattle Center's Carlton Playhouse, 200 seats, modified thrust stage. **Production considerations:** cast limit of 10; prefers unit set or simple sets. **Best submission time:** year-round. **Response time:** 4–6 weeks letter; 4–6 months script. **Special programs:** MultiCultural Theatre Works (see Development).

## THE GUTHRIE THEATER
725 Vineland Pl; Minneapolis, MN 55403; (612) 347-1100

**Submission procedure:** no unsolicited scripts; synopsis, 10 pages of dialogue and letter of inquiry. **Types of material:** full-length plays, translations, adaptations. **Facilities:** Guthrie Theater, 1309 seats, thrust stage. **Best submission time:** year-round. **Response time:** 2–3 weeks letter; 2–3 months script.

## HARTFORD STAGE COMPANY
50 Church St; Hartford, CT 06103; (203) 525-5601
Kim Euell, *Director of New Play Development*

**Submission procedure:** no unsolicited scripts; synopsis, 10 pages of dialogue and letter of inquiry. **Types of material:** full-length plays, translations, adaptations. **Facilities:** John W. Huntington Theatre, 489 seats, thrust stage. **Best submission time:** year-round. **Response time:** 10–14 days letter; 6–9 months script.

## HIP POCKET THEATRE
1627 Fairmount Ave; Fort Worth, TX 76104-4237; (817) 927-2833
Johnny Simons, *Artistic Director*

**Submission procedure:** accepts unsolicited scripts; include cassette for musicals.

**Types of material:** full-length plays, translations, adaptations, plays for young audiences, musicals, multi-media works. **Special interests:** well-crafted stories with poetic, mythic slant that incorporate ritual and ensemble; works utilizing masks, puppetry, music, dance, mime and strong visual elements. **Facilities:** Oak Acres Amphitheatre, 175 seats, outdoor amphitheatre; Magnolia Theatre, 85 seats, black box. **Production considerations:** prefers cast limit of 10–15; simple sets; no fly space in Magnolia. **Best submission time:** Oct–Feb. **Response time:** 4 weeks.

## THE HIPPODROME STATE THEATRE
25 Southeast Second Pl; Gainesville, FL 32601-6596; (904) 373-5968
David Boyce, *Dramaturg*

**Submission procedure:** no unsolicited scripts; professional recommendation or agent submission. **Types of material:** full-length plays, translations, adaptations. **Facilities:** Mainstage Theatre, 266 seats, thrust stage; Second Stage, 87 seats, flexible stage. **Production considerations:** prefers small cast, unit set. **Best submission time:** summer–fall. **Response time:** 8 months.

## HONOLULU THEATRE FOR YOUTH
2846 Ualena St; Honolulu, HI 96819-1910; (808) 839-9885
Jane Campbell, *Managing Director*

**Submission procedure:** no unsolicited scripts; synopsis, resume and letter of inquiry. **Types of material:** one-acts, plays for young audiences. **Special interests:** plays for audiences up to high school age, with contemporary themes; adaptations of fairy tales or literary classics; new works based on Pacific Rim cultures. **Facilities:** Leeward Community College Theatre, 650 seats, proscenium stage; Kaimuki High School Theatre, 650 seats, proscenium stage; McCoy Pavilion, 300 seats, flexible stage. **Production considerations:** cast limit of 10, simple production demands. **Best submission time:** year-round. **Response time:** 1 month letter; 4–5 months script.

## HORIZON THEATRE COMPANY
Box 5376, Station E; Atlanta, GA 31107; (404) 523-1477
Lisa Adler, *Co-Artistic Director*

**Submission procedure:** accepts unsolicited scripts from GA playwrights only; others send synopsis, resume and letter of inquiry. **Types of material:** full-length plays, translations, adaptations, musicals. **Special interests:** contemporary social and political issues; plays by women; southern urban themes; satires and comedies. **Facilities:** Horizon Theatre, 170–200 seats, flexible stage. **Production considerations:** plays cast from ensemble of up to 12 actors aged 20–40. **Best submission time:** May–Jun. **Response time:** 6 months letter; 12 months script. **Special programs:** Teen Ensemble: submit one-acts about teen issues to be performed by teens. Senior Citizens Ensemble: submit one-acts about senior-citizen issues to be performed by senior citizens.

## HORSE CAVE THEATRE
Box 215; Horse Cave, KY 42749; (502) 786-1200
Warren Hammack, *Artistic Director*

**Submission procedure:** no unsolicited scripts; professional recommendation. **Types of material:** full-length plays. **Special interests:** KY-based plays by KY playwrights. **Facilities:** Horse Cave Theatre, 345 seats, thrust stage. **Production considerations:** cast limit of 10, 1 set. **Best submission time:** Oct–Apr. **Response time:** varies.

## THE HUMAN RACE THEATRE COMPANY
126 North Main St, Suite 300; Dayton, OH 45402-1710; (513) 461-3823
Tony Dallas, *Playwright in Residence*

**Submission procedure:** no unsolicited scripts; professional recommendation. **Types of material:** full-length plays, one-acts, plays for young audiences. **Special interests:** OH playwrights; works for junior and senior high school audiences; contemporary issues. **Facilities:** The Loft, 219 seats, thrust stage. **Production considerations:** small casts; no fly space; plays for young audiences tour to schools. **Best submission time:** year-round. **Response time:** 6 months.

## HUNTINGTON THEATRE COMPANY
264 Huntington Ave; Boston MA 02115-4606; (617) 266-7900
Jayme Koszyn, *Literary Associate*

**Submission procedure:** no unsolicited scripts; synopsis and letter of inquiry. **Types of material:** full-length plays, translations, adaptations. **Special interests:** New England playwrights; plays of regional relevance. **Facilities:** Huntington Theatre, 850 seats, proscenium stage. **Best submission time:** May–Sep. **Response time:** 2 months letter; 6 months script.

## ILLINOIS THEATRE CENTER
400A Lakewood Blvd; Park Forest, IL 60466; (708) 481-3510
Steve S. Billig, *Artistic Director*

**Submission procedure:** no unsolicited scripts; synopsis and letter of inquiry with SASE for response. **Types of material:** full-length plays, musicals. **Facilities:** Illinois Theatre Center, 200 seats, proscenium-thrust stage. **Production considerations:** cast limit of 9 for plays, 14 for musicals. **Best submission time:** year-round. **Response time:** 1 month letter; 2 months script.

## ILLUSION THEATER
528 Hennepin Ave, Suite 704; Minneapolis, MN 55403; (612) 339-4944
Michael Robins, *Executive Producing Director*

**Submission procedure:** no unsolicited scripts; professional recommendation. **Types of material:** full-length plays, one-acts, translations, adaptations, musicals. **Special interests:** writers to collaborate on new works with company. **Facilities:**

Illusion Theater, 250 seats, semi-thrust stage. **Best submission time:** Jul–Nov. **Response time:** 6–12 months. **Special programs:** Fresh Ink Series: 5–6 plays each presented with minimal set and costumes for 1 weekend; post-performance discussion with audience, who are seated onstage; scripts selected through theatre's normal submission procedure.

## INDIANA REPERTORY THEATRE
140 West Washington St; Indianapolis, IN 46204-3465; (317) 635-5277
Janet Allen, *Associate Artistic Director*

**Submission procedure:** no unsolicited scripts; synopsis and letter of inquiry from playwright with SASE for response; inquiries only from agents (no scripts). **Types of material:** full-length plays, translations, adaptations. **Special interests:** adaptations of classic literature; plays that explore cultural/ethnic issues. **Facilities:** Mainstage, 600 seats, modified thrust stage; Upperstage, 250 seats, modified proscenium stage. **Production considerations:** cast limit of 6–8. **Best submission time:** year-round (season chosen by Jan each year). **Response time:** 3–4 months letter; 6 months script. **Special programs:** Family Plays: presentation of plays for family audiences with a focus on youth and culturally/ethnically diverse plays with an emphasis on history and literature; follow theatre's normal submission procedure above.

## INTAR HISPANIC AMERICAN ARTS CENTER
Box 788; New York, NY 10108; (212) 695-6134, -6135
Lorenzo Mans, *Literary Manager*

**Submission procedure:** accepts unsolicited scripts. **Types of material:** full-length plays, one-acts, translations, adaptations, musicals. **Special interests:** new plays by Hispanic-American writers and translations and adaptations of Hispanic works only. **Facilities:** INTAR on Theatre Row, 99 seats, proscenium stage; INTAR Stage Two, 75 seats, proscenium stage. **Production considerations:** prefers cast limit of 8; no wing space. **Best submission time:** year-round (season chosen late summer–early fall). **Response time:** 3–6 months. **Special programs:** Mini-Workshop Series leading to mainstage production.

## INTERACT THEATRE COMPANY
Box 42138; Philadelphia, PA 19101; (215) 568-8077
Seth Rozin, *Artistic Director*
Tom Gibbons, *Literary Manager*

**Submission procedure:** no unsolicited scripts; synopsis, resume and letter of inquiry. **Types of material:** full-length plays. **Special interests:** plays that theatrically explore issues of cultural conflict only (political, social, historical, etc.). **Facilities:** Harold Prince Theatre at Annenberg Center, 200 seats, proscenium or 3/4-arena stage. **Production considerations:** cast limit of 10. **Best submission time:** year-round. **Response time:** 1 month letter; 4 months script. **Special programs:** script-in-hand reading series.

## INTIMAN THEATRE COMPANY
Box 19760; Seattle, WA 98109; (206) 626-0775
Robert Menna, *Dramaturg/Literary Manager*

**Submission procedure:** no unsolicited scripts; synopsis, sample pages and letter of inquiry with SASE for response (indicate if play is unproduced). **Types of material:** full-length plays, translations, adaptations. **Special interests:** well-crafted plays that fully utilize the power of language and character relationships to explore enduring themes. **Facilities:** Intiman Playhouse, 424 seats, thrust stage. **Production considerations:** prefers cast limit of 12. **Best submission time:** year-round. **Response time:** 1 month letter; 4 months script. **Special programs:** New Voices at Intiman: developmental readings of unproduced new plays; scripts selected through theatre's normal submission procedure.

## INVISIBLE THEATRE
1400 North 1st Ave; Tucson, AZ 85719; (602) 882-9721
Deborah Dickey, *Literary Manager*

**Submission procedure:** no unsolicited scripts; professional recommendation. **Types of material:** full-length plays, one-acts, musicals. **Special interests:** mainly but not exclusively works with contemporary settings; works with strong female roles; social and political issues; small-cast musicals only. **Facilities:** Invisible Theatre, 78 seats, black box. **Production considerations:** cast limit of 10, simple set, minimal props. **Best submission time:** after 1 Sep 1996 only. **Response time:** 6–12 months.

## IRONDALE ENSEMBLE PROJECT
Box 1314, Old Chelsea Station; New York, NY 10011-1314; (212) 633-1292
Jim Niesen, *Artistic Director*

**Submission procedure:** no unsolicited scripts; letter of inquiry from playwright interested in developing work with ensemble through ongoing workshop process. **Types of material:** full-length plays, one-acts, adaptations, plays for young audiences, musicals. **Special interests:** works with political or social relevance. **Facilities:** no permanent facility. **Production considerations:** cast limit of 8–9, unit set. **Best submission time:** Sep–Jun. **Response time:** 10 weeks.

## JEWISH ENSEMBLE THEATRE
6600 West Maple Rd; West Bloomfield, MI 48322-3002; (810) 788-2900
Evelyn Orbach, *Artistic Director*

**Submission procedure:** accepts unsolicited scripts. **Types of material:** full-length plays, one-acts, plays for young audiences. **Special interests:** works on Jewish themes and/or by Jewish writers. **Facilities:** Aaron DeRoy Theatre, 194 seats, thrust stage. **Production considerations:** no fly space. **Best submission time:** late spring–early fall. **Response time:** 6 months. **Special programs:** Festival of New Plays in Staged Readings: 4 plays given readings during Feb series, possibly leading to main-stage production; scripts selected through theatre's normal submission procedure.

## JEWISH REPERTORY THEATRE

92nd Street Y; 1395 Lexington Ave; New York, NY 10128; (212) 415-5550
Ran Avni, *Artistic Director*

**Submission procedure:** accepts unsolicited scripts. **Types of material:** full-length plays, one-acts, musicals. **Special interests:** works that address some aspect of Jewish life. **Facilities:** Playhouse 91, 299 seats, thrust stage. **Production considerations:** small cast. **Best submission time:** Sep–May. **Response time:** 1 month. **Special programs:** Lee Guber Playwrights' Lab: readings of new plays.

## JOMANDI PRODUCTIONS

1444 Mayson St NE; Atlanta, GA 30324; (404) 876-6346
Julie Pradia, *Literary Manager*

**Submission procedure:** no unsolicited scripts; synopsis, dialogue sample, resume and letter of inquiry. **Types of material:** full-length plays, adaptations, plays for young audiences, musicals. **Special interests:** historical or contemporary portrayals of the African-American experience; adaptations of African-American literature. **Facilities:** 14th Street Playhouse main stage, 375 seats, proscenium/thrust stage. **Production considerations:** produces some large-cast plays but prefers average cast of 7; prefers unit set. **Best submission time:** spring–summer. **Response time:** 1 month letter; 4–6 months script.

## L. A. THEATRE WORKS

681 Venice Blvd; Venice, CA 90291; (310) 827-0808
Kirsten Dahl, *Literary Manager*

**Submission procedure:** no unsolicited scripts; agent submission. **Types of material:** full-length plays, one-acts, adaptations. **Special interests:** highly theatrical, nonrealistic new plays; contemporary adaptations of classic themes. **Facilities:** no permanent facility. **Best submission time:** year-round. **Response time:** 4–6 months. **Special programs:** Radio Theatre Series for New Plays: bimonthly performances; scripts selected from among those received through theatre's normal submission procedure. Writers Dialogue: series of advanced playwriting workshops; $250 fee for 10-week session; contact theatre for information.

## LA JOLLA PLAYHOUSE

Box 12039; La Jolla, CA 92039; (619) 550-1070
Robert Blacker, *Associate Artistic Director*
Gregory Gunter, *Literary Manager/Dramaturg*

**Submission procedure:** no unsolicited scripts; professional recommendation. **Types of material:** full-length plays, translations, musicals. **Special interests:** material pertinent to the lives we are leading at the end of this century; innovative form and language. **Facilities:** Mandell Weiss Center for the

Performing Arts, 500 seats, proscenium stage; Weiss Forum, 400 seats, thrust stage. **Best submission time:** Feb–Nov. **Response time:** 4 months.

## LA MAMA EXPERIMENTAL THEATER CLUB
74A East 4th St; New York, NY 10003; (212) 254-6468
Ellen Stewart, *Artistic Director*
Meryl Vladimer, *Associate Director*

**Submission procedure:** no unsolicited scripts; accepts unsolicited videotapes of projects with synopsis; prefers professional recommendation. **Types of material:** full-length plays, one-acts, musicals, performance art. **Special interests:** culturally diverse works with music, movement and media. **Facilities:** Annex Theater, 299 seats, flexible stage; Club, 125 seats, black box; 1st Floor Theater, 99 seats, black box. **Best submission time:** year-round. **Response time:** 2–6 months. **Special programs:** New Voices/New Plays: weekly series of readings followed by informal audience-response sessions. One Night Stand Series: weekly performance series for emerging multidisciplinary performance artists, including writers, who perform own work; theatre provides lighting, sound and stage management. Cross Cultural Institute of Theater Art Studies: texts promoting intercultural under-standing and artistic exchange developed or created through theatrical workshops, artistic explorations and premiere productions involving collaboration among artists of varying geographic and ethnic origins.

## LAGUNA PLAYHOUSE
606 Laguna Canyon Rd; Laguna Beach, CA 92651; (714) 494-8022
Andrew Barnicle, *Artistic Director*

**Submission procedure:** accepts unsolicited scripts. **Types of material:** full-length plays, plays for young audiences, musicals. **Facilities:** Moulton Theater, 418 seats, proscenium stage. **Best submission time:** year-round. **Response time:** 6–12 months.

## LINCOLN CENTER THEATER
150 West 65th St; New York, NY 10023; (212) 362-7600
Anne Cattaneo, *Dramaturg*

**Submission procedure:** no unsolicited scripts; agent submission. **Types of material:** full-length plays, one-acts, translations, adaptations, musicals. **Facilities:** Vivian Beaumont, 1000 seats, thrust stage; Mitzi E. Newhouse, 300 seats, thrust stage. **Best submission time:** year-round. **Response time:** 2–4 months.

## LIVE BAIT THEATRICAL COMPANY
3914 North Clark; Chicago, IL 60613; (312) 871-1212
Edward Thomas-Herrera, *Managing Director*

**Submission procedure:** no unsolicited scripts; synopsis and letter of inquiry from Chicago-area playwrights only; no other submissions accepted. **Types of material:** full-length plays, translations, adaptations, performance art. **Special interests:**

nonrealistic plays; performance poetry; performance art; multimedia works; works that emphasize visual aspects of staging. **Facilities:** Live Bait Theater, 70 seats, black box. **Production considerations:** prefers cast limit of 9; 1 set; no fly or wing space. **Best submission time:** year-round. **Response time:** 6 weeks letter; 6 months script.

## LIVE OAK THEATRE
200 Colorado St; Austin, TX 78701; (512) 472-5143
Tom Byrne, *Literary Manager*

**Submission procedure:** send SASE for submission guidelines. **Types of material:** full-length plays, adaptations. **Special interests:** strong character pieces with Texas or small-town feel. **Facilities:** Live Oak Theatre, 250 seats, proscenium-thrust stage. **Production considerations:** no fly space; limited wing space; smallish stage. **Best submission time:** year-round; scripts postmarked after 1 Nov will be considered for next season. **Response time:** guidelines sent in 10 days; scripts chosen in summer of year after submission. **Special programs:** Live Oak Theatre's Harvest Festival of New American Plays (see Prizes).

## LONG WHARF THEATRE
222 Sargent Dr; New Haven, CT 06511; (203) 787-4284
John Tillinger, *Literary Consultant*

**Submission procedure:** no unsolicited scripts; professional recommendation. **Types of material:** full-length plays, translations, adaptations. **Special interests:** plays about human relationships, social concerns, ethical and moral dilemmas; will also consider farces and comedies of manners. **Facilities:** Long Wharf Theatre, 484 seats, thrust stage; Stage II, 199 seats, flexible stage. **Best submission time:** year-round. **Response time:** 6 months. **Special programs:** in-house readings of new plays. Long Wharf Theatre Stage II Workshops (see Development).

## MABOU MINES
150 First Ave; New York, NY 10009; (212) 473-0559
Sharon Fogarty, *Company Manager*

**Submission procedure:** no unsolicited scripts; professional recommendation. **Types of material:** full-length plays, one-acts, translations, adaptations. **Special interests:** contemporary works on contemporary issues. **Facilities:** no permanent facility. **Best submission time:** year-round. **Response time:** 6 months.

## MAD RIVER THEATER WORKS
Box 248; West Liberty, OH 43357; (513) 465-6751
Jeff Hooper, *Producing Director*

**Submission procedure:** no unsolicited scripts; professional recommendation. **Types of material:** full-length plays, one-acts, adaptations. **Special interests:** midwestern or rural subject matter. **Facilities:** Center Stage, 150 seats, flexible stage. **Production considerations:** cast limit of 6, simple set and costumes. **Best submission time:** year-round. **Response time:** 3–4 months.

## MADISON REPERTORY THEATRE
122 State St, Suite 201; Madison, WI 53703-2500; (608) 256-0029
D. Scott Glasser, *Artistic Director*

**Submission procedure:** no unsolicited scripts; synopsis and letter of inquiry. **Types of material:** full-length plays, one-acts, translations, adaptations, musicals. **Special interests:** works with midwestern themes. **Facilities:** Isthmus Playhouse, 335 seats, thrust stage. **Production considerations:** cast limit of 15; no fly space. **Best submission time:** summer. **Response time:** 3–4 months letter; 3–4 months script.

## MAGIC THEATRE
Fort Mason Center, Bldg D; San Francisco, CA 94123; (415) 411-8001
Cathy Clark, *Literary Manager*

**Submission procedure:** no unsolicited scripts; synopsis, first 10 pages of play, resume and letter of inquiry. **Types of material:** full-length plays. **Special interests:** new plays that are innovative and/or nonlinear in form and content; political themes. **Facilities:** Magic Theatre Southside, 170 seats, proscenium stage; Magic Theatre Northside, 155 seats, thrust stage. **Production considerations:** prefers cast limit of 6. **Best submission time:** Sep–May. **Response time:** 6 weeks letter; 6–8 months script. **Special programs:** commissioning program; participation by invitation only. Also hosts Bay Area Playwrights Festival (see Development).

## MANHATTAN THEATRE CLUB
453 West 16th St; New York, NY 10011; (212) 645-5590
Kate Loewald, *Director of Play Development*

**Submission procedure:** no unsolicited scripts; agent submission. **Types of material:** full-length plays, musicals. **Facilities:** Stage I at City Center, 299 seats, proscenium stage; Stage II, 150 seats, thrust stage. **Production considerations:** casts average 6–8; 1 set or unit set. **Best submission time:** year-round. **Response time:** 6 months. **Special programs:** readings and workshop productions of new musicals. "First-hearing" readings: in-house readings of new plays or first drafts. Manhattan Theatre Club Playwriting Fellowships (see Fellowships and Grants).

## MARIN THEATRE COMPANY
397 Miller Ave; Mill Valley, CA 94941; (415) 388-5200
Lee Sankowich, *Artistic Director*

**Submission procedure:** no unsolicited scripts; agent submission. **Types of material:** full-length plays, translations, adaptations, plays for young audiences. **Facilities:** Marin Theatre, 250 seats, proscenium stage; 2nd theatre, 109 seats, black box. **Best submission time:** Jun–Aug. **Response time:** 6 months.

## MARK TAPER FORUM
135 North Grand Ave; Los Angeles, CA 90012; (213) 972-7574
Oliver Mayer, *Associate Literary Manager*

**Submission procedure:** no unsolicited scripts; description of work, 5–10 sample pages and letter of inquiry. **Types of material:** full-length plays, one-acts, translations, adaptations, plays for young audiences, musicals, literary cabaret, performance art. **Facilities:** Mark Taper Forum, 742 seats, thrust stage; Taper, Too, 80–90 seats, flexible stage. **Best submission time:** call for information. **Response time:** 4–6 weeks letter; 8–10 weeks script. **Special programs:** Mark Taper Forum Developmental Programs (see Development).

## McCARTER THEATRE CENTER FOR THE PERFORMING ARTS
91 University Pl; Princeton, NJ 08540; (609) 683-9100
Janice Paran, *Literary Manager/Dramaturg*

**Submission procedure:** no unsolicited scripts; synopsis and letter of inquiry. **Types of material:** full-length plays, musicals. **Facilities:** McCarter Theatre, 1077 seats, proscenium stage. **Best submission time:** Sep–May. **Response time:** 1 month letter; 3 months script. **Special programs:** New Play Festival: annual 2-week festival presenting commissioned one-acts and 1 full-length play; participation by invitation only.

## MERRIMACK REPERTORY THEATRE
Box 228; Lowell, MA 01853; (508) 454-6324
David G. Kent, *Artistic Director*

**Submission procedure:** no unsolicited scripts; synopsis and letter of inquiry. **Types of material:** full-length plays, translations, adaptations, plays for young audiences, musicals. **Special interests:** well-crafted stories with a poetic and human focus; varied ethnic tapestries of American life and love. **Facilities:** Liberty Hall, 386 seats, thrust stage. **Production considerations:** moderate cast size, simple set. **Best submission time:** spring–summer. **Response time:** 1 month letter (if interested); 6 months script.

## MERRY-GO-ROUND PLAYHOUSE
Box 506; Auburn, NY 13021; (315) 255-1305
Gregory Rapp, *Theatre Manager*

**Submission procedure:** accepts unsolicited scripts. **Types of material:** full-length plays, translations, adaptations, plays for young audiences, musicals. **Special interests:** participatory plays for young audiences with cast limit of 3–4; plays for grades K–12. **Facilities:** Merry-Go-Round Playhouse (adaptable), 325 seats, proscenium stage or 100 seats, thrust stage. **Production considerations:** cast limit of 5. **Best submission time:** Jan–Feb. **Response time:** 2 months.

## METRO THEATER COMPANY
524 Trinity Ave; St. Louis, MO 63130; (314) 727-3552
Carol North Evans, *Producing Director*

**Submission procedure:** no unsolicited scripts; professional recommendation. **Types of material:** plays and musicals for young audiences. **Special interests:** no works longer than 60 minutes; plays with music and musicals that are not dramatically limited by traditional concepts of "children's theatre." **Facilities:** touring company. **Production considerations:** works cast from ensemble of 5; sets suitable for touring. **Best submission time:** year-round. **Response time:** 2–3 months. **Special programs:** new plays readings; commissioning program; interested writers send letter of inquiry with recommendations from theatres who have produced writer's work.

## METROSTAGE
1816 Duke St; Alexandria, VA 22314; (703) 548-9044
Carolyn Griffin, *Producing Director*

**Submission procedure:** no unsolicited scripts; synopsis, first 10 pages of dialogue, list of productions and readings, and letter of inquiry. **Types of material:** full-length plays, one-acts, plays for young audiences, musicals. **Facilities:** MetroStage, 100 seats, thrust stage. **Production considerations:** cast limit of 8, prefers 4; prefers 1 set. **Best submission time:** year-round. **Response time:** 1 month letter; 1 month script. **Special programs:** First Stage: staged reading series Jan–May.

## MILL MOUNTAIN THEATRE
1 Market Square SE; Roanoke, VA 24011-1437; (703) 342-5730
Jo Weinstein, *Literary Manager*

**Submission procedure:** accepts unsolicited one-acts only; synopsis, 10 pages of dialogue and letter of inquiry for all other submissions. **Types of material:** full-length plays, one-acts, musicals. **Special interests:** plays with racially mixed casts. **Facilities:** Mill Mountain Theatre, 400 seats, flexible proscenium stage; Theatre B, 125 seats, flexible space. **Production considerations:** cast limit of 15 for plays, 24 for musicals; prefers unit set. **Best submission time:** year-round. **Response time:** 6 weeks letter; 6–8 months script. **Special programs:** Centerpieces: monthly lunchtime staged readings of one-acts by emerging playwrights; unpublished one-acts 25–35 minutes long (no 10-minute plays). The Mill Mountain Theatre New Play Competition: The Norfolk Southern Festival of New Works (see Prizes).

## MILWAUKEE CHAMBER THEATRE
158 North Broadway; Milwaukee, WI 53202; (414) 276-8842
Montgomery Davis, *Artistic Director*

**Submission procedure:** no unsolicited scripts; professional recommendation. **Types of material:** full-length plays, one-acts, translations, adaptations. **Special interests:** strong, well-crafted plays; plays about Shaw for annual Shaw Festival. **Facilities:** Broadway Theatre Center: main stage, 372 seats, proscenium stage;

studio, 99 seats, black box. **Production considerations:** 1 set or unit set. **Best submission time:** summer. **Response time:** 2 months.

## MILWAUKEE PUBLIC THEATRE
626 East Kilbourn Ave, #802; Milwaukee, WI 53202-3237; (414) 271-8484
Barbara Leigh, *Co-Artistic/Producing Director*

**Submission procedure:** no unsolicited scripts; synopsis and letter of inquiry with SASE for response. **Types of material:** full-length plays, one-acts, translations, adaptations, plays for young audiences, cabaret/revues, clown/vaudeville shows. **Special interests:** works with cast of 1–3 playing multiple roles; political satire; social-political and regional or local themes; plays dealing with disabilities; interart works; new clown/vaudeville shows; works for young and family audiences. **Facilities:** no permanent facility. **Production considerations:** simple production demands; productions tour. **Best submission time:** year-round for plays dealing with disabilities; Sep only for all other submissions. **Response time:** 6 months letter; 12 months script. **Special programs:** outdoor park performances.

## MILWAUKEE REPERTORY THEATER
108 East Wells St; Milwaukee, WI 53202; (414) 224-1761
Joseph Hanreddy, *Artistic Director*

**Submission procedure:** no unsolicited scripts; agent submission. **Types of material:** full-length plays, translations, adaptations, musicals, cabaret/revues. **Special interests:** works for cabaret space must not exceed 80 minutes in length. **Facilities:** Powerhouse Theatre, 720 seats, thrust stage; Stiemke Theatre, 200 seats, flexible stage; Stackner Cabaret, 100 seats, cabaret stage. **Best submission time:** year-round. **Response time:** 2–3 months.

## MISSOURI REPERTORY THEATRE
4949 Cherry St; Kansas City, MO 64110-2499; (816) 235-2727
George Keathley, *Artistic Director*

**Submission procedure:** no unsolicited scripts; synopsis and letter of inquiry. **Types of material:** full-length plays, translations, adaptations. **Facilities:** Helen F. Spencer Theatre, 740 seats, modified thrust stage. **Best submission time:** year-round. **Response time:** 1 month letter; script varies. **Special programs:** Playwrights' Stage: scripts developed through series of readings leading to production.

## MIXED BLOOD THEATRE COMPANY
1501 South Fourth St; Minneapolis, MN 55454; (612) 338-0937
David Kunz, *Script Czar*

**Submission procedure:** no unsolicited scripts; synopsis and letter of inquiry. **Types of material:** full-length plays, translations, musicals, cabaret/revues. **Facilities:** Main Stage, 200 seats, flexible stage. **Best submission time:** year-round. **Response time:** 1 month letter; 2–6 months script. **Special programs:** Mixed Blood Versus America (see Prizes).

## THE MONTANA REPERTORY THEATRE
Department of Drama and Dance; The University of Montana;
    Missoula, MT 59812-1582; (406) 243-6809
Greg Johnson, *Artistic Director*

**Submission procedure:** no unsolicited scripts; synopsis, resume and letter of inquiry. **Types of material:** full-length plays, one-acts, musicals. **Special interests:** plays by and about Native Americans. **Facilities:** touring company. **Best submission time:** summer. **Response time:** 3 months letter; 6 months script.

## MUSIC-THEATRE GROUP
29 Bethune St; New York, NY 10014; (212) 924-3108
Jun–Aug: Box 641; Stockbridge, MA 01262
Lyn Austin, *Producing Director*
Diane Wondisford, *General Director*

**Submission procedure:** no unsolicited scripts; direct solicitation to playwright or agent. **Types of material:** music-theatre works, operas, cabaret. **Special interests:** experimental musical works; collaborations between music-theatre, dance and the visual arts. **Facilities:** no permanent facility.

## NATIONAL JEWISH THEATER
5050 West Church St; Skokie, IL 60077; (708) 675-2200
Jeff Ginsberg and Susan Padveen, *Co-Artistic Directors*

**Submission procedure:** no unsolicited scripts; synopsis and letter of inquiry with SASE for response. **Types of material:** full-length plays, translations, adaptations, musicals. **Special interests:** American Jewish experience from early immigration to contemporary problems. **Facilities:** Mainstage, 250 seats, open stage. **Production considerations:** prefers cast limit of 8–10; no more than 2 sets; no fly space. **Best submission time:** year-round. **Response time:** 2 months letter; 4 months script.

## NATIONAL THEATRE OF THE DEAF
Box 659; Chester, CT 06412; (203) 526-4971 (voice), -4974 (TTY)
Will Rhys, *Artistic Director*

**Submission procedure:** no unsolicited scripts; synopsis, character breakdown, sample pages and letter of inquiry with SASE for response. **Types of material:** full-length plays, adaptations, plays for young audiences. **Special interests:** deaf issues; culturally diverse plays. **Facilities:** touring company. **Production considerations:** cast limit of 10; production must tour. **Best submission time:** year-round. **Response time:** 1 month letter; 3–6 months script.

## NEBRASKA REPERTORY THEATRE
215 Temple Bldg; 12th and R Sts; Lincoln, NE 68588-0201; (402) 472-2072
Kathy Fletcher, *Literary Manager*

**Submission procedure:** no unsolicited scripts; synopsis and letter of inquiry with SASE for response. **Types of material:** full-length plays, one-acts, musicals. **Special interests:** unpublished scripts for NEW THEATRE series (see below); plays that contribute to multicultural awareness. **Facilities:** Howell Theatre, 380 seats, proscenium stage; Studio Theatre, 180 seats, black box. **Production considerations:** simple set for Studio Theatre. **Best submission time:** Aug–Feb. **Response time:** 1 month letter; 2–6 months script. **Special programs:** NEW THEATRE reading and performance series.

## NEBRASKA THEATRE CARAVAN
6915 Cass St; Omaha, NE 68132; (402) 553-4890
Richard L. Scott, *Managing Director*

**Submission procedure:** no unsolicited scripts; synopsis and letter of inquiry. **Types of material:** full-length plays, adaptations, plays for young audiences, musicals. **Facilities:** touring company. **Production considerations:** cast limit of 12, 1 set. **Best submission time:** year-round. **Response time:** 1 month letter; 3 months script.

## NEW DRAMATISTS
See Membership and Service Organizations.

## NEW FEDERAL THEATRE
466 Grand St; New York, NY 10002; (212) 598-0400
Woodie King, Jr., *Producing Director*
Pat White, *Company Manager*

**Submission procedure:** no unsolicited scripts; professional recommendation. **Types of material:** full-length plays. **Special interests:** social and political issues; family and community themes related to minorities. **Facilities:** Henry Street Settlement Abron Arts Center: Theatre 1, 350 seats, proscenium stage; Theatre 2, 100 seats, 3/4-arena stage; Theatre 3, 100 seats, endstage. **Production considerations:** small cast, no more than 2 sets. **Best submission time:** year-round. **Response time:** 5 months.

## NEW JERSEY SHAKESPEARE FESTIVAL
c/o Drew University; 36 Madison Ave; Madison, NJ 07940; (201) 408-3278
Bonnie J. Monte, *Artistic Director*

**Submission procedure:** no unsolicited scripts; synopsis and letter of inquiry. **Types of material:** full-length plays, translations, adaptations. **Special interests:** translations and/or adaptations of classic works only. **Facilities:** Festival Theatre, 238 seats, thrust stage. **Production considerations:** modest technical demands; limited wing space. **Best submission time:** early fall. **Response time:** 2 months letter; 1 month script.

## NEW REPERTORY THEATRE
Box 418; Newton Highlands, MA 02161; (617) 332-7058
Larry Lane, *Artistic Director*

**Submission procedure:** no unsolicited scripts; direct solicitation to playwright or agent. **Types of material:** full-length plays, translations, adaptations. **Special interests:** multicultural themes; intimate, interpersonal themes. **Facilities:** New Repertory Theatre, 150 seats, thrust stage.

## NEW STAGE THEATRE
Box 4792; Jackson, MS 39296-4792; (601) 948-0143
John Maxwell, *Interim Artistic Director*

**Submission procedure:** no unsolicited scripts; synopsis and letter of inquiry. **Types of material:** full-length plays. **Facilities:** Meyer Crystal Auditorium, 364 seats, proscenium stage. **Production considerations:** cast of 3–8. **Best submission time:** summer–fall. **Response time:** 4 weeks letter; 3 months script. **Special programs:** New Play Series: public readings of 8 new plays every year; full production of a new play every season.

## NEW YORK STATE THEATRE INSTITUTE
The EGG; Empire State Plaza; Albany, NY 12223; (518) 274-3200
Patricia Di Benedetto Snyder, *Producing Director*

**Submission procedure:** accepts unsolicited scripts. **Types of material:** full-length plays, adaptations, musicals. **Special interests:** mainly presents works for family audiences. **Facilities:** Mainstage, 900 seats, flexible stage; Studio Theatre, 450 seats, thrust stage. **Best submission time:** Jun–Sep. **Response time:** 3–4 months. **Special programs:** New Works: developmental workshops, staged readings or workshop productions; playwright receives negotiable remuneration, travel, housing.

## NEW YORK THEATRE WORKSHOP
79 East 4th St; New York, NY 10003; (212) 780-9037
Gerard Manning, *Literary Manager*

**Submission procedure:** no unsolicited scripts; synopsis, 10-page sample scene and letter of inquiry. **Types of material:** full-length plays, one-acts, translations, music-theatre works, proposals for performance projects. **Special interests:** large issues; socially relevant and/or minority issues; innovative form and language. **Facilities:** 79 East 4th Street Theatre, 150 seats, proscenium stage. **Best submission time:** fall–spring. **Response time:** 4 weeks letter; 3–5 months script. **Special programs:** Mondays at Three: reading series, developmental workshops and symposiums. Playwrights Circle. Summer writing residency.

## NORTHLIGHT THEATRE
600 Davis St; Evanston, IL 60201; (708) 869-7732
Brian Russell, *Assistant Artistic Director*

**Submission procedure:** no unsolicited scripts; synopsis and letter of inquiry. **Types of material:** full-length plays, translations, adaptations, musicals. **Special interests:** translations and adaptations of "lost" plays; the public world and public issues; plays of ideas; works that are passionate and/or hilarious; stylistic exploration and complexity; no domestic realism. **Facilities:** no permanent facility; company performs in various proscenium- or thrust-stage venues with 250–500 seats. **Best submission time:** Sep–Feb. **Response time:** 1 month letter; 2–4 months script.

## NOVEL STAGES
Box 58879; Philadelphia, PA 19102-8879; (215) 546-0999
Clista Townsend, *Artistic Associate*

**Submission procedure:** no unsolicited scripts; synopsis and letter of inquiry with SASP for response. **Types of material:** full-length plays, one-acts, translations, adaptations, plays for young audiences. **Facilities:** Stage III at 1619 Walnut St, 130 seats, endstage. **Production considerations:** simple set; no fly space, very little wing space. **Best submission time:** year-round. **Response time:** 6 months letter; 9–12 months script.

## ODYSSEY THEATRE ENSEMBLE
2055 South Sepulveda Blvd; Los Angeles, CA 90025; (310) 477-2055
Jan Lewis, *Literary Manager/Dramaturg*

**Submission procedure:** no unsolicited scripts; synopsis, 8–10 pages of dialogue, play's production history (if any), resume and letter of inquiry; include cassette for musicals. **Types of material:** full-length plays, translations, adaptations, musicals. **Special interests:** culturally diverse works; works with innovative form or provocative subject matter; works exploring the enduring questions of human existence and the possibilities of the live-theatre experience; works with political or sociological impact. **Facilities:** Odyssey 1, 99 seats, flexible stage; Odyssey 2, 99 seats, thrust stage; Odyssey 3, 99 seats, endstage. **Production considerations:** plays must be 90 minutes or longer. **Best submission time:** year-round. **Response time:** 2–4 weeks letter; 6 months script.

## OLD GLOBE THEATRE
Box 2171; San Diego, CA 92112-2171; (619) 231-1941
Raúl Moncada, *Literary Manager*

**Submission procedure:** no unsolicited scripts; synopsis and letter of inquiry. **Types of material:** full-length plays, translations, adaptations, musicals. **Special interests:** well-crafted plays; strongly theatrical material. **Facilities:** Old Globe Theatre, 581 seats, modified thrust stage; Cassius Carter Centre Stage, 225 seats, arena stage; Lowell Davies Festival Stage, 620 seats, outdoor stage. **Production considerations:**

prefers cast limit of 8. **Best submission time:** year-round. **Response time:** 2–3 months letter; 6–10 months script.

## OLNEY THEATRE CENTER FOR THE ARTS
Box 550; Olney, MD 20830; (301) 924-4485
Jim Petosa, *Artistic Director*

**Submission procedure:** no unsolicited scripts; professional recommendation. **Types of material:** full-length plays, translations, adaptations. **Facilities:** Mainstage, 500 seats, proscenium stage. **Production considerations:** cast limit of 8. **Best submission time:** year-round. **Response time:** 6 months.

## OMAHA THEATER COMPANY FOR YOUNG PEOPLE
(formerly The Emmy Gifford Children's Theater)
3504 Center St; Omaha, NE 68105; (402) 345-4849
James Larson, *Artistic Director*

**Submission procedure:** no unsolicited scripts; professional recommendation. **Types of material:** plays for family audiences. **Special interests:** plays based on children's literature and contemporary issues; multicultural themes. **Facilities:** Omaha Theater Company, 500 seats, proscenium stage; second stage, 150 seats, black box. **Production considerations:** cast limit of 15; prefers unit set. **Best submission time:** year-round. **Response time:** 6 months.

## ONTOLOGICAL-HYSTERIC THEATER
260 West Broadway; New York, NY 10013; (212) 941-8911

**Submission procedure:** no unsolicited scripts; direct soliciation to playwright or agent. **Types of material:** full-length plays. **Facilities:** Ontological at St. Mark's Theater, 80 seats, black box.

## THE OPEN EYE THEATER
Box 204; Denver, NY 12421; (607) 326-4986
Amie Brockway, *Producing Artistic Director*

**Submission procedure:** no unsolicited scripts; synopsis and letter of inquiry with self-addressed, unstamped envelope for possible response. **Types of material:** full-length plays, one-acts, translations, adaptations. **Special interests:** plays for multigenerational audiences only; culturally diverse themes; plays with music; ensemble plays; plays of any length (10 minutes or more) by upstate NY residents, especially Catskill Mountain area writers, about life in rural upstate NY. **Facilities:** no permanent facility. **Production considerations:** minimal set. **Best submission time:** Oct–Apr. **Response time:** 1 week letter (if interested); 3–6 months script. **Special programs:** New Play Works: summer new-play developmental program of readings and workshop productions.

## OREGON SHAKESPEARE FESTIVAL

Box 158; Ashland, OR 97520; (503) 482-2111
Cynthia White, *Associate Director/Play Development*

**Submission procedure:** no unsolicited scripts; synopsis, 10 pages of dialogue and letter of inquiry. **Types of material:** full-length plays, translations. **Special interests:** Pacific Northwest playwrights; submissions by women and minorities encouraged. **Facilities:** Angus Bowmer Theatre, 600 seats, thrust stage; Elizabethan Theatre, 1194 seats, outdoor Elizabethan stage; Black Swan, 140 seats, black box. **Best submission time:** year-round. **Response time:** varies.

## ORGANIC THEATER COMPANY

3319 North Clark St; Chicago, IL 60657; (312) 327-2427
Paul Frellick, *Artistic Director*

**Submission procedure:** no unsolicited scripts; synopsis, 10 pages of dialogue and letter of inquiry. **Types of material:** full-length plays, long one-acts. **Special interests:** unproduced works only; imaginative plays that explore the theatrical medium; scripts by women and minorities; writers willing to work a year or more to bring script from initial idea through workshop to limited or full production. **Facilities:** Mainstage, 400 seats, modified thrust stage; Organic Greenhouse, 90 seats, proscenium stage; South Hall, up to 60 seats, flexible space. **Best submission time:** year-round. **Response time:** 4–6 weeks letter; 2–4 months script.

## PAN ASIAN REPERTORY THEATRE

47 Great Jones St; New York, NY 10012; (212) 505-5655
Tisa Chang, *Artistic/Producing Director*

**Submission procedure:** accepts unsolicited scripts with resume. **Types of material:** full-length plays, translations, adaptations, musicals. **Special interests:** Asian or Asian-American themes only. **Facilities:** 46th Street Playhouse, 150 seats, 38' x 40' open stage. **Production considerations:** prefers cast limit of 8. **Best submission time:** summer. **Response time:** 9 months. **Special programs:** staged readings and workshops.

## PEGASUS PLAYERS

1145 West Wilson; Chicago, IL 60640; (312) 878-9761
Arlene J. Crewdson, *Artistic Director*

**Submission procedure:** no unsolicited scripts; synopsis and letter of inquiry. **Types of material:** full-length plays, translations, adaptations, musicals. **Facilities:** The O'Rourke Center for the Performing Arts, 250 seats, proscenium stage. **Best submission time:** year-round. **Response time:** 1 month letter; 4–6 months script. **Special programs:** Chicago Young Playwrights Festival: annual Jan festival of plays by Chicago-area high school students; write for information.

## PENNSYLVANIA STAGE COMPANY
837 Linden St; Allentown, PA 18101; (610) 434-6110
Charles Richter, *Artistic Director*

**Submission procedure:** no unsolicited scripts; synopsis, cast list, 10 pages of dialogue and letter of inquiry. **Types of material:** full-length plays, musicals. **Facilities:** J. I. Rodale Theatre, 274 seats, proscenium stage. **Production considerations:** cast limit of 10 for musicals, 11 for plays; prefers 1 set. **Best submission time:** year-round. **Response time:** 1 month letter; 3 months script. **Special programs:** New Evolving Works Program: staged reading series.

## PENOBSCOT THEATRE COMPANY
183 Main St; Bangor, ME 04401; (207) 942-3333
Mark Torres, *Producing Artistic Director*

**Submission procedure:** no unsolicited scripts; synopsis and letter of inquiry. **Types of material:** full-length plays, plays for young audiences. **Special interests:** new American plays. **Facilities:** Penobscot Theatre, 132 seats, proscenium/thrust stage. **Production considerations:** small cast, limited production requirements; small performance space. **Best submission time:** late fall. **Response time:** 4 weeks letter; 2 months script. **Special programs:** play reading series in late spring; scripts selected through theatre's normal submission procedure.

## THE PENUMBRA THEATRE COMPANY
The Martin Luther King Bldg; 270 North Kent St; St. Paul, MN 55102-1794;
    (612) 224-4601
Lou Bellamy, *Artistic Director*

**Submission procedure:** accepts unsolicited scripts with resume. **Types of material:** full-length plays, one-acts, translations, adaptations, plays for young audiences, musicals. **Special interests:** works that address the African-American experience. **Facilities:** Hallie Q. Brown Theater, 260 seats, proscenium/thrust stage. **Best submission time:** year-round. **Response time:** 6–9 months. **Special programs:** Cornerstone Dramaturgy and Development Project (see Development).

## THE PEOPLE'S LIGHT AND THEATRE COMPANY
39 Conestoga Rd; Malvern, PA 19355-1798; (215) 647-1900
Alda Cortese, *Literary Manager*

**Submission procedure:** no unsolicited scripts; synopsis, cast list, 10 pages of dialogue and letter of inquiry. **Types of material:** full-length plays, translations, adaptations. **Facilities:** People's Light and Theatre, 350 seats, flexible stage; Steinbright Stage, 99–150 seats, flexible stage. **Production considerations:** prefers cast limit of 12, 1 set or unit set. **Best submission time:** year-round. **Response time:** 2 weeks letter; 8–10 months script.

## PERSEVERANCE THEATRE
914 3rd St; Douglas, AK 99824; (907) 364-2421, -2151
Molly Smith, *Artistic Director*

**Submission procedure:** no unsolicited scripts; synopsis, resume, list of previous productions and letter of inquiry. **Types of material:** full-length plays, one-acts. **Special interests:** new plays by AK playwrights; plays about ethnic experiences, gender, sexual orientation, disabilities, etc. **Facilities:** Mainstage, 150 seats, thrust stage; Phoenix Stage, 50–75 seats, flexible space; Voices Stage, 100 seats, flexible space. **Best submission time:** year-round. **Response time:** 1 month letter; 6 months script.

## PETERBOROUGH PLAYERS
Box 1; Peterborough, NH 03458; (603) 924-7585
Ellen M. Dinerstein, *Producing Director*

**Submission procedure:** no unsolicited scripts; synopsis and letter of inquiry. **Types of material:** full-length plays, one-acts, adaptations. **Facilities:** Hadley Barn, 193 seats, flexible stage. **Best submission time:** Sep–Jan. **Response time:** 2 months letter; 6 months script. **Special programs:** staged readings.

## PHILADELPHIA FESTIVAL THEATRE FOR NEW PLAYS AT ANNENBERG CENTER
3680 Walnut St; Philadelphia, PA 19104; (215) 898-3900
Sally de Sousa, *General Manager*

**Submission procedure:** no unsolicited scripts; synopsis, 10 pages of dialogue, resume and letter of inquiry. **Types of material:** full-length plays. **Special interests:** only plays not previously given full production; plays which reflect larger social issues through strong character relationships. **Facilities:** Zellerbach Theatre, 900 seats, proscenium/thrust stage; Harold Prince Theatre, 200 seats, proscenium or 3/4-arena stage. **Best submission time:** year-round. **Response time:** 3–4 weeks letter; 6–9 months script. **Special programs:** Previewers: series of script-in-hand readings; scripts selected through theatre's normal submission procedure. The Dennis McIntyre Playwriting Award (see Prizes).

## THE PHILADELPHIA THEATRE COMPANY
The Bourse Bldg; 21 South 5th St; Philadelphia, PA 19106; (215) 592-8333
Sara Garonzik, *Producing Artistic Director*

**Submission procedure:** no unsolicited scripts; agent submission. **Types of material:** full-length plays. **Special interests:** new American plays; social/humanistic themes; sense of theatricality; minority playwrights. **Facilities:** Plays and Players Theater, 324 seats, proscenium stage. **Best submission time:** Jan–Jun. **Response time:** 6–8 months. **Special programs:** STAGES: program of staged readings.

## THE PHOENIX THEATRE

See Festival of Emerging American Theatre (FEAT) Competition in Prizes.


## THE PHOENIX THEATRE COMPANY
Box 236; Purchase, NY 10577; (914) 251-6288
Bram Lewis, *Artistic Director*

**Submission procedure:** accepts unsolicited scripts. **Types of material:** full-length plays, one-acts, translations, adaptations, plays for young audiences, musicals, cabaret/revues, performance art. **Special interests:** mainstream works for main stage; more provocative works for second stage. **Facilities:** main stage, 516 seats, proscenium stage; second stage, 300 seats, black box. **Best submission time:** Jan. **Response time:** 10 weeks.


## PILLSBURY HOUSE THEATRE
3501 Chicago Ave S; Minneapolis, MN 55407; (612) 824-0708
Ralph Remington, *Producing Artistic Director*

**Submission procedure:** accepts unsolicited scripts. **Types of material:** full-length plays, one-acts, translations, adaptations, plays for young audiences, musicals, performance art. **Special interests:** only works that speak to issues of sociopolitical change; works that address marginalized groups, e.g., people of color, women, lesbians, gays, the disabled and the economically disenfranchised; nonlinear works. **Facilities:** Pillsbury House Theatre, 120 seats, black box/proscenium stage. **Production considerations:** cast limit of 12; no fly space. **Best submission time:** year-round. **Response time:** 10 weeks.


## PIONEER THEATRE COMPANY
University of Utah; Salt Lake City, UT 84112; (801) 581-6356
Charles Morey, *Artistic Director*

**Submission procedure:** no unsolicited scripts; synopsis and letter of inquiry. **Types of material:** full-length plays, translations, adaptations, musicals. **Facilities:** Pioneer Memorial Theatre, 1000 seats, proscenium stage. **Best submission time:** fall. **Response time:** 1 month letter; 6 months script.


## PIRATE PLAYHOUSE—ISLAND THEATRE
2200 Periwinkle Way; Sanibel Island, FL 33957; (813) 472-0006
Robert Cacioppo, *Artistic Director*

**Submission procedure:** no unsolicited scripts; synopsis, 10 pages of dialogue, character breakdown and letter of inquiry with SASP for response. **Types of material:** plays for young audiences. **Facilities:** Pirate Playhouse, 180 seats, thrust/proscenium/arena. **Best submission time:** year-round. **Response time:** 1–3 months letter; 3–5 months script.

## PITTSBURGH PUBLIC THEATER
Allegheny Square; Pittsburgh, PA 15212-5349; (412) 323-8200
Rob Zellers, *Literary Manager*

**Submission procedure:** no unsolicited scripts; synopsis, dialogue sample and letter of inquiry with SASE for response. **Types of material:** full-length plays, translations, adaptations, musicals. **Facilities:** Theodore L. Hazlett, Jr. Theater, 457 seats, thrust or arena stage. **Best submission time:** year-round. **Response time:** 1 month letter; 3 months script.

## PLAYHOUSE ON THE SQUARE
51 South Cooper St; Memphis, TN 38104; (901) 725-0776
Jackie Nichols, *Executive Producer*

**Submission procedure:** accepts unsolicited scripts. **Types of material:** full-lcngth plays, musicals. **Facilities:** Playhouse on the Square, 250 seats, proscenium stage; Circuit Playhouse, 136 seats, proscenium stage. **Best submission time:** year-round. **Response time:** 3–5 months. **Special programs:** Playhouse on the Square New Play Competition (see Prizes).

## PLAYMAKERS REPERTORY COMPANY
CB# 3235 Graham Memorial Bldg, 052A; Chapel Hill, NC 27599-3235;
    (919) 962-1132
David Hammond, *Associate Producing Director*

**Submission procedure:** no unsolicited scripts; professional recommendation. **Types of material:** full-length plays, translations, adaptations. **Facilities:** Paul Green Theatre, 498 seats, thrust stage. **Best submission time:** Apr–Sep. **Response time:** 6 months.

## THE PLAYWRIGHTS' CENTER

See Membership and Service Organizations.

## PLAYWRIGHTS HORIZONS
416 West 42nd St; New York, NY 10036-6896; (212) 564-1235
Tim Sanford, *Literary Manager*
Dana Williams, *Director of Musical Theater Program*

**Submission procedure:** prefers unsolicited scripts with resume and cover letter; if necessary, will accept synopsis, dialogue sample and letter of inquiry; for musicals, send script and cassette (no synopses). **Types of material:** full-length plays, musicals. **Special interests:** works by American writers only; works with strong sense of language that take theatrical risks; works by minority writers. **Facilities:** Mainstage, 145 seats, proscenium stage; Studio Theater, 72 seats, black box. **Best submission time:** year-round. **Response time:** 6 weeks letter; 3–6 months script.

## POPE THEATRE COMPANY
262 South Ocean Blvd; Manalapan, FL 33462; (407) 585-3404
Louis Tyrrell, *Producing Director*

**Submission procedure:** no unsolicited scripts; agent submission. **Types of material:** full-length plays, plays for young audiences. **Special interests:** contemporary issues and ideas. **Facilities:** Lois Pope Theatre, 250 seats, thrust stage. **Production considerations:** cast of 2–6, 1 set. **Best submission time:** year-round. **Response time:** 3–4 months. **Special programs:** reading series.

## PORTLAND REPERTORY THEATRE
2 World Trade Center; 25 Southwest Salmon St; Portland, OR 97204-3233;
    (503) 224-4491
Kit Koenig, *Literary Manager/Dramaturg*

**Submission procedure:** no unsolicited scripts; synopsis with cast breakdown and number of sets, first 10–15 pages of script (including character and set descriptions) and letter of inquiry with SASE for response. **Types of material:** full-length plays, translations, adaptations. **Facilities:** Portland Repertory Theatre, 230 seats, proscenium stage; Stage II, 160 seats, thrust stage. **Production considerations:** cast limit of 10, not more than 2 sets. **Best submission time:** May–Aug. **Response time:** 4 months letter; 6–12 months script. **Special programs:** staged reading series, play development for Portland-area playwrights.

## PORTLAND STAGE COMPANY
Box 1458; Portland, ME 04104; (207) 774-1043
Matthew Arbour, *Literary Manager*

**Submission procedure:** no unsolicited scripts; synopsis, dialogue sample and letter of inquiry. **Types of material:** full-length plays, translations, adaptations. **Facilities:** Performing Arts Center Theatre, 290 seats, proscenium stage; PSC Rehearsal Hall, 90 seats, flexible space (readings only). **Best submission time:** year-round. **Response time:** 2 months letter; 3–6 months script. **Special programs:** in-house play readings.

## THE PUBLIC THEATER/NEW YORK SHAKESPEARE FESTIVAL
Joseph Papp Public Theater; 425 Lafayette St; New York, NY 10003;
    (212) 598-7129
Shelby Jiggetts, *Play Development Department*

**Submission procedure:** accepts unsolicited scripts; also accepts synopsis, 10-page sample scene and letter of inquiry; include cassette of 3–5 songs for musicals and operas. **Types of material:** full-length plays, translations, adaptations, musicals, operas. **Facilities:** Newman Theater, 299 seats, proscenium stage; Anspacher Theater, 275 seats, thrust stage; Martinson Hall, 200 seats, proscenium stage; LuEsther Hall, 150 seats, flexible stage; Shiva Theater, 100 seats, flexible stage. **Best submission time:** year-round. **Response time:** 3 weeks letter; 6 months script.

## THE PURPLE ROSE THEATRE COMPANY
137 Park St; Chelsea, MI 48118; (313) 475-5817
Anthony Caselli, *Literary Coordinator*

**Submission procedure:** accepts unsolicited scripts. **Types of material:** full-length plays. **Special interests:** plays that speak to a middle-American audience. **Facilities:** Garage Theatre, 119 seats, thrust stage. **Production considerations:** cast limit of 10; no fly or wing space. **Best submission time:** year-round. **Response time:** 6–9 months. **Special programs:** Playwrights Unit: area playwrights meet monthly to discuss works; interested playwrights send letter of introduction addressed to unit. Developmental workshops: members of Playwrights Unit or playwrights found through theatre's normal submission procedure work with company to develop scripts through readings and conferences.

## REMAINS THEATRE
750 North Orleans, 4th Floor; Chicago, IL 60610; (312) 335-9595
Neel Keller, *Artistic Director*

**Submission procedure:** no unsolicited scripts; synopsis and letter of inquiry. **Types of material:** full-length plays, adaptations. **Special interests:** political plays; plays of local interest; adaptations. **Facilities:** no permanent space. **Best submission time:** year-round. **Response time:** 3 weeks letter; 3 months script.

## REPERTORIO ESPAÑOL
138 East 27th St; New York, NY 10016; (212) 889-2850
Robert Weber Federico, *Artistic Associate Producer*

**Submission procedure:** no unsolicited scripts; synopsis and letter of inquiry. **Types of material:** full-length plays, adaptations, plays for young audiences, musicals, operas. **Special interests:** plays dealing with Hispanic themes. **Facilities:** Gramercy Arts Theatre, 127 seats, proscenium stage. **Production considerations:** small cast. **Best submission time:** summer. **Response time:** 1 month letter; 6 months script.

## THE REPERTORY THEATRE OF ST. LOUIS
Box 191730; St. Louis, MO 63119; (314) 968-7340
Susan Gregg, *Associate Artistic Director*

**Submission procedure:** no unsolicited scripts; synopsis and letter of inquiry. **Types of material:** full-length plays. **Special interests:** nonnaturalistic plays; contemporary social and political issues. **Facilities:** Main Stage, 750 seats, thrust stage; Studio Theatre, 130 seats, black box. **Production considerations:** small cast, modest production demands. **Best submission time:** year-round. **Response time:** 1 month letter; 2 years script. **Special programs:** developmental workshop for new plays; scripts selected through theatre's normal submission procedure.

## RIVERSIDE THEATRE
Box 3788; Vero Beach, FL 32964; (407) 231-5860
Brian Spitler, *Production Manager*

**Submission procedure:** no unsolicited scripts; synopsis and letter of inquiry. **Types of material:** full-length plays, translations, adaptations, plays for young audiences, musicals. **Facilities:** Riverside Theatre, 633 seats, proscenium stage; Agnes Wahlstrom Youth Playhouse, 200 seats, flexible stage. **Production considerations:** cast limit of 10. **Best submission time:** fall. **Response time:** 1 month letter (if interested); 3–5 months script.

## RIVERSIDE THEATRE
Box 1651; Iowa City, IA 52244; (319) 338-7672
Ron Clark, *Artistic Director*

**Submission procedure:** no unsolicited scripts; synopsis and letter of inquiry. **Types of material:** full-length plays, translations, adaptations, cabaret/revues. **Facilities:** Riverside Theatre, 110 seats, flexible stage. **Production considerations:** small cast, simple set. **Best submission time:** year-round. **Response time:** 1 month letter (if interested); 3–5 months script.

## THE ROAD COMPANY
Box 5278 EKS; Johnson City, TN 37603-5278; (615) 926-7726
Christine Murdock, *General Manager*

**Submission procedure:** no unsolicited scripts; synopsis and letter of inquiry. **Types of material:** full-length plays, one-acts, adaptations, cabaret/revues. **Special interests:** southern playwrights; experimental work. **Facilities:** Beeson Hall, 100–150 seats, flexible space. **Production considerations:** small cast, simple sets. **Best submission time:** year-round. **Response time:** 1 month letter (if interested); 6–12 months script. **Special programs:** salaried writer-in-residence each season.

## ROADSIDE THEATER
306 Madison St; Whitesburg, KY 41858; (606) 633-0108
Dudley Cocke, *Director*

**Submission procedure:** no unsolicited scripts; synopsis, dialogue sample and letter of inquiry. **Types of material:** full-length plays. **Special interests:** plays about the Appalachian region only. **Facilities:** Appalshop Theater, 150 seats, thrust stage. **Production considerations:** small cast, simple sets suitable for touring. **Best submission time:** year-round. **Response time:** 2 weeks letter; 1 month script. **Special programs:** reading and workshop series. Playwright residencies initiated by theatre; playwright may not apply.

## ROUND HOUSE THEATRE
12210 Bushey Dr; Silver Spring, MD 20902; (301) 933-9530
Jerry Whiddon, *Producing Artistic Director*

**Submission procedure:** no unsolicited scripts; synopsis, dialogue sample, cast breakdown, technical requirements and letter of inquiry. **Types of material:** full-length plays, translations, adaptations, plays for young audiences, musicals. **Special interests:** contemporary social and political issues; new translations of lesser-known classics; experimental works. **Facilities:** Round House Theatre, 216 seats, modified thrust stage. **Production considerations:** cast limit of 10; prefers 1 set. **Best submission time:** year-round. **Response time:** 2 months letter (if interested); at least 12 months script.

## SACRAMENTO THEATRE COMPANY
1419 H St; Sacramento, CA 95814; (916) 446-7501
Patrick Elkins-Zeglarski, *Artistic Coordinator*

**Submission procedure:** no unsolicited scripts; synopsis, resume and letter of inquiry with SASE for response. **Types of material:** full-length plays, adaptations, cabaret/revues. **Special interests:** contemporary social and political issues; craftsmanship; theatricality; vital language; characters an audience will care about. **Facilities:** McClatchy Mainstage, 300 seats, proscenium stage; Stage II, 90 seats, black box. **Production considerations:** cast of 3–5. **Best submission time:** Jun–Dec. **Response time:** 1 month letter; 3 months script.

## THE SALT LAKE ACTING COMPANY
168 West 500 N; Salt Lake City, UT 84103; (801) 363-0526
David Mong, *Literary Manager*

**Submission procedure:** no unsolicited scripts; synopsis, 5–10 pages of dialogue, resume and letter of inquiry with SASE for response. **Types of material:** full-length plays, translations, adaptations, musicals. **Special interests:** western American writers who understand the unique synergistic effect that playwright, actor and audience enjoy when a work is produced for the stage. **Facilities:** Upstairs, 99–130 seats, thrust stage; Downstairs, 49 seats, black box. **Best submission time:** year-round. **Response time:** 4 months letter; 8 months script. **Special programs:** reading series in winter and spring.

## SAN DIEGO REPERTORY THEATRE
79 Horton Plaza; San Diego, CA 92101; (619) 231-3586
*Literary Manager*

**Submission procedure:** no unsolicited scripts; synopsis and letter of inquiry. **Types of material:** full-length plays, translations, adaptations, musicals, literary cabaret, mixed-media events. **Special interests:** multiethnic work; hard-hitting social and political work; offbeat hip musicals; dramatic work with unusual incorporation of music; women's issues; sharp-edged comedy; poetic visions; Hispanic plays suitable for presentation in both Spanish and English. **Facilities:** Lyceum Stage, 550 seats, modified thrust stage; Lyceum Space, 225 seats, flexible stage. **Production considerations:** no fly loft. **Best submission time:** year-round. **Response time:** 3 months letter; 12 months script. **Special programs:** readings and workshop productions.

## SAN JOSE REPERTORY THEATRE
Box 2399; San Jose, CA 95109-2399; (408) 291-2266
J. R. Orlando, *Assistant to the Artistic Director*

**Submission procedure:** no unsolicited scripts; synopsis, dialogue sample and letter of inquiry with SASP for response. **Types of material:** full-length plays, translations, adaptations, musicals. **Special interests:** small-cast musicals. **Facilities:** Montgomery Theatre, 537 seats, proscenium stage; Louis B. Mayer Theatre, 505 seats, proscenium stage. **Best submission time:** Sep–Nov. **Response time:** 1 month letter; 6 months script.

## SANTA MONICA PLAYHOUSE
1211 4th St; Santa Monica, CA 90401-1391; (310) 394-9779
Chris DeCarlo, *Co-Artistic Director*

**Submission procedure:** no unsolicited scripts; synopsis and letter of inquiry. **Types of material:** full-length plays, one-acts, translations, adaptations, plays for young audiences, musicals. **Facilities:** Santa Monica Playhouse, 88 seats, arena/thrust stage. **Production considerations:** cast limit of 8, simple production demands. **Best submission time:** year-round. **Response time:** 3 months letter; 6 months script.

## SEACOAST REPERTORY THEATRE
125 Bow St; Portsmouth, NH 03801; (603) 433-4793
Roy M. Rogosin, *Producing Artistic Director*

**Submission procedure:** no unsolicited scripts; agent submission (1-page synopsis only; include cassette for musicals). **Types of material:** full-length plays, one-acts, plays for young audiences, musicals. **Special interests:** new American plays; small-scale musicals; plays for young audiences. **Facilities:** Seacoast Repertory Theatre of the Portsmouth Academy of Performing Arts, 175 seats, thrust stage. **Best submission time:** year-round. **Response time:** 3–6 months.

## SEASIDE MUSIC THEATER
Box 2835; Daytona Beach, FL 32120; (904) 252-3394
Lester Malizia, *General Manager*

**Submission procedure:** no unsolicited scripts; synopsis, cassette of music and letter of inquiry. **Types of material:** musicals for young and adult audiences, cabaret/revues. **Facilities:** Winter Theater, 600 seats, proscenium stage; Summer Repertory Theater, 500 seats, proscenium stage; Theater for Children, 150 seats, modified thrust stage. **Production considerations:** cast limit of 8 for Winter Theater, 30 for Summer Repertory Theater, 10 for Theater for Children; small musical combo for Theater for Children and Winter Theater, 25-member orchestra for Summer Repertory Theater; no wing or orchestra space in Winter Theater, no fly space except in Summer Repertory Theater. **Best submission time:** Sep–Nov. **Response time:** 1 month letter; 3 months script.

## SEATTLE CHILDREN'S THEATRE
Box 9640; Seattle, WA 98109-0640; (206) 443-0807
Deborah Frockt, *Dramaturg/Literary Manager*

**Submission procedure:** no unsolicited scripts; synopsis, 10 pages of dialogue, resume and letter of inquiry with SASP for response. **Types of material:** works for young audiences, including full-length plays, one-acts, translations, adaptations and musicals. **Special interests:** sophisticated work for young audiences only; scripts dealing with contemporary life and concerns which do not "talk down" to young audiences. **Facilities:** Charlotte Martin Theatre, 485 seats, proscenium stage; Eve Alvord Theatre, 280 seats, black box. **Best submission time:** year-round. **Response time:** 2 months letter; 6 months script.

## SEATTLE REPERTORY THEATRE
155 Mercer St; Seattle, WA 98109; (206) 443-2210
Kurt Beattie, *Artistic Associate/Literary Manager*

**Submission procedure:** no unsolicited scripts; professional recommendation. **Types of material:** full-length plays, translations, adaptations, musicals. **Facilities:** Seattle Repertory Theatre, 856 seats, proscenium stage; Poncho Forum, 142 seats, arena stage. **Best submission time:** year-round. **Response time:** 2–3 months. **Special programs:** New Plays in Process Project: program of workshop productions; playwright receives travel and per diem.

## SECOND STAGE THEATRE
Box 1807, Ansonia Station; New York, NY 10023; (212) 787-8302
(Mr.) Erin Sanders, *Literary Manager/Dramaturg*

**Submission procedure:** no unsolicited scripts; synopsis, 5–10 pages of dialogue, resume and letter of inquiry. **Types of material:** full-length plays, adaptations, musicals. **Special interests:** new and previously produced American plays (include production history with script); "heightened" realism; sociopolitical issues; plays by women and minority writers. **Facilities:** McGinn/Cazale Theatre, 110 seats, endstage. **Best submission time:** year-round. **Response time:** 1 month letter; 4–6 months script. **Special programs:** annual series of 4–6 readings of new and previously produced plays.

## 7 STAGES
1105 Euclid Ave NE; Atlanta, GA 30307; (404) 522-0911
Del Hamilton, *Artistic Director*

**Submission procedure:** no unsolicited scripts; synopsis, dialogue sample, resume and letter of inquiry. **Types of material:** full-length plays, translations, adaptations, musicals, performance pieces. **Special interests:** Southeast playwrights; nontraditional plays and performance texts focusing on social, political or spiritual themes, especially by young black writers and women. **Facilities:** 7 Stages, 250 seats, thrust stage; Back Door, 100 seats, flexible stage. **Best submission time:** year-round. **Response time:** 4 months letter; 8–10 months script. **Special programs:** Workshop Program: year-round development of nontraditional, process-oriented pieces that involve collaboration with other theatre artists (dancers, musicians, designers, etc.); send letter of inquiry.

## SHAKESPEARE & COMPANY
The Mount; Box 865; Lenox, MA 01240; (413) 637-1199, ext 112
Dennis Krausnick, *Director of Training*

**Submission procedure:** no unsolicited scripts; synopsis, 4 pages of dialogue and letter of inquiry. **Types of material:** full-length and one-act adaptations. **Special interests:** plays based on or adapted from works by Edith Wharton or Henry James only. **Facilities:** Mainstage Theatre, 500 seats, outdoor amphitheatre; Oxford Court, 250 seats, outdoor amphitheatre; Stables Theatre, 108 seats, thrust stage; Salon Theatre, 75–90 seats, endstage. **Production considerations:** minimal set pieces only; all theatre spaces part of historic estate (former home of Edith Wharton). **Best submission time:** fall–winter. **Response time:** 6 months letter (if interested); 6 months script.

## SHAKESPEARE SANTA CRUZ
Performing Arts Complex; University of California–Santa Cruz;
    Santa Cruz, CA 95064; (408) 459-2121
*Literary Manager*

**Submission procedure:** no unsolicited scripts; will accept synopsis, resume and letter of inquiry; prefers professional recommendation. **Types of material:** full-length plays, one-acts, plays for young audiences. **Special interests:** Shakespearean spinoffs, i.e., plays that use Shakespeare's characters or plots. **Facilities:** Sinsheimer-Stanley Glen, 500–800 seats, outdoor amphitheatre; Performing Arts Theater, 500 seats, thrust stage. **Production considerations:** small cast, minimal set. **Best submission time:** fall–winter. **Response time:** 1 month letter; 1 month script.

## THE SHAKESPEARE THEATRE
301 East Capitol St SE; Washington, DC 20003; (202) 547-3230
Michael Kahn, *Artistic Director*

**Submission procedure:** no unsolicited scripts; professional recommendation. **Types of material:** translations, adaptations. **Special interests:** translations and adaptations of classics only. **Facilities:** Lansburgh Theatre, 449 seats, thrust stage. **Best submission time:** summer. **Response time:** 2 months.

## SIGNATURE THEATRE
3806 South Four Mile Run Dr; Arlington, VA 22206; (703) 820-9771
Marcia Gardner, *Literary Manager*

**Submission procedure:** accepts unsolicited scripts. **Types of material:** full-length plays, adaptations, musicals. **Special interests:** social issues; comedies. **Facilities:** Signature Theatre, 126 seats, black box. **Production considerations:** prefers cast limit of 10; no fly space. **Best submission time:** Sep–May. **Response time:** 4 months. **Special programs:** Stages: staged readings of new plays-in-process; scripts selected through theatre's normal submission procedure. Emerging Playwrights Series: full production of 1 new play a year.

## SOCIETY HILL PLAYHOUSE
507 South 8th St; Philadelphia, PA 19147; (215) 923-0210
Walter Vail, *Literary Manager*

**Submission procedure:** no unsolicited scripts; synopsis and letter of inquiry with SASE for response. **Types of material:** full-length plays, translations, adaptations, musicals. **Special interests:** musicals and comedies with casts of 5–7. **Facilities:** Society Hill Playhouse, 223 seats, proscenium stage; Second Space, 90 seats, flexible stage. **Production considerations:** prefers small cast. **Best submission time:** year-round. **Response time:** 1 month letter; 6 months script.

## SOURCE THEATRE COMPANY
1835 14th St NW; Washington, DC 20009; (202) 462-1073
Elizabeth Robelen, *Director of Script Development*

**Submission procedure:** accepts unsolicited scripts that have not been professionally produced with synopsis, resume and letter-size SASE for response (scripts not returned); new works normally produced as part of Washington Theatre Festival (see below) before being considered for main-stage production. **Types of material:** full-length plays, one-acts, musicals. **Facilities:** Source Theatre Company, 101 seats, thrust stage. **Best submission time:** 15 Sep–15 Jan only. **Response time:** 4–8 months. **Special programs:** 16th Annual Washington Theatre Festival: new-play workshop productions; scripts selected through competition (see below); *deadline:* 15 Jan 1996; *dates:* 6 Jul–4 Aug 1996. Source Theatre Company National Playwriting Competition (see Prizes).

## SOUTH COAST REPERTORY
Box 2197; Costa Mesa, CA 92628-2197; (714) 957-2602
Jerry Patch, *Dramaturg*
John Glore, *Literary Manager*

**Submission procedure:** no unsolicited scripts; synopsis, optional dialogue sample, and letter of inquiry. **Types of material:** full-length plays, one-acts, translations, adaptations, musicals. **Facilities:** Mainstage, 507 seats, modified thrust stage; Second Stage, 161 seats, thrust stage. **Best submission time:** year-round. **Response time:** 1–3 weeks letter; 2–4 months script. **Special programs:** COLAB (Collaboration Laboratory) New Play Program: developmental program involving readings, staged readings, workshop and full productions; participation and all commissions offered by David Emmes and Martin Benson, artistic directors; playwright receives grant, commission and/or royalties depending on nature of project. Hispanic Playwrights Project (see Development).

## SPOKANE INTERPLAYERS ENSEMBLE
Box 1961; Spokane, WA 99210; (509) 455-7529
Robert A. Welch, *Managing Director*

**Submission procedure:** no unsolicited scripts; synopsis with cast list, set requirements, play's production history and reviews (if any), dialogue sample and letter of inquiry. **Types of material:** full-length plays, bills of related one-acts, translations, adaptations, cabaret/revues. **Facilities:** Spokane Interplayers Ensemble, 255 seats, thrust stage. **Production considerations:** prefers cast limit of 8, 1 set. **Best submission time:** year-round. **Response time:** 3 months letter (if interested); 3–6 months script.

## ST. LOUIS BLACK REPERTORY COMPANY
634 North Grand Blvd, Suite 10-F; St. Louis, MO 63103; (314) 534-3807
Ronald J. Himes, *Producing Director*

**Submission procedure:** no unsolicited scripts; synopsis, 3–5 pages of dialogue, resume and letter of inquiry. **Types of material:** full-length plays, plays for young audiences, musicals. **Special interests:** works by African-American and Third World playwrights. **Facilities:** Grandel Square Theatre, 470 seats, thrust stage. **Best submission time:** Jun–Aug. **Response time:** 2 months letter; 2 months script. **Special programs:** touring company presenting works for young audiences.

## STAGE ONE: THE LOUISVILLE CHILDREN'S THEATRE
425 West Market St; Louisville, KY 40202-3300; (502) 589-5946
Moses Goldberg, *Producing Director*

**Submission procedure:** accepts unsolicited scripts. **Types of material:** plays for young audiences. **Special interests:** plays about young people in the real world; good, honest treatments of familiar titles. **Facilities:** Moritz von Bomard Theater, 610 seats, thrust stage; Louisville Gardens, 300 seats, arena stage. **Production considerations:** prefers cast limit of 12; some productions tour. **Best submission time:** Oct–Dec. **Response time:** 3 months. **Special programs:** Tomorrow's Playwrights: annual one-act competition open to high school students throughout KY region; 3 finalists receive staged readings and prepare rewrite to determine placement; scholarship check for winner, cash awards for 2 runners-up and 3 sponsoring schools; submit play through school; *deadline:* 15 Jan 1996.

## STAGE WEST
Box 2587; Fort Worth, TX 76113; (817) 924-9454
Jerry Russell, *Artistic Director*

**Submission procedure:** no unsolicited scripts; synopsis and letter of inquiry. **Types of material:** full-length plays, translations, adaptations, musicals, cabaret/revues. **Special interests:** plays with universal themes; contemporary issues. **Facilities:** Stage West, 190 seats, thrust stage. **Production considerations:** prefers cast limit of 9. **Best submission time:** Jan–Mar. **Response time:** 1 month letter; 3 months script.

## STAGES
210 South Westgate Ave; Los Angeles, CA 90049; (213) 463-5356
Paul Verdier, *Artistic Director*

**Submission procedure:** no unsolicited scripts; synopsis and letter of inquiry. **Types of material:** full-length plays, one-acts, translations, adaptations. **Special interests:** plays by foreign writers both in original language and in translation; theatre regularly produces plays in Spanish, French and English but can also find actors fluent in other languages; challenging, experimental work. **Facilities:** Mainstage, 49 seats, proscenium stage; Lab, 25 seats, classroom; Amphitheatre, 99 seats, outdoor flexible stage. **Production considerations:** prefers cast limit of 5. **Best submission time:** year-round. **Response time:** 1 month letter; 3 months script.

## STAGEWEST
One Columbus Center; Springfield, MA 01103; (413) 781-4470
Eric Hill, *Artistic Director*

**Submission procedure:** no unsolicited scripts; synopsis and letter of inquiry. **Types of material:** full-length plays, translations, adaptations. **Special interests:** new translations or adaptations of neglected classic and 20th-century European plays; adaptations of nondramatic material. **Facilities:** Mainstage, 480 seats, thrust stage; Studio, 99 seats, flexible stage. **Best submission time:** year-round. **Response time:** 6 months letter; 3 months script. **Special programs:** Theatre for Young Audiences: touring company presents works for local schools.

## STAMFORD THEATRE WORKS
95 Atlantic St; Stamford, CT 06901; (203) 359-4414
Steve Karp, *Artistic Director*

**Submission procedure:** accepts unsolicited scripts; include cassette for musicals. **Types of material:** full-length plays, translations, adaptations, musicals. **Special interests:** plays that are innovative and thought-provoking, socially and culturally relevant, challenging and entertaining. **Facilities:** Center Stage, 150 seats, modified thrust stage. **Production considerations:** prefers small cast, unit set. **Best submission time:** year-round. **Response time:** 6 months. **Special programs:** Plays-in-Process Series: 3 staged readings a year of unproduced plays or musicals for purpose of developing future STW productions.

## STEPPENWOLF THEATRE COMPANY

1650 North Halsted; Chicago, IL 60614; (312) 335-1888
Martha Lavey, *Artistic Associate*

**Submission procedure:** no unsolicited scripts; professional recommendation. **Types of material:** full-length plays, one-acts, translations, adaptations. **Special interests:** ensemble pieces with dynamic acting roles. **Facilities:** Mainstage, 510 seats, proscenium stage; Studio, 50–300 seats, flexible stage. **Best submission time:** year-round.

## STUDIO ARENA THEATRE

710 Main St; Buffalo, NY 14202-1990; (716) 856-8025
Gavin Cameron-Webb, *Artistic Director*

**Submission procedure:** no unsolicited scripts; agent submission. **Types of material:** full-length plays, translations, adaptations. **Special interests:** plays of local interest; plays of a theatrical nature; American history and culture; ethnic cultures, including plays about minorities. **Facilities:** Studio Arena Theatre, 637 seats, thrust stage. **Production considerations:** cast limit of 12 (prefers smaller-cast plays); no fly system, limited wing space. **Best submission time:** year-round. **Response time:** 6 months.

## THE STUDIO THEATRE

1333 P St NW; Washington, DC 20005; (202) 232-7267
Serge Seiden, *Literary Manager*

**Submission procedure:** no unsolicited scripts; direct solicitation to playwright or agent. **Types of material:** full-length plays, translations, adaptations, musicals. **Special interests:** American lyric realism; ethnic American themes; translations of new European and Asian plays. **Facilities:** The Studio Theatre, 200 seats, modified thrust stage; Secondstage, 50 seats, flexible stage.

## SYRACUSE STAGE

820 East Genesee St; Syracuse, NY 13210-1508; (315) 443-4008
Lenora Inez Brown, *Dramaturg*

**Submission procedure:** no unsolicited scripts; synopsis, 10-page sample and letter of inquiry. **Types of material:** full-length plays, translations, adaptations, musicals. **Special interests:** plays for a multicultural company; plays by and about people of color and women. **Facilities:** John D. Archbold Theatre, 499 seats, flexible stage. **Production considerations:** prefers cast limit of 8. **Best submission time:** early summer. **Response time:** 6 weeks letter; 6–9 months script.

## TACOMA ACTORS GUILD

901 Broadway, 6th Floor; Tacoma, WA 98402-4404; (206) 272-3107
Bruce K. Sevy, *Artistic Director*

**Submission procedure:** no unsolicited scripts; synopsis and letter of inquiry. **Types**

of material: full-length plays, translations, adaptations, musicals. **Facilities:** Theatre on the Square, 302 seats, proscenium stage. **Production considerations:** prefers small cast; 1 set or unit set. **Best submission time:** spring–summer. **Response time:** 1–2 months letter; 8–12 months script.

## TENNESSEE REPERTORY THEATRE

427 Chestnut St; Nashville, TN 37203-4826; (615) 244-4878
Don Jones, *Associate Artistic Director*

**Submission procedure:** no unsolicited scripts; synopsis, dialogue sample, cassette of music and lyrics, and letter of inquiry. **Types of material:** musicals. **Special interests:** new American musicals. **Facilities:** Polk Theatre, 1050 seats, proscenium stage. **Best submission time:** Jun–Sep. **Response time:** 4–6 weeks letter; 9–12 months script.

## THALIA SPANISH THEATRE

Box 4368; Sunnyside, NY 11104; (718) 729-3880
Silvia Brito, *Artistic/Executive Director*

**Submission procedure:** accepts unsolicited scripts. **Types of material:** full-length plays, translations, adaptations. **Special interests:** plays in Spanish only. **Facilities:** Thalia Spanish Theatre, 74 seats, proscenium stage. **Production considerations:** cast limit of 6, 1 set. **Best submission time:** Dec–Jan. **Response time:** 3 months.

## THEATER AT LIME KILN

Lime Kiln Arts; Box 663; Lexington, VA 24450; (703) 463-7088
Barry Mines, *Artistic Director*

**Submission procedure:** accepts unsolicited scripts. **Types of material:** full-length plays, adaptations, musicals. **Special interests:** issues, language and music indigenous to VA and region; nontraditional staging. **Facilities:** The Kiln, 299 seats, outdoor amphitheatre. **Production considerations:** prefers cast limit of 9. **Best submission time:** fall. **Response time:** 3 months. **Special Programs:** Theater at Lime Kiln Regional Playwriting Contest (see Prizes).

## THE THEATRE AT MONMOUTH

Box 385; Monmouth, ME 04259-0385; (207) 933-2952
Richard Sewell, *Artistic Director*

**Submission procedure:** no unsolicited scripts; synopsis and letter of inquiry. **Types of material:** plays for young audiences. **Special interests:** small-cast traditional plays for young audiences (no musicals). **Facilities:** Cumston Hall, 275 seats, raked thrust stage. **Production considerations:** simple set. **Best submission time:** Nov. **Response time:** 4–6 weeks letter; 4–6 months script.

## THEATRE DE LA JEUNE LUNE
105 First St N; Minneapolis, MN 55401; (612) 332-3968
Barbara Berlovitz Desbois, *Co-Artistic Director*

**Submission procedure:** no unsolicited scripts; synopsis and letter of inquiry. **Types of material:** full-length plays, translations, adaptations, musicals, cabaret/revues. **Special interests:** large-cast plays dealing with universal themes. **Facilities:** Theatre de la Jeune Lune, 500 seats, flexible stage. **Best submission time:** year-round. **Response time:** 8–10 weeks letter; 4 months script.

## THEATRE FOR A NEW AUDIENCE
154 Christopher St, Suite 3D; New York, NY 10014-2839; (212) 229-2819

**Submission procedure:** no unsolicited scripts; direct solicitation to playwright or agent. **Types of material:** full-length plays, one-acts. **Special interests:** plays in which there is a compelling use of language. **Facilities:** Theatre at St. Clement's, 175 seats, proscenium stage. **Special programs:** commissioning program; participation by invitation only.

## THEATER FOR THE NEW CITY
155 First Ave; New York, NY 10003-2906; (212) 254-1109
Crystal Field, *Artistic Director*

**Submission procedure:** accepts unsolicited scripts. **Types of material:** full-length plays. **Special interests:** experimental American works; plays with poetry, music and dance; social issues. **Facilities:** Joyce and Seward Johnson Theater, 200 seats, flexible space; 2nd theatre, 75 seats, flexible space; 3rd theatre, 100 seats, flexible space; also cabaret space. **Best submission time:** summer. **Response time:** 9–12 months.

## THEATRE IV
114 West Broad St; Richmond, VA 23220; (804) 783-1688
Bruce Miller, *Artistic Director*

**Submission procedure:** no unsolicited scripts; synopsis and letter of inquiry. **Types of material:** full-length plays, translations, adaptations, plays for young audiences. **Special interests:** plays for young audiences. **Facilities:** Empire Theatre, 604 seats (150 for adult-audience productions), proscenium stage; Little Theatre, 84 seats, flexible stage. **Production considerations:** moderate budget for all productions. **Best submission time:** year-round. **Response time:** 6 months letter; 6 months script.

## THEATRE GAEL
Box 77156; Atlanta, GA 30357; (404) 876-1138
John Stephens, *Artistic Director*

**Submission procedure:** no unsolicited scripts; synopsis and letter of inquiry. **Types of material:** full-length plays, translations, adaptations, plays for young audiences.

**Special interests:** plays depicting life in Ireland, Scotland, Wales; plays about Americans of Celtic heritage; plays that compare different cultural backgrounds, e.g., the African-American versus Irish-American experiences. **Facilities:** no permanent facility; company tours to 80–330-seat flexible-stage theatres. **Production considerations:** productions tour to local schools. **Best submission time:** year-round. **Response time:** 1 month letter; 3 months script. **Special programs:** Worldsong Children's Theatre: company tours to local schools, recreational areas and libraries.

## THEATRE IN THE SQUARE
11 Whitlock Ave; Marietta, GA 30064; (404) 422-8369
Melanie Parker, *Public Relations/Administration Manager*

**Submission procedure:** no unsolicited scripts; synopsis and letter of inquiry. **Types of material:** full-length plays, one-acts, translations, musicals. **Special interests:** world and southeastern premieres. **Facilities:** Mainstage, 225 seats, proscenium stage; Alley Stage, up to 80 seats, flexible stage. **Production considerations:** cast limit of 9, unit set; no fly space. **Best submission time:** Jan–Feb. **Response time:** 1 month letter (if interested); 6 months script.

## THEATER OF THE FIRST AMENDMENT
MS 3E6; George Mason University; Fairfax, VA 22030-4444; (703) 993-2195
Rick Davis, *Artistic Director*

**Submission procedure:** no unsolicited scripts; synopsis, sample pages, resume and letter of inquiry. **Types of material:** full-length plays, one-acts, translations, adaptations. **Special interests:** cultural history made dramatic as distinct from history dramatized; large battles joined; hard questions asked; word and image stretched. **Facilities:** TheaterSpace, 150–200 seats, flexible space. **Production considerations:** roles for younger actors welcome as TFA works with training program. **Best submission time:** Aug–Jan. **Response time:** 2 weeks letter; 6 months script. **Special programs:** readings, workshops and other development activities tailored to work under serious consideration for production.

## THEATRE WEST
3333 Cahuenga Blvd W; Los Angeles, CA 90068; (213) 851-4839
Arden Lewis and Doug Haverty, *Workshop Moderators*

**Submission procedure:** no unsolicited scripts; scripts developed in weekly workshops open to member playwrights only; submit script, resume and letter of intent; dues of $40 per month upon acceptance. **Types of material:** full-length plays, one-acts, translations, adaptations, plays for young audiences, musicals. **Facilities:** Theatre West, 180 seats, proscenium stage. **Best submission time:** year-round. **Response time:** 2 months.

## THEATRE X

Box 92206; Milwaukee, WI 53202; (414) 278-0555
John D. Schneider, *Artistic Director*

**Submission procedure:** no unsolicited scripts; recommendation from professional familiar with company's work. **Types of material:** full-length plays, performance art. **Special interests:** plays written for or with the company; performance art and avant-garde works. **Facilities:** Black Box, 99 seats, flexible stage. **Production considerations:** small cast. **Best submission time:** year-round. **Response time:** 6 months.

## THEATREVIRGINIA

2800 Grove Ave; Richmond, VA 23221-2466; (804) 367-0840
George Black, *Producing Artistic Director*

**Submission procedure:** no unsolicited scripts; agent submission. **Types of material:** full-length plays, musicals. **Facilities:** Main Stage, 500 seats, proscenium stage. **Best submission time:** year-round. **Response time:** 3–8 months. **Special programs:** New Voices for the Theatre: playwriting competition open to VA students grades 5–12; winners grades 9–12 attend 3-week summer residency program and receive dramaturgical assistance and professional staged reading; contact Education and Outreach Department for more information; *deadline:* 1 Feb 1996.

## THEATREWORKS

470 San Antonio Rd; Palo Alto, CA 94306; (415) 812-7550
Jeannie Barroga, *Literary Manager*

**Submission procedure:** accepts unsolicited full-length plays and musicals; also accepts synopsis, dialogue sample and letter of inquiry with SASP for response; for translations and adaptations, send only letter of inquiry with SASP for response. **Types of material:** full-length plays, translations, adaptations, musicals. **Special interests:** works offering opportunities for multicultural casting. **Facilities:** Mountain View Center, 625 seats, proscenium stage; Stage II, 117 seats, thrust stage. **Best submission time:** Aug–Nov. **Response time:** 1 month letter; 4 months script.

## THEATREWORKS/USA

890 Broadway, 7th Floor; New York, NY 10003; (212) 677-5959
Barbara Pasternack, *Associate Artistic Director*

**Submission procedure:** accepts unsolicited scripts; prefers synopsis, sample scene(s) and songs (include cassette and lyric sheet) and letter of inquiry. **Types of material:** plays and musicals for young audiences. **Special interests:** literary adaptations; historical/biographical themes; fairy tales; contemporary issues. **Facilities:** Promenade Theatre, 398 seats, proscenium stage; also tours. **Production considerations:** cast limit of 5 (can play multiple roles), sets suitable for touring. **Best submission time:** summer. **Response time:** 1 month letter; 6 months script.

**Special programs:** developmental workshops. Theatreworks/USA Commissioning Program (see Prizes).

## THEATRICAL OUTFIT
Box 7098; Atlanta, GA 30357; (404) 872-0665
Mary Fisher, *Literary Manager*

**Submission procedure:** no unsolicited scripts; synopsis and letter of inquiry. **Types of material:** music-theatre works. **Special interests:** new music-theatre only; no mainstream works. **Facilities:** Theatrical Outfit, 200 seats, black box. **Best submission time:** summer. **Response time:** 2 months letter; 2 months script.

## TOUCHSTONE THEATRE
321 East 4th St; Bethlehem, PA 18015; (215) 867-1689
Mark McKenna, *Artistic Director*

**Submission procedure:** no unsolicited scripts; letter of inquiry. **Types of material:** proposals for works to be created in collaboration with company's ensemble only. **Facilities:** Touchstone Theatre, 74 seats, black box. **Production considerations:** 18' x 21' playing area. **Best submission time:** year-round. **Response time:** 1 month.

## TRINITY REPERTORY COMPANY
201 Washington St; Providence, RI 02903; (401) 521-1100
Oskar Eustis, *Artistic Director*

**Submission procedure:** no unsolicited scripts; dialogue sample, resume and letter of inquiry. **Types of material:** full-length plays, translations, adaptations. **Facilities:** Upstairs Theatre, 440 seats, thrust stage; Downstairs Theatre, 297 seats, thrust stage. **Best submission time:** year-round. **Response time:** 12 months letter; 12 months script.

## TRUSTUS THEATRE

See South Carolina Playwrights' Festival in Prizes.

## UBU REPERTORY THEATER
15 West 28th St; New York, NY 10001; (212) 679-7540
Françoise Kourilsky, *Artistic Director*

**Submission procedure:** no unsolicited scripts; synopsis and letter of inquiry. **Types of material:** full-length plays, one-acts, translations. **Special interests:** French-language plays or their translations only; contemporary plays from French-speaking countries and regions. **Facilities:** Ubu Repertory Theater, 99 seats, proscenium stage. **Production considerations:** cast limit of 10, 1 set or simple sets. **Best submission time:** year-round. **Response time:** 2 months letter; 6 months script.

## UNICORN THEATRE

See Unicorn Theatre National Playwrights' Award in Prizes.


## UTAH SHAKESPEAREAN FESTIVAL

351 West Center St; Cedar City, UT 84720-2498; (801) 586-7880
Douglas N. Cook, *Producing Artistic Director*

**Submission procedure:** no unsolicited scripts; professional recommendation. **Types of material:** full-length plays for Aug staged reading series. **Special interest:** plays by writers from western intermountain region; plays about minorities or the underserved. **Facilities:** Thorley Recital Hall, 235 seats, modified thrust stage. **Production considerations:** cast limit of 10–12; no sets, minimal props and costumes; 5-rehearsal limit per production. **Best submission time:** Oct–Dec. **Response time:** 2 months.


## VICTORY GARDENS THEATER

2257 North Lincoln Ave; Chicago, IL 60614; (312) 549-5788
Sandy Shinner, *Associate Artistic Director*

**Submission procedure:** accepts unsolicited scripts from Chicago-area writers only; others send synopsis, 10 pages of dialogue and letter of inquiry. **Types of material:** full-length plays, adaptations, musicals. **Special interests:** Chicago and Midwest playwrights; plays by women and writers of color. **Facilities:** Mainstage, 195 seats, thrust stage; Studio, 70 seats, proscenium stage. **Production considerations:** prefers cast limit of 10; small-cast musicals only; simple set. **Best submission time:** Mar–Jun. **Response time:** 1 month letter; 6 months script. **Special programs:** Readers Theater: staged readings of works-in-progress by area writers twice a month.


## VINEYARD THEATRE

108 East 15th St; New York, NY 10003-9689; (212) 353-3366
Douglas Aibel, *Artistic Director*

**Submission procedure:** accepts unsolicited scripts; prefers synopsis, 10-page sample and letter of inquiry; include cassette for musicals. **Types of material:** full-length plays, musicals. **Special interests:** plays which incorporate music in a unique way; musicals with strong narrative. **Facilities:** Vineyard Theatre, 70 seats, thrust stage; Vineyard at Union Square, 130 seats, flexible stage. **Best submission time:** year-round. **Response time:** 6 months letter; 6 months script. **Special programs:** New Works at the Vineyard: play reading series. The Lab Program: developmental workshops for new plays and musicals.


## VIRGINIA STAGE COMPANY

Box 3770; Norfolk, VA 23514; (804) 627-6988

**Submission procedure:** no unsolicited scripts; synopsis and letter of inquiry. **Types of material:** full-length plays, musicals. **Special interests:** world premieres; plays by VA writers; poetic drama and comedy; hard-hitting, issue-oriented plays; no "kitchen-sink" drama. **Facilities:** main stage, 700 seats, proscenium stage; laboratory theatre, 99 seats, flexible space. **Best submission time:** year-round. **Response time:** 1 month letter; 6 months script.

## THE WALNUT STREET THEATRE COMPANY

825 Walnut St; Philadelphia, PA 19107-5107; (215) 574-3550
Beverly Elliott, *Literary Manager*

**Submission procedure:** no unsolicited scripts; synopsis, cast list, 14 pages of dialogue and letter of inquiry with SASE for response from Dramatist Guild members only; include professional-quality cassette for musicals. **Types of material:** full-length plays, musicals. **Special interests:** original, socially relevant musicals with uplifting themes; commercially viable works for Main Stage; meaningful comedies and dramas with some broad social relevance for Studio 3. **Facilities:** Main Stage, 1050 seats, proscenium stage; Studio 3, 80 seats, flexible stage. **Production considerations:** cast limit of 4 for Studio 3. **Response time:** 3 months letter; 6 months script.

## WEST COAST ENSEMBLE

Box 38728; Los Angeles, CA 90038; (213) 871-8673
Les Hanson, *Artistic Director*

**Submission procedure:** accepts unsolicited scripts. **Types of material:** full-length plays, one-acts, translations, adaptations, plays for young audiences, musicals, cabaret/revues. **Special interests:** world premieres; musicals; translations and adaptations. **Facilities:** Theatre A, 65 seats, proscenium stage; Theatre B, 99 seats, flexible stage. **Production considerations:** simple set; no fly space. **Best submission time:** Jun–Dec. **Response time:** 6 months. **Special programs:** Playwrights Unit: member playwrights meet weekly; staged readings of new plays developed in unit; local playwrights apply by submitting script. West Coast Ensemble Contests (see Prizes).

## WILLIAMSTOWN THEATRE FESTIVAL

Box 517; Williamstown, MA 01267; (413) 458-3200
Peter Hunt, *Artistic/Executive Director*

**Submission procedure:** no unsolicited scripts; synopsis, dialogue sample and letter of inquiry. **Types of material:** full-length plays, adaptations, musicals. **Facilities:** Main Stage, 521 seats, proscenium stage; 2nd stage, 96 seats, thrust stage. **Production considerations:** cast limit of 10 for musicals. **Best submission time:** 1 Nov–15 Mar. **Response time:** 1 month letter; several months script. **Special programs:** New Play Staged Readings Series.

## THE WILMA THEATER

2030 Sansom St; Philadelphia, PA 19103-4417; (215) 963-0249
Michael Hollinger, *Literary Manager/Dramaturg*

**Submission procedure:** no unsolicited scripts; synopsis, dialogue sample and letter of inquiry. **Types of material:** full-length plays, translations, adaptations, musicals. **Special interests:** new translations and adaptations from the international repertoire with emphasis on innovative, bold staging; world premieres; ensemble works; works with poetic dimension; plays with music; multimedia works; social issues. **Facilities:** Wilma Theater, 100 seats, proscenium stage. **Production considerations:** prefers cast limit of 8, limited scene changes; stage 30' x 22'. **Best submission time:** year-round. **Response time:** 8–10 weeks letter; 4–6 months script.

## WISDOM BRIDGE THEATRE CHICAGO COMPANY

332 South Michigan, Suite 1540; Chicago, IL 60604; (312) 341-2550
Jeffrey Ortmann, *Producing Director*

**Submission procedure:** no unsolicited scripts; synopsis and letter of inquiry. **Types of material:** full-length plays, adaptations, musicals. **Special interests:** contemporary themes; musicals with high literary value; adaptations of American classics. **Facilities:** Ivanhoe Theatre, 497 seats, thrust stage. **Best submission time:** year-round. **Response time:** 1–2 months letter; 3 months script.

## WOMEN'S PROJECT & PRODUCTIONS

10 Columbus Circle, Suite 2270; New York, NY 10019; (212) 765-1706
Susan Bougetz, *Literary Manager*

**Submission procedure:** no unsolicited scripts; synopsis, 10-page dialogue sample and letter of inquiry with SASE for response. **Types of material:** full-length plays. **Special interests:** plays by women only. **Facilities:** no permanent space. **Best submission time:** year-round. **Response time:** 2–4 weeks letter; 3–6 months script. **Special programs:** developmental program including play readings, work-in-progress presentations, playwright's lab and directors' forum; participation by invitation only. Commissioning program.

## WOOLLY MAMMOTH THEATRE COMPANY

1401 Church St NW; Washington, DC 20005; (202) 393-3939
Jim Byrnes, *Literary Manager*

**Submission procedure:** accepts unsolicited scripts. **Types of material:** full-length plays, translations, adaptations. **Special interests:** offbeat topics and styles; non-realism. **Facilities:** Woolly Mammoth, 132 seats, thrust stage. **Production considerations:** small cast, minimal staging requirements. **Best submission time:** year-round. **Response time:** 4 months.

## WORCESTER FOOTHILLS THEATRE COMPANY
100 Front St, Suite 137; Worcester, MA 01608; (508) 754-3314
Marc P. Smith, *Executive Producer/Artistic Director*

**Submission procedure:** no unsolicited scripts; synopsis and letter of inquiry. **Types of material:** full-length plays, translations, adaptations, musicals. **Special interests:** plays suited to multigenerational audiences. **Facilities:** Worcester Foothills Theatre, 349 seats, proscenium stage. **Production considerations:** prefers cast limit of 10, simple set; small-scale musicals only. **Best submission time:** year-round. **Response time:** 3 months letter; 4 months script.

## YALE REPERTORY THEATRE
Box 1903A, Yale Station; New Haven, CT 06520-7434; (203) 432-1560
*Resident Dramaturg*

**Submission procedure:** no unsolicited scripts; synopsis and letter of inquiry. **Types of material:** full-length plays, translations, adaptations. **Special interests:** new work; new translations of classics; contemporary foreign plays. **Facilities:** Yale Repertory Theatre, 487 seats, modified thrust stage; University Theatre, 654 seats, proscenium stage. **Best submission time:** year-round. **Response time:** 6 weeks letter; 3 months script.

## YOUNG PLAYWRIGHTS INC.
See Young Playwrights Festival in Prizes and Young Playwrights Inc. in Organizations.

## ZACHARY SCOTT THEATRE CENTER (ZACH)
1510 Toomey Rd; Austin, TX 78704-1078; (512) 476-0594
Alice Wilson, *Producing Artistic Director*

**Submission procedure:** no unsolicited scripts; synopsis, dialogue sample, resume and letter of inquiry. **Types of material:** full-length plays, plays for young audiences. **Facilities:** Mainstage 1, 200 seats, thrust stage; Mainstage 2, 130 seats, arena stage. **Production considerations:** plays for young audiences tour. **Best submission time:** Jul–Aug. **Response time:** 6 weeks letter; 4–6 months script.

# Prizes

**What competitions are included here?**

All the playwriting contests we've heard of that offer prizes of at least $200 or, in the case of awards to playwrights under the age of 19, the equivalent in production or publication. Most awards for which the playwright cannot apply—the Joseph Kesselring Award, the Pulitzer Prize—are not listed. Exceptions are made when, as with the Susan Smith Blackburn Prize, the nominating process allows playwrights to encourage nomination of their work by theatre professionals who are familiar with it.

**How can I give myself the best chance of winning?**

When a prize entry lists a notification date, make sure you don't mistake it for the deadline for submission. (One prize sponsor asked us to delete their notification date because so many playwrights were confusing the two!) If a listing specifies "write for guidelines," be sure to follow this instruction. It usually means that we don't have space in our brief listing to give you all the information you'll need to enter the contest. Write for the guidelines (and entry form, where applicable) several months ahead. Don't wait till the last minute since contests may occasionally change their rules or their deadlines after this book has been published. Follow the guidelines precisely. Send your script in well before the deadline, when the readers are fresh and enthusiastic rather than buried by an avalanche of submissions. If you can't submit well in advance, assume the deadline is the date your script must be received (not the postmark date). Except in the few cases where sponsors note that scripts won't be returned, always send an SASE with your submission. Many competitions enclose their response letter with the script when returning it.

### Should I enter contests that charge entry fees?

It's true that a number of listings in this section (and in other sections as well) require a payment of a fee. You need not conclude from this that the whole world is out to rip off playwrights. It is unfortunately the case that many contest sponsors do not secure sufficient funding to cover their costs, which are considerable. Some playwrights as a matter of principle will not pay fees, and are prepared to protest their imposition. Other writers are willing to add an entry fee to the costs of copying and postage as a part of doing business. It's up to you.

### Aren't new playwriting contests being created all the time?

Yes. As soon as we hear about them, we publish details of major new contests in the "Opportunities" column of our monthly magazine *American Theatre*. See Membership and Service Organizations and Useful Publications for other sources of current contest news.

### A couple of *Sourcebook* reminders:

Throughout the *Sourcebook*, "full-length play" means just that—a full-length, original work without a score or libretto. One-acts, muscials, adaptations, translations and plays for young audiences are not called full-length plays for our purposes. If an organization is interested in those dramatic works, we'll list them separately.

This year, *Sourcebook* entries are alphabetized by first word (excluding "the") even if the title starts with a proper name. So, for instance, you'll find the David James Ellis Memorial Award under D. In the index, you will also find this prize cross-listed under E. We have also expanded this section to include full listings of biennial prizes whose next deadline falls after the dates of this *Sourcebook* (after August 1996). By providind this added information, we hope to give you as much lead time as possible, but please read the deadlines carefully—don't mistake a March 1997 deadline for 1996!

## ACME ORIGINALS

ACME Acting Company; 3841 Northeast 2nd Ave, Suite 302A; Miami, FL 33137; (305) 576-7500
Betsy Cardwell, *Producing Director*

**Types of material:** full-length plays, one-acts. **Frequency:** annual. **Remuneration:**

$500–1000, production, travel and housing to attend rehearsals, and publication in arts and entertainment magazine for 3 winners; staged reading for 10 runners-up. **Guidelines:** play not produced professionally; prefers contemporary issues. **Submission procedure:** script only; script will not be returned. **Deadline:** ongoing (plays to be produced in 1996 chosen by 15 Apr 1996). **Dates:** summer.

## ALASKA NATIVE PLAYS CONTEST
Department of Theatre; University of Alaska, Anchorage; 3211 Providence Dr; Anchorage, AK 99508-8120
David Edgecombe, *Associate Professor*

**Types of material:** full-length plays, one-acts, adaptations, plays for young audiences. **Frequency:** annual. **Remuneration:** $500 1st prize; $300 2nd prize; $200 3rd prize; possible production, travel to performance for Alaska playwrights only. **Guidelines:** Native American characters and/or themes. **Submission procedure:** script only. **Deadline:** 20 Mar 1996. **Notification:** 10 May 1996.

## AMERICAN SHORTS CONTEST
Florida Studio Theatre; 1241 North Palm Ave; Sarasota, FL 34236

**Types of material:** very short plays. **Frequency:** annual. **Remuneration:** $500; production for winning script and up to 12 others as part of evening of short works. **Guidelines:** play of 5 pages or less on specified theme TBA; write for guidelines. **Submission procedure:** script only. **Deadline:** TBA (15 Jun in 1995).

## AMERICAN TRANSLATORS ASSOCIATION AWARDS
Honors Division; 324 North Jordan; Indiana University; Bloomington, IN 47405; (812) 855-3555
Breon Mitchell, *Chair, ATA Honors and Awards*

### German Literary Translation Prize

**Types of material:** translations of full-length and one-act plays. **Frequency:** biennial. **Remuneration:** $1000. **Guidelines:** translation from German published in U.S. by American publisher during 2 years before deadline as single volume or in collection. **Submission procedure:** translation nominated by publisher; 2 copies of book plus 10 consecutive pages of German original, extra jacket and any advertising copy; brief vita of translator. **Deadline:** 15 Apr 1997. **Notification:** Sep 1997.

### Lewis Galantiere Literary Translation Prize

**Types of material:** translations of full-length plays and one-acts. **Frequency:** biennial. **Remuneration:** $500; up to $500 travel, and housing to attend ATA annual conference. **Guidelines:** translation from any language except German published in U.S. by American publisher during 2 years before deadline as single volume or in collection. **Submission procedure:** no submission by translator; publisher nominates translation and submits 2 copies of book plus 10 consecutive pages of original, extra jacket and any advertising copy. **Deadline:** 15 May 1996. **Notification:** 1 Oct 1996.

### ANNA ZORNIO MEMORIAL CHILDREN'S THEATRE PLAYWRITING AWARD

Department of Theater and Dance; University of New Hampshire;
Paul Creative Arts Center; 30 College Rd; Durham, NH 03824-3538;
(603) 862-3288
Peggy Rae Johnson

**Types of material:** plays and musicals for young audiences. **Frequency:** every 4 years. **Remuneration:** $1000; production by UNH Theatre in Education Program. **Guidelines:** U.S. or Canadian resident; unpublished work not produced professionally and not more than 1 hour long; prefers single or unit set; 2-submission limit; write for rules. **Submission procedure:** script with brief synopsis, character breakdown and statement of design/technical considerations; SASP for acknowledgment of receipt; include cassette for musical. **Deadline:** Dec 1997. **Notification:** Jun 1997.

### THE ANNUAL BLANK THEATRE COMPANY YOUNG PLAYWRIGHTS FESTIVAL

1301 Lucile Ave; Los Angeles, CA 90026; (213) 662-7734
April Dawn, *Producer*

**Types of material:** full-length plays, one-acts, translations, adaptations, plays for young audiences, musicals, operas. **Frequency:** annual. **Remuneration:** workshop production for approximately 9 playwrights. **Guidelines:** playwright 19 years of age or younger as of deadline date; original play of any length on any subject. **Submission procedure:** script with cover sheet containing name, date of birth, home address, phone number, and name of school (if any). **Deadline:** 18 Apr 1996. **Notification:** May 1996.

### ASF TRANSLATION PRIZE

The American-Scandinavian Foundation; 725 Park Ave; New York, NY 10021;
(212) 879-9779
*Publishing Office*

**Types of material:** translations. **Frequency:** annual. **Remuneration:** $2000; publication of excerpt in *Scandinavian Review*, $500 for runner-up. **Guidelines:** unpublished translation from a Scandinavian language into English of work written by a Scandinavian author after 1800; manuscript must be at least 50 pages long if prose, 25 pages if poetry, and must be conceived as part of a book; write for guidelines. **Submission procedure:** 4 copies of translation, 1 of original; permission letter from copyright holder. **Deadline:** 1 Jun 1996. **Notification:** fall 1996.

## BAKER'S PLAYS HIGH SCHOOL PLAYWRITING CONTEST
Baker's Plays; 100 Chauncy St; Boston, MA 02111; (617) 482-1280
Raymond Pape, *Associate Editor*

**Types of material:** full-length plays, one-acts, plays for young audiences, musicals. **Frequency:** annual. **Remuneration:** 1st prize $500 and publication; 2nd prize $250; 3rd prize $100. **Guidelines:** high school student, sponsored by high school drama or English teacher; prefers play which has been produced or given public reading; write for guidelines. **Submission procedure:** script with signature of sponsoring teacher. **Deadline:** 31 Jan 1996. **Notification:** May 1996.

## BEVERLY HILLS THEATRE GUILD–
## JULIE HARRIS PLAYWRIGHT AWARD
2815 North Beachwood Dr; Los Angeles, CA 90068-1923; (213) 465-2703
Marcella Meharg, *Coordinator*

**Types of material:** full-length plays. **Frequency:** annual. **Remuneration:** $5000 1st prize plus $2000 to help finance production in Los Angeles area within 1 year; $2000 2nd prize; $1000 3rd prize. **Guidelines:** U.S. citizen; 1 submission, not previously submitted, published, produced or optioned, or winner of major competition; send SASE for guidelines. **Submission procedure:** completed entry form and script. **Deadline:** 1 Nov 1995. **Notification:** Jun 1996.

## BIENNIAL PROMISING PLAYWRIGHT AWARD
Colonial Players, Inc; 108 East St; Annapolis, MD 21401
*Contest Coordinator*

**Types of material:** full-length plays, bills of 2 related one-acts, adaptations. **Frequency:** biennial. **Remuneration:** $750; production (playwright must be available to attend rehearsals). **Guidelines:** resident of DC, DE, MD, PA, VA or WV; play, not produced professionally, suitable for arena stage; between 90–120 minutes; 2-set limit; cast limit of 10; only adaptations of material in public domain; send SASE for guidelines. **Submission procedure:** script only. **Deadline:** 31 Dec 1996; no submission before 1 Sep 1996. **Notification:** Jun 1997.

## CALIFORNIA YOUNG PLAYWRIGHTS CONTEST
Playwrights Project; 1450 Frazee Rd, Suite 215; San Diego, CA 92108;
(619) 298-9242
Deborah Salzer, *Director*

**Types of material:** full-length plays, one-acts, musicals. **Frequency:** annual. **Remuneration:** $100, production or staged reading, travel and housing to attend rehearsals to each of several winners (4 in 1994); all entrants receive written evaluation of work. **Guidelines:** CA writer or collaborating writers under 19 years of age as of deadline date; work at least 10 pages long; previous submissions ineligible; write for guidelines. **Submission procedure:** script, cover letter and brief bio; script will not be returned. **Deadline:** 1 Apr 1996. **Notification:** late fall 1996.

## CENTER THEATER INTERNATIONAL
## PLAYWRIGHTING CONTEST
1346 West Devon Ave; Chicago, IL 60660; (312) 508-0200
Dale Calandra, *Literary Manager*

**Types of material:** full-length plays. **Frequency:** annual. **Remuneration:** $300; production; winner and runners-up receive listings in mailing sent to all TCG Constituent and Associate theatres. **Guidelines:** unpublished play, not produced or optioned; cast limit of 4, minimal technical requirements; send SASE for rules. **Submission procedure:** completed entry form, script, 1-page synopsis, character breakdown, resume, $15 fee per submission and SASE for response; script will not be returned. **Deadline:** 15 Feb 1996. **Notification:** Aug 1996.

## CHICANO/LATINO LITERARY CONTEST
Department of Spanish and Portuguese; University of California at Irvine; Irvine, CA 92717; (714) 824-5702
Alejandro Morales, *Director*

Prize awarded for different genres (novel, short story, poetry, drama) in successive years; next deadline for drama 30 Apr 1998.

## CHRISTOPHER COLUMBUS
## SCREENPLAY DISCOVERY AWARDS
Christopher Columbus Society; 433 North Camden Dr, Suite 600; Beverly Hills, CA 90210; (310) 288-1881
Carlos de Abreu and Janice Pennington, *Co-Founders*

**Types of material:** screenplays. **Frequency:** annual. **Remuneration:** Discovery of the Month Award: up to 3 scripts a month selected for development and may be referred to industry professionals; all winners become eligible for Discovery of the Year Award: up to 3 scripts a year optioned by society for up to $10,000. **Guidelines:** unproduced feature screenplay not under current option; write for guidelines. **Submission procedure:** screenplay, completed application, release form and $45 fee; screenplay will not be returned. **Deadline:** last day of each month for monthly selection; 1 Dec each year for annual cycle.

## CLAUDER COMPETITION FOR EXCELLENCE IN PLAYWRITING
Box 383259; Cambridge, MA 02238-3259; (617) 322-3187
Betsy Carpenter, *Director*

**Types of material:** full-length plays. **Frequency:** biennial. **Remuneration:** $3000 1st prize; production by professional New England theatre; $500 prize and staged reading for several runners-up. **Guidelines:** resident of or student attending school or college in CT, MA, ME, NH, RI or VT; play not produced professionally and minimum 45 minutes long; write for guidelines. **Submission procedure:** script and production history, if any. **Deadline:** 30 Jun 1997. **Notification:** fall 1997.

## COE COLLEGE NEW WORKS FOR THE STAGE COMPETITION

Department of Theatre Arts; 1220 First Ave NE; Cedar Rapids, IA 52402;
(319) 399-8689
Susan Wolverton, *Chair, Playwriting Festival*

**Types of material:** full-length plays, plays for young audiences. **Frequency:** biennial, contingent on funding. **Remuneration:** $325; staged reading; travel, room and board for 1-week residency during Jan term. **Guidelines:** unproduced, unpublished play dealing with theme of Playwriting Festival and Symposia (theme different each year); festival includes workshops and public discussions; no translations, adaptations or musicals; send SASE for guidelines. **Submission procedure:** script only. **Deadline:** Jun 1996; exact date TBA. **Notification:** 1 Nov 1996.

## CONNECTIONS

Delaware Theatre Company; 200 Water St; Wilmington, DE 19801-5030
Cleveland Morris, *Artistic Director*

**Types of material:** full-length plays, musicals. **Frequency:** biennial. **Remuneration:** $10,000 1st prize; staged reading; possible full production with travel to rehearsals, housing and royalties; $500 each to 2nd and 3rd prize winners. **Guidelines:** full-length play, which has not received full professional production, that deals dealing with interracial dynamics in America. **Submission procedure:** 3 copies of script with production history, if any, and brief bio. **Deadline:** 1 Apr 1996. **Notification:** Aug 1996.

## THE CUNNINGHAM PRIZE FOR PLAYWRITING

Theatre School; DePaul University; 2135 North Kenmore;
Chicago, IL 60614-4111; (312) 325-7938
Lara Goetsch, *Public Relations Director*

**Types of material:** full-length plays, plays for young audiences, musicals. **Frequency:** annual. **Remuneration:** $5000. **Guidelines:** Chicago-area playwright; play which "affirms the centrality of religion, broadly defined, and the human quest for meaning, truth and community"; write for guidelines. **Submission procedure:** script and brief statement making connection to purpose of prize. **Deadline:** 1 Dec 1995. **Notification:** Mar 1996.

## DALE WASSERMAN DRAMA AWARD

Council for Wisconsin Writers; Box 55322; Madison, WI 53705; (608) 233-2484
Russell King, *President*

**Types of material:** full-length plays, one-acts, translations, adaptations, plays for young audiences, musicals, operas. **Frequency:** annual. **Remuneration:** $1000. **Guidelines:** current or former WI resident; work produced during preceding season. **Submission procedure:** completed entry form, script and $15 fee. **Deadline:** 1 Jan 1996.

## DAVID JAMES ELLIS MEMORIAL AWARD
Theatre Americana; Box 245; Altadena, CA 91001; (818) 397-1740
Hertha Donato, *Playreading Committee*

**Types of material:** full-length plays. **Frequency:** annual. **Remuneration:** $500 to best of 4 plays selected for production; color videotape of produced play. **Guidelines:** unpublished original play, not more than 2 hours in length; prefers American writers and plays on the American scene; 2-submission limit; write for guidelines. **Submission procedure:** script and resume. **Deadline:** 31 Jan 1996.

## DAYTON PLAYHOUSE FUTUREFEST
1301 East Siebenthaler Ave; Dayton, OH 45414; (513) 277-0144
Jean Howat Berry, *Interim Managing Director*

**Types of material:** full-length plays. **Frequency:** annual. **Remuneration:** 3 plays selected for full production, 3 for reading at Jul 1996 FutureFest weekend; possible travel, room and board to attend rehearsals; judges view full productions and select winner of $1000 prize. **Guidelines:** unproduced, unpublished play; send SASE for guidelines. **Submission procedure:** script and resume. **Deadline:** 30 Sep 1995. **Notification:** Apr 1996.

## DEEP SOUTH WRITERS CONFERENCE
c/o English Department; Box 44691; University of Southwestern Louisiana;
      Lafayette, LA 70504-4691
John W. Fiero, *Director*

### James H. Wilson Full-Length Play Award

**Types of material:** full-length plays. **Frequency:** annual. **Remuneration:** $300 1st prize, $100 2nd prize. **Guidelines:** original, unpublished play (no adaptations or musicals) not produced commercially; send SASE for guidelines. **Submission procedure:** script, brief bio and $15 fee per submission; script will not be returned. **Deadline:** 15 Jul 1996. **Notification:** Sep 1996.

### Miller Award

**Types of material:** full-length plays. **Frequency:** biennial. **Remuneration:** not less than $500. **Guidelines:** unpublished play, readily adaptable for film or TV, dealing with some aspect of the English Renaissance and/or the life of Edward de Vere, Earl of Oxford; write for guidelines, which are subject to change. **Submission procedure:** script and brief bio; script will not be returned. **Deadline:** 15 Jul 1997. **Notification:** Sep 1997.

### Paul T. Nolan One-Act Play Award

**Types of material:** one-acts. **Frequency:** annual. **Remuneration:** $200 1st prize, $100 2nd prize; possible publication in DSWC *Chapbook*. **Guidelines:** original, unpublished play (no adaptations or musicals) less than 50 pages long, not produced commercially; publication rights to winning plays reserved until 1 Jun

1997; send SASE for guidelines. **Submission procedure:** script, brief bio and $10 fee per submission; script will not be returned. **Deadline:** 15 Jul 1996. **Notification:** Sep 1996.

## THE DENNIS MCINTYRE PLAYWRITING AWARD
Philadelphia Festival Theatre for New Plays at Annenberg Center;
  3680 Walnut St; Philadelphia, PA 19104; (215) 898-3900
Sally de Sousa, *General Manager*

**Types of material:** full-length plays. **Frequency:** annual. **Remuneration:** cash award; production with travel and 4 weeks' room and board to attend rehearsals, or staged reading with travel and housing to attend reading. **Guidelines:** unproduced play by emerging "playwright of conscience" examining society's problems with honest scrutiny. **Submission procedure:** synopsis, 10 pages of dialogue, resume and letter of inquiry. **Deadline:** ongoing.

## DOROTHY SILVER PLAYWRITING COMPETITION
Jewish Community Center of Cleveland; 3505 Mayfield Rd;
  Cleveland Heights, OH 44118; (216) 382-4000, ext 275
Elaine Rembrandt, *Director of Cultural Arts*

**Types of material:** full-length plays. **Frequency:** annual. **Remuneration:** $1000 (including $500 to cover residency expenses); staged reading; possible production. **Guidelines:** unproduced play that provides fresh and significant perspective on the range of Jewish experience. **Submission procedure:** script only. **Deadline:** 15 Dec 1995. **Notification:** 15 Jul 1996.

## DRAMAFEST '98
Lodi Arts Commission; 125 South Hutchins St, Suite D; Lodi, CA 95240;
  (209) 369-4952
Julia Gillespie, *Commissioner*

**Types of material:** full-length plays, plays for young audiences, musicals. **Frequency:** biennial. **Remuneration:** $1000 for full-length play or musical, $500 for play for young audiences; production; travel, housing and board to attend rehearsals. **Guidelines:** unproduced, unpublished work; write for guidelines. **Submission procedure:** completed entry form and script. **Deadline:** 1 Apr 1997; no submission before 1 Jan 1997. **Notification:** fall 1997.

## DRAMARAMA
The Playwrights' Center of San Francisco; Box 460466;
  San Francisco, CA 94146-0466; (415) 626-4603
Sheppard Kominers, *Chairman*

**Types of material:** full-length plays, one-acts. **Frequency:** annual. **Remuneration:** up to 8 scripts given 4–5 rehearsals and staged readings at fall festival; $500 prize awarded on basis of readings. **Guidelines:** unproduced play; send SASE for guidelines and application. **Submission procedure:** see guidelines; submission requirements include $25 fee. **Deadline:** 15 Mar 1996. **Dates:** Oct 1996.

## DRURY COLLEGE ONE-ACT PLAY COMPETITION

Drury College; 900 North Benton Ave; Springfield, MO 65802; (417) 873-7430
Sandy Asher, *Writer-in-Residence*

**Types of material:** one-acts. **Frequency:** biennial. **Remuneration:** $300 1st prize, 2 runners-up receive $150; possible production; winners recommended to the Open Eye Theater (see entry in Production). **Guidelines:** unproduced, unpublished play 20–45 minutes long; prefers small cast, 1 set; 1 submission; send SASE for guidelines. **Submission procedure:** script only. **Deadline:** 1 Dec 1996. **Notification:** 1 Apr 1997.

## DUBUQUE FINE ARTS PLAYERS
## NATIONAL ONE-ACT PLAYWRITING CONTEST

1321 Tomahawk Dr; Dubuque, IA 52003; (319) 583-6748
Jennie G. Stabenow, *Coordinator*

**Types of material:** one-acts, one-act adaptations. **Frequency:** annual. **Remuneration:** $600 1st prize, $300 2nd prize, $200 3rd prize; possible production for all 3 plays. **Guidelines:** unproduced, unpublished play maximum 35 pages and 40 minutes long; prefers cast limit of 5, 1 set; no submission limit but playwright may not win more than 1 prize; only adaptations of material in public domain; send SASE for guidelines. **Submission procedure:** completed entry form with 2 copies of script, 1-paragraph synopsis and $10 fee per submission; SASP if acknowledgment of receipt is desired. **Deadline:** 31 Jan 1996; no submission before 1 Nov 1995. **Notification:** 30 Jun 1996.

## EMERGING PLAYWRIGHT AWARD

Playwrights' Preview Productions; 17 East 47th St;
    New York, NY 10017; (212) 289-2168
Pamela Faith Jackson, *Literary Associate*

**Types of material:** full-length plays, one-acts. **Frequency:** annual. **Remuneration:** $500; production; travel to attend rehearsals. **Guidelines:** play unproduced in New York; submissions from minority playwrights and plays with ethnically diverse casts encouraged. **Submission procedure:** script, production history (if any) and bio. **Deadline:** ongoing; best submission time Jul–Aug and Dec.

## FERNDALE REPERTORY THEATRE
## NEW WORKS COMPETITION

Box 892; Ferndale, CA 95536-0892; (707) 725-2378
Clinton Rebik, *Artistic Director*

**Types of material:** full-length plays, musicals. **Frequency:** annual. **Remuneration:** production with $250 royalty; set of all photos and promotional materials.

**Guidelines:** unpublished work which has not received full production; minimal technical demands; write for guidelines. **Submission procedure:** script, cast list and synopsis; resume, SASP. **Deadline:** 15 Oct 1995. **Notification:** 1 Jun 1996.

## THE FESTIVAL OF EMERGING AMERICAN THEATRE (FEAT) COMPETITION

The Phoenix Theatre; 749 North Park Ave; Indianapolis, IN 46202;
    (317) 635-7529
Bryan Fonseca, *Producing Director*

**Types of material:** full-length plays, one-acts. **Frequency:** annual. **Remuneration:** $750 for full-length play, $375 for one-act; 2 full-production slots will be filled, each with a full-length play or a bill of one-acts; housing to attend rehearsals. **Guidelines:** unpublished play not professionally produced and suitable for theatre with 150-seat and 75-seat houses that produces contemporary, issue-oriented works; moderate cast size and production demands; availability of playwright for rehearsals a consideration; 1 submission. **Submission procedure:** script, production history, 1- or 2-page synopsis, bio and $5 entry fee; optional SASE for critique. **Deadline:** 28 Feb 1996. **Notification:** May/Jun 1996. **Dates:** summer 1996.

## FESTIVAL OF FIRSTS PLAYWRITING COMPETITION

Sunset Center; Box 5066; Carmel, CA 93921; (408) 624-3996
*Director*

**Types of material:** full-length plays. **Frequency:** annual. **Remuneration:** up to $1000; possible production. **Guidelines:** unproduced play; send SASE for guidelines. **Submission procedure:** completed entry form, script, cast list, synopsis and $15 entry fee. **Deadline:** 31 Aug 1996.

## FMCT NATIONAL PLAYWRIGHTS COMPETITION

Fargo-Moorhead Community Theatre; Box 644; Fargo, ND 58107;
    (701) 235-1901
*Contest Administrator*

**Types of material:** full-length plays. **Frequency:** biennial. **Remuneration:** $1000; or $500, production and housing to attend rehearsals. **Guidelines:** 1 unproduced, unpublished submission; cast limit of 8; write for guidelines. **Submission procedure:** script and resume. **Deadline:** 1 Jul 1996. **Notification:** 1 Dec 1996.

## FRANCESCA PRIMUS SOUTHERN PLAYWRITING COMPETITION

(formerly Festival of Southern Theatre Playwriting Competition)
Department of Theatre Arts; University of Mississippi; University, MS 38677;
(601) 232-5816
Scott McCoy, *Producing Director*

**Types of material:** full-length plays. **Frequency:** annual. **Remuneration:** up to 3 awards: $1500; production. **Guidelines:** southern playwright or markedly southern theme; 1 submission, unpublished and not professionally produced. **Submission procedure:** script and bio. **Deadline:** 30 Nov 1995. **Notification:** 28 Feb 1996.

## GEORGE HAWKINS PLAYWRITING CONTEST

The Ensemble Theatre; 3535 Main St; Houston, TX 77002; (713) 520-0055
Eileen Morris, *Artistic Director*

**Types of material:** one-acts and musicals for young audiences. **Frequency:** annual. **Remuneration:** $500 1st prize; production; travel and housing to attend final week of rehearsals; 2nd and 3rd prizewinners receive staged reading. **Guidelines:** original work, not professionally produced, that illuminates the African-American experience for young people aged 6–18; prefers works maximum 45 minutes long with cast limit of 7 and simple set and props; write for guidelines. **Submission procedure:** completed entry form and script. **Deadline:** 20 Mar 1996; no submission before 1 Dec 1995. **Notification:** 20 May 1996.

## GEORGE HOUSTON BASS PLAY-RITES FESTIVAL AND MEMORIAL AWARD

Rites and Reason Theatre; Box 1148; Brown University; Providence, RI 02912;
(401) 863-3558
Elmo Terry-Morgan *Artistic Director*

**Types of material:** full-length plays, one-acts, musicals. **Frequency:** annual. **Remuneration:** 4 winners receive $250, staged reading at festival, travel and housing to attend rehearsals; winner of best play of festival receives $1000, workshop production, housing and travel to attend rehearsals. **Guidelines:** generally but not exclusively works depicting aspects of African-American life and history; prefers long one-acts but will consider short full-length plays; writer must be willing to develop work further. **Submission procedure:** script only; include cassette for musicals. **Deadline:** 1 Mar 1996. **Notification:** May 1996. **Dates:** Jun 1996.

## GEORGE R. KERNODLE PLAYWRITING CONTEST

Department of Drama; 619 Kimpel Hall; University of Arkansas;
Fayetteville, AR 72701; (501) 575-2953
*Director*

**Types of material:** one-acts. **Frequency:** annual. **Remuneration:** $300 1st prize, $200 2nd prize, $100 3rd prize; possible staged reading or production. **Guide-**

lines: U.S. or Canadian playwright; unproduced, unpublished play, not more than 1 hour long; cast limit of 8; 3-submission limit; write for guidelines. **Submission procedure:** script with statement that play has not received full production, $3 fee per submission and optional SASE or SASP for acknowledgment of receipt. **Deadline:** 1 Jun 1996; no submission before 1 Jan 1996. **Notification:** 1 Oct 1996.

## GILMAN AND GONZALEZ-FALLA THEATRE FOUNDATION MUSICAL THEATRE AWARD
109 East 64th St; New York, NY 10021; (212) 734-8011
Sarah Smith, *Coordinator*

**Types of material:** musicals. **Frequency:** annual. **Remuneration:** $25,000. **Guidelines:** writer(s) must have had a musical produced by commercial or nonprofit theatre; contact foundation for guidelines after 1 Jan 1996. **Submission procedure:** see guidelines. **Deadline:** TBA (1 Aug in 1995).

## GILMORE CREEK PLAYWRITING COMPETITION
Campus Box 78; St. Mary's College of Minnesota; Winona, MN 55987;
(507) 457-1606
Robert Pevitts, *Dean of School of Arts and Humanities*

**Types of material:** full-length plays, translations, adaptations, plays for young audiences, musicals. **Frequency:** biennial. **Remuneration:** $2500; production; stipend to cover travel, room and board for 2-week residency. **Guidelines:** full-length work not produced professionally. **Submission procedure:** completed application and script. **Deadline:** 15 Jan 1997. **Notification:** 15 May 1997.

## GOSHEN COLLEGE PEACE PLAYWRITING CONTEST
Goshen College; 1700 South Main St; Goshen, IN 46526; (219) 535-7393
Lauren Friesen, *Director of Theatre*

**Types of material:** one-acts. **Frequency:** biennial. **Remuneration:** $500; production; room and board to attend rehearsals and/or production. **Guidelines:** 1 unproduced submission, 30–50 minutes long, exploring a contemporary peace theme. **Submission procedure:** script only. **Deadline:** 31 Dec 1995. **Notification:** 1 May 1996.

## GREAT PLATTE RIVER PLAYWRIGHTS' FESTIVAL
University of Nebraska-Kearney Theatre; Kearney, NE 68849-5260;
(308) 865-8406
*Artistic Director*

**Types of material:** full-length plays, one-acts, plays for young audiences, musicals. **Frequency:** annual. **Remuneration:** $500 1st prize, $300 2nd prize, $200 3rd prize; production; travel and housing to attend rehearsals. **Guidelines:** unproduced, unpublished original work; submission of works-in-progress for possible development encouraged. **Submission procedure:** script with cover letter; include cassette for musical. **Deadline:** 1 Apr 1996. **Notification:** 1 May 1996.

## THE GREGORY KOLOVAKOS AWARD

PEN American Center; 568 Broadway; New York, NY 10012; (212) 334-1660
John Morrone, *Awards Coordinator*

**Types of material:** translations. **Frequency:** biennial. **Remuneration:** $2000. **Guidelines:** award to U.S. writer, critic or translator whose work has made a sustained contribution over time to the cause of Latin American literatures, as well as their Iberian counterparts, in English; primarily recognizes work from Spanish but contributions from other Hispanic languages also considered; candidate must be nominated by editor or colleague; write for guideline. **Submission procedure:** letter from nominator documenting candidate's qualifications with particular attention to depth and vision of his or her work; candidate's vita; supporting materials may be requested from finalists. **Deadline:** 1 Dec 1995. **Notification:** finalists mid-Dec 1995 (supporting materials due 6 Jan 1996); winner mid-Mar 1996.

## HAROLD MORTON LANDON TRANSLATION AWARD

The Academy of American Poets; 584 Broadway, Suite 1208;
New York, NY 10012; (212) 274-0343
Matthew Brogan, *Program Director*

**Types of material:** translations. **Frequency:** annual. **Remuneration:** $1000. **Guidelines:** U.S. citizen; published translation of verse, including verse drama, from any language into English verse; book published in 1995. **Submission procedure:** 2 copies of book (no manuscripts). **Deadline:** 31 Dec 1995.

## HENRICO THEATRE COMPANY
## PLAYWRITING COMPETITIONS

The County of Henrico; Division of Recreation and Parks; Box 27032;
Richmond, VA 23273; (804) 672-5100
J. Larkin Brown, Cultural Arts Coordinator

### Full-Length Play Competition

**Types of material:** full-length plays and plays with music. **Remuneration:** $250; production; videotape of production. **Guidelines:** full-length work relating to Christmas season (specific Christmas story or general seasonal theme); prefers small cast, simple set; write for guidelines. **Submission procedure:** 2 copies of script. **Deadline:** 1 Jul 1996. **Notification:** 15 Nov 1996.

### One-Act Playwriting Competition

**Types of material:** one-acts, one-act musicals. **Frequency:** annual. **Remuneration:** $250; production; $125 and possible production for each of 2 runners-up. **Guidelines:** unproduced, unpublished work; no controversial themes; prefers small cast, simple set; write for guidelines. **Submission procedure:** 2 copies of script. **Deadline:** 1 Jul 1996. **Notification:** 15 Nov 1996.

## HRC's Annual Playwriting Contest
Hudson River Classics, Inc; Box 940; Hudson, NY 12534; (518) 828-1329
W. Keith Hedrick, *President*

**Types of material:** full-length plays, one-acts. **Frequency:** annual. **Remuneration:** $500; staged reading; room, board and travel to attend performance. **Guidelines:** 60–90-minute unpublished play by New York State playwright. **Submission procedure:** script and $5 fee. **Deadline:** 1 Jun 1996; no submission before 15 Jan 1996. **Notification:** 15 Aug 1996.

## Inner City Cultural Center Competition
The Ivar Theater; 1605 North Ivar Ave; Los Angeles, CA 90028; (213) 962-2102
C. Bernard Jackson, *Executive Director*

**Types of material:** one-acts, translations, adaptations, plays for young audiences, musicals, operas. **Frequency:** annual. **Remuneration:** cash award ($1000 1st prize, $500 2nd prize, $250 3rd prize) or paid professional internship with film studio to winner (past winners awarded internships with Warner Brothers and Universal Studios). **Guidelines:** fully mounted productions compete in series of elimination rounds; maximum 40 minutes running time; small cast, minimal set; translations and adaptations must be of unpublished work; write for guidelines. **Submission procedure:** completed application and $45 fee. **Deadline:** 22 Jul 1996. **Dates:** Jul–Oct 1996.

## Jackie White Memorial National Children's Playwriting Contest
309 Parkade Blvd; Columbia, MO 65202; (314) 874-5628
Betsy Phillips, *Chair*

**Types of material:** plays and musicals to be performed by young actors. **Frequency:** annual. **Remuneration:** $250; production by Columbia Entertainment Company Children's Theatre School; room, board and partial travel to attend performance; all entrants receive written evaluation. **Guidelines:** unpublished original work, 60–90 minutes in length, with 20–30 speaking characters of all ages, at least 10 developed in some detail, to be played by students aged 10–15; send SASE for guidelines. **Submission procedure:** completed entry form, script, character description, act/scene synopsis, resume and $10 fee; include cassette for musical. **Deadline:** 30 May 1996. **Notification:** 30 Jul 1996.

## James D. Phelan Award in Literature
The San Francisco Foundation; 685 Market St, Suite 910;
    San Francisco, CA 94105; (415) 495-3100 or (510) 436-3100
Robert Uyeki, *Awards Program Coordinator*

**Types of material:** full-length plays, one-acts, plays for young audiences. **Frequency:** annual. **Remuneration:** $2000. **Guidelines:** unpublished play-in-progress; author CA born and aged 20–35 years as of 31 Jan 1996. **Submission**

**procedure:** completed application and script. **Deadline:** 31 Jan 1996; no submission before 15 Nov 1995. **Notification:** 15 Jun 1996.

## JANE CHAMBERS PLAYWRITING AWARD

English Department; Box 1852; Brown University; Providence, RI 02912;
   (401) 247-2911
Tori Haring-Smith, *Coordinator*

**Types of material:** full-length plays, one-acts, performance-art texts. **Frequency:** annual. **Remuneration:** $1000; rehearsed reading at national conference of Association for Theatre in Higher Education's Women and Theatre Program, which sponsors award; travel to attend rehearsals; student submissions eligible for $250 Student Award. **Guidelines:** work by a woman that reflects a feminist perspective and contains a majority of roles for women; special interest in works by and about women from a diversity of positions in respect to race, class, sexual preference, physical ability, age and geographical region; experimentation with dramatic form encouraged; no 1-woman shows; winner must be available to attend reading and part of conference in late Jul/early Aug; 1-submission limit; send SASE for guidelines and application. **Submission procedure:** completed application form, script, synopsis and resume; if possible, letter of endorsement by theatre professional familiar with writer's work; optional SASP for acknowledgment of receipt. **Deadline:** 15 Feb 1996. **Notification:** 30 May 1996. **Dates:** late Jul/early Aug.

## JEWEL BOX THEATRE PLAYWRIGHTING AWARD

3700 North Walker; Oklahoma City, OK 73118-7099; (405) 521-1786
Charles Tweed, *Production Director*

**Types of material:** full-length plays. **Frequency:** annual. **Remuneration:** $500; possible production. **Guidelines:** unproduced full-length play of strong ensemble nature with emphasis on character rather than spectacle; write for guidelines and forms. **Submission procedure:** completed entry form, playwright's agreement and 2 copies of script. **Deadline:** 15 Jan 1996. **Notification:** Apr 1996.

## JOHN GASSNER MEMORIAL PLAYWRITING AWARD

The New England Theatre Conference; c/o Department of Theatre;
   Northeastern University; 306 Huntington Ave; Boston, MA 02115;
   (617) 424-9275

**Types of material:** full-length plays. **Frequency:** annual. **Remuneration:** $500 1st prize, $250 2nd prize; staged reading at NETC annual convention; possible publication. **Guidelines:** New England resident or NETC member; unpublished play that has not had professional full production and is not under consideration for publication or professional production; 1 submission. **Submission procedure:** script with cover page, cast list with character descriptions, brief synopsis and statement that play has not been published or professionally produced and is not under consideration; SASP for acknowledgment of receipt; $10 fee, except for NETC members. **Deadline:** 15 Apr 1996. **Notification:** 1 Sep 1996 (winners only).

## KATHERINE AND LEE CHILCOTE AWARD

Cleveland Public Theatre; 6415 Detroit Ave; Cleveland, OH 44102;
    (216) 631-2727
Terence Cranendonk, *Director, New Plays Festival*

**Types of material:** full-length plays, one-acts. **Frequency:** annual. **Remuneration:** 10–13 plays receive staged reading at Jan festival; of those, 1 chosen to receive award of $8000 and full production. **Guidelines:** to be eligible for award, play, by OH playwright, which has socio/political content; write for guidelines. **Submission procedure:** script and $10 fee (waivable). **Deadline:** 1 Sep 1995. **Notification:** 1 Dec 1995 for festival; 1 Jan 1996 for award.

## KENNEDY CENTER AMERICAN COLLEGE THEATER FESTIVAL: MICHAEL KANIN PLAYWRITING AWARDS PROGRAM

The John F. Kennedy Center for the Performing Arts;
    Washington, DC 20566-0001; (202) 416-8850
John Lion, *Producing Director*

### The Fourth Freedom Forum Playwriting Award

**Types of material:** full-length plays. **Remuneration:** 1st prize: for playwright, $2500 plus all-expense-paid 2-week residency at Sundance Playwrights Laboratory (see Development), which includes consultation with Sundance directors and dramaturgs and reading by Lab actors; $750 to producing college or university; 2nd prize: $1000 to playwright; $500 to producing college or university. **Guidelines:** play on themes of world peace and international disarmament; produced by an ACTF-participating college or university; writer enrolled as full-time student at college or university during year of production; write for KC/ACTF brochure. **Submission procedure:** college or university which has entered production of work in ACTF registers work for awards program. **Deadline:** 1 Dec 1995. **Dates:** 15–24 Apr 1996.

### The KC/ACTF Musical Theater Award

**Types of material:** musicals. **Frequency:** annual. **Remuneration:** $1000 for lyrics; $1000 for music; $1000 for book; $1000 to producing college or university. **Guidelines:** original and copyrighted work produced by ACTF-participating college or university; at least 50% of writing team must be enrolled as full-time student(s) at college or university during year of production or during either of the 2 years preceding the production; write for KC/ACTF brochure. **Submission procedure:** college or university which has entered production of work in ACTF registers work for awards program. **Deadline:** 1 Dec 1995. **Dates:** 15–24 Apr 1996.

### The Lorraine Hansberry Playwriting Award

**Types of material:** full-length plays. **Frequency:** annual. **Remuneration:** 1st prize: $2500 plus all-expenses-paid fellowship to attend Shenandoah Playwrights Retreat (see Development) to playwright; $750 to producing college or university; 2nd prize: $1000 to playwright; $500 to producing college or university. **Guidelines:**

play dealing with the black experience produced by an ACTF-participating college or university; writer enrolled as full-time student at college or university during year of production or during either of the 2 years preceding the production; write for KC/ACTF brochure. **Submission procedure:** college or university which has entered production of work in ACTF registers work for awards program. **Deadline:** 1 Dec 1995. **Dates:** 15–24 Apr 1996.

### The National Student Playwriting Award

**Types of material:** full-length plays, adaptations, musicals. **Frequency:** annual. **Remuneration:** $2500; production at Kennedy Center during festival; publication by Samuel French with royalties; offer of William Morris Agency management contract; fellowship to attend Mount Sequoyah New Play Retreat (see Development); Dramatists Guild membership (see Membership and Service Organizations). **Guidelines:** work must be produced by ACTF-participating college or university; writer enrolled as full-time student at college or university during year of production or during either of the 2 years preceding the production; write for KC/ACTF brochure. **Submission procedure:** college or university which has entered production of work in ACTF registers work for awards program. **Deadline:** 1 Dec 1995. **Dates:** 15–24 Apr 1996.

### The Short Play Awards Program

**Types of material:** one-acts, one-act adaptations. **Frequency:** annual. **Remuneration:** up to 3 awards: $1000; publication by Samuel French; Dramatists Guild membership (see Membership and Service Organizations). **Guidelines:** one-act must be produced by ACTF-participating college or university; writer enrolled as full-time student at college or university during year of production or during either of the 2 years preceding the production; simple production demands (minimal setup and strike time); write for KC/ACTF brochure. **Submission procedure:** college or university which has entered production of work in ACTF registers work for awards program. **Deadline:** 1 Dec 1995. **Dates:** 15–24 Apr 1996.

## KUMU KAHUA PLAYWRITING CONTEST
Department of Theatre and Dance; University of Hawaii at Manoa;
        1770 East-West Rd; Honolulu, HI 96822; (808) 956-2588
Dennis Carroll, *Chair, Theatre and Dance*

**Types of material:** full-length plays, one-acts. **Frequency:** annual. **Remuneration:** *first category:* $500 for full-length play, $200 for one-act; *second category:* $250 for full-length play, $100 for one-act; reading and/or production if playwright present. **Guidelines:** unproduced play; previous entries ineligible; *first category:* play set in HI and dealing with some aspect of HI experience; *second category:* play not dealing with HI by HI resident only. **Submission procedure:** write for entry brochure. **Deadline:** 1 Jan 1996. **Notification:** 1 May 1996.

## L. ARNOLD WEISSBERGER PLAYWRITING COMPETITION

New Dramatists; 424 West 44th St; New York, NY 10036; (212) 757-6960
*Coordinator*

**Types of material:** full-length plays. **Frequency:** annual. **Remuneration:** $5000. **Guidelines:** 1 unpublished submission, not produced professionally; write for guidelines. **Submission procedure:** play must be nominated, then playwright submits script with optional SASP for acknowledgment of receipt. **Deadline:** 31 May 1996; no submission before 15 Sep 1995. **Notification:** May 1997.

## LAMIA INK! INTERNATIONAL ONE-PAGE PLAY COMPETITION

Box 202, Prince St Station; New York, NY 10012
Cortland Jessup, *Editor*

**Types of material:** 1-page plays. **Frequency:** annual. **Remuneration:** $200; reading in New York City and publication in magazine (see entry in Publication) for winner and 11 other best plays. **Guidelines:** 3-submission limit; send SASE for guidelines. **Submission procedure:** completed application, script, SASE for response and $1 fee per submission. **Deadline:** 15 Mar 1996. **Notification:** 15 Apr 1996.

## LAWRENCE S. EPSTEIN PLAYWRITING AWARD

115 Hatteras Rd; Barnegat, NJ 08005-2814
Lawrence S. Epstein, *Director*

**Types of material:** full-length plays, bills of related one-acts. **Frequency:** annual. **Remuneration:** $250. **Guidelines:** unproduced play. **Submission procedure:** script and optional $1 fee to help cover expenses. **Deadline:** 31 Mar 1996; no submission before 1 Jan 1996. **Notification:** Dec 1996.

## THE LEE KORF PLAYWRITING AWARDS

The Original Theatre Works; Burnight Center; Cerritos College;
    11110 Alondra Blvd; Norwalk, CA 90650-6298; (310) 860-2451, ext 2638
Gloria Manriquez, *Production Coordinator*

**Types of material:** full-length plays, musicals, theatre pieces, extravaganzas. **Frequency:** annual. **Remuneration:** $750; production. **Guidelines:** special interest in works with multicultural themes. **Submission procedure:** send SASE for guidelines and application. **Deadline:** 1 Jan 1996. **Notification:** 1 Apr 1996.

## LESBIAN PLAY AWARD

See LEND (Lesbian Exchange of New Drama) in Membership and Service Organizations.

## LETRAS DE ORO SPANISH LITERARY PRIZE COMPETITION

University of Miami; 1531 Brescia Ave; Coral Gables, FL 33124-3010;
(305) 284-3266
Joaquin Roy, *Graduate School of International Studies*

**Types of material:** full-length plays. **Frequency:** annual. **Remuneration:** $2500;
publication. **Guidelines:** U.S. resident; unpublished play written in Spanish that
has not won a previous award; 1 submission; write for rules. **Submission
procedure:** 3 copies of script. **Deadline:** 12 Oct 1995. **Notification:** Mar 1996.

## THE LITTLE THEATRE OF ALEXANDRIA
## NATIONAL ONE-ACT PLAYWRITING COMPETITION

Little Theatre of Alexandria; 600 Wolfe St; Alexandria, VA 22314;
(703) 683-5778
*Chairman, Playwriting Competition*

**Types of material:** one-acts. **Frequency:** annual. **Remuneration:** $350 1st prize,
$250 2nd prize, $150 3rd prize; possible production. **Guidelines:** U.S. citizen; 1
unpublished, unproduced submission; prefers plays with running times of 20–60
minutes, few scenes and 1 set. **Submission procedure:** script, synopsis, character
descriptions and $5 fee; send SASE for guidelines. **Deadline:** 31 Mar 1996.
**Notification:** Sep 1996.

## LIVE OAK THEATRE'S HARVEST FESTIVAL OF NEW AMERICAN PLAYS

200 Colorado St; Austin, TX 78701; (512) 472-5143
Tom Byrne, *Literary Manager*

**Types of material:** full-length plays. **Frequency:** annual. **Remuneration:** $1000 for
best American play; $500 Larry L. King Playwriting Award for Best Texas
Playwright; $500 for University of Texas student "who makes outstanding
contribution towards new play development"; full production with royalty; travel,
room and board to attend fall festival of staged readings. **Guidelines:** 1
submission, not produced professionally. **Submission procedure:** send SASE for
guidelines. **Deadline:** 1 Nov 1995. **Notification:** summer 1996.

## LOIS AND RICHARD ROSENTHAL NEW PLAY PRIZE

Cincinnati Playhouse in the Park; Box 6537; Cincinnati, OH 45206;
(513) 345-2242
Madeleine Pabis, *Artistic Associate*

**Types of material:** full-length plays, musicals. **Frequency:** annual. **Remuneration:**
$10,000; production; travel and housing to attend rehearsals. **Guidelines:** 1
unpublished submission, not produced professionally. **Submission procedure:** no
scripts; 5 pages of dialogue, 2-page maximum abstract including synopsis,
character breakdown and playwright's bio, submitted by playwright or agent.
**Deadline:** 1 Feb 1996; no submission before 15 Oct 1995. **Notification:** 2 months;
6 months if script is requested.

## LOS ANGELES DESIGNERS' THEATRE COMMISSIONS
Box 1883; Studio City, CA 91614-0883;
    (213) 650-9600 (voice), (818) 769-9000 (TDD)
Richard Niederberg, *Artistic Director*

**Types of material:** full-length plays, bills of related one-acts, translations, adaptations, plays for young audiences, musicals, operas. **Frequency:** ongoing. **Remuneration:** negotiable commissioning fee; possible travel to attend rehearsals if developmental work is needed. **Guidelines:** work with commercial potential which has not received professional full production, is not under option and is free of commitment to specific director, actors or other personnel; large casts and multiple sets welcome; prefers controversial material. **Submission procedure:** script or synopsis and resume; include cassette for musical; materials will not be returned. **Deadline:** ongoing. **Notification:** at least 4 months.

## LOVE CREEK ONE-ACT FESTIVALS
Love Creek Productions; c/o 75 Liberty Pl; Weehawken, NJ 07087-7014
Cynthia Granville, *Festival Literary Manager/Chair, Reading Committee*

### Annual Short Play Festival

**Types of material:** one-acts. **Frequency:** annual. **Remuneration:** approximately 40 finalists receive mini-showcase production in New York City during festival; $300 prize for best play of festival. **Guidelines:** unpublished play, not produced in NYC area within past year; maximum length of 40 minutes; cast of 2 or more, simple sets and costumes; 2-submission limit; send SASE for guidelines. **Submission procedure:** script with letter giving theatre permission to produce play if chosen and specifying whether Equity showcase is acceptable. **Deadline:** 30 Sep 1995. **Dates:** Jan–Feb 1996.

### One-Act Mini-Festivals

**Types of material:** one-acts. **Frequency:** 2–4 times per year. **Remuneration:** approximately 25 finalists receive mini-showcase production in New York City during each festival; $200 prize for best play of festival. **Guidelines:** unpublished play on specified theme, not produced in NYC area within past year; maximum length of 40 minutes; cast of 2 or more, simple sets and costumes; 2-submission limit; for Gay and Lesbian Festival, scripts with gay/lesbian themes, special interest in lesbian themes, positive, life-affirming depictions of gay and lesbian life, and mature portrayals of gay and lesbian sexuality; for second festival, "Fear of God: Religion in the '90s," scripts with "nonsatirical examination of religion and spirituality"; send SASE for other festival topics and guidelines. **Submission procedure:** script with letter giving theatre permission to produce play if chosen and specifying whether Equity showcase acceptable. **Deadline:** 15 Oct 1995 for Gay and Lesbian Festival; TBA for other festivals (send SASE for information).

## The Marc A. Klein Playwriting Award

Department of Theater Arts; Case Western Reserve University; 10900 Euclid Ave; Cleveland, OH 44106-7077; (216) 368-2858

John Orlock, *Chair, Reading Committee*

**Types of material:** full-length plays, bills of related one-acts. **Frequency:** annual. **Remuneration:** $1000, including $500 to cover residency expenses; production. **Guidelines:** student currently enrolled at U.S. college or university; work, endorsed by faculty member of university theatre department, that has not received professional full production or trade-book publication. **Submission procedure:** completed entry form and script. **Deadline:** 15 May 1996. **Notification:** 15 Jul 1996.

## Margaret Bartle Playwriting Award

Community Children's Theatre; 8021 East 129th Terr; Grandview, MO 64030-2114; (816) 761-5775

Blanche Sellens, *Chairman, Playwriting Contest*

**Types of material:** plays and musicals for young audiences. **Frequency:** annual. **Remuneration:** $500. **Guidelines:** unpublished, unproduced work 55–60 minutes long, suitable for grades 1–6; 8-character limit; all parts played by adult women. **Submission procedure:** script only; include cassette for musical. **Deadline:** 31 Jan 1996. **Notification:** Apr 1996.

## Marvin Taylor Playwriting Award

Sierra Repertory Theatre; Box 3030; Sonora, CA 95370; (209) 532-3120

Dennis Jones, *Producing Director*

**Types of material:** full-length plays, adaptations, musicals. **Frequency:** annual. **Remuneration:** $500; possible production. **Guidelines:** 1 submission that has received no more than 2 productions or staged readings; cast limit of 15, prefers 6; not more than 2 sets. **Submission procedure:** script only. **Deadline:** 31 Aug 1996. **Notification:** Mar 1997.

## Maxim Mazumdar New Play Competition

Alleyway Theatre; 1 Curtain Up Alley; Buffalo, NY 14202-1911; (716) 852-2600

Joyce Stilson, *Dramaturg*

**Types of material:** full-length plays, one-acts, musicals. **Frequency:** annual. **Remuneration:** $400, production with royalty, and travel and housing to attend rehearsals for full-length play or musical; $100 and production for one-act play or musical. **Guidelines:** unproduced full-length work minimum 90 minutes long with cast limit of 10 and unit set or simple set, or unproduced one-act work less than 60 minutes long with cast limit of 6 and simple set; prefers work with unconventional setting that explores the boundaries of theatricality; limit of 1 submission in each category. **Submission procedure:** script and resume; $5 fee per playwright. **Deadline:** 1 Sep 1995. **Notification:** 1 Jan 1996 for finalists; 1 Feb 1996 for winners.

## McLaren Memorial Comedy Playwriting Competition

Midland Community Theatre; 2000 West Wadley Ave; Midland, TX 79705;
   (915) 682-2544
Mary Lou Cassidy, *Coordinator*

**Types of material:** full-length plays, one-acts, translations, adaptations, plays for young audiences, musicals. **Frequency:** annual. **Remuneration:** $400; staged reading; housing while attending rehearsals. **Guidelines:** comedies only; prefers work that has not received professional full production but will consider work with 1 nonprofit-theatre production. **Submission procedure:** script and $5 fee. **Deadline:** 31 Jan 1996; no submission before 1 Dec 1995. **Notification:** 15 May 1996.

## Midwest Theatre Network Original Play Competition/ Rochester Playwright Festival

5031 Tongen Ave NW; Rochester, MN 55901; (507) 281-1472
Joan Sween, *Executive Director*

**Types of material:** full-length plays, collections of one-acts, musicals, experimental works. **Frequency:** annual. **Remuneration:** 4–8 awards of $1000 each (contingent on funding); full production at 1 of 7 cooperating theatres; possible travel, room and board to attend performance. **Guidelines:** unpublished work that has not received professional production; send SASE for guidelines and entry form. **Submission procedure:** 1 completed entry form with each script; first submission free, $5 fee for each additional script; include score and/or cassette for musical. **Deadline:** 18 Nov 1995. **Notification:** Feb 1996.

## Midwestern Playwrights Festival

The University of Toledo; Department of Theatre, Film and Dance;
   Toledo, OH 43606-3390; (419) 537-2202
John S. Kuhn, *Playwriting Festival Coordinator*

**Types of material:** full-length plays, translations, adaptations, musicals. **Frequency:** annual. **Remuneration:** winner receives $1000, staged reading in fall 1996, production at Toledo Repertoire Theatre in spring 1997, and travel, room and board for reading and 2-week residency during production; 1st runner-up receives $350 and staged reading; 2nd runner-up receives $150 and staged reading. **Guidelines:** resident of IL, IN, MI or OH; 1 full-length, 2-act submission not published or produced professionally; cast limit of 10; prefers 1 set; write for guidelines. **Submission procedure:** 2 copies of script, 1-page synopsis, resume and cover letter. **Deadline:** 1 May 1996. **Notification:** 1 Aug 1996.

## MILDRED AND ALBERT PANOWSKI PLAYWRITING AWARD

Forest A. Roberts Theatre; Northern Michigan University; Marquette, MI 49855; (906) 227-2553

James A. Panowski, *Director*

**Types of material:** full-length plays, adaptations. **Frequency:** annual. **Remuneration:** $2000; production; travel, room and board for 1-week residency. **Guidelines:** 1 unpublished, unproduced submission; rewrites of previous entries ineligible; production will be entered in Kennedy Center American College Theater Festival (see entry in this section) if playwright is eligible; write for guidelines. **Submission procedure:** completed entry form and script. **Deadline:** 17 Nov 1995. **Notification:** Apr 1996.

## THE MILL MOUNTAIN THEATRE NEW PLAY COMPETITION: THE NORFOLK SOUTHERN FESTIVAL OF NEW WORKS

1 Market Square SE, 2nd Floor; Roanoke, VA 24011-1437; (703) 342-5730

Jo Weinstein, *Literary Manager*

**Types of material:** full-length plays, one-acts. **Frequency:** annual. **Remuneration:** $1000; staged reading with possibility of production; travel stipend and housing for limited residency. **Guidelines:** U.S. resident; 1 unproduced, unpublished submission; cast limit of 10; no 10-minute plays; send SASE for guidelines. **Submission procedure:** script, brief synopsis of scenes, character descriptions, history of play and resume. **Deadline:** 1 Jan 1996; no submission before 1 Oct 1995. **Notification:** Aug 1996.

## MIXED BLOOD VERSUS AMERICA

Mixed Blood Theatre Company; 1501 South 4th St; Minneapolis, MN 55454; (612) 338-0937

David Kunz, *Script Czar*

**Types of material:** full-length plays, musicals. **Frequency:** annual. **Remuneration:** $2000; production. **Guidelines:** unproduced, unpublished work by U.S. citizen who has had at least 1 work produced or workshopped professionally or by educational institution; 2-submission limit; write for guidelines. **Submission procedure:** script and resume or other evidence of work produced or workshopped; include cassette of songs for musical; mark all contest submissions "Mixed Blood Versus America." **Deadline:** 15 Mar 1996. **Notification:** fall 1996.

## MOBIL PLAYWRITING COMPETITION

Royal Exchange Theatre Company; St. Ann's Sq; Manchester M2 7DH; UK; 441-61-833-9333

Alan Pollock, *Literary Manager*

**Types of material:** full-length plays. **Frequency:** biennial. **Remuneration:** up to about £40,000 divided among several winners; possible production. **Guidelines:** original play written in English and not previously produced or optioned in any medium; send SASE for guidelines. **Submission procedure:** script with pseudonymous playwright's name, and sealed envelope addressed with pseudonym and play title and containing card with play title, author's actual name, address and telephone number. **Deadline:** TBA (5 Aug in 1994).

## MORTON R. SARETT MEMORIAL AWARD
Department of Theatre Arts; University of Nevada, Las Vegas;
  4505 Maryland Pkwy, Box 455036; Las Vegas, NV 89154-5036;
  (702) 895-3666
Corrine A. Bonate, *Coordinator*

**Types of material:** full-length plays, musicals. **Frequency:** biennial. **Remuneration:** $3000; production; travel and housing to attend rehearsals. **Guidelines:** unpublished, unproduced play or musical; send SASE for guidelines. **Submission procedure:** completed application, 2 copies of script and 50-word synopsis. **Deadline:** mid-Dec 1995; exact date TBA. **Notification:** Jun 1996.

## MRTW SCRIPT CONTEST
Midwest Radio Theatre Workshop; KOPN Radio; 915 East Broadway;
  Columbia, MO 65201; (314) 874-5676
Steve Donofrio, *Director*

**Types of material:** short radio plays. **Frequency:** annual. **Remuneration:** $800 to be divided among 2–4 winners; possible radio production for local broadcast and national distribution via satellite and tape sales; scholarship to attend fall 1996 Midwest Radio Theatre Workshop (see Development); publication in MRTW Scriptbook. **Guidelines:** original radio play 15–30 minutes long (no adaptations) by established or emerging writer; special interest in plays by women, gay and lesbian writers and writers of color and in issue-oriented plays on contemporary themes; 1 submission; write for guidelines. **Submission procedure:** 3 copies of script in radio format and cover letter indicating if play has been produced; $10 fee. **Deadline:** 15 Nov 1995. **Notification:** 1 Mar 1996.

## NANTUCKET SHORT PLAY FESTIVAL AND COMPETITION
Nantucket Theatrical Productions; Box 2177; Nantucket, MA 02584;
  (508) 228-5002
Jim Patrick, *Literary Manager*

**Types of material:** one-acts. **Frequency:** annual. **Remuneration:** $200; 1 or more staged readings for winning play and selected additional plays as part of summer festival. **Guidelines:** unpublished play which has not received Equity production; maximum length of 1 hour; special interest in multiracial themes and plays by playwrights of color; simple production demands; send SASE for rules. **Submission procedure:** completed entry form, script and $5 fee. **Deadline:** 1 Mar 1996. **Notification:** 1 May 1996. **Dates:** Jul 1996.

## National Children's Theatre Festival

Actors' Playhouse at the Miracle Theatre; 280 Miracle Mile;
    Coral Gables, FL 33134
Judy Buckland, *Education Director*

**Types of material:** works for young audiences. **Frequency:** annual. **Remuneration:** 3 awards in each of 2 categories (plays and musicals): $1200 1st prize plus production, travel and housing to attend fall festival; $500 2nd prize; $250 3rd prize. **Guidelines:** unpublished play for young people aged 12–17, 45–60 minutes long, with cast limit of 6 (may play multiple roles) and minimal sets suitable for touring; or unpublished musical for young people aged 5–12, 45–60 minutes long, with cast limit of 8 (may play multiple roles) and maximum of 2 major or 4 simple sets; translations and adaptations eligible only if writer owns copyright to material; special interest in works dealing with social issues including multiculturalism in today's society; write for guidelines. **Submission procedure:** completed entry form, script and $10 fee; include score and cassette for musical. **Deadline:** 1 Dec 1995. **Notification:** 1 Mar 1996. **Dates:** 22–28 Apr 1996.

## National Hispanic Playwriting Contest

Arizona Theatre Company; Box 1631; Tucson, AZ 85702; (602) 884-8210
Matthew Wiener, *Associate Artistic Director*

**Types of material:** full-length plays, adaptations. **Frequency:** annual. **Remuneration:** $1000; staged reading; travel, room and board to attend rehearsals and performance. **Guidelines:** playwright of Hispanic heritage residing in U.S., territories or Mexico; 1 unproduced submission written in English or in Spanish with English translation with Hispanic-American themes or setting. **Submission procedure:** script (with English translation if original in Spanish), synopsis, production history and bio. **Deadline:** 1 Sep 1995. **Notification:** Jan 1996.

## National Play Award

Box 286; Hollywood, CA 90078; (213) 465-9517
Raul Espinova, *Project Director*

**Types of material:** full-length plays. **Frequency:** biennial. **Remuneration:** $5000. **Guidelines:** original unpublished play, not produced with paid Equity cast, that has not won major award or been previously submitted to NPA; send SASE for guidelines after 1 Jan 1996. **Submission procedure:** script with optional SASP for acknowledgment of receipt. **Deadline:** 30 Jun 1997; no submission before 1 Jan 1997. **Notification:** spring 1998.

## National Ten-Minute Play Contest

Actors Theatre of Louisville; 316 West Main St; Louisville, KY 40202-4218;
    (502) 584-1265
Michael Bigelow Dixon, *Literary Manager*
Michele Volansky, *Assistant Literary Manager*

**Types of material:** 10-minute plays. **Frequency:** annual. **Remuneration:** Heideman

Award of $1000; possible production with royalty. **Guidelines:** U.S. citizen or resident; play 10 pages long or less which has not had Equity production; 2-submission limit; previous entries ineligible; write for guidelines. **Submission procedure:** script only. **Deadline:** 1 Dec 1995. **Notification:** fall 1996.

## NEW AMERICAN COMEDY (NAC) FESTIVAL
Ukiah Players Theatre; 1041 Low Gap Rd; Ukiah, CA 95482; (707) 462-1210
Catherine Babcock Magruder, *NAC Producer*

**Types of material:** full-length plays. **Frequency:** biennial. **Remuneration:** 2 awards: $1000; staged reading; up to $400 travel, housing and $25 per diem to attend 2-week festival. **Guidelines:** unproduced, unpublished comedy; prefers small cast, simple set; playwright must be available to participate in 2-week developmental process during festival; write for guidelines. **Submission procedure:** completed application, script with 1-page summary of plot, scenic requirements, character breakdown and estimated running time; optional resume. **Deadline:** 31 Dec 1995. **Notification:** 1 Mar 1996. **Dates:** 3–19 May 1996.

## NEW AMERICAN MUSICAL WRITERS COMPETITION AND FESTIVAL
NEW STAGES Musical Arts; 270 West 17th St, #17C; New York, NY 10011
Joe Miloscia, *Artistic Director*

**Types of material:** music-theatre works, including musicals, operettas and revues. **Frequency:** annual. **Remuneration:** cash award, contingent on funding; staged reading in NEW STAGES festival for 3–5 works; possible selection for additional development in NEW STAGES Musical Workshop Program (see Development). **Guidelines:** U.S. citizen or resident who has not received significant recognition in the musical theatre field; unpublished original work or adaptation (adapter must obtain rights for work not in public domain); unfinished work eligible if writer(s) can submit 80% of book and songs plus detailed outline of unwritten scenes; 2-submission limit. **Submission procedure:** project synopsis, latest draft of libretto, cassette of songs (do not submit score), list of any previous productions of work, and resumes of composer, librettist and lyricist. **Deadline:** 1 Mar 1996; no submission before 1 Nov 1995.

## NEW CHRISTIAN PLAYS AWARD
Ensemble Theatre Company/Colorado Christian University;
        180 South Garrison St; Lakewood, CO 80226; (303) 238-5386, ext 132
Patrick Rainville Dorn, *Literary Manager*

**Types of material:** full-length plays, one-acts, adaptations, plays for young audiences, musicals. **Frequency:** annual. **Remuneration:** $200 1st prize; possible production and publication in *Christian Drama Magazine* or *Encore Performance Publishing* for winner and 3 finalists. **Guidelines:** unpublished play that is "good theatre with a Christian worldview and not preachy or didactic"; send SASE for guidelines. **Submission procedure:** script and $15 fee. **Deadline:** 31 Mar 1996. **Notification:** 1 Jun 1996.

## NEW CITY THEATER AND ART CENTER PLAYWRIGHT'S FESTIVAL

1634 11th Ave; Seattle, WA 98122; (206) 323-6801
*Festival Manager*

**Types of material:** one-acts, one-act musicals, mixed media pieces. **Frequency:** annual. **Remuneration:** $500 to playwright selected as Best of Festival. **Guidelines:** unproduced work or work-in-progress, not more than 50 minutes in length and with minimal production requirements; 40–50 playwrights invited to participate in festival; playwright finds director, mounts production and is responsible for costs, including $70 production fee; each production receives 1 performance, or 2 if selected for Best of Fest weekend; write for guidelines. **Submission procedure:** completed application form with one-act work sample (need not be festival project), synopsis including running time, and resume. **Deadline:** 4–15 Sep 1995; exact date TBA. **Notification:** by 30 Sep 1995 for festival selection; Jan 1996 for Best of Festival award. **Dates:** Nov/Dec 1995.

## NEW ENGLAND NEW PLAY COMPETITION AND SHOWCASE

The Vineyard Playhouse; Box 2452; Vineyard Haven, MA 02568-2452;
   (508) 693-6450
M. J. Munafo, *Artistic Director*

**Types of material:** full-length plays. **Frequency:** annual. **Remuneration:** $500 grand prize; staged reading for grand prizewinner and 3 other finalists; travel and housing to attend rehearsals and reading. **Guidelines:** New England resident; 1 full-length, unpublished submission, not produced professionally; prefers cast of 10 or fewer, simple set suitable for small stage; guidelines subject to change; send SASE for information. **Submission procedure:** completed application with 2 copies of script and $5 fee. **Deadline:** 1 Jun 1996. **Notification:** 1 Sep 1996. **Dates:** Oct 1996.

## NEW WOMEN PLAYWRIGHT'S CONTEST

Off Center Theater; Tampa Bay Performing Arts Center; Box 518;
   Tampa, FL 33601-0518; (813) 222-1033, -1021
Wendy Leigh, *Artistic Director*

**Types of material:** full-length plays, musicals. **Frequency:** annual. **Remuneration:** 1st prize $1000, full production, travel and housing to attend rehearsals and performance; 2nd prize $100, staged reading, travel and housing; 3rd prize $50, reading. **Guidelines:** plays by and about women with casts at least 50% female; prefers unproduced comedies depicting "strong, intelligent, contemporary women with keen senses of humor." **Submission procedure:** script and synopsis. **Deadline:** 15 Sep 1995. **Notification:** 1 Jan 1996.

## NEW YORK COMEDY PLAYWRITING COMPETITION

The 11th HOUR Theatre Collective; 55 Mercer St; New York, NY 10013;
(212) 802-7298
Lara Koritzke, *Coordinator*

**Types of material:** full-length plays. **Frequency:** annual. **Remuneration:** $300, full production. **Guidelines:** unpublished comedy, not produced in New York City, suitable for production in 70-seat black box theatre; simple set; no screenplays; 1 submission limit. **Submission procedure:** script, production history (if any), resume. **Deadline:** 15 Jan 1996. **Notification:** spring 1996.

## NPT SCREENPLAY/PLAYWRITING FESTIVAL

New Professional Theatre; 443 West 50th St; New York, NY 10019;
(212) 484-9811
Sheila K. Davis, *Producer*

**Types of material:** full-length plays, screenplays. **Frequency:** annual. **Remuneration:** 3 awards of $2000 and professional staged reading. **Guidelines:** special interest in minority women writers. **Submission procedure:** script only. **Deadline:** 1 Jun 1996; no submission before 1 Apr 1996. **Notification:** 1 Sep 1996.

## OFF-OFF BROADWAY ORIGINAL SHORT PLAY FESTIVAL

45 West 25th St; New York, NY 10010-2751; (212) 206-8990
William Talbot, *Festival Coordinator*

**Types of material:** one-acts, segments of full-length plays. **Frequency:** annual. **Remuneration:** festival production hosted by Love Creek Productions on Theatre Row in New York City; possible publication by Samuel French. **Guidelines:** presentation less than 40 minutes long of work developed and produced by theatre, professional school or college that has playwriting program. **Submission procedure:** no submission by playwright; completed application submitted by organization producing work. **Deadline:** Jan–Mar 1996; exact date TBA. **Notification:** within 2 weeks. **Dates:** late spring 1996.

## OGLEBAY INSTITUTE TOWNGATE THEATRE
## PLAYWRITING CONTEST

Oglebay Institute; Stifel Fine Arts Center; 1330 National Rd;
Wheeling, WV 26003; (304) 242-7700
*Performing Arts Department*

**Types of material:** full-length plays. **Frequency:** annual. **Remuneration:** $300; production; partial travel to attend performances. **Guidelines:** unpublished, unproduced play; simple set. **Submission procedure:** script with resume. **Deadline:** 1 Jan 1996. **Notification:** 31 Mar 1996.

## PACIFIC NORTHWEST WRITERS CONFERENCE LITERARY CONTEST
2033 Sixth Ave, Suite 804; Seattle, WA 98121; (206) 443-3807
Shirley Bishop, *Executive Director*

**Types of material:** one-acts. **Frequency:** annual. **Remuneration:** 3 prizes awarded to writers chosen from 13 categories, 1 of which is playwriting; $300 1st prize, $200 2nd prize, $150 3rd prize; all finalists receive written critiques; award-winning play receives reading at summer conference. **Guidelines:** unpublished, unproduced play; maximum 40 pages long and cast limit of 4; 1-submission limit per category per writer; send SASE for guidelines and registration form. **Submission procedure:** completed registration form, 2 copies of script submitted anonymously with separate sheet giving 1-sentence plot summary and playwright's name and contact information; $30 fee for nonmembers or $20 fee for members; include SASE for critique and SASP for acknowledgment of receipt. **Deadline:** 15 Mar 1996. **Notification:** Jul 1996.

## PAUL GREEN PLAYWRIGHTS PRIZE
North Carolina Writers' Network; Box 954; Carrboro, NC 27510; (919) 967-9540
Rachel Hunsinger, *Program Director*

**Types of material:** full-length plays, one-acts. **Frequency:** annual. **Remuneration:** $500, possible production. **Guidelines:** unpublished, unproduced play. **Submission procedure:** 2 copies of script, synopsis and $10 fee for nonmembers or $7.50 fee for members; do not list name on manuscript, include separate cover sheet with title, name and contact information; include SASE for winners list. **Deadline:** 30 Sep 1995. **Notification:** Jan 1996.

## PEN CENTER USA WEST LITERARY AWARDS
672 South Lafayette Park Pl, Suite 41; Los Angeles, CA 90057; (213) 365-8500
Nathalie Geld, *Program Coordinator*

**Types of material:** full-length plays, screenplays, teleplays. **Frequency:** annual. **Remuneration:** $500 award in each of several categories, including drama, screenwriting and television writing. **Guidelines:** writer residing west of Mississippi River; only full-length (original or adapted) screenplays and teleplays; script first produced during 1995 calendar year. **Submission procedure:** 4 copies of script with cover letter giving title of work, author's name and state of residence, name of producer and production dates. **Deadline:** 31 Dec 1995.

## PEN–BOOK-OF-THE-MONTH CLUB TRANSLATION PRIZE
PEN American Center; 568 Broadway; New York, NY 10012; (212) 334-1660
John Morrone, *Program Coordinator*

**Types of material:** translations. **Frequency:** annual. **Remuneration:** $3000. **Guidelines:** book-length translation from any language into English published in U.S. during current calendar year. **Submission procedure:** 3 copies of book. **Deadline:** 20 Dec 1995. **Notification:** spring 1996.

## PERISHABLE THEATRE WOMEN'S PLAYWRITING FESTIVAL
Box 23132; Providence, RI 02903; (401) 331-2695
Kathleen Jenkins, *Festival Director*

**Types of material:** one-acts. **Frequency:** annual. **Remuneration:** 3 awards of $200; production. **Guidelines:** unproduced one-act, less than 1 hour in length, by woman playwright; prefers plays that address women's issues. **Submission procedure:** script and resume. **Deadline:** 30 Jan 1996. **Notification:** 15 Mar 1996.

## PLAYHOUSE ON THE SQUARE NEW PLAY COMPETITION
Playhouse on the Square; 51 South Cooper St; Memphis, TN 38104;
(901) 725-0776, 726-4498
Jackie Nichols, *Executive Director*

**Types of material:** full-length plays, musicals. **Frequency:** annual. **Remuneration:** $500; production. **Guidelines:** unproduced work; small cast; full arrangement for piano for musical; prefers southern playwrights. **Submission procedure:** script only. **Deadline:** 1 Apr 1996.

## PLAYWRIGHTS FIRST PLAYS-IN-PROGRESS AWARD
c\o The Players; 16 Gramercy Park South; New York, NY 10003;
(212) 249-6299, 677-1966

**Types of material:** full-length plays. **Frequency:** annual. **Remuneration:** $1000 for best play; possible reading for selected plays; useful introductions to theatre professionals. **Guidelines:** 1 unproduced play (no adaptations or translations). **Submission procedure:** script and resume. **Deadline:** 15 Oct 1995. **Notification:** May 1996.

## PLAYWRIGHTS' THEATER OF DENTON PLAYWRITING COMPETITION
Box 732; Denton, TX 76202-0732
Mark Pearce, *Artistic Director*

**Types of material:** full-length plays, one-acts. **Frequency:** annual. **Remuneration:** $1000. **Submission procedure:** script and $15 fee (check payable to Sigma Corporation). **Deadline:** 15 Dec 1995.

## QRL POETRY SERIES AWARDS
Quarterly Review of Literature; Princeton University; 26 Haslet Ave;
Princeton, NJ 08540
Renée Weiss, *Co-Editor*

**Types of material:** full-length plays, one-acts, translations. **Frequency:** annual. **Remuneration:** $1000; publication in QRL Poetry Series; 100 complimentary paperback copies. **Guidelines:** up to 6 awards a year for poetry and poetic drama only; play 50–100 pages in length; send SASE for guidelines. **Submission**

**procedure:** submissions accepted in Nov and May only; must be accompanied by $20 subscription for books published in series.

## RENATO POGGIOLI AWARD

PEN American Center; 568 Broadway; New York, NY 10012; (212) 334-1660
John Morrone, *Program Coordinator*

**Types of material:** translations. **Frequency:** annual. **Remuneration:** $3000. **Guidelines:** book-length translation from Italian into English by promising young translator; work-in-progress eligible. **Submission procedure:** curriculum vitae, sample of translation and original Italian text. **Deadline:** 20 Dec 1995. **Notification:** Mar 1996.

## REVA SHINER FULL-LENGTH PLAY CONTEST

Bloomington Playwrights Project; 308 South Washington St;
 Bloomington, IN 47401; (812) 334-1188
Amy Kaliszewski, *Literary Manager*

**Types of material:** full-length plays, musicals. **Frequency:** annual. **Remuneration:** $500; staged reading; production. **Guidelines:** unpublished, unproduced work 75–135 minutes long, suitable for production in small 75-seat theatre; welcomes innovative works; simple set; write for guidelines. **Submission procedure:** script, cover letter and $5 fee; include cassette for musical. **Deadline:** 15 Jan 1996. **Notification:** Apr 1996.

## ROBERT BONE MEMORIAL PLAYWRITING AWARD

The Playwrights' Project; Sammons Center for the Arts, #12;
 3630 Harry Hines Blvd; Dallas, TX 75219; (214) 497-1752
Rafael Parry, *Director of Programming*

**Types of material:** full-length plays, musicals. **Frequency:** annual. **Remuneration:** $250. **Guidelines:** resident of AR, AZ, CO, NM, OK or TX; 1 unproduced submission. **Submission procedure:** script, synopsis, bio and $15 fee; optional SASE for acknowledgment of receipt; include cassette for musical. **Deadline:** 1 May 1996. **Notification:** Aug 1996.

## ROBERT J. PICKERING AWARD
## FOR PLAYWRITING EXCELLENCE

Coldwater Community Theater; c/o 89 South Division; Coldwater, MI 49036;
 (517) 279-7963
J. Richard Colbeck, *Chairman, Play Selection Committee*

**Types of material:** full-length plays, plays for young audiences, musicals. **Frequency:** annual. **Remuneration:** 1st prize $200, production and housing to attend performance; 2nd prize $100; 3rd prize $50. **Guidelines:** unproduced play. **Submission procedure:** script only. **Deadline:** 31 Dec 1995. **Notification:** 1 Feb 1996.

## SAM EDWARDS DEAF PLAYWRIGHTS COMPETITION

New York Deaf Theatre; 305 Seventh Ave, 11th Floor;
   New York, NY 10001-6008; (212) 924-9491 (voice), -9535 (teletypewriter)
Tony Allicino, *General Manager*

**Types of material:** full-length plays, one-acts. **Frequency:** annual. **Remuneration:** $400 for full-length play, $200 for one-act; possible full or workshop production or staged reading. **Guidelines:** unproduced play by deaf playwright; write for guidelines. **Submission procedure:** completed application, script, short synopsis and bio; fee of $10 for U.S. playwright, $15 for non-U.S. playwright. **Deadline:** 1 Sep 1995. **Notification:** Jan 1996.

## SCHOLASTIC WRITING AWARDS

555 Broadway; New York, NY 10012; (212) 343-6892

**Types of material:** for high school seniors only, portfolios of 3–8 pieces (fiction, poetry, drama, etc.); for students grades 7–12, individual pieces in various categories, including drama (stage, film, television and radio scripts). **Frequency:** annual. **Remuneration:** $5000 scholarship towards college tuition for author of each of 5 best portfolios; $1000 merit award, to be applied toward tuition for New York University's Tisch School of the Arts dramatic writing program, for best work in any category by high school senior; cash prizes totaling $14,000 awarded to several top students in each category, including dramatic writing. **Guidelines:** portfolio totaling not more than 50 pages; for dramatic category, unpublished script not more than 30 minutes long; write for further information by 1 Oct 1995. **Submission procedure:** completed application and portfolio or script. **Deadline:** mid-Jan 1996; exact date TBA. **Notification:** May 1996.

## SHUBERT FENDRICH MEMORIAL PLAYWRITING CONTEST

Pioneer Drama Service; Box 4267; Englewood, CO 80155-4267; (303) 779-4035
Terri Johnson, *Assistant Editor*

**Types of material:** full-length plays, one-acts, translations, adaptations, plays for young audiences, musicals. **Frequency:** annual. **Remuneration:** publication with $1000 advance on royalties (10% book royalty, 50% performance royalty). **Guidelines:** produced, unpublished work not more than 90 minutes long; subject matter and language appropriate for schools and community theatres; prefers works with a preponderance of female roles and minimal set requirements; all entries considered for publication; send SASE for guidelines. **Submission procedure:** script with proof of production (e.g., program, reviews). **Deadline:** 1 Mar 1996 (scripts received after deadline will be considered for 1997 contest).

## SIENA COLLEGE INTERNATIONAL
## PLAYWRIGHTS COMPETITION

Department of Creative Arts; Siena College; 515 Loudon Rd;
    Loudonville, NY 12211-1462; (518) 783-2381
Mark Heckler, *Director of Theatre*

**Types of material:** full-length plays. **Frequency:** biennial. **Remuneration:** $2000; production; $1000 to cover residency expenses. **Guidelines:** play that has had no previous reading, workshop or full production; prefers play suitable for college audience and featuring college-age characters and contemporary situations; prefers small cast; playwright must be available for 6-week residency in Jan/Feb 1997. **Submission procedure:** send SASE for application form and guidelines after 1 Nov 1995; mail completed application with letter-size SASE in advance of script. **Deadline:** 30 Jun 1996; no submission before 1 Feb 1996. **Notification:** 30 Sep 1996.

## THE SOCIETY OF MIDLAND AUTHORS DRAMA AWARD

29 East Division St; Chicago, IL 60610; (312) 337-1482
Phyllis Ford-Choyke, *President*

**Types of material:** full-length plays. **Frequency:** annual. **Remuneration:** at least $300. **Guidelines:** playwright currently living and working in IA, IL, IN, KS, MI, MN, MO, ND, NE, OH, SD or WI; new play given its first professional (not community theatre or college) production in 1995. **Submission procedure:** send SASE for guidelines and application form. **Deadline:** 15 Jan 1996. **Notification:** spring 1996.

## SOURCE THEATRE COMPANY
## NATIONAL PLAYWRITING COMPETITION

1835 14th St NW; Washington, DC 20009; (202) 462-1073
Keith Parker, *Literary Manager*

**Types of material:** full-length plays, one-acts, musicals. **Frequency:** annual. **Remuneration:** $250; workshop production in Washington Theatre Festival (see theatre's entry in Production). **Guidelines:** work not produced professionally. **Submission procedure:** script, synopsis, resume and letter-size SASE for response; materials will not be returned. **Deadline:** 15 Jan 1996. **Notification:** 15 May 1996.

## SOUTH CAROLINA PLAYWRIGHTS' FESTIVAL

Trustus Theatre; Box 11721; Columbia, SC 29211; (803) 771-9153
Jayce T. Tromsness, *Literary Manager*

**Types of material:** full-length plays, one-acts. **Frequency:** annual. **Remuneration:** 1st prize of $500 and production with travel and housing to attend rehearsals and opening; 2nd prize of $250 and staged reading; one-acts eligible only for $50 prize and reading as part of Late Night series. **Guidelines:** play not produced professionally; cast limit of 8; prefers 1 set; full-length play not less than 80 minutes long; send SASE for guidelines and application. **Submission procedure:**

completed application and $5 fee. **Deadline:** 1 Mar 1996; no submission before 1 Jan 1996. **Notification:** 1 Jun 1996.

## SOUTHEASTERN THEATRE CONFERENCE NEW PLAY PROJECT
Box 9868; Greensboro, NC 27429-0868; (910) 272-3645
*Coordinator*

**Types of material:** full-length plays, bills of 2 related one-acts. **Frequency:** annual. **Remuneration:** $1000; staged reading at SETC Annual Convention; travel, room and board to attend convention; submission of work by SETC to O'Neill Center for favored consideration for National Playwrights Conference (see Development). **Guidelines:** resident of state in SETC region (AL, FL, GA, KY, MS, NC, SC, TN, VA, WV); unproduced work; bills of one-acts bound in 1 cover; limit of 1 full-length submission or bill of 2 one-acts. **Submission procedure:** completed application and script. **Deadline:** 1 Jun 1996; no submission before 1 Mar 1996. **Notification:** Dec 1996.

## SOUTHERN PLAYWRIGHTS COMPETITION
Center for Southern Studies; 228 Stone Center; Jacksonville State University;
    Jacksonville, AL 36265; (205) 782-5411
Steven J. Whitton, *Coordinator*

**Types of material:** full-length plays. **Frequency:** annual. **Remuneration:** $1000; production; housing to attend rehearsals. **Guidelines:** native or resident of AL, AR, FL, GA, KY, LA, MS, NC, SC, TN, TX, VA or WV; 1 unpublished original submission that deals with the southern experience and has not received Equity production; write for guidelines. **Submission procedure:** completed entry form, script and synopsis. **Deadline:** 15 Feb 1996. **Notification:** 1 May 1996.

## SUMMERFIELD G. ROBERTS AWARD
The Sons of the Republic of Texas; 5942 Abrams Rd, Suite 222;
    Dallas, TX 75231; (214) 343-2145
Maydee J. Scurlock

**Types of material:** full-length plays. **Frequency:** annual. **Remuneration:** $2500 given to work from 1 of several genres, including playwriting. **Guidelines:** play about living in the Republic of Texas, completed during calendar year preceding deadline. **Submission procedure:** 5 copies of script; scripts will not be returned. **Deadline:** 15 Jan 1996. **Notification:** early Apr 1996.

## THE SUSAN SMITH BLACKBURN PRIZE
3239 Avalon Pl; Houston, TX 77019; (713) 522-8529
Emilie S. Kilgore, *Board of Directors*

**Types of material:** full-length plays. **Frequency:** annual. **Remuneration:** $5000 1st prize plus signed Willem de Kooning print, made especially for Blackburn Prize; $2000 2nd prize; $500 to each of 8–10 other finalists. **Guidelines:** woman playwright of any nationality writing in English; unproduced play or play produced within one year of deadline. **Submission procedure:** no submission by playwright; professional artistic director, literary manager or dramaturg invited to submit play and submits 2 copies of script; playwright may bring script to attention of eligible nominator; send SASE for list of theatres eligible to nominate. **Deadline:** 20 Sep 1995. **Notification:** Jan 1996 for finalists; Feb 1996 for winners.

## SWTA ANNUAL NEW PLAY CONTEST

Southwest Theatre Association; University of Oklahoma School of Drama;
    563 Elm Ave; Norman, OK 73019-0310; (405) 325-4021
Ray Paolino, *New Plays Committee*

**Types of material:** full-length plays, one-acts, adaptations. **Frequency:** annual. **Remuneration:** $200 1st prize; staged reading at SWTA convention in Nov 1996; possible publication in SWTA journal, *Theatre Southwest.* **Guidelines:** unproduced, unpublished play. **Submission procedure:** script, brief synopsis, character breakdown and $10 fee (check payable to SWTA); letter of recommendation helpful. **Deadline:** 31 Mar 1996.

## TADA! SPRING STAGED READING SERIES

120 West 28th St; New York, NY 10001; (212) 627-1732
Janine Nina Trevens, *Artistic Director*

**Types of material:** plays and musicals for young audiences. **Frequency:** annual. **Remuneration:** 3 awards of $200; staged reading; possible production. **Guidelines:** unproduced play or musical by professional or student playwright written for child actors who do not play adult characters; prefers works with human characters, as opposed to "animal" plays. **Submission procedure:** script and character breakdown; include cassette for musical. **Deadline:** 1 Feb 1996. **Notification:** 15 Mar 1996.

## TENNESSEE WILLIAMS/NEW ORLEANS LITERARY FESTIVAL ONE-ACT PLAY COMPETITION

Metro College Conference Services, ED 122; University of New Orleans;
    New Orleans, LA 70148

**Types of material:** one-acts. **Frequency:** annual. **Remuneration:** $1000; reading in spring 1996 festival; production in spring 1997 festival. **Guidelines:** unpublished play on an American subject, not more than 1 hour long and not produced professionally. **Submission procedure:** script with SASE for notification and $15 fee (check payable to University of New Orleans); script will not be returned. **Deadline:** 31 Dec 1995.

## THEATER AT LIME KILN REGIONAL PLAYWRITING CONTEST
Lime Kiln Arts; Box 663; Lexington, VA 24450; (703) 463-7088
Eleanor Connor, *Community Liaison/Dramaturg*

**Types of material:** full-length plays, one-acts, musicals. **Frequency:** annual. **Remuneration:** $1000 1st prize, $500 2nd prize; staged reading; possible production. **Guidelines:** 1 unproduced, unpublished submission relating to the Appalachian region; plays with music encouraged; write for guidelines. **Submission procedure:** completed entry form, script, short synopsis, history of play and bio; include letter-size SASE if notification is desired. **Deadline:** 30 Sep 1995. **Notification:** 1 Mar 1996 (if SASE is enclosed).

## THEATRE MEMPHIS NEW PLAY COMPETITION
630 Perkins St Extended; Memphis, TN 38117-4799; (901) 682-8323
Kim Ford, *Chair, New Play Competition*

**Types of material:** full-length plays. **Frequency:** triennial. **Remuneration:** $1500 (may be split between 2 winners); possible production with travel and housing to attend performance. **Guidelines:** original work not produced with royalty payment prior to deadline date; write for guidelines. **Submission procedure:** script submitted anonymously with detached title page giving playwright's name and address; resume. **Deadline:** 1 Jul 1996. **Notification:** Dec 1996.

## THEATREWORKS/USA COMMISSIONING PROGRAM
Theatreworks/USA; 890 Broadway; New York, NY 10003; (212) 677-5959
Barbara Pasternack, *Associate Artistic Director*

**Types of material:** plays with music and musicals for young and family audiences. **Frequency:** ongoing. **Remuneration:** step commissioning process; 2-week developmental workshop and production. **Guidelines:** works dealing with issues relevant to target audiences; special interest in historical/biographical subject matter and musical adaptations of fairy tales and traditional or contemporary classics; 1 hour long; cast of 5 actors, set suitable for touring. **Submission procedure:** prefers treatment with sample scenes, lyric sheets and cassette of music preferred; will accept script only. **Deadline:** ongoing.

## THEODORE WARD PRIZE FOR AFRICAN-AMERICAN PLAYWRIGHTS
Columbia College Chicago Theater/Music Center; 72 East 11th St;
    Chicago, IL 60605; (312) 663-9462
Chuck Smith, *Facilitator*

**Types of material:** full-length plays, translations, adaptations. **Frequency:** annual. **Remuneration:** 1st prize $2000, production, travel and housing to attend rehearsals; 2nd prize $500, staged reading; 3rd prize, staged reading at Goodman Theatre. **Guidelines:** U.S. resident of African-American descent; 1 full-length submission not professionally produced; translations and adaptations of material in public domain only; write for guidelines. **Submission procedure:** script, short synopsis, production history and brief resume. **Deadline:** 1 Aug 1996; no submission before 1 May 1996. **Notification:** Nov 1996.

### THE THREE-GENRES SHORT PLAY COMPETITION
2225 Mt. Vernon Ave; Riverside, CA 92507; (909) 369-3938
Stephen Minot, *Editor*

**Types of material:** one-acts. **Frequency:** every 4 years. **Remuneration:** $500, publication. **Guidelines:** innovative, experimental play between 10–15 minutes long; previously published plays accepted; send SASE for application and guidelines after 1 Oct 1995. **Submission procedure:** script and application. **Deadline:** 15 Jan 1996. **Notification:** 15 Mar 1996.

### THRESHOLD THEATER METAPHYSICAL PLAY CONTEST
1907 Cannonwood Ln; Austin, TX 78745; (512) 448-4373
Jennifer Mellett, *Executive Director*

**Types of material:** full-length plays. **Frequency:** annual. **Remuneration:** $200. **Guidelines:** play, not professionally produced, whose theme involves two contrasting levels of theatrical reality (e.g. the dead and the living, waking and dreaming, body and soul, material and nonmaterial) and the crossing of the "threshold" between them; 100–135 minutes long; must have at least 3 substantial speaking roles and maximum cast of 8; prefers 1 set; write for guidelines by 1 Jan 1996. **Submission procedure:** script, synopsis, resume and $15 fee. **Deadline:** 1 Apr 1996. **Notification:** 31 Mar 1997.

### TOWNGATE THEATRE PLAYWRITING CONTEST
Oglebay Institute Stifel Fine Arts Center; 1330 National Rd; Wheeling, WV 26003

**Types of material:** full-length plays. **Frequency:** annual. **Remuneration:** $300; production; partial travel expenses. **Guidelines:** unproduced, unpublished play; no submission limit. **Submission procedure:** script only. **Deadline:** 1 Jan 1996. **Notification:** 31 Mar 1996.

### TOWSON STATE UNIVERSITY PRIZE FOR LITERATURE
Towson State University; Towson, MD 21204-7097; (410) 830-2128
Annette Chappell, *Dean, College of Liberal Arts*

**Types of material:** book or book-length manuscript; all literary genres eligible, including plays. **Frequency:** annual. **Remuneration:** $1000. **Guidelines:** work published within 3 years prior to submission or scheduled for publication within the year; author no more than 40 years of age, MD resident for 3 years and at time prize awarded. **Submission procedure:** publisher or playwright submits completed application and 5 copies of work; write for guidelines. **Deadline:** 15 May 1996. **Notification:** 1 Dec 1996.

## Unicorn Theatre National Playwrights' Award
3820 Main St; Kansas City, MO 64111; (816) 531-7529
*Literary Manager*

**Types of material:** full-length plays. **Frequency:** no set dates. **Remuneration:** $1000; production; possible travel and residency. **Guidelines:** unpublished play not produced professionally; special interest in social issues; contemporary (post-1950) themes and settings only; cast limit of 10; 2-submission limit. **Submission procedure:** no scripts; send synopsis, at least 10 pages of dialogue, resume, letter of inquiry and SASE for response. **Deadline:** ongoing. **Notification:** 2 weeks; 2–4 months if script is requested.

## University of Louisville Grawemeyer Award
## for Music Composition
Grawemeyer Music Award Committee; School of Music; University of Louisville; Louisville, KY 40292; (502) 852-6907
Paul Brink, *Executive Secretary*

**Types of material:** works in major musical genres, including music-theatre works and operas. **Frequency:** annual. **Remuneration:** $150,000 (paid in 5 annual installments of $30,000). **Guidelines:** work premiered during previous 5 years; entry must be sponsored by professional music organization or individual; write for guidelines. **Submission procedure:** completed application, score, cassette, supporting materials and $50 fee submitted jointly by composer and sponsor. **Deadline:** 29 Jan 1996. **Notification:** late spring 1996.

## Urban Stages Award
17 East 47th St; New York, NY 10017; (212) 289-2168

**Types of material:** one-acts. **Frequency:** annual. **Remuneration:** $200, 4–6 "radio style" staged readings in libraries throughout New York City's boroughs. **Guidelines:** play no more than 1 hour long with cast limit of 5 which has not been produced in New York; special interest in minority playwrights and ethnically diverse casts; send SASE for guidelines. **Submission procedure:** script, production history and author bio. **Deadline:** 15 Jun 1996.

## Utah Playfest
Theatre Arts Department; Utah State University; Logan, UT 84322-4025; (801) 797-3021
Roger Held, *Director*

**Types of material:** full-length plays, one-acts. **Frequency:** biennial. **Remuneration:** $100–500; possible publication and production; if produced, writer receives travel and housing; $5000 royalty for produced full-length play. **Guidelines:** submission limit of 1 full-length and 1 one-act play. **Submission procedure:** 2 copies of script and $10 fee. **Deadline:** 15 May 1996. **Notification:** 1 Jan 1997.

## VERMONT PLAYWRIGHTS AWARD

The Valley Players; Box 441; Waitsfield, VT 05673; (802) 496-3927
Tony Egan, *Coordinator*

**Types of material:** full-length plays. **Frequency:** annual. **Remuneration:** $1000; probable production. **Guidelines:** resident of ME, NH or VT; unproduced, unpublished play, suitable for community group, that has not won playwriting competition; moderate production demands; send SASE for guidelines. **Submission procedure:** completed entry form and 2 copies of script. **Deadline:** 1 Oct 1995.

## VERY SPECIAL ARTS YOUNG PLAYWRIGHTS PROGRAM

Education Office; The John F. Kennedy Center for the Performing Arts;
    Washington, DC 20566; (202) 628-2800 (voice), 737-0645 (TDD)
Elena Widder, *Coordinator, National Programs*

**Types of material:** full-length plays, one-acts. **Frequency:** annual. **Remuneration:** professional production at Kennedy Center; travel, room and board to attend performance. **Guidelines:** play dealing with some aspect of disability by writer aged 12–18 years; write for guidelines. **Submission procedure:** 3 copies of script and short bio. **Deadline:** Apr 1996; exact date TBA.

## WALDO M. AND GRACE C. BONDERMAN IUPUI PLAYWRITING COMPETITION FOR YOUNG AUDIENCES

IUPUI University Theatre; 525 North Blackford St; Indianapolis, IN 46202-3120;
    (317) 274-2095
Mark McCreary, *Literary Manager*

**Types of material:** plays for young audiences. **Frequency:** biennial. **Remuneration:** 4 prizes of $1000; 1 week of developmental work culminating in showcase reading at National Youth Theatre Playwriting Symposium; travel, room and board for residency. **Guidelines:** well-crafted play with strong storyline, compelling characters and careful attention to language; unpublished play at least 45 minutes long and not previously produced by Equity company; writer must be available for week-long residency. **Submission procedure:** send SASE for entry form and guidelines. **Deadline:** 1 Sep 1996. **Notification:** Dec 1996. **Dates:** 30 Mar–1 Apr 1997.

## WAREHOUSE THEATRE COMPANY ONE-ACT COMPETITION

Stephens College; Columbia, MO 65215; (314) 876-7194
*Artistic Director*

**Types of material:** one-acts. **Frequency:** annual. **Remuneration:** $200; production as part of company's Evening of One-Acts. **Guidelines:** unpublished, unproduced script by undergraduate or graduate student; special interest in scripts by, for or about women; write for guidelines. **Submission procedure:** script with $8 fee. **Deadline:** 31 Dec 1995. **Notification:** 1 Feb 1996.

## West Coast Ensemble Contests
Box 38728; Los Angeles, CA 90038; (213) 871-8673
Les Hanson, *Artistic Director*

### West Coast Ensemble Full-Length Play Competition

**Types of material:** full-length plays. **Frequency:** annual. **Remuneration:** $500; production; royalty on any performances beyond 8-week run. **Guidelines:** 1 submission not produced in southern CA; cast limit of 12. **Submission procedure:** script with SASE or SASP for acknowledgment of receipt. **Deadline:** 31 Dec 1995. **Notification:** within 6 months of deadline.

### West Coast Ensemble Musical Stairs

**Types of material:** musical theatre works. **Frequency:** annual. **Remuneration:** $500; production; royalty on any performances beyond 8-week run. **Guidelines:** 1 unpublished musical submission not produced in southern CA; all genres and styles eligible, including pop, rock, country and western, etc.; cast limit of 12. **Submission procedure:** script, cassette of music (include score and lead sheets if available). **Deadline:** 30 Jun 1996. **Notification:** within 6 months.

## Western Great Lakes Playwriting Competition
South Bend Civic Theatre; Box 11375; South Bend, IN 46634; (219) 234-1112
Tom Vander Ven, *Competition Chair*

**Types of material:** full-length plays. **Frequency:** annual. **Remuneration:** $500; staged reading; possible production; travel, room and board to attend reading or production. **Guidelines:** resident of IL, IN, MI, MN, OH or WI; play not produced professionally; send SASE for guidelines. **Submission procedure:** script and signed statement that play has not been professionally produced. **Deadline:** 3 Jun 1996. **Notification:** Sep 1996.

## White Bird Annual Playwriting Contest
White Bird Productions; Box 20233, Columbus Circle Station;
New York, NY 10023; (718) 788-5984
Kathryn Dickinson, *Artistic Director*

**Types of material:** full-length plays, one-acts. **Frequency:** annual. **Remuneration:** $200; staged reading; possible travel to attend rehearsals. **Guidelines:** play whose theme, plot and/or central idea deals in a general or specific way with the environment; 2-submission limit. **Submission procedure:** script and resume. **Deadline:** 15 Feb 1996. **Notification:** Apr 1996.

## The White-Willis New Playwrights Contest
The White-Willis Theatre; 5266 Gate Lake Rd; Fort Lauderdale, FL 33319;
(305) 722-4371
Ann White, *Founder/Executive Director*

**Types of material:** full-length plays. **Frequency:** annual. **Remuneration:** $500;

production. **Guidelines:** unpublished, unproduced play; small cast, simple set preferred; after closing of Fort Lauderdale production, theatre retains option to produce first-class production for 120 days and requires 5% of all playwright's earnings from play for 3 years; send SASE for guidelines. **Submission procedure:** script only. **Deadline:** 1 Sep 1995. **Notification:** Jan 1996.

## WICHITA STATE UNIVERSITY PLAYWRITING CONTEST

University Theatre; Wichita State University; Wichita, KS 67260-0153;
(316) 689-3368
Leroy Clark, *Contest Director*

**Types of material:** full-length plays, bills of related one-acts. **Frequency:** annual. **Remuneration:** production; expenses for playwright to attend production. **Guidelines:** unpublished, unproduced work at least 90 minutes long by student currently enrolled at U.S. college or university; write for guidelines. **Submission procedure:** script only. **Deadline:** 15 Feb 1996. **Notification:** 15 Apr 1996.

## WRITER'S DIGEST WRITING COMPETITION

1507 Dana Ave; Cincinnati, OH 45207-1005; (513) 531-2690, ext 580
*Competition Coordinator*

**Types of materials:** full-length plays, screenplays, teleplays. **Frequency:** annual. **Remuneration:** Grand Prize: Apple PowerBook computer, expenses-paid trip to New York City to meet with editors and agents; $500 1st prize, $250 2nd prize, $100 3rd prize, each with $100 worth of Writer's Digest books; $50 4th prize with current *Writer's Market* and 1-year subscription to *Writer's Digest* magazine; $25 5th prize with 1-year subscription to *Writer's Digest* magazine. **Guidelines:** unproduced, unpublished work, not accepted by publisher or producer at time of submission; previous entries ineligible; send SASE for guidelines. **Submission procedure:** completed entry form, first 15 pages of script, 1-page synopsis and indication of projected market for work, and $7 fee. **Deadline:** 31 May 1996. **Notification:** fall 1996.

## YEAR-END-SERIES (Y.E.S.) NEW PLAY FESTIVAL

Department of Theatre; Northern Kentucky University;
Highland Heights, KY 41099; (606) 572-6362
Michael King, *Project Director*

**Types of material:** full-length plays, adaptations, musicals. **Frequency:** biennial. **Remuneration:** 3 prizes: $400; production; travel and expenses to attend late rehearsals and performance. **Guidelines:** unproduced work in which majority of roles can be handled by students; small orchestra for musicals; 1 submission; playwright available for visit in Apr 1995. **Submission procedure:** completed application and script. **Deadline:** 15 Oct 1996. **Notification:** Jan 1997. **Dates:** late Apr 1997.

## YOUNG PLAYWRIGHTS FESTIVAL

Young Playwrights Inc.; 321 West 44th St, Suite 906; New York, NY 10036;
(212) 307-1140
Sheri M. Goldhirsch, *Artistic Director*

**Types of material:** full-length plays, one-acts. **Frequency:** annual. **Remuneration:** staged reading or production with royalty; travel and residency; 1-year Dramatists Guild membership (see Membership and Service Organizations). **Guidelines:** playwright under the age of 19 on 15 Oct 1995; submissions from minority playwrights encouraged; write for guidelines. **Submission procedure:** script with playwright's name, date of birth, home address and phone number on title page. **Deadline:** 15 Oct 1995.

# Publication

**What is listed in this section?**

Those who are primarily or exclusively play publishers and who consider work of unpublished writers. In addition, we list literary magazines and other small presses which have indicated they publish plays.

**How can I determine the best places to submit my play?**

Think of these publishers as highly individual people looking for very particular kinds of material, which means you should find out as much as possible about their operations before submitting scripts. One of the best ways to do research is by contacting the Council of Literary Magazines and Presses: 154 Christopher St, Suite 3C; New York, NY 10014-2839; (212) 741-9110. Ask for *The 1995-96 Directory of Literary Magazines* ($11.95 paper, plus $3.05 for 1st-class postage and handling), a descriptive listing of hundreds of magazines, including many which say they publish plays. You may be able to look at copies of some of these in a local library or bookstore. Other leads may be found in the *1995-96 International Directory of Little Magazines and Small Presses* (Dustbooks; Box 100; Paradise, CA 95967; (916) 877-6110; $29.95 paper, $45.95 cloth, plus $6.00 shipping and handling). You can also write to individual publishers listed here and ask for style sheets, catalogues, sample copies, etc. Don't forget that when publishers say they accept unsolicited scripts, they *always* require you to enclose an SASE for return of the manuscript.

## ALABAMA LITERARY REVIEW
253 Smith Hall; Troy State University; Troy, AL 36082; (205) 670-3307
Theron Montgomery, *Chief Editor*

**Types of material:** full-length plays, one-acts, translations, adaptations. **Remuneration:** 3 complimentary copies (more on request); $5–10 a page when funds are available. **Guidelines:** biannual literary journal publishing 1 play a year; plays less than 50 pages long, less than 30 pages preferred. **Submission procedure:** accepts unsolicited scripts. **Response time:** 2–3 months.

## AMELIA MAGAZINE
329 "E" St; Bakersfield, CA 93304; (805) 323-4064
Frederick A. Raborg, Jr., *Editor*

**Types of material:** one-acts, including translations. **Remuneration:** $150 prize; 10 complimentary copies. **Guidelines:** winner of annual Frank McClure One-Act Play Award published in magazine Oct 1996; unpublished play maximum 45 minutes long. **Submission procedure:** submit script, including note of any productions, and $15 fee (includes copy of magazine containing winning entry). **Deadline:** 15 May 1996. **Notification:** 15 Jul 1996.

## AMERICAN THEATRE
Theatre Communications Group; 355 Lexington Ave; New York, NY 10017-0217;
    (212) 697-5230
Jim O'Quinn, *Editor*
Wendy Weiner, *Play Editor*

**Types of material:** full-length plays, one-acts, translations, adaptations, plays for young audiences. **Remuneration:** fee for one-time serial rights; 25 complimentary copies. **Guidelines:** national magazine publishing 6 plays a year; significant works from the contemporary world theatre. **Submission procedure:** no unsolicited scripts; submissions at play editor's request only.

## AMERICAN WRITING: A MAGAZINE
4343 Manayunk Ave; Philadelphia, PA 19128
Alexandra Grilikhes, *Editor*

**Types of material:** translations, short experimental theatre pieces, performance pieces, performance artists' in-process notes and diaries. **Remuneration:** 3 complimentary copies. **Guidelines:** biannual literary/arts journal publishing 1 or 2 theatrical works a year; seeks new writing that takes risks and explores new forms; interested in "the voice of the loner"; 10,000 words maximum. **Submission procedure:** accepts unsolicited scripts. **Response time:** 2–3 months.

## THE AMERICAS REVIEW

Arte Público Press; University of Houston; Houston, TX 77204-2090;
    (713) 743-2841
Nicolás Kanellos, *Publisher*
Lauro Flores, *Editor*

**Types of material:** full-length plays, one-acts, adaptations, plays for young audiences, musicals. **Remuneration:** fee; 2 complimentary copies. **Guidelines:** unpublished works in English or Spanish by Hispanic writers only. **Submission procedure:** accepts unsolicited scripts. **Response time:** 3 months.

## ANCHORAGE PRESS

Box 8067; New Orleans, LA 70182; (504) 283-8868
Orlin Corey, *Editor*

**Types of material:** works for young audiences, including full-length plays, one-acts, translations, adaptations and musicals. **Remuneration:** negotiated royalty. **Guidelines:** specialty house publishing quality works for young audiences only; works produced at least 3 times. **Submission procedure:** accepts unsolicited scripts with proof of production. **Response time:** 45–90 days.

## ARAN PRESS

1320 South 3rd St; Louisville, KY 40208-2306; (502) 636-0115
Tom Eagan, *Editor and Publisher*

**Types of material:** full-length plays, one-acts, translations, adaptations. **Remuneration:** 10% book royalty, 50% production royalty; playwright contributes to publishing costs: $300 for full-length play, $150 for one-act. **Guidelines:** plays suitable for marketing to community, college and university, summer stock, dinner and professional theatres. **Submission procedure:** accepts unsolicited scripts; prefers letter of inquiry with SASE for response. **Response time:** 3 weeks.

## ART CRAFT PUBLISHING COMPANY

Box 1058; Cedar Rapids, IA 52406; (319) 364-6311
C. Emmett McMullen, *Editor and Publisher*

**Types of material:** full-length plays, one-acts, musicals. **Remuneration:** outright purchase or performance royalty; complimentary copies. **Guidelines:** works suitable for middle school and junior and senior high school market. **Submission procedure:** accepts unsolicited scripts. **Response time:** 1–2 months.

## ARTE PÚBLICO PRESS

University of Houston; Houston, TX 77204-2090; (713) 743-2841
Nicolás Kanellos, *Publisher*

**Types of material:** full-length plays, one-acts, adaptations, plays for young audiences, musicals. **Remuneration:** negotiated royalty; complimentary copies. **Guidelines:** unpublished works in English or Spanish by Hispanic writers only;

usually writers whose work has previously been published in *The Americas Review* (see entry in this section). **Submission procedure:** accepts unsolicited scripts. **Response time:** 6 months.

## ASIAN PACIFIC AMERICAN JOURNAL

37 Saint Marks Pl, Suite B; New York, NY 10003-7801; (212) 228-6718
Soo Mee Kwon and Julie Koo, *Co-Editors*

**Types of material:** one-acts. **Remuneration:** 2 complimentary copies. **Guidelines:** biannual literary journal devoted to the work of Asian-American writers; plays maximum 4000 words. **Submission procedure:** accepts unsolicited scripts; contact editors for theme of upcoming issue and deadline; send 2 copies of script plus copy on Macintosh disk. **Response time:** 3 months.

## BAKER'S PLAYS

100 Chauncy St; Boston, MA 02111; (617) 482-1280
Raymond Pape, *Associate Editor*

**Types of material:** full-length plays, one-acts, plays for young audiences, musicals, chancel dramas. **Remuneration:** negotiated book and production royalty. **Guidelines:** prefers produced plays; prefers plays suitable for high school, community and regional theatres; "Plays from Young Authors" division features plays by high school playwrights. **Submission procedure:** accepts unsolicited scripts with resume; include press clippings if play has been produced. **Response time:** 2–6 months. **Special programs:** Baker's Plays High School Playwriting Contest (see Prizes).

## THE BELLINGHAM REVIEW

The Signpost Press; Mail Stop 9055; Western Washington University;
    Bellingham, WA 98225
Robin Hemley, *Editor*

**Types of material:** one-acts. **Remuneration:** 1 complimentary copy; 1-year subscription. **Guidelines:** biannual small-press periodical featuring short plays, fiction and poetry; unpublished plays, preferably less than 5000 words long. **Submission procedure:** accepts unsolicited scripts; submit 1 Sep–1 Mar only. **Response time:** 4 months.

## BELLOWING ARK

Box 45637; Seattle, WA 98145; (206) 545-8302
Robert R. Ward, *Editor*

**Types of material:** full-length plays, one-acts, translations, adaptations. **Remuneration:** 2 complimentary copies. **Guidelines:** bimonthly literary journal featuring work in the American Romantic tradition that "demonstrates that life is both meaningful and worth living"; prefers plays less than 40 pages long. **Submission procedure:** accepts unsolicited scripts; write for guidelines (sample copy $3). **Response time:** 2–10 weeks.

## BLIZZARD PUBLISHING
73 Furby St; Winnipeg, MB R3C 2A2; Canada;
   (204) 775-2923, (800) 694-9256
Anna Synenko, *Marketing Manager*

**Types of material:** full-length plays, one-acts, translations, adaptations, plays for young audiences. **Remuneration:** advance against royalties; 10% book royalty; complimentary copies. **Guidelines:** publishes 11 plays a year and critical literature on theatre; special interest in contemporary or provocative themes and educational works; write for guidelines. **Submission procedure:** no unsolicited scripts; synopsis and letter of inquiry; submit Mar–Nov only. **Response time:** 4 months.

## BROADWAY PLAY PUBLISHING
56 East 81st St; New York, NY 10028; (212) 772-8334

**Types of material:** full-length plays. **Remuneration:** 10% book royalty, 80% amateur royalty, 90% stock royalty; 10 complimentary copies. **Guidelines:** major interest is in original, innovative work by American playwrights; no historical or autobiographical plays. **Submission procedure:** no unsolicited scripts; letter of inquiry. **Response time:** 3 months.

## CALLALOO
Department of English; University of Virginia; Bryan Hall;
   Charlottesville, VA 22903; (804) 924-6637
Charles H. Rowell, *Editor*

**Types of material:** one-acts, including translations. **Remuneration:** complimentary copies and offprints; payment when grant money is available. **Guidelines:** journal of Afro-American and African arts and letters published by Johns Hopkins University Press. **Submission procedure:** accepts unsolicited scripts. **Response time:** 6 months.

## CHICAGO PLAYS
2632 North Lincoln; Chicago, IL 60614; (312) 348-4658
Jill Murray

**Types of material:** full-length plays, one-acts, adaptations, plays for young audiences, musicals. **Remuneration:** book and performance royalties; complimentary copies (usually 10). **Guidelines:** publishes for professional and amateur market. **Submission procedure:** accepts unsolicited scripts with proof of or notice of application for copyright, programs, reviews and publicity material; write or call for guidelines. **Response time:** 3 months.

## Collages & Bricolages
Box 86; Clarion, PA 16214; (814) 226-5799
Marie-José Fortis, *Editor*

**Types of material:** one-acts, minimalist plays. **Remuneration:** 2 complimentary copies. **Guidelines:** annual journal of international writing publishing poetry, fiction, drama and criticism, including 1–5 plays a year; for 1996 issue, works on or inspired by Beckett or Ionesco only; avant-garde and feminist work; innovative plays less than 30 pages long reflecting philosophical and social concerns. **Submission procedure:** accepts unsolicited scripts; submit only 1 Aug–1 Dec for following year's issue. **Response time:** 2 weeks–3 months.

## Confrontation
English Department; C.W. Post College of Long Island University;
      Greenvale, NY 11548; (516) 299-2391
Martin Tucker, *Editor*

**Types of material:** one-acts. **Remuneration:** $15–75; 1 complimentary copy. **Guidelines:** general magazine for literate audience; unpublished plays. **Submission procedure:** accepts unsolicited scripts. **Response time:** 8–10 weeks.

## Contemporary Drama Service
Meriwether Publishing, Ltd; 885 Elkton Dr; Colorado Springs, CO 80907
Arthur L. Zapel, *Executive Editor*

**Types of material:** full-length plays, one-acts, adaptations, plays for young audiences, musicals, readers' theatre, monologues. **Remuneration:** book and performance royalties or payment for amateur and publishing rights. **Guidelines:** publishes works suitable for teenage, high school and college market, as well as collections of scenes and practical books on theatre arts; no works for preteen audiences; prefers comedies; prefers produced works. **Submission procedure:** accepts unsolicited scripts; send $2 for sample catalogue and guidelines. **Response time:** 2 months.

## CrazyQuilt Quarterly
Box 632729; San Diego, CA 92163-2729; (619) 688-1023
Marsh Cassady, *Drama Editor*

**Types of material:** one-acts. **Remuneration:** 2 complimentary copies. **Guidelines:** quarterly literary journal publishing 4–6 plays a year. **Submission procedure:** accepts unsolicited scripts. **Response time:** 3 months.

## The Cream City Review
English Department; Box 413; University of Wisconsin–Milwaukee;
      Milwaukee, WI 53201; (414) 229-4708
Mark Drechsler and Andrew Rivera, *Editors-in-Chief*

**Types of material:** one-acts. **Remuneration:** $5 per printed page; 2 complimentary copies. **Guidelines:** biannual literary magazine publishing mainstream and experimental work, including an average of 1 play a year; plays maximum 30 pages long. **Submission procedure:** accepts unsolicited scripts. **Response time:** 6–8 weeks.

## DESCANT

Box 314, Station P; Toronto, Ontario; Canada M5S 2S8; (416) 593-2557
Tracy Jenkins, *Managing Editor*

**Types of material:** full-length plays, one-acts, performance-art texts. **Remuneration:** $100 honorarium; 1 complimentary copy (additional copies at 40% discount). **Guidelines:** quarterly literary magazine publishing an average of 2 plays a year; unpublished plays. **Submission procedure:** accepts unsolicited scripts. **Response time:** 6 months.

## THE DRAMATIC PUBLISHING COMPANY

311 Washington St; Box 129; Woodstock, IL 60098; (815) 338-7170
Susan Sergel, *Editor*

**Types of material:** full-length plays, one-acts, translations, adaptations, plays for young audiences, musicals. **Remuneration:** standard royalty; 10 complimentary copies (30% discount on additional copies). **Guidelines:** works for stock and amateur market; at least 30 minutes long; prefers produced plays. **Submission procedure:** accepts unsolicited scripts. **Response time:** 2–4 months.

## DRAMATICS MAGAZINE

3368 Central Pkwy; Cincinnati, OH 45225; (513) 559-1996
Don Corathers, *Editor*

**Types of material:** full-length plays, one-acts. **Remuneration:** payment for 1-time publication rights; complimentary copies. **Guidelines:** educational theatre magazine; plays suitable for high school production; prefers produced plays. **Submission procedure:** accepts unsolicited scripts. **Response time:** 2–3 months.

## DRAMATISTS PLAY SERVICE

440 Park Ave South; New York, NY 10016; (212) 683-8960
Stephen Sultan, *President*

**Types of material:** full-length plays, one-acts, translations, adaptations, plays for young audiences, musicals. **Remuneration:** usually advance against royalties; 10% book royalty, 80% amateur royalty, 90% stock royalty; 10 complimentary copies. **Guidelines:** works for stock and amateur market; prefers works produced in New York City. **Submission procedure:** no unsolicited scripts; letter of inquiry. **Response time:** 2–4 months.

## EARTH'S DAUGHTERS
Box 41, Central Park Station; Buffalo, NY 14215; (716) 837-7778

**Types of material:** full-length plays, one-acts, translations, adaptations, plays for young audiences. **Remuneration:** 2 complimentary copies. **Guidelines:** triannual feminist literary and art periodical with focus on experience and creative expression of women; frequently publishes play excerpts with occasional issue devoted to complete text of play. **Submission procedure:** accepts unsolicited scripts. **Response time:** 2 months.

## ELDRIDGE PUBLISHING COMPANY
Box 1595; Venice, FL 34284-1595; (800) HI-STAGE
Nancy S. Vorhis, *Editor*

**Types of material:** full-length plays, one-acts, musicals. **Remuneration:** outright purchase of religious material only; all other works, 10% book royalty, 50% amateur and educational royalty; complimentary copies (50% discount on additional copies). **Guidelines:** publishes 40–50 plays and musicals a year for school, church and community theatre; comedies, mysteries or serious drama; special interest in full-length plays for junior and senior high school market; seeks Christmas plays. **Submission procedure:** accepts unsolicited scripts; if possible, include cassette for musicals. **Response time:** 2 months.

## ENCORE PERFORMANCE PUBLISHING
Box 692; Orem, UT 84057; (801) 225-0605
Michael C. Perry, *President*

**Types of material:** full-length plays, one-acts, translations, adaptations, plays for young audiences, musicals. **Remuneration:** 10% book royalty, 50% performance royalty; 10 complimentary copies (discount on additional copies). **Guidelines:** publishes 10–30 plays and musicals a year; works must have had at least 2 amateur or professional productions; special interest in works with strong family or Judeo-Christian message and in Christmas, Halloween and other holiday plays. **Submission procedure:** no unsolicited scripts; synopsis, production information and letter of inquiry; best submission time May–Aug. **Response time:** 2–4 weeks letter; 2–3 months script.

## THE FOUR DIRECTIONS
## AMERICAN INDIAN LITERARY QUARTERLY
Snowbird Publishing Company; Box 729; Tellico Plains, TN 37385;
    (615) 253-3680
William Meyer, *Publisher*

**Types of material:** one-acts, including translations, adaptations and plays for young audiences. **Remuneration:** 1.5¢ a word; 4 complimentary copies. **Guidelines:** quarterly magazine publishing fiction, poetry, plays and articles by and of interest to American Indians; one-acts by American Indian playwrights only. **Submission procedure:** accepts unsolicited scripts with statement of tribal affiliation and brief bio listing any other publications in which playwright's work appears. **Response time:** 4–6 weeks.

## FREELANCE PRESS

Box 548; Dover, MA 02030; (508) 785-1260
Narcissa Campion, *Managing Editor*

**Types of material:** musicals. **Remuneration:** 10% book royalty, 70% performance royalty; 1 complimentary copy. **Guidelines:** unpublished issue-oriented musicals and musical adaptations of classics; approximately 1 hour long, suitable for performing by young people only. **Submission procedure:** accepts unsolicited scripts. **Response time:** 3 months.

## HAWAI'I REVIEW

c/o UH Mānoa Department of English; 1733 Donaghho Rd; Honolulu, HI 96822; (808) 956-3030
Michelle Viray, *Editor-in-Chief*

**Types of material:** one-acts, translations, adaptations. **Remuneration:** U.S. citizens/Social Security cardholders: $10 a page, 2 complimentary copies; non-citizens: books of value equivalent to per-page payment, complimentary copies. **Guidelines:** triquarterly literary journal; submit up to 28 double-spaced pages. **Submission procedure:** accepts unsolicited scripts with SASE for response. **Response time:** 3–4 months.

## HEUER PUBLISHING COMPANY

Box 248; Cedar Rapids, IA 52406; (319) 364-6311
C. Emmett McMullen, *Editor and Publisher*

**Types of material:** full-length plays, one-acts, musicals. **Remuneration:** outright purchase or performance royalty; complimentary copies. **Guidelines:** works suitable for middle school and junior and senior high school markets. **Submission procedure:** accepts unsolicited scripts. **Response time:** 1–2 months.

## HOLVOE BOOKS

Box 62; Hewlett, NY 11557-0062; (516) 357-9607
Steven Fisch, *Associate Editor*

**Types of material:** full-length plays, one-acts, translations, adaptations, plays for young audiences, libretti. **Remuneration:** complimentary copies; possible advance and royalties. **Guidelines:** publishes play anthologies for libraries and colleges and limited trade distribution; publishes *This Month ON STAGE* (see entry this section). **Submission procedure:** accepts unsolicited scripts with resume and cover letter; send SASE for guidelines. **Response time:** 6–8 months.

## I. E. CLARK

Saint John's Rd; Box 246; Schulenburg, TX 78956-0246; (409) 743-3232
Debra Drabek, *Editorial Department*

**Types of material:** full-length plays, one-acts, translations, adaptations, plays for young audiences, musicals. **Remuneration:** book and performance royalties. **Guidelines:** publishes for worldwide professional, amateur and educational market; prefers produced works. **Submission procedure:** accepts unsolicited scripts; cassette or videotape must accompany musical; include proof of production with reviews and photos for produced works; send $2 for catalogue; send SASE for submission guidelines. **Response time:** 3–6 months.

## KALLIOPE, A JOURNAL OF WOMEN'S ART

Florida Community College; 3939 Roosevelt Blvd; Jacksonville, FL 32205;
(904) 381-3511
Mary Sue Koeppel, *Editor*

**Types of material:** one-acts. **Remuneration:** 3 complimentary copies or free 1-year subscription. **Guidelines:** triannual journal of women's art publishing short fiction, poetry, artwork, photography, interviews, reviews and an average of 1 play a year; unpublished plays, less than 25 pages long, by women only; no trite themes or erotica. **Submission procedure:** accepts unsolicited scripts. **Response time:** 3–6 months.

## THE KENYON REVIEW

Kenyon College; Gambier, OH 43022; (614) 427-3339
David H. Lynn, *Editor*

**Types of material:** one-acts, excerpts from full-length plays. **Remuneration:** cash payment; 2 complimentary copies. **Guidelines:** literary journal publishing an average of 2 plays a year; 30-page maximum. **Submission procedure:** accepts unsolicited scripts (typed and double-spaced only) with SASE for response. **Response time:** 3 months.

## LAMIA INK!

Box 202, Prince St Station; New York, NY 10012
Cortland Jessup, *Editor*

**Types of material:** very short monologues and performance pieces; 1-page plays for contest (see below). **Remuneration:** 4 complimentary copies. **Guidelines:** triannual "art rag" magazine; experimental theatre pieces maximum 5 pages long, prefers 2–3 pages; special interest in Japanese, Pacific Rim and Native American writers, and poets' theatre, performance poems, theatre manifestos and essays. **Submission procedure:** accepts unsolicited scripts with SASE for response. **Deadline:** 30 Sep for Dec issue; 30 Dec for Feb issue; 30 Mar for May issue. **Response time:** 2–3 weeks after deadline. **Special programs:** Lamia Ink! International One-Page Play Competition (see Prizes).

## LIBRETO/AS

The Presbyter's Peartree; 15 Alta Vista Dr; Princeton, NJ 08540-7416;
(609) 737-7065
Laurence M. Leive, *Publisher*

**Types of material:** full-length plays, one-acts, translations, adaptations, plays for young audiences, musicals. **Remuneration:** royalty; complimentary copies. **Guidelines:** theatre press publishing an average of 12 works a year by writers of Cuban origin. **Submission procedure:** accepts unsolicited scripts; prefers synopsis and letter of inquiry. **Response time:** 1 week letter; 1 month script.

## LILLENAS DRAMA RESOURCES

Lillenas Publishing Company; Box 419527; Kansas City, MO 64141;
(816) 931-1900
Paul M. Miller, *Consultant/Editor*

**Types of material:** full-length plays, one-acts, musicals, collections of sketches, skits, playlets, recitations. **Remuneration:** outright purchase or royalty. **Guidelines:** unpublished "creatively conceived and practically producible scripts and outlines that provide church and school with an opportunity to glorify God and his creation in drama." **Submission procedure:** accepts unsolicited scripts; send SASE for contributor's guidelines and current need sheet. **Response time:** 3 months.

## MODERN INTERNATIONAL DRAMA

Theatre Department; State University of New York–Binghamton; Box 6000;
Binghamton, NY 13902-6000; (607) 777-2704
George E. Wellwarth and Anthony M. Pasquariello, *Editors*

**Types of material:** translations. **Remuneration:** 3 complimentary copies. **Guidelines:** biannual journal; unpublished translations of plays not previously translated only; style guide sent on request. **Submission procedure:** accepts unsolicited scripts. **Response time:** 1 month.

## NEW PLAYS

Box 5074; Charlottesville, VA 22905; (804) 979-2777
Patricia Whitton, *Publisher*

**Types of material:** plays for young audiences. **Remuneration:** 10% book royalty, 50% performance royalty. **Guidelines:** innovative material not duplicated by other sources of plays for young audiences; produced plays, directed by someone other than author. **Submission procedure:** accepts unsolicited scripts. **Response time:** at least 1–2 months.

## PACIFIC REVIEW
English Department; California State University; 5500 University Pkwy;
 San Bernardino, CA 92407-2397; (909) 880-5894
James Brown and Juan Delgado, *Faculty Editors*

**Types of material:** one-acts. **Remuneration:** 2 complimentary copies. **Guidelines:**
annual literary journal; prefers realistic plays with contemporary themes; plays
maximum 25 pages long. **Submission procedure:** accepts unsolicited scripts;
submit 1 Sep–1 Feb only. **Response time:** 2 months.

## PAJ BOOKS
Box 260, Village Station; New York, NY 10014-0260; (212) 243-3885
Bonnie Marranca and Gautam Dasgupta, *Editors*

**Types of material:** full-length plays, one-acts, translations. **Remuneration:** royalty
and/or fee. **Guidelines:** plays and critical literature on the performing arts from
the international repertoire published by John Hopkins University Press; special
interest in translations. **Submission procedure:** no unsolicited scripts; synopsis and
letter of inquiry. **Response time:** 1–2 months.

## PASSAIC REVIEW
442 Stuyvesant Ave; Lyndhurst, NJ 07071; (201) 939-5510
Richard Quatrone, *Publisher and Editor*

**Types of material:** short one-acts, including plays for young audiences. **Remuneration:** 1 complimentary copy. **Guidelines:** biannual literary review publishing an
average of 1 play a year; seeks work which is passionate, powerful, free, personal
and alive and which deals with the human condition; plays under 5 pages long.
**Submission procedure:** accepts unsolicited scripts. **Response time:** up to 12
months.

## PERFORMING ARTS JOURNAL
Box 260, Village Station; New York, NY 10014-0260; (212) 243-3885
Bonnie Marranca and Gautam Dasgupta, *Co-Publishers and Editors*

**Types of material:** short full-length plays, one-acts, translations. **Remuneration:**
fee. **Guidelines:** publishes plays and critical literature on the performing arts from
the international repertoire; special interest in translations; plays less than 40
pages long. **Submission procedure:** no unsolicited scripts; synopsis and letter of
inquiry. **Response time:** 1–2 months.

## PIONEER DRAMA SERVICE
Box 4267; Englewood, CO 80155-4267; (303) 779-4035

**Types of material:** full-length plays, one-acts, plays for young audiences, musicals.
**Remuneration:** outright purchase or royalty. **Guidelines:** produced work suitable
for educational theatre, including melodramas and Christmas plays. **Submission
procedure:** accepts unsolicited scripts; prefers synopsis and letter of inquiry.

**Response time:** 3–12 weeks. **Special programs:** Shubert Fendrich Memorial Playwriting Contest (see Prizes).

## PLAYERS PRESS
Box 1132; Studio City, CA 91614-0132; (818) 789-4980
Robert W. Gordon, *Senior Editor*

**Types of material:** full-length plays, one-acts, translations, adaptations, plays for young audiences, musicals, monologues, scenes, teleplays, screenplays. **Remuneration:** cash option and/or outright purchase or royalty; complimentary copies (additional copies at 20% discount). **Guidelines:** theatre press publishing technical and reference books and scripts; produced works for professional, amateur and educational markets. **Submission procedure:** accepts unsolicited scripts with proof of production, resume and 2 business-size SASEs; prefers synopsis, proof of production, resume and letter of inquiry with SASE for response. **Response time:** 1–6 weeks letter; 1–6 months script.

## PLAYS, THE DRAMA MAGAZINE FOR YOUNG PEOPLE
120 Boylston St; Boston, MA 02116-4615; (617) 423-3157
Elizabeth Preston, *Managing Editor*

**Types of material:** one-act plays for young audiences, including adaptations of material in the public domain. **Remuneration:** payment on acceptance. **Guidelines:** publishes about 70 plays and programs a year; prefers work 20–30 minutes long for junior and senior high, 15–20 minutes for middle grades, 8–15 minutes for lower grades; no religious plays. **Submission procedure:** accepts unsolicited original scripts; letter of inquiry for adaptations; prefers format used in magazine (send SASE for style sheet). **Response time:** 2 weeks.

## PLAYSOURCE
Theatre Communications Group; 355 Lexington Ave; New York, NY 10017-0217;
    (212) 697-5230
Wendy Weiner, *Editor*

**Types of material:** full-length plays, one-acts, translations, adaptations, plays for young audiences, musicals. **Remuneration:** brief descriptive listing of work circulated in quarterly bulletin to potential producers; 1 complimentary copy. **Guidelines:** works that have received full production at TCG Constituent or Associate theatre, or workshop or staged reading as part of major developmental program; bulletin mailed Oct, Jan, Apr and Jul to 300-plus TCG theatres and to subscribers, including other nonprofit theatres, college and university theatres and libraries, and some film and television production companies. **Submission procedure:** TCG Constituent and Associate theatres or developmental organizations supply TCG with list of new works they have produced or developed in their current or most recent season; TCG sends playwright listing form to complete. **Deadline:** ongoing.

## POEMS & PLAYS

English Department; Middle Tennessee State University; Murfreesboro, TN 37132; (615) 898-2712

Gay Brewer, *Editor*

**Types of material:** one-acts, short plays. **Remuneration:** 1 complimentary copy. **Guidelines:** annual magazine of poetry and short plays published Apr/May and including an average of 2–3 plays in each issue; unpublished plays; prefers short one-acts. **Submission procedure:** accepts unsolicited scripts; submissions read 1 Oct–15 Jan only. **Response time:** 1–2 months. **Special programs:** Tennessee Chapbook Prize: annual award for one-act (or combination of short one-acts) maximum 24–30 pages long; winning script published as interior chapbook in magazine; playwright receives 50 complimentary copies; submit script and $10 for reading fee and copy of next issue; *deadline:* 15 Jan 1996; no submissions before 1 Oct 1995.

## PORTLAND REVIEW

Box 751-SD; Portland, OR 97207; (503) 725-4533

*Editor*

**Types of material:** short plays. **Remuneration:** 1 complimentary copy. **Guidelines:** triannual journal of the arts published Sep, Jan and May; plays less than 4000 words long. **Submission procedure:** accepts unsolicited scripts. **Response time:** 2 months.

## PRISM INTERNATIONAL

Department of Creative Writing; University of British Columbia; Buch E462–1866 Main Mall; Vancouver, BC; Canada V6T 1Z1; (604) 822-2514

Leah Postman, *Editor*

**Types of material:** one-acts, translations, excerpts from full-length plays. **Remuneration:** $20 per printed page; 1-year subscription. **Guidelines:** quarterly literary magazine; unpublished plays, maximum 40 pages long; send SASE for guidelines. **Submission procedure:** accepts unsolicited scripts. **Response time:** 2–4 months.

## PROVINCETOWN ARTS/PROVINCETOWN ARTS PRESS

650 Commercial St; Provincetown, MA 02657; (508) 487-3167

Christopher Busa, *Editor and Publisher*

**Types of material:** one-acts, translations, performance-art texts. **Remuneration:** $50–300; 2 complimentary copies. **Guidelines:** annual magazine focusing broadly on artists and writers who inhabit or visit the tip of Cape Cod, and publishing an average of 1 play a year; also small press publishing 1 play or collection of plays a year; especially interested in performance-art texts; unpublished plays not more than 30 pages long. **Submission procedure:** accepts unsolicited scripts; submissions read Sep–Mar. **Response time:** 2 months.

## Rag Mag

Box 12; Goodhue, MN 55027; (612) 923-4590
Beverly Voldseth, *Editor and Publisher*

**Types of material:** full-length plays, one-acts. **Remuneration:** 1 complimentary copy. **Guidelines:** biannual small-press literary magazine publishing artwork, prose and poetry, and interested in receiving play submissions; for Oct issue, works on theme "mothers" only; for Apr issue, works on theme "fathers" only; innovative character plays; prefers short one-acts but will consider longer plays with a view to publishing extracts or scenes. **Submission procedure:** accepts unsolicited short one-acts; send maximum 10-page sample, bio and letter of inquiry for longer plays; submit Apr-Jun for Oct issue, Jul-Sep for Apr issue. **Response time:** 1–2 months.

## Resource Publications

160 East Virginia St, #290; San Jose, CA 95112-5848; (408) 286-8505
Ken Guentert, *Editorial Director*

**Types of material:** plays 7–15 minutes long. **Remuneration:** royalty. **Guidelines:** unpublished plays or collections of plays suitable for celebrations, religious education classes, youth ministry, and education, counseling and therapy. **Submission procedure:** accepts unsolicited scripts. **Response time:** 2 months.

## Rockford Review

Box 858; Rockford, IL 61105
David Ross, *Editor*

**Types of material:** one-acts. **Remuneration:** one-acts selected for publication eligible for quarterly "Editor's Choice" prize of $25 (winner invited to reading and reception as guest of honor in Oct); 1 complimentary copy. **Guidelines:** quarterly journal publishing poetry, fiction, satire, artwork and an average of 4–5 plays a year; one-acts not more than 15 pages long, preferably of a satirical nature; interested in work that provides new insight into the human dilemma ("to cope or not to cope"). **Submission procedure:** accepts unsolicited scripts; sample copy $5. **Response time:** 1–2 months.

## Samuel French

45 West 25th St; New York, NY 10010-2751; (212) 206-8990
Lawrence Harbison, *Editor*

**Types of material:** full-length plays, one-acts, plays for young audiences, musicals. **Remuneration:** generally, advance against royalties; 10% book royalty, 80% amateur royalty, 90% stock royalty; 10 complimentary copies (40% discount on additional copies). **Guidelines:** "Many of our publications have never been produced in New York; these are generally comprised of light comedies, mysteries, mystery-comedies, a handful of one-acts and plays for young audiences, and plays with a preponderance of female roles; however, do not hesitate to send in your Future Pulitzer Prize Winner"; prefers script format presented in

*Guidelines* booklet ($4 postpaid). **Submission procedure:** accepts unsolicited scripts. **Response time:** 2–12 months.

## Scripts and Scribbles
141 Wooster St; New York, NY 10012-3163; (212) 473-6695
Daryl Chin, *Consulting Editor*

**Types of material:** full-length plays, one-acts, performance-art texts or scenarios. **Remuneration:** 25 complimentary copies. **Guidelines:** series initiated to publish texts for nontraditional theatre work and works produced outside New York City. **Submission procedure:** no unsolicited scripts; synopsis and letter of inquiry. **Response time:** 6 months.

## Sinister Wisdom
Box 3252; Berkeley, CA 94703
Akiba Onada-Sikwoia, *Editor*

**Types of material:** one-acts, excerpts from full-length plays (3000 words maximum). **Remuneration:** 2 complimentary copies. **Guidelines:** lesbian/feminist quarterly of art and literature; works by lesbians reflecting the diversity of lesbians; no heterosexual themes; send SASE for current themes. **Submission procedure:** accepts unsolicited scripts. **Response time:** 2–9 months.

## Smith and Kraus
Box 127; Lyme, NH 03768; (603) 795-4331
Marisa Smith, *President*

**Types of material:** full-length plays, one-acts, translations, adaptations, plays for young audiences, monologues. **Remuneration:** usually fee or royalty; at least 10 complimentary copies. **Guidelines:** theatre press publishing works of interest to theatrical community, especially to actors, including collections of monologues and an average of 50 full-length plays a year. **Submission procedure:** accepts unsolicited scripts. **Response time:** 1–2 months.

## Stet Magazine
Box 75; Cambridge, MA 02238-0075; (508) 264-4938
Cassandra Oxley, *Editor and Publisher*

**Types of material:** one-acts, performance-art texts. **Remuneration:** 2 complimentary copies. **Guidelines:** quarterly literary magazine publishing an average of 2 plays a year; unpublished works maximum 20 pages long; special interest in short pieces and in innovative, experimental work. **Submission procedure:** accepts unsolicited scripts with bio; sample copy $4. **Response time:** 2–3 months.

## SUN & MOON PRESS
6026 Wilshire Blvd; Los Angeles, CA 90036; (213) 857-1115
*American Theater and Literature Program*

**Types of material:** full-length plays, one-acts, translations. **Remuneration:** royalty; 10 complimentary copies. **Guidelines:** press publishing average of 10 single-play volumes a year including 2 winners of *American Theater and Literature Program Contest*; unpublished plays. **Submission procedure:** accepts unsolicited script for prize only, submit with $25 fee. **Response time:** 2–6 months.

## THEATER
222 York St; New Haven, CT 06520; (203) 432-1568
Erika Munk, *Editor*

**Types of material:** full-length plays, one-acts, translations, adaptations. **Remuneration:** minimum fee of $150; complimentary copies. **Guidelines:** triannual theatre journal publishing an average of 2 plays in each issue; special interest in experimental, innovative work; "no standard psychological realism or TV-script clones." **Submission procedure:** accepts unsolicited scripts with resume. **Response time:** 3 months.

## THEATREFORUM
Theatre Department; University of California–San Diego;
    9500 Gilman Dr; La Jolla, CA 92093-0344; (619) 534-6598
Jim Carmody, Adele Edling Shank and Theodore Shank, *Editors*

**Types of material:** full-length plays, translations, adaptations. **Remuneration:** varies by length; 10 complimentary copies. **Guidelines:** biannual international journal focusing on innovative work. **Submission procedure:** no unsolicited scripts; professional recommendation. **Response time:** 3 months.

## THIS MONTH ON STAGE
Box 62; Hewlett, NY 11557-0062; (516) 357-9607
Editorial Department

**Types of material:** full-length plays, one-acts, translations, adaptations, libretti. **Remuneration:** $1; 2 complimentary copies. **Guidelines:** monthly theatre magazine; special interest in short plays and one-acts. **Submission procedure:** accepts unsolicited scripts with resume, cover letter and SASE for response; send SASE for guidelines. **Response time:** 6–8 months.

## TOMORROW MAGAZINE
Box 148486; Chicago, IL 60614; (312) 984-6092
Tim W. Brown, *Editor*

**Types of material:** one-acts, monologues, performance-art texts. **Remuneration:** 1 complimentary copy. **Guidelines:** biannual magazine publishing all literary genres, including an average of 1–2 plays a year; works maximum 15 pages long;

special interest in comedy. **Submission procedure:** accepts unsolicited scripts; sample copy $5. **Response time:** 3 weeks–3 months.

## UBU REPERTORY THEATER PUBLICATIONS

See Membership and Service Organizations.

## UNITED ARTS
141 Wooster St; New York, NY 10012-3163; (212) 473-6695
Daryl Chin, *Editor*

**Types of material:** one-acts, translations, performance-art texts, scenarios, manifestos. **Remuneration:** complimentary copies. **Guidelines:** journal of analysis and opinion covering visual arts, film, video, theatre and dance, published 3–4 times a year by University Arts Resources; nontraditional, avant-garde plays. **Submission pro-cedure:** accepts unsolicited scripts; prefers synopsis and letter of inquiry. **Re-sponse time:** 6 months.

## VENTANA PRODUCTIONS/PUBLICATIONS
Box 191973; San Francisco, CA 94119; (415) 522-8989
Vicky Simmons, *Literary Manager*

**Types of material:** full-length plays, one-acts, monologues. **Remuneration:** 10% book royalty, 90% production royalty; 10 complimentary copies. **Guidelines:** independent production company and small press publishing original single- and multiple-play volumes; prefers produced plays or plays with significant accomplishments. **Submission procedure:** no unsolicited scripts; synopsis and letter of inquiry. **Response time:** 3 months. **Special programs:** Ventana Publications Play Award: annual award for full-length or one-act play with significant accomplishments; winning script receives publication and public reading, playwright receives book and performance royalties and 10 complimentary copies; submit script with proof of production/accomplishments and $10 fee; send SASE for guidelines; *deadline:* 15 Feb 1996.

# Development

**What's in this section?**

Conferences, festivals, workshops and programs whose primary purpose is to develop plays and playwrights, including a substantial number devoted to music-theatre. Also listed are some playwright groups and membership organizations whose main activity is play development. Developmental organizations such as New Dramatists whose many programs cannot be adequately described in the brief format used in this section are listed in Membership and Service Organizations. Some programs listed in Prizes also include a developmental element.

**How can I get into these programs?**

Keep applying to those for which you are convinced your work is suited. If you're turned down one year, you may be accepted the next on the strength of your latest piece. If you're required to submit a script with your application, don't forget your SASE!

## ACADEMY THEATRE NEW PLAY DEVELOPMENT PROGRAM
501 Mean St NW; Atlanta, GA 30318; (404) 525-4111
Sabina M. Angel, *New Play Development Coordinator*

**Open to:** playwrights. **Description:** year-round program of 6–8 week workshops; 8–10 plays developed each workshop in collaboration with actors, directors and dramaturgs, culminating in readings and staged readings; playwright receives access to theatre's studio spaces and conference room for independent rehearsals. **Financial arrangement:** $120–150 fee per workshop. **Guidelines:** resident of metro-Atlanta area or Southeast region. **Application procedure:** script of new play or 10-page dialogue sample of work-in-progress, synopsis, bio and letter of inquiry. **Deadline:** ongoing.

## ALCAZAR SCRIPTS IN PROGRESS
650 Geary St; San Francisco, CA 94102; (415) 441-6655
Alan Ramos, *Script Supervisor*

**Open to:** playwrights, composers, screenwriters. **Description:** 1 play developed through 3-month process, including 2 staged readings; possible full production with 4 weeks of rehearsal. **Financial arrangement:** room and board; royalties, if produced. **Guidelines:** unproduced play. **Application procedure:** script and resume. **Deadline:** 31 Dec 1995. **Notification date:** 28 Feb 1996. **Dates:** 19 Jun 1996–Sep 1996.

## AMERICAN PLAYWRIGHT PROGRAM
Westbeth Theatre Center; 151 Bank St; New York, NY 10014; (212) 691-2272
Steven Bloom, *Literary Manager*

**Open to:** playwrights. **Description:** program to develop full-length plays through critiques, story conferences and staged readings; possible production by Westbeth Theatre Center or through referral to other producing organizations. **Financial arrangement:** free. **Guidelines:** contemporary themes; cast limit of 8, minimal set; welcomes work by minority playwrights; send SASE for guidelines. **Application procedure:** script only. **Deadline:** ongoing. **Notification:** 4–6 months.

## ASCAP MUSICAL THEATRE WORKSHOP
1 Lincoln Plaza; New York, NY 10023; (212) 621-6234
Michael A. Kerker, *Director of Musical Theatre*

**Open to:** composers, lyricists. **Description:** 10-week workshop meeting once a week for 3 hours under the direction of Stephen Schwartz; works presented to panels of musical theatre professionals. **Financial arrangement:** free; $500 Bernice Cohen Musical Theatre Fund Award given to most promising participating individual or team. **Guidelines:** write for press release. **Application procedure:** resume and cassette of 4 theatrical songs (no pop songs). **Deadline:** 1 Sep 1995. **Notification:** Sep 1995. **Dates:** workshop begins Dec 1995.

## ASIAN AMERICAN THEATER COMPANY
## NEW PLAYS & PLAYWRIGHTS DEVELOPMENT PROGRAM
403 Arguello Blvd; San Francisco, CA 94118; (415) 751-2600
Diane Emito Takei, *Artistic Director*

**Open to:** playwrights. **Description:** developmental workshop for 2–4 plays, leading
to staged reading or production; plays not selected for workshop considered for
inclusion in series of 8–10 readings presented each season. **Financial arrangement:**
fee; amount contingent on funding. **Guidelines:** American, Canadian or U.K.
playwright of Asian-Pacific descent writing in English; prefers plays depicting
Asian-Pacific American perspective. **Application procedure:** script and letter of
inquiry. **Deadline:** ongoing. **Dates:** TBA.

## THE AUDREY SKIRBALL-KENIS THEATRE
9478 West Olympic Blvd, Suite 304; Beverly Hills, CA 90212; (310) 284-8965
Mead Hunter, *Director of Literary Programs*

**Open to:** playwrights. **Description:** 15–20 plays receive staged readings; of those,
2–3 selected for workshop production. **Financial arrangement:** playwright receives
$100 for staged reading, $1000 for workshop production. **Guidelines:** full-length
play-in-progress not produced or scheduled for production. **Application
procedure:** script submissions accepted only from agents or with professional
recommendation; playwrights may submit synopsis, sample pages and resume.
**Deadline:** ongoing. **Notification:** 4–6 months.

## BAY AREA PLAYWRIGHTS FESTIVAL
The Playwrights Foundation; Box 460357; San Francisco, CA 94114;
    (415) 255-2254
Mame Hunt, *Artistic Director*

**Open to:** playwrights. **Description:** 6–9 scripts given dramaturgical attention and
2 rehearsed readings separated by 5–6 days for rewrites during 3-week festival at
Magic Theatre; prefestival weekend retreat for initial brainstorming with directors
and dramaturgs. **Financial arrangement:** small stipend, travel. **Guidelines:**
unproduced original full-length play only. **Application procedure:** script and
resume. **Deadline:** 1 Mar 1996. **Notification:** May 1996. **Dates:** prefestival weekend
Jun 1996; festival late Jul–early Aug 1996.

## BMI–LEHMAN ENGEL MUSICAL THEATRE WORKSHOP
Broadcast Music, Inc.; 320 West 57th St; New York, NY 10019; (212) 830-2515
Norma Grossman, *Director, Musical Theatre*

**Open to:** composers, librettists, lyricists. **Description:** 2-year program of weekly
workshop meetings; showcase presentation to invited members of entertainment
industry each year. **Financial arrangement:** free. **Application procedure:** completed
application and work samples. **Deadline:** 1 May 1996 for librettists; 1 Aug 1996 for
composers and lyricists.

## BORDER PLAYWRIGHTS PROJECT
Borderlands Theater; Box 2791; Tucson, AZ 85702; (602) 882-8607

**Open to:** playwrights. **Description:** 3 plays developed over 10-day residency with actors, director and dramaturg, culminating in staged reading. **Financial arrangement:** small stipend, travel, housing. **Guidelines:** unproduced full-length play which reflects the culturally diverse realities of the border region, or uses the border as metaphor; English, Spanish and bilingual scripts accepted; special interest in works by writers of color; write for information. **Application procedure:** 2 copies of script. **Deadline:** 30 Mar 1996. **Notification:** Jun 1996. **Dates:** Sep 1996.

## BROADWAY TOMORROW
191 Claremont Ave, Suite 53; New York, NY 10027; (212) 864-4736
Elyse Curtis, *Artistic Director*

**Open to:** composers, librettists, lyricists. **Description:** new musicals presented in concert with writers' involvement. **Financial arrangement:** free. **Guidelines:** resident of NY metropolitan area. **Application procedure:** submissions accepted with professional recommendation from past participant only; cassette of 3 songs with description of 3 scenes in which they occur, synopsis, resume, reviews if available and SASE for response. **Deadline:** 31 Aug 1996.

## CAC PLAYWRIGHT'S UNIT
Contemporary Arts Center; Box 30498; New Orleans, LA 70190; (504) 523-1216
Pamela Marquis, *Theatre Coordinator*

**Open to:** playwrights. **Description:** 9-month workshop for 8–10 writers; participants' works developed and given staged readings. **Financial arrangement:** write or call for information. **Guidelines:** writer living in New Orleans area. **Application procedure:** script only. **Deadline:** ongoing. **Dates:** Sep–May.

## CARNEGIE-MELLON SHOWCASE OF NEW PLAYS
Drama Department; Carnegie-Mellon University; Schenley Park;
    Pittsburgh, PA 15213; (412) 268-3284
Frank Gagliano, *Artistic Director* (submissions)
Mary Chlipala, *Assistant Literary Manager* (phone inquiries)

**Open to:** playwrights, translators. **Description:** 5 playwrights each brought in for 2 weeks' work on play with director and Equity company of actors, culminating in 3 public script-in-hand performances. **Financial arrangement:** $1200 stipend, travel and housing. **Guidelines:** full-length play, bill of related one-acts, or one-act which writer is developing into full-length play; program seeks "plays of risk; no subjects are taboo; all forms are acceptable; the more audacious and the richer the language, the better." **Application procedure:** script with resume of past productions and readings; submissions accepted only from agents or when accompanied by a letter of recommendation from literary manager of a major theatre. **Deadline:** 1 Dec 1995. **Notification:** Apr 1996. **Dates:** Jul 1996.

## CHARLOTTE FESTIVAL/NEW PLAYS IN AMERICA
Charlotte Repertory Theatre; 2040 Charlotte Plaza; Charlotte, NC 28244;
   (704) 375-4796
Claudia Carter Covington, *Literary Manager*
Carol Bellamy, *Literary Associate*

**Open to:** playrights, translators. **Description:** 4 plays each given 12–16 hours of rehearsal with Equity company, culminating in 2 public staged readings, during week-long festival; some scripts subsequently receive full production as part of theatre's regular season. **Financial arrangement:** honorarium, travel, housing. **Guidelines:** only full-length plays and translations that have not received professional production. **Application procedure:** script only. **Deadline:** ongoing.

## THE CHESTERFIELD FILM COMPANY/WRITER'S FILM PROJECT
Universal Studios; 100 Universal City Plaza, Bldg 447;
   Universal City, CA 91608; (818) 777-0998

**Open to:** playwrights, screenwriters. **Description:** up to 10 writers annually chosen for year-long screenwriting workshop meeting 3–5 times a week; writer creates 2 feature-length screenplays; company intends to produce best of year's work. **Financial arrangement:** $20,000 stipend. **Guidelines:** current and former writing-program students encouraged to apply; write or call for information. **Application procedure:** 2 copies of completed application, writing samples and $37 fee. **Deadline:** May 1996; exact date TBA. **Notification:** Sep 1996. **Dates:** Oct 1996–Sep 1997.

## CORNERSTONE DRAMATURGY AND DEVELOPMENT PROJECT
Penumbra Theatre Company; 270 North Kent St; St. Paul, MN 55102-1794;
   (612) 224-4601
Lou Bellamy, *Artistic Director*

**Open to:** playwrights. **Description:** 1 playwright a year offered mainstage production with possible 3–4 week residency; 1 playwright offered 4-week workshop-residency culminating in staged reading; 3 playwrights offered staged reading. **Financial arrangement:** varies according to needs of project. **Guidelines:** full-length play dealing with the African-American and/or Pan African experience which has not received professional full production; one-acts considered; write for guidelines. **Application procedure:** script and resume. **Deadline:** ongoing.

## DENVER CENTER THEATRE COMPANY
## U S WEST WORKSHOPS
1050 13th St; Denver, CO 80204; (303) 893-4000
Tom Szentgyorgyi, *Associate Artistic Director/New Play Development*

**Open to:** playwrights. **Description:** new plays receive workshops and rehearsed readings throughout company's season; most plays given 15–30 hours of rehearsal, culminating in 1 public presentation. **Financial arrangement:** stipend, travel, housing. **Guidelines:** unproduced full-length play only; no plays for young audiences, musicals or 1-person shows. **Application procedure:** write for guidelines. **Deadline:** ongoing. **Dates:** Sep–Jun.

## DIAMOND HEAD THEATRE DEVELOPMENTAL PROGRAMS
520 Makapuu Ave; Honolulu, HI 96816; (808) 734-8763
Ernest E. Fulton, *Producing Director*

### Originals

**Open to:** playwrights. **Description:** ongoing playwrights' workshop led by Jim Hutchison in which playwrights meet regularly to develop their scripts through reading and discussion; monthly public readings of works-in-progress. **Financial arrangement:** participant pays $5 a session. **Application procedure:** attend workshop session; check date and time of sessions (currently every other Wednesday 7–10 p.m.).

### Pacific Rim Play Festival

**Open to:** playwrights. **Description:** 2 plays each rehearsed with participation of playwright and given 2 staged readings a week apart, followed by discussion with audience (playwright has opportunity to revise script between readings). **Financial arrangement:** free. **Guidelines:** current HI resident. **Application procedure:** script and cover letter indicating that submission is for festival. **Deadline:** 30 Nov 1995. **Dates:** Jan/Feb 1996.

## DRAMA LEAGUE DEVELOPING ARTISTS SERIES
The Drama League of New York; 165 West 46th St, Suite 601;
    New York, NY 10036; (212) 302-2100
Aimée K. Michel, *Artistic Director*

**Open to:** playwrights. **Description:** 10–15 scripts or performance projects at different stages of development given 1 rehearsal and public reading as part of year-long series. **Financial arrangement:** free. **Application procedure:** script, or 1-page proposal describing project for which script has yet to be developed, submitted by playwright, director or playwright-director team; optional SASE for acknowledgment of receipt. **Deadline:** ongoing.

## FAIRCHESTER PLAYWRIGHTS
24 Spruce Dr; Wilton, CT 06897; (203) 762-8343
Sherman K. Poultney, *Director*

**Open to:** playwrights, screenwriters, television writers. **Description:** Sep–Jun workshop meets monthly for public staged readings of members' works by professional actors. **Financial arrangement:** writer receiving reading pays for room rental and refreshments for public and fellow writers. **Guidelines:** writer must be able to attend regular meetings; unproduced work; plays may be full-length or one-act; adaptations eligible. **Application procedure:** write or call for guidelines, or to arrange to attend a reading. **Deadline:** ongoing.

## FIRST STAGE
6817 Franklin Ave; Los Angeles, CA 90028; (213) 850-6271
Dennis Safren, *Literary Manager*

**Open to:** playwrights, screenwriters. **Description:** organization providing year-round developmental services using professional actors, directors and dramaturgs; weekly staged readings of plays and screenplays followed by discussions; bimonthly playwriting and screenwriting workshops; periodic dramaturgy workshops; annual short-play marathon. **Financial arrangement:** subscription of $115 a year or $35 a quarter for resident of L.A., Orange or Ventura counties; $58 annual subscription for nonresident; nonmember may submit script for reading. **Application procedure:** script only. **Deadline:** ongoing.

## THE FRANK SILVERA WRITERS' WORKSHOP
317 West 125th St, Top Floor; New York, NY 10027; (212) 662-8463
Garland Lee Thompson, *Founding Executive Director*

**Open to:** playwrights. **Description:** program includes Monday series of readings of new plays by new and established writers, followed by critiques; Wednesday seminars conducted by master playwrights; staged readings and 2–3 showcase productions a year. **Financial arrangement:** $35 annual fee plus $10 per Wednesday class; Monday-night readings free. **Guidelines:** interested in new plays by writers of all colors and backgrounds. **Application procedure:** Sep open house; attending a Monday-night session encouraged; call for information.

## FREDERICK DOUGLASS CREATIVE ARTS CENTER
## WRITING WORKSHOPS
270 West 96th St; New York, NY 10025; (212) 864-3375
Fred Hudson, *Artistic Director*

**Open to:** playwrights, screenwriters, television writers. **Description:** 4 cycles a year of 8-week workshops; beginning and advanced playwriting; latter includes readings and possible productions; also film and television writing workshops; weekly meetings. **Financial arrangement:** $100 fee per workshop; author of play given staged reading receives $50, author of produced play receives $500. **Application procedure:** contact FDCAC for information. **Deadline:** 8 Sep 1995 for 1st cycle; 5 Jan 1996 for 2nd cycle; 5 Apr 1996 for 3rd cycle; 7 Jun 1996 for 4th cycle. **Dates:** Oct–Dec 1995; Jan–Mar 1996; Apr–Jun 1996; Jul–Sep 1996.

## FULL MOON PLAYWRIGHT'S EXCHANGE
160 West 71st St, PHA; New York, NY 10023; (212) 787-1945
Stuart Warmflash, *Manager*

**Open to:** playwrights. **Description:** members meet weekly to develop their scripts through supportive critical process. **Financial arrangement:** free. **Application procedure:** script and resume; following favorable script review, playwright attends 2 trial meetings. **Deadline:** ongoing. **Notification:** 3 months.

## HAROLD PRINCE MUSICAL THEATRE PROGRAM

The Directors Company; 311 West 43rd St, Suite 206; New York, NY 10036;
    (212) 246-5877
*Selection Committee*

**Open to:** playwrights, composers, librettists, lyricists, screenwriters. **Description:** writers and composers of 3 musicals meet monthly with director in developmental program; 30-minute segments of each musical given 4 weeks of rehearsal, which includes weekly critiques by Harold Prince, culminating in production for invited audience in New York City; possible future full production at Denver Center Theatre Company. **Financial arrangement:** writer paid fee for option on first production. **Guidelines:** full-length musical or operetta that has not received professional New York production. **Application procedure:** script with at least 1 complete act, tape of score, synopsis, resume, 3 letters of recommendation and letter of interest. **Deadline:** 1 Sep 1995. **Notification date:** Oct 1995. **Dates:** fall 1995–Jun 1996.

## THE HBO NEW WRITERS PROJECT

2049 Century Park East, Suite 4100; Los Angeles, CA 90067-3215;
    (310) 201-9200
Steve Kaplan, *Executive Director*

**Open to:** playwrights, writer-performers. **Description:** project designed to encourage and cultivate emerging, multicultural comic writers and performers; Home Box Office, in conjunction with Wavy Line Productions, will offer authors of 25 one-act works the opportunity to participate in writers workshop with a view to nurturing the works for possible stage, TV or film development. **Financial arrangement:** small honorarium, travel and housing. **Guidelines:** writer not currently writing for, or contracted to write for, network TV show, national cable TV show or feature film; one-act play, solo performance piece or half-hour TV play (no spec episodes) that meets a broad definition of comedy and reflects the multicultural world in which we live; work not more than 60 pages long and not currently under option; 3-submission limit; write for guidelines. **Application procedure:** completed application/release form (unless submitted by agent), script and resume; optional VHS videotape of performance. **Deadline:** 1 Feb 1996. **Notification:** 30 Mar 1996. **Dates:** spring/summer 1996.

## HISPANIC PLAYWRIGHTS PROJECT

South Coast Repertory; Box 2197; Costa Mesa, CA 92628-2197;
    (714) 957-2602, ext. 215
José Cruz González, *Project Director*

**Open to:** playwrights. **Description:** up to 3 scripts given 6-day workshop with director, dramaturg and professional cast, culminating in public reading and discussion; playwright meets with director and dramaturg prior to workshop. **Financial arrangement:** honorarium, travel, housing. **Guidelines:** Hispanic-American playwright; unproduced play preferred but produced play which would benefit from further development will be considered; play must not be written entirely in Spanish; no musicals. **Application procedure:** script with synopsis and bio. **Deadline:** 29 Mar 1996. **Notification:** 10 May 1996. **Dates:** preworkshop meeting weekend of 15 Jun 1996; workshop 23 Jul–4 Aug 1996.

## THE ISIDORA AGUIRRE PLAYWRIGHTING LAB

El Teatro de la Esperanza; Box 40578; San Francisco, CA 94140-0578;
    (415) 255-2320
Chela Cadwell, *Program Manager*

**Open to:** playwrights. **Description:** 1–3 plays developed through individual sessions and weekly seminars with professional dramaturg over 6-week period, culminating in public staged reading; possible future full production for 1 or more plays. **Financial arrangement:** stipend to cover room and board. **Guidelines:** Chicano/Latino playwright; full-length play-in-progress reflective of or adaptable to the Chicano experience; prefers bilingual plays, but accepts monolingual plays in Spanish or English; prefers cast limit of 6 (doubling allowed) and set suitable for touring, but will consider larger-cast plays with nontourable sets; write for guidelines. **Application procedure:** 3 copies of script and resume (material will not be returned). **Deadline:** 15 Mar 1996. **Notification:** 15 May 1996. **Dates:** Jun–Jul 1996.

## KEY WEST THEATRE FESTIVAL

Box 992; Key West, FL 33041
Joan McGillis, *Artistic Director*

**Open to:** playwrights, translators. **Description:** up to 5 plays each given up to 12 hours of rehearsal, culminating in public staged readings during 10-day festival which also includes full productions of new plays, workshops and seminars, and which brings together a wide range of professional theatre artists from diverse cultural and ethnic backgrounds. **Financial arrangement:** travel and housing. **Guidelines:** unproduced full-length play, one-act, musical, work for young audiences. **Application procedure:** script, resume and letter of recommendation. **Deadline:** ongoing. **Dates:** early fall.

## L. A. BLACK PLAYWRIGHTS

Box 191535; Los Angeles, CA 90019; (213) 292-9438
James Graham Bronson, *President*

**Open to:** playwrights, librettists, lyricists. **Description:** group meets every second Sunday for guest speakers, private and public readings, and showcases. **Financial arrangement:** free. **Guidelines:** resident of L.A. area; members mainly but not exclusively black; prefers produced playwright. **Application procedure:** submit full-length play. **Deadline:** ongoing. **Dates:** year-round.

## THE LEHMAN ENGEL MUSICAL THEATRE WORKSHOP

6425 Hollywood Blvd; Hollywood, CA 90028; (213) 465-8818
John Sparks, *Co-Director*

**Open to:** composers, librettists, lyricists. **Description:** Sep–Jun workshop; in-house staged readings; skeletal productions (Equity contract). **Financial arrangement:** 1st-year workshop members pay dues of $500, which include nonrefundable application fee (see below); in subsequent years, members pay dues of $300. **Application procedure:** completed application; 1-page resume; cassette of 3 songs or equivalent for composer; 3 lyrics for lyricist; short scene for librettist; nonrefundable $25 fee. **Deadline:** 1 Aug 1996. **Notification:** Sep 1996. **Dates:** Sep 1996–Jun 1997.

## THE LOFT FEST '96—FESTIVAL OF SHORTS
1441 East Fletcher Ave; Tampa, FL 33612; (813) 972-1200
Kelly Smith, *Artistic Director*

**Open to:** playwrights. **Description:** 4-6 plays each given full production during 3–4 week festival; some scripts receive subsequent staged readings. **Financial arrangement:** $100 honorarium; possible travel and housing. **Guidelines:** unproduced one-act, 10-minute play or monologue. **Application procedure:** script, synopsis and letter of interest. **Deadline:** 30 Apr 1996. **Notification date:** 31 May 1996. **Dates:** 19 Jul–25 Aug 1996.

## LONG WHARF THEATRE STAGE II WORKSHOPS
222 Sargent Dr; New Haven, CT 06511; (203) 787-4284
Sari Bodi, *Literary Analyst*

**Open to:** playwrights, translators, composers, librettists, lyricists. **Description:** 4 scripts given 3 weeks of rehearsal, 3 weeks of performance with playwright in residence; optional discussion after performance with audience members, who complete comment sheets (no critics); unit set, costumes and props from stock. **Financial arrangement:** stipend. **Application procedure:** script and professional recommendation, or agent submission. **Deadline:** ongoing. **Notification:** 6 months. **Dates:** Sep–May.

## MANHATTAN PLAYWRIGHTS UNIT
338 West 19th St, #6B; New York, NY 10011-3982; (212) 989-0948
Saul Zachary, *Artistic Director*

**Open to:** playwrights, screenwriters. **Description:** developmental workshop meeting weekly for in-house readings and discussions of members' works-in-progress; end-of-season series of staged readings of new plays. **Financial arrangement:** free. **Guidelines:** produced or published writer. **Application procedure:** letter of inquiry, resume and SASE for response. **Deadline:** ongoing.

## Mark Taper Forum Developmental Programs

135 North Grand Ave; Los Angeles, CA 90012; (213) 972-7574
Oliver Mayer, *Associate Literary Manager*

### Asian-Pacific American Friends of the Center Theater Group (APAF-CTG) Reading Series

**Open to:** playwrights. **Description:** 3–5 plays a year each given 2–4 days of rehearsal and reading followed by discussion with audience. **Financial arrangement:** honorarium. **Guidelines:** Asian-Pacific playwright; program designed to bring Asian-Pacific artists and audiences into CTG on an ongoing basis; scripts selected by APAF-CTG and Taper staff. **Application procedure:** script and resume. **Deadline:** call for information.

### New Work Festival

**Open to:** playwrights. **Description:** 16–18 plays given workshops (2 weeks of rehearsal, 2 public presentations) or rehearsed readings. **Financial arrangement:** remuneration varies. **Guidelines:** unproduced, unpublished play. **Application procedure:** call for information. **Deadline:** TBA.

## The Maxwell Anderson Playwrights Series (MAPS)

11 Esquire Rd; Norwalk, CT 06851-2206; (203) 847-4124
Muriel Nussbaum and Ken Parker, *Artistic Directors*

**Open to:** playwrights. **Description:** 6 new plays a year each given 3 staged readings with professional director and actors, followed by audience discussion and critique, as part of developmental series presented at small studio theatre in Greenwich, CT. **Financial arrangement:** free. **Guidelines:** unproduced play; write for guidelines. **Application procedure:** script only. **Deadline:** ongoing.

## Merely Players

49 Murray St, #1; New York, NY 10007; (212) 349-0369
Monica M. Hayes, *Artistic Director*

**Open to:** playwrights. **Description:** nonprofit theatre organization with a membership of more than 65 actors, directors and writers develops new scripts through Directors Lab, bimonthly readings and critiques, Second Step staged readings and full productions. **Financial arrangement:** members pay annual dues of $80; initial free participation for playwright not yet enrolled as member. **Guidelines:** playwrights willing to participate in development of their plays may submit scripts; playwright who has had at least 1 full-length script developed through the group's process may be invited to become a member. **Application procedure:** script only. **Deadline:** ongoing.

## MIDWEST RADIO THEATRE WORKSHOP
KOPN Radio; 915 East Broadway; Columbia, MO 65201; (314) 874-5676
Steve Donofrio, *Director*

**Open to:** playwrights, radio writers. **Description:** annual program of 6-day radio-theatre workshops for writers, actors, directors and sound designers; Live Performance Workshop: 55 participants of all disciplines take workshops in production, direction, acting, writing and engineering; commissioned plays or scripts selected through MRTW Script Contest (see Prizes) produced for radio broadcast and live performance with audience; biennial Writers' Workshop: for approximately 16 writers. **Financial arrangement:** $200–300 fee for each workshop; some partial and full scholarships available based on financial need and experience, with priority given to women and people of color; possibility of free housing in community. **Application procedure:** completed registration form with deposit; write for information. **Deadline:** 1 Sep 1995 for scholarship applications; most workshops filled at least 1 month before starting date. **Dates:** Live Performance Workshop 16–21 Oct 1995; next Writers' Workshop spring 1997.

## MOUNT SEQUOYAH NEW PLAY RETREAT
c/o Department of Drama; Kimpel Hall 619; The University of Arkansas;
        Fayetteville, AR 72701; (501) 575-2953
Roger Gross, *Director*

**Open to:** playwrights. **Description:** 3-week developmental workshop for 6 playwrights; personal writing time combined with workshop sessions in which plays are developed with participating directors and resident acting company under supervision of retreat's staff of directors and produced playwrights; each play receives public staged reading. **Financial arrangement:** workshop free; playwright pays travel; fellowships cover room and board. **Application procedure:** previously completed one-act or full-length play; draft or partial draft of play to be worked on at retreat, resume, and names and phone numbers of 3 theatre professionals who have worked with applicant. **Deadline:** 1 Feb 1996. **Notification:** 1 Apr 1996. **Dates:** 19 May–9 Jun 1996.

## MULTICULTURAL THEATRE WORKS
The Group: Seattle's MultiCultural Theatre; 305 Harrison St; Seattle, WA 98109;
        (206) 441-9480
Talvin Wilks, *Literary Manager*

**Open to:** playwrights. **Description:** 1–3 playwrights a year each offered 2-week residency, during which script is developed; possible public workshop production. **Financial arrangement:** stipend, travel, housing. **Guidelines:** full-length play, translation, adaptation or play for young audiences that has not been fully produced by Equity company; play dealing with contemporary social, political and/or cultural issues relevant to the world community. **Application procedure:** synopsis, dialogue sample, resume, letter of inquiry and SASE for response. **Deadline:** ongoing. **Notification:** 4–6 weeks; 4–6 months if script is requested.

## MUSICAL THEATRE WORKS

440 Lafayette St; New York, NY 10003; (212) 677-0040
Anthony J. Stimac, *Artistic Director*

**Open to:** composers, librettists, lyricists. **Description:** new composers, librettists and lyricists work with established musical-theatre professionals to develop projects through meetings, informal readings, staged readings and full Off Broadway productions. **Financial arrangement:** free. **Guidelines:** completed unproduced work. **Application procedure:** script and cassette of music. **Deadline:** ongoing.

## NATIONAL MUSIC THEATER CONFERENCE

O'Neill Theater Center; 234 West 44th St, Suite 901; New York, NY 10036-3909;
(212) 382-2790
Paulette Haupt, *Artistic Director*
Suzanne Munkelt, *Administrator*

**Open to:** composers, librettists, lyricists. **Description:** development period of 2–4 weeks at O'Neill Center, Waterford, CT for new music-theatre works of all genres, traditional and nontraditional; some works developed privately, others presented as staged readings. **Financial arrangement:** stipend, round-trip travel from NYC, room and board. **Guidelines:** U.S. citizen; unproduced work; adaptations acceptable if rights have been obtained. **Application procedure:** send SASE for guidelines and application form after 15 Sep 1995. **Deadline:** 1 Feb 1996; no submission before 1 Nov 1995. **Dates:** Aug 1996.

## NATIONAL MUSIC THEATER NETWORK

1697 Broadway, Suite 902; New York, NY 10019
Timothy Jerome, *President*

**Open to:** composers, librettists, lyricists. **Description:** national screening of submitted musical theatre works; written evaluations sent to all writers; descriptive listings of recommended works published in catalogue distributed to producers/ theatres and 12 of these given staged readings in annual "Broadway Dozen," a showcase for potential producers. **Financial arrangement:** free. **Guidelines:** completed work with original music which has not received a major production. **Application procedure:** completed application and $45 fee; write for details. **Deadline:** ongoing.

## NATIONAL PLAYWRIGHTS CONFERENCE

O'Neill Theater Center; 234 West 44th St, Suite 901; New York, NY 10036-3909;
(212) 382-2790
Lloyd Richards, *Artistic Director*

**Open to:** playwrights, screenwriters, television writers. **Description:** 4-week conference at O'Neill Center, Waterford, CT; 9–12 plays developed and presented as staged readings; 1–3 screenplays/teleplays developed and read; preconference weekend for initial reading and planning. **Financial arrangement:** stipend, travel, room and board. **Guidelines:** U.S. citizen or resident; unoptioned and unproduced work; no adaptations or translations. **Application procedure:** send SASE for guidelines after 15 Sep 1995. **Deadline:** 1 Dec 1995. **Notification:** Apr 1996. **Dates:** preconference weekend TBA; conference Jul 1996.

## THE NEW HARMONY PROJECT CONFERENCE/LABORATORY
613 North East St; Indianapolis, IN 46202; (317) 464-9405
Jeffrey L. Sparks, *Executive Director*
Andrew Tsao, *Artistic Director*

**Open to:** playwrights, composers, librettists, screenwriters, television writers. **Description:** 4–6 scripts given up to 2 weeks of intensive development with professional community of directors, actors, producers, dramaturgs and musical directors. **Financial arrangement:** stipend of $100–200, depending on length of stay; travel, room and board. **Guidelines:** narrative works that "emphasize the dignity of the human spirit and the worth of the human experience." **Application procedure:** 10-page writing sample, project proposal and statement of artistic purpose. **Deadline:** 15 Nov 1995. **Notification:** 15 Mar 1996. **Dates:** 18 May–5 Jun 1996.

## NEW STAGES MUSICAL WORKSHOP PROGRAM
NEW STAGES Musical Arts; 270 West 17th St, #17C; New York, NY 10011
Joe Miloscia, *Artistic Director*

**Open to:** composers, librettists, lyricists. **Description:** up to 5 musicals each developed with resident company in workshop of 6–8 weeks, culminating in public reading or workshop production. **Financial arrangement:** varies with level of production. **Guidelines:** U.S. citizen or resident who has not received significant recognition in the musical theatre field; unpublished original work or adaptation (adapter must obtain rights for work not in public domain); unfinished work eligible if writer(s) can submit 80% of book and songs plus detailed outline of unwritten scenes; 2-submission limit. **Submission procedure:** project synopsis, latest draft of libretto, cassette of songs (do not submit score), list of any previous productions of work, and resumes of composer, librettist and lyricist. **Deadline:** ongoing.

## NEW VOICES FOR A NEW AMERICA
Arena Stage; 6th & Maine Ave, SW; Washington, DC 20024; (202) 554-9066
Cathy Madison, *Literary Manager*

**Open to:** playwrights. **Description:** 4-part program that includes PlayQuest: 3 plays each given 4 weeks of rehearsal in text-intensive workshop with playwright in residence, culminating in a mini-season of minimally staged public performances; commissioning program; full production of 1 new play a year in Old Vat Room and 1 in Fichandler Stage or Kreeger Theater (see theatre's entry in Production). **Financial arrangement:** varies. **Guidelines:** unproduced full-length play, translation, adaptation or musical; special interest in works for a multicultural company and works by writers of color. **Submission procedure:** synopsis, 10-page dialogue sample and letter of inquiry; participation in commissioning program by invitation only. **Deadline:** ongoing (early summer best time to submit). **Notification:** 3 months; 5 months to respond to script, if requested.

## NEW VOICES PLAY DEVELOPMENT PROGRAM

Plowshares Theatre Company; Fisher Building Station; Box 11399;
    Detroit, MI 48211; (810) 353-5591
Gary Anderson, *Artistic Director*

**Open to:** playwrights, translators. **Description:** up to 6 plays-in-progress given 2 weeks of rehearsal with professional company of actors, directors and dramaturgs, culminating in 2 staged readings followed by audience discussion; program provides marketing assistance following development; possible future full production. **Financial arrangement:** free; some travel stipends available. **Guidelines:** African-American playwright; unproduced play addressing the African-American experience. **Application procedure:** completed application, synopsis and resume. **Deadline:** 30 Oct 1995. **Notification date:** Mar 1996. **Dates:** 11–28 Jul 1996.

## NEW YORK FOUNDATION FOR THE ARTS
## ARTISTS' NEW WORKS

155 Ave of the Americas, 14th Floor; New York, NY 10013-1507;
    (212) 366-6900
Lynda A. Hansen, *Director*

**Open to:** playwrights, translators, composers, librettists, lyricists, screenwriters, radio and television writers. **Description:** program supports development, production and distribution of creative new projects by individual artists, both emerging talents and established professionals, with strong emphasis on independent film and video but also including radio, literature, performance art, theatre, music, dance and visual arts; as sponsoring organization for nonprofit status, NYFA provides fiscal management assistance and proposal reviews with focus on fundraising counsel; program does not offer grants. **Financial arrangement:** as a service fee, NYFA retains 8% of grants and contributions it receives on behalf of a project; $50 contract fee payable on signing. **Guidelines:** majority of sponsored artists located in NY metropolitan area; solid project proposal with realistic budget (most selected projects budgeted at not less than $25,000); selection based on artistic excellence, uniqueness and fundability of project, and on artist's previous work and proven ability to complete proposed work. **Application procedure:** write for application form and further information. **Deadline:** 13 Oct 1995; mid-Jan 1996, mid-Apr 1996, mid-Jul 1996 (exact dates TBA). **Notification:** 3 months.

## NEWGATE THEATRE NEW PLAY DEVELOPMENT

134 Mathewson St; Providence, RI 02906
Julia Steiny, *Literary Manager*

**Open to:** playwrights. **Description:** organization providing year-round developmental services; bimonthly meetings for local playwrights; 4–8 scripts each season receive staged reading, in some cases leading to workshop production; at least 1 play receives mainstage production; 2–6 plays receive workshop productions in annual Short Play Festival. **Financial arrangement:** free; small stipend and possible housing for main stage production. **Guidelines:** resident of southern New England. **Application procedure:** script, resume and SASE for response. **Deadline:** 1 Feb 1996 for reading; 1 Jun 1996 for festival. **Dates:** Short Play Festival Sep 1996.

## THE NEXT STAGE

The Cleveland Play House; Box 1989; Cleveland, OH 44106-0189;
      (216) 795-7010
Scott Kanoff, *Director of Playwrights Unit/Resident Dramaturg*
Coleen Hubbard, *Director of New Play Development*

**Open to:** playwrights. **Description:** 3-tier developmental program: Stage One: The Playwrights Unit, ongoing playwrights' workshop; new plays developed through discussion and readings; members allowed to attend rehearsals, performances and all other theatre programming. Stage Two: in Oct, 4–8 plays each given 1 week of rehearsal with Play House company, culminating in public reading. Stage Three: at least 1 play developed in Stages One or Two offered main stage production. **Financial arrangement:** for Stage One: free; possible small stipend; for Stage Two: stipend, transportation and housing; for Stage Three: royalties, transportation and housing. **Guidelines:** for Stage One, resident of Northern Ohio area, produced or unproduced full-length play; for Stage Two, unproduced full-length play. **Application procedure:** script only. **Deadline:** for Stage One, submit 1–30 Apr only; for Stage Two, submit 15 May–30 Jun only.

## PADUA HILLS PLAYWRIGHTS' WORKSHOP/FESTIVAL

Box 461450; Los Angeles, CA 90046; (213) 650-6401
Murray Mednick, *Founder/Artistic Director*

**Open to:** playwrights. **Description:** 7-week program combines development of site-specific, environmental theatre works by professional playwrights with student workshop taught by invited playwrights and Padua Hills staff, and culminates in outdoor theatre festival open to the public. **Financial arrangement:** professional playwright receives $500 for production and/or $500 teaching honorarium, plus travel and housing; student playwright pays $1000 workshop fee. **Guidelines:** festival produces an eclectic range of work but looks for professional playwrights who can fit into a collegial creative atmosphere and are not exclusively focused on own work and career; student playwrights write for information. **Application procedure:** professional playwright send resume, letter of inquiry and letter of recommendation from theatre professional familiar with festival's work; student playwright send small representative work sample (monologue, scene, short story or poetry), letter of intention and SASE for response. **Deadline:** ongoing for professional playwrights; 20 May 1996 for students. **Dates:** late Jun–mid-Aug 1996.

## PKE THEATRE
Patchett Kaufman Entertainment; 8621 Hayden Pl; Culver City, CA 90232
Dan Lauria, *Artistic Director*

**Open to:** playwrights. **Description:** 1 play per week given staged reading for audience including theatre, film and TV professionals. **Financial arrangement:** free. **Guidelines:** unproduced play. **Application procedure:** script only. **Deadline:** ongoing.

## PLAYFORMERS
20 Waterside Plaza, Apt 11G; New York, NY 10010; (212) 213-9835
John Fritz, *Executive Director*

**Open to:** playwrights. **Description:** playwrights' support group meeting 1 or 2 times a month Sep–Jun for readings of works-in-progress and critiques; selected plays receive staged readings with director and professional actors. **Financial arrangement:** $15 initiation fee on acceptance; $135 annual dues. **Guidelines:** playwright invited to attend meetings as guest before applying for membership. **Application procedure:** letter of recommendation from theatre professional, sample script and resume. **Deadline:** ongoing.

## PLAYLABS
The Playwrights' Center; 2301 Franklin Ave East; Minneapolis, MN 55406-1099; (612) 332-7481
Elissa Adams, *Artistic Director*

**Open to:** playwrights, writer-performers. **Description:** 4–8 new works given 2 weeks of development with playwright's choice of professional director, dramaturg and Twin Cities actors, culminating in staged reading followed by audience discussion. **Financial arrangement:** travel, housing and per diem. **Guidelines:** U.S. citizen or permanent resident; unproduced, unpublished play, solo performance piece or mixed-media piece; full-length works preferred; writer must be available to attend entire conference and preconference weekend. **Application procedure:** completed application and script; send SASE for application after 16 Oct 1995. **Deadline:** 15 Dec 1995. **Notification:** 1 May 1996. **Dates:** preconference weekend May/June 1996 (exact dates TBA); conference 28 Jul–11 Aug 1996.

## PLAYS-IN-PROGRESS FESTIVALS OF NEW WORKS
615 4th St; Eureka, CA 95501; (707) 443-3724
Susan Bigelow-Marsh, *Executive Director*

**Open to:** playwrights. **Description:** 5 scripts each given full production and 8–10 scripts each given 3–4 weeks of development with actors and directors, culminating in staged reading followed by discussion, in spring or fall festival of new work; ongoing development and Monday night reading series for local writers. **Financial arrangement:** negotiable; travel, housing. **Guidelines:** primarily CA writers; 1 out-of-state writer selected for each festival; unproduced, unpublished play. **Application procedure:** script with resume. **Deadline:** 1 Mar 1995; 1 Aug 1995. **Dates:** Apr 1995; Oct 1995.

## PLAYWORKS FESTIVAL

Theatre Department; Fox Fine Arts Center; University of Texas at El Paso;
El Paso, TX 79968-0549; (915) 747-5146, -7854
Michael Wright, *Head of Playwriting and Directing*

**Open to:** playwrights. **Description:** 3 playwrights each given 3-week residencies to write new play, culminating in public presentation of work-in-progress followed by critique; possible future full production. **Financial arrangement:** stipend TBA (amount contingent on funding); travel, room and board. **Guidelines:** student playwright enrolled in college or university in AR, AZ, LA, NM, NV, OK or TX; submissions from Latino and Native American playwrights especially encouraged. **Submission procedure:** work sample, proposal for script to be developed in residence and names of at least two faculty references. **Deadline:** 31 Jan 1996. **Notification:** 1 Apr 1996. **Dates:** Jun 1996.

## PLAYWRIGHTS FORUM

Box 11488; Washington, DC 20008-0688; (301) 816-0569
Ernest Joselovitz, *President*

**Open to:** playwrights. **Description:** ongoing developmental program including 3-tier range of membership options: Forum 2, professional playwriting groups meeting biweekly; Forum 1, workshop program offering three 3-month sessions a year for apprentice playwrights; and Associate membership offering participation in many of Forum's auxiliary programs but not in workshops; depending on type of membership, members variously eligible for in-house and public readings, Musical Theatre Wing, special classes including Rewrites and screenwriting, production observerships, free theatre tickets, annual conference, organization's newsletter and handbook, and new published series of members' scripts. **Financial arrangement:** for Forum 2, $90 every 4 months; for Forum 1, $90 per 15-week session; Associate membership $25 a year. **Guidelines:** resident of mid-Atlantic area only; for Forum 2, prefers produced playwright or former Forum 1 participant, willing to make long-term commitment; send SASE for further information. **Application procedure:** for Forum 2, script and bio; for Forum 1, send SASE or call for information; for Associate membership, send annual fee. **Deadline:** for Forum 2, ongoing; for Forum 1, 1 Sep 1995, 1 Jan 1996, 1 May 1996. **Notification:** 6 weeks.

## PLAYWRIGHTS' PLATFORM

164 Brayton Rd; Boston, MA 02135; (617) 254-4482
Beverly Creasey, *President*

**Open to:** playwrights. **Description:** ongoing developmental program including weekly workshop held at Massachusetts College of Art, staged readings, summer festival of full productions, dramaturgical and referral services. **Financial arrangement:** playwright receives percentage of gate for festival productions;

participants encouraged to become members of organization ($15 annual dues). **Guidelines:** MA resident only; unpublished, unproduced play; write for membership information. **Application procedure:** letter of inquiry only. **Deadline:** ongoing.

## PLAYWRIGHTS' PREVIEW PRODUCTIONS
17 East 47th St; New York, NY 10017; (212) 289-2168
Frances Hill, *Artistic Director*
Pamela Faith Jackson, *Literary Associate*

**Open to:** playwrights. **Description:** 8–12 plays receive staged readings, some chosen for full production or further development; see also Urban Stages Award and Emerging Playwright Award in Prizes. **Financial arrangement:** free. **Guidelines:** play not produced in NY metropolitan area. **Application procedure:** script, production history, bio and SASE for response. **Deadline:** ongoing; best submission times Jul, Aug, Dec. **Dates:** Oct–Nov, Feb–Mar.

## THE PLAYWRIGHTS THEATRE OF LOS ANGELES
2522 Veteran Ave; Los Angeles, CA 90064
Richard Polak, *Artistic Director*

**Open to:** playwrights, composers (only if involved in collaborating on musical-theatre work), librettists, lyricists. **Description:** ongoing membership-based developmental workshop; activities include bimonthly readings of members' works, showcase productions, and full productions of excerpts from members' works to raise money for charitable causes. **Financial arrangement:** free. **Guidelines:** serious theatre writer who has completed at least 2 full-length works; work must be suitable for commercial theatre; no experimental works or teleplays. **Application procedure:** synopsis and letter of inquiry. **Deadline:** ongoing.

## PLAYWRIGHTS THEATRE OF NEW JERSEY
## NEW PLAY DEVELOPMENT PROGRAM
33 Green Village Rd; Madison, NJ 07940; (201) 514-1787
Kate McAteer, *Literary Associate*

**Open to:** playwrights. **Description:** new plays developed through sit-down readings, staged readings and productions; liaison with other producing theatres provided. **Financial arrangement:** playwright receives royalty. **Guidelines:** unproduced play by American playwright; write for brochure. **Application procedure:** script, 1-page synopsis and developmental history, if any; resume and SASP for acknowledgment of receipt. **Deadline:** submit 1 Sep–30 Apr only.

## PLAYWRIGHTS WEEK
The Lark Theatre Company; 395 Riverside Dr, Suite 12B;
    New York, NY 10025; (212) 727-3626
*Marjorie Wampole*, Literary Manager

**Open to:** playwrights. **Description:** 8 plays-in-progress given up to 15 hours of rehearsal, culminating in staged reading followed by optional audience discussion or critique; at least 1 script receives subsequent full production. **Financial arrangement:** free; possible travel and housing. **Application procedure:** script only. **Deadline:** 1 Dec 1995. **Notification date:** 1 Mar 1996. **Dates:** 9–13 May 1996.

### PRIMARY STAGES COMPANY

584 Ninth Ave; New York, NY 10036; (212) 333-7471
Andrew Leynse, *Literary Manager*

**Open to:** playwrights. **Description:** organization committed to developing new plays through readings and full productions. **Financial arrangement:** varies. **Guidelines:** play or musical, not produced in New York City, by American playwright. **Application procedure:** script or synopsis, 10-page dialogue sample, letter of inquiry and SASE for response. **Deadline:** ongoing.

### PUERTO RICAN TRAVELING THEATRE
### PLAYWRIGHTS' WORKSHOP

141 West 94th St; New York, NY 10025; (212) 354-1293
Allen Davis III, *Director*

**Open to:** playwrights. **Description:** 3 units, 1 for professional playwrights, 2 for beginners; weekly meetings; spring staged reading series; City "In Sight" showcase production series. **Financial arrangement:** free. **Guidelines:** resident of New York City area; Latino or other minority playwright or playwright interested in multicultural theatre. **Application procedure:** for professional unit, submit full-length play; beginners contact director. **Deadline:** 30 Sep 1995. **Notification:** within 2 weeks. **Dates:** Oct 1995–Jul 1996.

### RED OCTOPUS THEATRE COMPANY
### ORIGINAL SCRIPTS WORKSHOP

Box 1403; Newport, OR 97365
Bo Harrington, *Executive Committee*

**Open to:** playwrights. **Description:** short plays or excerpts from plays developed over period of 3 weeks in collaboration with director and actors, culminating in staged reading. **Financial arrangement:** free housing. **Guidelines:** unproduced, unpublished work-in-progress, approximately 30 minutes long; cast limit of 6; 1 submission; previous submissions ineligible. **Application procedure:** script only; playwright's name on cover page only (not on script). **Deadline:** 1 Dec 1995. **Notification:** 1 Apr 1996. **Dates:** spring 1996.

### REMEMBRANCE THROUGH THE PERFORMING ARTS
### NEW PLAY DEVELOPMENT

3300 Bee Caves Rd, Suite 650; Austin, TX 78746; (512) 465-8084
Marla Macdonald, *Director of New Play Development*

**Open to:** playwrights. **Description:** 3-phase, 18-month developmental process: 2

6-week developmental workshops, each for 8 playwrights, culminating in public staged readings, followed by discussions; 4 plays subsequently selected for production in works-in-progress series with playwright in residence for last 2 weeks of rehearsal and 1st week of performances; 2 of these plays subsequently given world-premiere full productions in cooperation with professional theatre in Seattle or New York City. **Financial arrangement:** free. **Guidelines:** resident of central TX; full-length play that has not received Equity production; currently also accepting one-acts with teenage cast of characters for "youth-at-risk" project. **Application procedure:** script and resume. **Deadline:** 1 Apr 1996; no submission before 1 Jul 1995. **Notification:** 1 May 1996.

## THE RICHARD RODGERS AWARDS
American Academy of Arts and Letters; 633 West 155th St;
    New York, NY 10032-7599; (212) 368-5900
Kathryn Talalay, *Program Assistant*

**Open to:** playwrights, composers, librettists, lyricists. **Description:** 1 or more works a year given full production, studio/lab production or staged reading by nonprofit theatre in New York City; writer(s) participate in rehearsal process. **Financial arrangement:** free. **Guidelines:** U.S. citizen or permanent resident; new work by writer/composer not already established in musical theatre; innovative, experimental works encouraged; 1 submission; previous submissions ineligible. **Application procedure:** send SASE for application and information. **Deadline:** 1 Nov 1995. **Notification:** Mar 1995.

## THE SCHOOLHOUSE
Owens Rd; Croton Falls, NY 10519; (914) 234-7232
Douglas Michael, *Literary Manager*

**Open to:** playwrights. **Description:** about 6 plays a year receive development with director and actors, culminating in public reading and possible full production; ongoing weekly writer's group. **Financial arrangement:** small fee to help offset costs. **Guidelines:** resident of Westchester or Putnam counties, NY or Fairfield County, CT, who can participate in program; prefers full-length plays. **Application procedure:** script or excerpt (at least 10 pages) and letter of inquiry. **Deadline:** ongoing. **Notification:** 1 month.

## THE SCRIPTEASERS
3404 Hawk St; San Diego, CA 92103-3862; (619) 295-4040
Jonathan Dunn-Rankin, *Corresponding Secretary*

**Open to:** playwrights, screenwriters, television writers. **Description:** writers, directors and actors meet every other Friday evening in private home for cold readings of new scripts, followed by period of constructive criticism and light refreshments; 1 or 2 rehearsed staged readings a year presented at local theatres as showcases. **Financial arrangement:** donations of $1 accepted at each reading. **Guidelines:** membership by invitation only; guest writer must attend at least 2 readings before submitting script; unproduced script by new or established writer who is resident of San Diego County; write or call for guidelines. **Submission procedure:** see guidelines. **Deadline:** ongoing.

### SHENANDOAH INTERNATIONAL PLAYWRIGHTS RETREAT
ShenanArts; Rt 5, Box 167-F; Staunton, VA 24401; (540) 248-1868
Robert Graham Small, *Director*
Kathleen Tosco, *Managing Director*

**Open to:** playwrights, screenwriters. **Description:** 3-week retreat for 4–6 American writers and 6 international writers at Pennyroyal farm in Shenandoah Valley; program geared to facilitate major rewrite or new draft of existing script; personal writing balanced by workshops and staged readings with professional company of dramaturgs, directors and actors. **Financial arrangement:** fellowships cover costs. **Guidelines:** competitive admission based on submitted work. **Application procedure:** 2 copies of completed draft of script to be worked on at retreat; personal statement of applicant's background as a writer; SASP for acknowledgment of receipt; call or write for guidelines. **Deadline:** 1 Mar 1996. **Notification:** after Jun 10 1996. **Dates:** 4–25 Aug 1996.

### SOUTHERN APPALACHIAN PLAYWRIGHTS' CONFERENCE
Southern Appalachian Repertory Theatre; Box 620; Mars Hill, NC 28754-0620; (704) 689-1384
Gaynelle M. Caldwell, Jr., *Assistant Managing Director*

**Open to:** playwrights. **Description:** up to 5 writers selected to participate in annual 3-day conference at which 1 work by each writer is given informal reading and critiqued by panel of theatre professionals; 1 work selected for production as part of summer 1997 season. **Financial arrangement:** room and board; writer of work selected for production receives $500 honorarium. **Guidelines:** unproduced, unpublished play. **Application procedure:** script with cast list and synopsis; resume. **Deadline:** 1 Oct 1995. **Dates:** Jan 1996.

### SUMMERNITE, NEW PLAY STUDIO
Stevens Bldg; Northern Illinois University; DeKalb, IL 60115-2854; (815) 753-8258
Gene Terruso, *Artistic Director*

**Open to:** playwrights. **Description:** up to 10 plays receive staged readings during 15-week program; 2 plays chosen for subsequent full production. **Financial arrangement:** free; royalties for plays chosen for production. **Guidelines:** full-length play or one-act not previously produced in Chicago area. **Application procedure:** synopsis. **Deadline:** 31 Aug 1996. **Notification date:** May 1997. **Dates:** Feb–May 1997.

## THE SUNDANCE INSTITUTE
## INDEPENDENT FEATURE FILM PROGRAM
225 Santa Monica Blvd, 8th Floor; Santa Monica, CA 90401; (310) 394-4662

**Open to:** playwrights, screenwriters, filmmaking teams (e.g., writer/director, writer/producer). **Description:** program includes 5-day Screenwriters Labs each Jan and Jun offering participants one-on-one problem-solving sessions with professional screenwriters; 3-week Filmmakers Lab in Jun in which projects are explored through work with directors, writers, actors, cinematographers, producers, designers, editors and other resource personnel; network/advisory service offers practical and creative assistance to selected projects. **Financial arrangement:** travel, room and board for at least 1 writer/filmmaker per project; possible room and board for additional members of team. **Guidelines:** "compelling, original narrative scripts (they can be based on a true story or be adaptations of plays, novels, short stories, etc.) which represent the unique vision of the writer and/or director"; special interest in supporting new talent and artists in transition (e.g., theatre artist who wants to work in film, writer who wants to direct); send SASE for guidelines. **Submission procedure:** completed application, cover letter, first 5 pages of screenplay, synopsis, bios of project participants and $25 fee; after review process, applicants who pass 1st round of selection will be asked to send full screenplay. **Deadline:** Nov 1995 for Jun 1996 Screenwriters Lab and Filmmakers Lab; Jun 1996 for Jan 1997 Screenwriters Lab (exact dates TBA).

## THE SUNDANCE PLAYWRIGHTS LABORATORY
Box 16450; Salt Lake City, UT 84116; (801) 328-3456
David Kirk Chambers, *Managing Director*

**Open to:** playwrights. **Description:** 10–18 days of intensive developmental workshops and readings of 8–12 scripts; each assigned cast, director and dramaturg. **Financial arrangement:** travel, room and board. **Guidelines:** unproduced play for young or adult audiences; playwright and script must be nominated by nonprofit theatre. **Application procedure:** letter of nomination from theatre, script and playwright's resume. **Deadline:** 15 Dec 1995. **Notification:** Apr 1996. **Dates:** Jul 1996.

## THE TEN-MINUTE MUSICALS PROJECT
Box 461194; West Hollywood, CA 90046; (213) 656-8751
Michael Koppy, *Producer*

**Open to:** composers, librettists, lyricists. **Description:** up to 10 brief pieces selected during annual cycle for possible inclusion in full-length anthology-musicals to be produced at Equity theatres in U.S. and Canada; occasionally some pieces workshopped using professional actors and director. **Financial arrangement:** $250 royalty advance with equal share of licensing royalties when produced. **Guidelines:** complete work with a definite beginning, middle and end, 8–14 minutes long, in any musical style or genre; adaptations of strongly structured material in the public domain, or for which rights have been obtained, are encouraged; cast of 2–9, prefers 6–9; write for guidelines. **Application procedure:** script, lead sheets and cassette of sung material. **Deadline:** 31 Aug 1996. **Notification:** 2 months.

## TEXAS PLAYWRIGHTS FESTIVAL

Stages Repertory Theatre; 3201 Allen Pkwy, #101; Houston, TX 77019;
(713) 527-0240
Beth Sanford, *Associate Artistic Director*

**Open to:** playwrights. **Description:** up to 5 plays chosen for development with
dramaturg, director and actors over period of approximately 30 days, culminating
in staged readings. **Financial arrangement:** small stipend, contingent on funding.
**Guidelines:** TX native or resident or non-TX playwright writing on TX theme;
play not produced professionally; prefers small cast. **Application procedure:** script
only. **Deadline:** 31 Jan 1996. **Notification:** May 1996. **Dates:** Jun 1996.

## THEATRE ARTISTS WORKSHOP OF WESTPORT

17 Morningside Dr S; Westport, CT 06880; (203) 227-5836
*Admissions Committee*

**Open to:** playwrights, composers, librettists, lyricists. **Description:** laboratory where
professional writers can exercise their craft and develop projects in collaboration
with member directors, actors and allied theatre artists; ongoing workshop
meetings; work presented for peer evaluation. **Financial arrangement:** annual
membership dues and contributions of $220; $50 initiation fee. **Guidelines:**
serious, theatre-oriented writer of professional caliber. **Application procedure:**
completed application and 3 copies of script. **Deadline:** ongoing.

## UNIVERSITY OF ALABAMA NEW PLAYWRIGHTS' PROGRAM

Department of Theatre and Dance; University of Alabama; Box 870239;
Tuscaloosa, AL 35487-0239; (205) 348-9032
Paul C. Castagno, *Director and Dramaturg*

**Open to:** playwrights, composers, librettists, lyricists. **Description:** opportunity for
writer to develop unproduced script or to pursue further development of
produced work, culminating in full production; writer may visit campus several
times during rehearsal process and required to offer limited playwriting
workshops during visit(s); recent MFA playwrights encouraged to apply;
production considered for entry in the Kennedy Center American College
Theater Festival (see Prizes). **Financial arrangement:** substantial stipend, travel
and expenses. **Guidelines:** writer with some previous experience and script that
has had some development; can consider works with large casts and complex
production demands. **Application procedure:** script or synopsis and cover letter.
**Deadline:** ongoing. **Notification:** 6 months. **Dates:** fall–spring. **Other programs:**
department will also consider writers' proposals for workshops with its playwriting
and acting students.

## VENTURE'S PLAYWRIGHT CONNECTION

Venture Theatre; 43 South 3rd St; Philadelphia, PA 19106; (215) 923-2766
H. German Wilson, *Artistic Director*

### National Playwright Residencies

**Open to:** playwrights. **Description:** 1 playwright brought in for intensive week of script development hosted by Philadelphia's Balch Institute of Ethnic Studies, culminating in staged reading; possible future full production by Venture Theatre. **Financial arrangement:** $1000 award, travel and housing. **Guidelines:** playwright who has had at least 1 professional full production; full-length play grounded within a particular culture or ethnic group or that explores dynamics between such groups, and that has not received more than 2 previous workshops and/or 1 professional or other production; experienced playwrights, especially playwrights of color, encouraged to apply; write for guidelines. **Application procedure:** completed application and script. **Deadline:** 1 Jul 1996. **Dates:** exact dates TBA (May/Jun in 1995).

### Venture to Write

**Open to:** playwrights. **Description:** emerging and experienced playwrights meet biweekly in self-directed membership program to develop their scripts through group readings and discussions; critiques by resident dramaturgs and playwrights, group theatre trips, guest speakers and occasional script-in-hand readings with professional actors. **Financial arrangement:** member playwright pays dues of $75 a year. **Guidelines:** resident of Philadelphia or Delaware valley. **Application procedure:** completed application and script. **Deadline:** ongoing.

## VOICE AND VISION
## RETREAT FOR WOMEN THEATRE ARTISTS

Box 021529; Brooklyn, NY 11202; (212) 502-1151
Marya Mazor and Jean Wagner, *Artistic Directors*

**Open to:** playwrights, translators, composers, librettists, lyricists. **Description:** up to 5 works-in-progress given 1 week of rehearsal and workshop performance or staged reading at Smith College in Northampton, MA; projects chosen to reflect broad range of aesthetics, ethnic backgrounds, artistic experiences and age groups. **Financial arrangement:** travel, housing, some meals. **Guidelines:** project initiator must be a woman; emerging or established artist; submission of dance-theatre, multimedia and performance-art projects encouraged. **Application procedure:** script or project description; resumes of project's main participants; statement of goals to be accomplished during retreat, number of project participants, whether additional participants will be needed (director, actors, etc.) and any special equipment needs. **Deadline:** 15 Jan 1996 for retreat. **Dates:** summer 1996. **Other programs:** year-round developmental services in New York City; *deadline:* ongoing.

## THE WATERFRONT ENSEMBLE
Box 1486; Hoboken, NJ 07030
*Artistic Director*

**Open to:** playwrights, translators. **Description:** actors, directors and writers meet weekly to develop plays through supportive criticism and improvisation; 5–10 public staged readings and 1–2 productions a year of selected plays; showcase readings of selected plays for possible production by outside companies; organization also sponsors playwrights for grants, fellowships, awards and festivals. **Financial arrangement:** annual membership dues of $75; $2 a meeting for guests. **Guidelines:** NJ or NY resident; unproduced material in need of further development; write for additional information. **Submission procedure:** script and resume. **Deadline:** ongoing. **Notification:** 2 months.

## WHETSTONE THEATRE COMPANY PLAYWRIGHTS PROGRAM
Box 1580; Brattleboro, VT 05302; (802) 257-2600
Bill Hickok, *Artistic Director*

**Open to:** playwrights, translators. **Description:** selected plays, translations and adaptations enter program of public workshop sessions, staged readings and discussions aimed at assisting development of writer's work, providing new opportunities for the company and informing audience about the playwriting process; possibility of selection for full production (1 new play produced each season). **Financial arrangement:** stipend of $100–500, depending on project; possible travel and housing. **Guidelines:** play not produced professionally; prefers small cast and simple technical requirements. **Application procedure:** script and resume. **Deadline:** ongoing.

## WORDSMITHS
City of Los Angeles Cultural Affairs Dept/
    Performing Arts Division; Los Angeles Theatre Center;
    514 South Spring St; Los Angeles, CA 91030; (213) 485-2437
Ernest D. Dillihay, *Director, Performing Arts Division*

**Open to:** playwrights. **Description:** 10–12 playwrights chosen quarterly for 10–12 week developmental workshop offering script analysis and critique; 6–12 plays each year receive staged reading with professional director and actors; at least 3 plays chosen for full production. **Financial arrangement:** free; writers of work selected for production receive stipend. **Guidelines:** resident of Los Angeles area; unproduced full-length play or one-act. **Application procedure:** script with cover sheet listing title and playwright, synopsis and production history. **Deadline:** TBA (23 Jun in 1995). **Notification:** 2 weeks. **Dates:** year-round.

# Career Opportunities

- Agents
- Fellowships and Grants
- Emergency Funds
- State Arts Agencies
- Colonies and Residencies
- Membership and Service Organizations

# Agents

**I'm wondering whether or not I should have an agent. Where can I get information to help me decide?**

Write to the Association of Authors' Representatives at 10 Astor Pl, 3rd Floor; New York, NY 10003. Send a check or money order for $5 and a 55¢ SASE to receive the AAR's brochure describing the role of the literary agent and how to find an agent, and its membership list and canon of ethics. See Useful Publications for books you can consult on the subject. Ask fellow playwrights what they think.

**How do I select the names of appropriate agents to contact?**

All of the agents listed here represent playwrights. (In some cases, the name of the agency contains the name of the agent.) The Dramatists Guild also has a list of agents available to its members, and provides advice on relationships with agents (see Membership and Service Organizations). You may come across names that appear on none of these lists, but be wary, especially if someone tries to charge you a fee to read your script. Again, talk to other playwrights about their experiences. Look at copies of scripts for the names of agents representing specific playwrights. See what kinds of plays various agents handle in order to make an intelligent guess as to whether they would be interested in representing you and your work.

**How do I approach an agent?**

Do not telephone, do not drop in, do not send manuscripts. Write a brief letter describing your work and asking if the agent would like to see a script. Enclose your professional resume; it should show that you have had work produced or published and make clear that you look at writing as an ongoing career, not an occasional hobby. If you're a beginning writer who's just finished your first play, you'd probably do better to work on getting a production rather than an agent.

### ABE NEWBORN ASSOCIATES
1365 York Ave, #25G; New York, NY 10021; (212) 861-4635
Abe Newborn, Joyce Newborn, *Agents*

### THE AGENCY
1800 Ave of the Stars, Suite 400; Los Angeles, CA 90067; (310) 551-3000
Dino Carlaftes, Emile Gladstone, Nick Mechanic, Walter Morgan, James Scott, Michael Van Dyck, Jerome Zeitman, *Agents*

### AGENCY FOR THE PERFORMING ARTS
888 Seventh Ave, Suite 602; New York, NY 10106; (212) 582-1500
Ana Maria Allessi, *Agent*

### ANN ELMO AGENCY
60 East 42nd St; New York, NY 10165; (212) 661-2880
Letti Lee, *Agent*

### THE BARBARA HOGENSON AGENCY, INC.
19 West 44th St, Suite 1000; New York, NY 10036; (212) 730-7306

### BERMAN, BOALS & FLYNN
225 Lafayette St, Suite 1207; New York, NY 10012; (212) 966-0339
Lois Berman, Judy Boals, Jim Flynn, *Agents*

### BERTHA KLAUSNER INTERNATIONAL LITERARY AGENCY
71 Park Ave; New York, NY 10016; (212) 685-2642

### THE BETHEL AGENCY
360 West 53rd St, Suite BA; New York, NY 10019; (212) 664-0455
Lewis Chambers, *Agent*

### BRET ADAMS LTD.
448 West 44th St; New York, NY 10036; (212) 765-5630
Bret Adams, Mary Harden, *Agents*

## DON BUCHWALD & ASSOCIATES
10 East 44th St; New York, NY 10017; (212) 867-1200
Traci Ching Weinstein, *Agent*

## DORESE AGENCY LTD.
37965 Palo Verde Dr; Cathedral City, CA 92234; (619) 321-1115
Alyss Dorese, *Agent*

## THE DRAMATIC PUBLISHING COMPANY
311 Washington St; Box 129; Woodstock, IL 60098; (815) 338-7170
Susan Sergel, Julie Kunzie, Dana Wolworth (musicals), *Agents*

## ELISABETH MARTON AGENCY
1 Union Square, Room 612; New York, NY 10003-3303; (212) 255-1908
Tonda Marton, *Agent*

## FIFI OSCARD ASSOCIATES
24 West 40th St, 17th Floor; New York, NY 10018; (212) 764-1100
Carmen LaVia, Kevin McShane, Fifi Oscard, Bruce Ostler, *Agents*

## FLORA ROBERTS
157 West 57th St; New York, NY 10019; (212) 355-4165
Sarah Douglas, Flora Roberts, *Agents*

## FREIDA FISHBEIN, LTD.
2556 Hubbard St; Brooklyn, NY 11235; (212) 247-4398
Janice Fishbein, Douglas Michael, *Agents*

## THE GERSH AGENCY
130 West 42nd St; New York, NY 10036; (212) 997-1818
Jason Fogelson, David Guc, Scott Yoselow, *Agents*

## GRAHAM AGENCY
311 West 43rd St; New York, NY 10036; (212) 489-7730
Earl Graham, *Agent*

## HELEN MERRILL
435 West 23rd St, Suite 1A; New York, NY 10011; (212) 691-5326
Clyde Kuemmerle, Helen Merrill, *Agents*

## INTERNATIONAL CREATIVE MANAGEMENT
40 West 57th St; New York, NY 10019; (212) 556-5600
Bridget Aschenberg, Mitch Douglas, Brad Kalos, *Agents*

## THE JOYCE KETAY AGENCY
1501 Broadway, Suite 1910; New York, NY 10036; (212) 354-6825
Joyce P. Ketay, Carl Mulert, *Agents*

## THE KOPALOFF COMPANY
1800 Ave of the Stars, Suite 400; Los Angeles, CA 90067; (310) 551-3000
Don Kopaloff, *Agent*

## LANTZ-HARRIS LITERARY AGENCY
888 Seventh Ave, Suite 2500; New York, NY 10106; (212) 586-0200
Robert Lantz, *Agent*
156 Fifth Ave, Suite 617; New York, NY 10010; (212) 924-6269
Joy Harris, *Agent*
*In association with:* The Roberts Company; 10345 West Olympic Blvd,
Penthouse; Los Angeles, CA 90064; (310) 552-7800
Nancy Roberts, *Agent*

## MICHAEL IMISON PLAYWRIGHTS
28 Almeida St; London N1 1TD; England; 441-71-354-3174

## PARAMUSE ARTISTS ASSOCIATES
1414 Ave of the Americas; New York, NY 10019; (212) 758-5055
Shirley Bernstein, *Agent*

## THE PARNESS AGENCY
1424 4th St, Suite 404; Santa Monica, CA 90401; (310) 319-1664
Leslie Parness, *Agent*

## PEREGRINE WHITTLESEY AGENCY
345 East 80th St, #31F; New York, NY 10021; (212) 737-0153

## ROBERT A. FREEDMAN DRAMATIC AGENCY
1501 Broadway, Suite 2310; New York, NY 10036; (212) 840-5760
Robert A. Freedman, Selma Luttinger, *Agents*

## ROSENSTONE/WENDER
3 East 48th St, 4th Floor; New York, NY 10017; (212) 832-8330
Ronald Gwiazda, Howard Rosenstone, *Agents*

## SAMUEL FRENCH
45 West 25th St; New York, NY 10010-2751; (212) 206-8990
Lawrence Harbison, *Editor*

## SHUKAT COMPANY, LTD.
340 West 55th St, Suite 1A; New York, NY 10019; (212) 582-7614
Scott Shukat, Patricia McLaughlin, *Agents*

## STEPHEN PEVNER, INC.
248 West 73rd St, 2nd Floor; New York, NY 10023; (212) 496-0474

## THE SUSAN GURMAN AGENCY
865 West End Ave, #4B; New York, NY 10025; (212) 864-5243

## SUSAN SCHULMAN LITERARY AGENCY
454 West 44th St; New York, NY 10036; (212) 713-1633

## THE TANTLEFF OFFICE
375 Greenwich St, Suite 603; New York, NY 10013; (212) 941-3939
John B. Santoianni, Jack Tantleff, *Agents*

## WILLIAM MORRIS AGENCY
1325 Ave of the Americas; New York, NY 10019; (212) 586-5100
Peter Franklin, George Lane, Owen Laster, Biff Liff, Mary Meagher,
Gilbert Parker, Erica Silverman, *Agents*

## WRITERS & ARTISTS AGENCY
19 West 44th St, Suite 1000; New York, NY 10036; (212) 391-1112
William Craver, Peter Hagan, Scott Hudson, *Agents*

# Fellowships and Grants

**Can I apply directly to all the programs listed in this section?**

No. You will see that a number of the grant programs we list must be applied to by a producing or presenting organization. However, you should be aware that these programs exist so that you can bring them to the attention of organizations with which you have a working relationship. All or most of the funds disbursed directly benefit the individual artist since they go to cover commissioning fees, residencies and other expenses related to the creation of new works.

**How can I enhance my chances of winning an award?**

Start early. This is so important that we give full listings to the increasing number of awards offered in alternate years, even when the deadline falls outside the period this *Sourcebook* covers. Use the Submission Calendar in the back of this book to help you plan your campaign. In the case of all awards for which you can apply directly, write for guidelines and application forms months ahead. Study the guidelines carefully and follow them meticulously. Don't hesitate to ask for advice and assistance from the organization to which you are applying. Submit a well thought-out, excellently written, neatly typed application—and make sure it arrives in the organization's office by the deadline. (Never assume, without checking, that the deadline is the postmark date.) Apply for as many awards as you qualify for; once you have written the first grant proposal, you can often, with little additional work, adapt it to fit others' guidelines.

## THE ALFRED HODDER FELLOWSHIP
The Council of the Humanities; 122 East Pyne; Princeton University;
Princeton, NJ 08544-5264

Annual fellowship for writers and scholars, including playwrights and translators.
Next deadline for dramatic writers TBA.

## THE AMERICAN-SCANDINAVIAN FOUNDATION
725 Park Ave; New York, NY 10021; (212) 879-9779
*Exchange Division*

**Open to:** playwrights, translators, composers, librettists, lyricists. **Frequency:**
annual. **Remuneration:** $2500–15,000. **Guidelines:** grants and fellowships for
research and study in Scandinavian countries; U.S. citizen or permanent resident
with undergraduate degree; Scandinavian language competence expected.
**Application procedure:** completed application, supplementary materials and $10
fee. **Deadline:** 1 Nov 1995. **Notification:** Mar 1996.

## ARTISTS-IN-BERLIN PROGRAMME
German Academic Exchange Service (DAAD); 950 Third Ave, 19th Floor;
New York, NY 10022; (212) 758-3223

**Open to:** playwrights, composers. **Frequency:** annual. **Remuneration:** monthly
grant to cover living costs and rent during 1-year residency in Berlin (6 months
in exceptional cases); workspace provided or paid for; travel for writer and any
members of immediate family who will be staying in Berlin for period of
residency; health and accident insurance; in some cases specific projects such as
readings or publications can be subsidized. **Guidelines:** to enable 15–20
internationally known and qualified young artists to pursue own work while
participating in the cultural life of the city and making contact with local artists;
must reside in Berlin for period of grant; German nationals and foreign writers
who are resident in Germany ineligible; write for guidelines. **Application
procedure:** completed application; samples of published work, preferably in
German, otherwise in English or French, (no manuscripts) for playwrights; scores,
records, tapes or published work for composers. **Deadline:** 31 Dec 1995. **Notification:** May 1996. **Dates:** residency begins between 1 Jan and 30 Jun 1997.

## ARTIST TRUST
1402 Third Ave, Suite 404; Seattle, WA 98101-2118; (206) 467-8734
Marschel Paul, *Director*

### Fellowships

**Open to:** playwrights, composers, librettists, lyricists, screenwriters, radio and
television writers. **Frequency:** awards rotate among disciplines. **Remuneration:**
$5000 award. **Guidelines:** WA resident only; practicing professional artist of
exceptional talent and demonstrated ability; award based on creative excellence
and continuing dedication to an artistic discipline; send SASE for guidelines.
**Application procedure:** completed application and work sample. **Deadline:** late

spring 1996 for playwrights; late spring 1997 for composers, librettists, lyricists, screenwriters, radio and television writers; exact dates TBA.

## GAP (Grants for Artist Projects)

**Open to:** playwrights, composers, librettists, lyricists, screenwriters, radio and television writers. **Frequency:** annual. **Remuneration:** grant of up to $1000. **Guidelines:** WA resident only; grant for the initiation, continuation or completion of specific creative project undertaken by individual artist; award based on quality of work as represented by supporting material and on creativity and feasibility of proposed project; write for guidelines. **Application procedure:** completed application and work sample. **Deadline:** 28 Feb 1996.

## ASIAN CULTURAL COUNCIL
1290 Ave of the Americas; New York, NY 10104; (212) 373-4300

**Open to:** playwrights, composers, librettists, lyricists. **Frequency:** annual. **Remuneration:** amount varies. **Guidelines:** to support residencies in Japan for American artists for a variety of purposes, including creative activities (other than performances), research projects, professional observation tours and specialized training. **Application procedure:** write describing project and requesting application. **Deadline:** 1 Feb 1996.

## ATLANTA BUREAU OF CULTURAL AFFAIRS
675 Ponce de Leon Ave; Atlanta, GA 30308; (404) 817-6815
Sophia Lyman, *Project Adminstrator*

### Artists Project

**Open to:** playwrights, composers, librettists, lyricists. **Frequency:** annual. **Remuneration:** grant of up to $3000. **Guidelines:** practicing professional artist resident in city of Atlanta for at least 1 year prior to deadline. **Application procedure:** write for guidelines and application. **Deadline:** Nov 1995; exact date TBA. **Notification:** 3 months.

### Mayor's Fellowships in the Arts

**Open to:** playwrights, composers, librettists, lyricists. **Frequency:** awards rotate among disciplines. **Remuneration:** $6600 award. **Guidelines:** practicing professional artist resident in city of Atlanta for at least 3 consecutive years prior to deadline; playwright may apply under literary or theatre arts; composer, librettist, lyricist applies under music. **Application procedure:** write for guidelines and application. **Deadline:** Feb 1996 for playwrights (exact date TBA); subsequent rotation not yet set. **Notification:** 3 months.

## BRODY ARTS FUND

California Community Foundation; 606 South Olive St, Suite 2400;
Los Angeles, CA 90014-1526; (213) 413-4042
*Program Officer, Arts*

**Open to:** playwrights, composers, librettists, lyricists, screenwriters, radio and television writers. **Frequency:** awards rotate among disciplines. **Remuneration:** fellowship of $5000. **Guidelines:** L.A. county resident; emerging artist; prefers artist in "expansion arts" field (minority, inner-city, rural and tribal arts); write for guidelines; application available in Jan of application year. **Application procedure:** completed application and supporting materials. **Deadline:** Mar 1996 for composers, librettists, lyricists; Mar 1997 for playwrights, screenwriters, radio and television writers; exact dates TBA. **Notification:** Jun.

## BUNTING FELLOWSHIP PROGRAM

The Mary Ingraham Bunting Institute of Radcliffe College; 34 Concord Ave;
Cambridge, MA 02138; (617) 495-8212
*Fellowships Coordinator*

**Open to:** playwrights, composers, librettists. **Frequency:** annual. **Remuneration:** $33,000 1-year fellowship. **Guidelines:** to provide opportunity and support for professional woman of demonstrated accomplishment and exceptional promise to complete substantial project in her field; full-time appointment; fellow required to reside in Boston area and expected to present work-in-progress in public colloquia during year; office or studio space, auditing privileges and access to libraries and other resources of Radcliffe and Harvard provided. **Application procedure:** completed application with $45 fee. **Deadline:** 15 Oct 1995. **Notification:** Apr 1996. **Dates:** 15 Sep 1996–15 Aug 1997.

## BUSH ARTIST FELLOWSHIPS

The Bush Foundation; E-900 First National Bank Bldg; 332 Minnesota St;
St. Paul, MN 55101; (612) 227-5222
Sally Dixon, *Program Director*

**Open to:** playwrights, composers, screenwriters. **Frequency:** biennial for "scriptworks" (i.e., plays and screenplays) and music. **Remuneration:** stipend of $2166 a month for 6–11 months or total of $26,000 for 12–18 months, plus $7000 for production costs and travel. **Guidelines:** MN, ND, SD or western WI resident at least 25 years old; playwright must have had at least 1 play given full production or workshop production by professional (not necessarily Equity) theatre; screenwriter must have had 1 public staged reading, professional workshop production, or screenplay sale or option. **Application procedure:** write for guidelines and application. **Deadline:** late Oct 1996; exact date TBA. **Notification:** late Mar 1997.

## CINTAS FELLOWSHIP PROGRAM

Arts International; Institute of International Education; 809 United Nations Plaza;
New York, NY 10017-3580; (212) 984-5370
*Associate Program Officer*

**Open to:** playwrights, composers. **Frequency:** annual. **Remuneration:** $10,000 fellowship. **Guidelines:** professional artist of Cuban citizenship or parentage (at least 1 parent must have been Cuban citizen) but not presently residing in Cuba; composer must be writing for the concert stage or opera, not in the popular idiom. **Application procedure:** completed application with work sample; letters of reference. **Deadline:** 1 Mar 1996. **Notification:** 1 Aug 1996.

## DOBIE-PAISANO FELLOWSHIP

University of Texas at Austin; Main Bldg 101; Austin, TX 78712; (512) 471-7213
Audrey Slate, *Coordinator*

**Open to:** playwrights. **Frequency:** annual. **Remuneration:** $7200 stipend to cover 6-month residency at 265-acre ranch; free housing; families welcome. **Guidelines:** native Texan, or playwright who lived in TX for at least 2 years or is writing about TX subject; ordinarily 2 writers selected each year. **Application procedure:** write for application after 1 Oct 1995. **Deadline:** 26 Jan 1996. **Notification:** May 1996.

## THE DON AND GEE NICHOLL
## FELLOWSHIPS IN SCREENWRITING

Academy of Motion Picture Arts and Sciences; 8949 Wilshire Blvd;
Beverly Hills, CA 90211-1972; (310) 247-3059
Greg Beal, *Program Coordinator*

**Open to:** playwrights, screenwriters. **Frequency:** annual. **Remuneration:** up to 5 fellowships of $25,000. **Guidelines:** playwright, screenwriter or fiction writer who has not worked as a professional screenwriter for theatrical films or television or sold screen or television rights to any original story, treatment, stage play, screenplay or teleplay; 1st-round selection based on submission of original screenplay or screen adaptation of writer's own original work, 100–130 pages, written in standard screenplay format; send SASE for guidelines after 1 Jan 1996. **Application procedure:** completed application, screenplay and $30 application fee. **Deadline:** 1 May 1996. **Notification:** 1st-round selection Aug 1996; winners late Oct 1996.

## ELECTRONIC ARTS GRANT PROGRAM

Experimental Television Center; 180 Front St; Owego, NY 13827;
(607) 687-4341
Sherry Miller Hocking, *Program Director*

**Finishing Funds**

**Open to:** artists, including writers and composers, involved in creation of audio, video or computer-generated time-based works. **Frequency:** annual. **Remunera-**

tion: 20–25 grants of up to $500. **Guidelines:** resident of NY State; funds to be used to assist completion of work which is time-based in conception and execution and is to be presented as tape or installation; work must be completed before 30 Sep 1996; write for guidelines. **Application procedure:** 3 copies of completed application, project description, work samples and resume. **Deadline:** 15 Mar 1996. **Notification:** 6 weeks.

## Presentation Funds

**Open to:** nonprofit organizations presenting audio, video or computer-generated time-based works. **Frequency:** ongoing. **Remuneration:** grant of approximately $150–300 to assist presentation of work and artist's involvement in activities related to presentation. **Guidelines:** New York State organization; event must be open to public and should emphasize work of NY State artist(s); write for guidelines. **Application procedure:** individual may not apply; completed application and supporting materials submitted by organization well in advance of event. **Notification:** 15th of month following month of submission.

## FULBRIGHT SCHOLAR AWARDS

Council for International Exchange of Scholars (CIES); 3007 Tilden St NW,
    Suite 5M, Box FEL; Washington, DC 20008-3009; (202) 686-7877

**Open to:** scholars and professionals in all areas of theatre and the arts, including playwrights, translators, composers, librettists and lyricists. **Frequency:** annual. **Remuneration:** grant for university lecturing or research in one of more than 135 countries for 2–9 months; amount varies with country of award; travel; maintenance allowance for living costs of grantee and possibly family. **Guidelines:** U.S. citizen; MFA, Ph.D. or comparable professional qualifications; university or college teaching experience for lecturing awards; for selected countries, proficiency in a foreign language. **Application procedure:** completed application. **Deadline:** 1 Aug 1996. **Notification:** up to 11 months, depending on country; average 8 months.

## FUND FOR NEW AMERICAN PLAYS

The John F. Kennedy Center for the Performing Arts; 2700 F St NW;
    Washington, DC 20566; (202) 416-8024
Sophy Burnham, *Manager*

**Open to:** nonprofit professional theatres. **Frequency:** annual. **Remuneration:** $10,000 grant to playwright whose work theatre is producing, plus grant (amount dependent on quality of proposal and need) to theatre (5 in 1994); $2,500 Roger L. Stevens award to playwright whose work shows "extraordinary promise" (5 in 1994). **Guidelines:** $10,000 playwright grant to cover living and travel expenses during minimum of 4 weeks of rehearsal and during any necessary additional rehearsals and rewrites in course of run; theatre grant to cover expenses exceeding theatre's budget allocation for hiring of director, designer and guest actors; limit of 1 proposal per theatre; translations and musicals ineligible; write for guidelines. **Application procedure:** playwright may not apply; proposal and supporting materials submitted by theatre. **Deadline:** 15 Mar 1996.

## GEORGE BENNETT FELLOWSHIP

Phillips Exeter Academy; Exeter, NH 03833-1104
Charles Pratt, *Coordinator, Selection Committee*

**Open to:** playwrights. **Frequency:** annual. **Remuneration:** academic-year stipend of $5000; free room and board for fellow and family. **Guidelines:** individual who is seriously contemplating or pursuing a career as a writer and who needs time and freedom from material considerations to complete a project in progress; fellow expected to make self and talents available in informal and unofficial way to students interested in writing; send SASE for guidelines and application (no phone inquiries). **Application procedure:** completed application, work sample, statement concerning work-in-progress, names of 2 references and $5 fee. **Deadline:** 1 Dec 1995. **Notification:** 15 Mar 1996. **Dates:** Sep 1996–Jun 1997.

## INSTITUTE OF INTERNATIONAL EDUCATION

809 United Nations Plaza; New York, NY 10017-3580; (212) 984-5330
*U.S. Student Programs Division*

**Open to:** playwrights, translators, composers, librettists, lyricists. **Frequency:** annual. **Remuneration:** fellowship or grant; amount varies with country of award. **Guidelines:** specific opportunities for study abroad in the arts; write for brochure. **Application procedure:** completed application and supporting materials. **Deadline:** 23 Oct 1995. **Notification:** Jan 1996.

## THE JAPAN FOUNDATION

152 West 57th St, 39th Floor; New York, NY 10019; (212) 489-0299
*Artists Fellowship Program*

**Open to:** specialists in the fields of fine arts, performing arts, music, journalism and creative writing, including playwrights, composers, librettists, lyricists and screenwriters. **Frequency:** annual. **Remuneration:** monthly stipend of ¥370,000 (about $4400) or ¥430,000 (about $5100), depending on grantee's professional career; travel; other allowances. **Guidelines:** U.S. citizen or permanent resident; fellowship of 1–6 months, not to be held concurrently with another major grant, to support project substantially related to Japan. **Application procedure:** write for guidelines and application, stating theme of project, present position and citizenship. **Deadline:** 1 Dec 1995. **Notification:** late Mar/early Apr 1996. **Dates:** between 1 Apr 1996 and 31 Mar 1997.

## JOHN SIMON GUGGENHEIM MEMORIAL FOUNDATION

90 Park Ave; New York, NY 10016; (212) 687-4470

**Open to:** playwrights, composers. **Frequency:** annual. **Remuneration:** 1-year fellowship (in 1994 147 fellowships with average grant of $27,667). **Guidelines:** citizen or permanent resident of North or South America or recipient must demonstrate exceptional creative ability; grant to support research in any field of knowledge or creation in any of the arts under the freest possible conditions.

**Application procedure:** write for information. **Deadline:** 1 Oct 1995. **Notification:** Mar 1996.

## THE KLEBAN AWARD

c/o Zissu, Stein & Mosher; 270 Madison Ave, Suite 1410; New York, NY 10016;
(212) 683-5320
Alan J. Stein, *Secretary*

**Open to:** TBA (librettists and/or lyricists). **Frequency:** annual. **Remuneration:** TBA ($100,000 each to lyricist and librettist, payable in installments of $50,000 a year, in 1995–96). **Guidelines:** applicant whose work has received a full or workshop production, or who has been a member or associate of a professional musical workshop or theatre group (e.g., ASCAP or BMI workshop or Dramatists Guild Musical Theater Development Program); writer whose work has been performed on the Broadway stage for a cumulative period of 2 years ineligible; write for guidelines. **Application procedure:** completed application and work sample. **Deadline:** TBA (30 Sep in 1994).

## MANHATTAN THEATRE CLUB PLAYWRITING FELLOWSHIPS

453 West 16th St; New York, NY 10011; (212) 645-5590
Bruce E. Whitacre, *Associate Director of Play Development*

**Open to:** playwrights. **Frequency:** annual. **Remuneration:** $10,000 fellowship. **Guidelines:** New York-based playwright, age 35 or younger, who has completed formal education and can demonstrate financial need; writers from diverse cultural groups encouraged to apply; fellowship includes commission for new play, production assistantship, 1-year residency at MTC; send SASE for further information. **Application procedure:** sample script, resume, statement of purpose and letter of recommendation from theatre professional or professor. **Deadline:** spring 1996; exact date TBA.

## MARY FLAGLER CARY CHARITABLE TRUST
## COMMISSIONING PROGRAM

122 East 42nd St, Room 3505; New York, NY 10168; (212) 953-7705
Gayle Morgan, *Music Program Director*

**Open to:** performance institutions including theatre and opera companies. **Frequency:** biennial. **Remuneration:** grant to help nonprofit professional organization commission new musical work from established or emerging composer; amount varies (total of $300,000 available for 1995 grants). **Guidelines:** New York City organization only; funds to be used to compensate composer and librettist for creative work and to cover copying costs; write for guidelines. **Application procedure:** individual may not apply; letter of application and representative audiotape of composer's music submitted by organization. **Deadline:** 30 Jun 1997.

## THE MARY ROBERTS RINEHART AWARDS
English Department; MSN 3E4; George Mason University;
    Fairfax, VA 22030-4444; (703) 993-1185
*Director, Writing Program*

**Open to:** playwrights. **Frequency:** biennial. **Remuneration:** grant; amount varies with fund's income (currently around $900). **Guidelines:** playwright who lacks financial means to complete a definitely projected work; playwrights who have had a play professionally produced or published, or who have previously received a Rinehart Fund Grant, are ineligible. **Application procedure:** playwright may not apply; nominations accepted from established authors, editors, agents or writing program faculty members. **Deadline:** 30 Nov 1996. **Notification:** Mar 1997.

## MEET THE COMPOSER GRANT PROGRAMS
2112 Broadway, Suite 505; New York, NY 10023; (212) 787-3601

### Meet the Composer/Reader's Digest Commissioning Program
Tracy Williams, *Program Manager*

**Open to:** opera, theatre and music-theatre companies and presenting organizations. **Frequency:** annual. **Remuneration:** commissioning grant of $5000–100,000 per composer to cover composer and librettist fees and copying costs (amount dependent on scope and length of work). **Guidelines:** consortium of no fewer than 2 American producing or presenting organizations with annual budgets of at least $100,000 commissioning opera or music-theatre work by American composer; plans must involve full production of work and at least 6 performances with no fewer than 2 performances to be presented by each consortium member within 18 months of premiere; write for guidelines. **Application procedure:** individual may not apply; completed application and supporting materials submitted by 1 member of consortium. **Deadline:** 15 Apr 1996. **Notification:** Jul 1996.

### New Residencies
Theodore Wiprud, *Program Manager*

**Open to:** performing and community organizations, including opera and theatre companies. **Frequency:** annual. **Remuneration:** grant for composer's salary ($30,000 per annum for 2 years; $15,000 towards 3rd-year salary, to be matched by host organizations); up to $10,000 for host organizations' additional production costs (extra rehearsal, instrument rental, studio costs, etc.); up to $5000 for copying costs; possible limited assistance with composer's relocation costs. **Guidelines:** 2 performing organizations and 1 community organization form Residency Partnership to sponsor 3-year residency by composer who, as creator, educator and arts ambassador, helps hosts to grow artistically and deepen their roots in community, and brings citizens into contact with the creative process; composer, who must be U.S. citizen or permanent resident, works 20 hours a week with host organizations during residency (including composing time) and writes 1 major work, 1 shorter work and occasional pieces for host organizations and community; host performing organizations produce works composed during residency, including at least 2 public performances of major residency commission; write for guidelines. **Application procedure:** individual may not apply; 1 of 2 performing organizations in Residency Partnership submits Letter of Intent before making formal application. **Deadline:** Oct 1995 for Letter of Intent; Nov 1995 for formal application; exact dates TBA. **Notification:** Apr 1996. **Dates:** residencies begin Sep 1996.

## NATIONAL ENDOWMENT FOR THE ARTS
## INTERNATIONAL PROGRAM
1100 Pennsylvania Ave NW, Room 618; Washington, DC 20506;
    (202) 682-5422
Merianne Liteman, *Director*

### ArtsLink Collaborative Projects
All applications and inquiries to Citizen Exchange Council; 12 West 31st St; New York, NY 10001-4415; (212) 643-1985

**Open to:** creative, interpretive and traditional artists, including playwrights, translators, composers, librettists and lyricists. **Frequency:** annual. **Remuneration:** grant of up to $6000 (most grants $1500–3500). **Guidelines:** U.S. citizen or permanent resident; to enable individual artists or groups of up to 5 artists to work with their counterparts in Central or Eastern Europe, the former Soviet Union or the Baltics; mutually beneficial collaborative project that will enrich artists' work and/or create new work that draws inspiration from knowledge and experience gained in country visited; write for guidelines. **Application procedure:** completed application and supporting materials. **Deadline:** 15 Feb 1996. **Notification:** 15 Jun 1996.

### The Fund for U.S. Artists at International Festivals and Exhibitions
All applications and inquiries to: Arts International; Institute of International Education; 809 United Nations Plaza; New York, NY 10017-3580; (212) 984-5370

**Open to:** performing artists and groups, including playwrights, composers, librettists and lyricists who perform their own work. **Frequency:** triannual. **Remuneration:** grant of up to $25,000 (most grants $500–10,000) to cover foreign travel, housing, per diem and production costs. **Guidelines:** U.S. citizen or permanent resident who has been invited to international festival. **Application procedure:** completed application; copy of invitation from festival; full budget showing all costs of participation in festival and festival's contribution to these costs. **Deadline:** early Sep; mid-Jan; early May (exact dates TBA).

### International Projects Initiative

**Open to:** U.S. nonprofit professional cultural organizations including theatre and opera companies, and units of city, county, tribal or state government. **Frequency:** annual. **Remuneration:** matching grant of up to $35,000 (most grants $10,000–25,000). **Guidelines:** projects involving sustained partnerships, artistic exchange or collaborations with artists and arts organizations abroad; individual writers and composers may benefit from eligible projects, which include collaborative development and commissioning of new works, residencies for U.S. artists abroad and projects which involve interaction among the diverse cultural communities of the U.S. and their cultures of origin. **Application procedure:** individual may not apply; completed application and supporting materials submitted by organization. **Deadline:** Oct 1995; exact date TBA.

### United States/Japan Creative Artists' Fellowships

**Open to:** creative, interpretive or traditional artists, including playwrights, translators, composers, librettists and lyricists. **Frequency:** annual. **Remuneration:** monthly stipend to cover housing, living expenses and modest professional support services; roundtrip transportation for artist and family members; stipend to study Japanese language in U.S., if necessary. **Guidelines:** U.S. citizen or permanent resident; to enable established artist to pursue discipline in Japan for 6 consecutive months; artists who have spent more than 3 months in Japan ineligible. **Application procedure:** write or call for guidelines and application materials. **Deadline:** Feb 1996; exact date TBA.

### The U.S./Canada/Mexico Creative Artists' Residencies

**Open to:** creative, interpretive or traditional artists, including playwrights, translators, composers, librettists and lyricists. **Frequency:** annual. **Remuneration:** residency costs, travel and health insurance for 20 artists. **Guidelines:** U.S. citizen or permanent resident; residency of 2 consecutive months in Canada or Mexico; visiting artists meet with artists in their field, expand their understanding of their art form, may create new work inspired by residency experience, and participate in activities that benefit host community during stay (master classes, workshops, lecture/demonstrations, etc.); proficiency in Spanish not required for Mexican residencies. **Application procedure:** write or call for guidelines and application materials. **Deadline:** Feb 1996; exact date TBA.

## NATIONAL ENDOWMENT FOR THE ARTS
## LITERATURE PROGRAM
1100 Pennsylvania Ave NW, Room 722; Washington, DC 20506;
(202) 682-5451
Gigi Bradford, *Director*

### Fellowships for Translators

**Open to:** translators. **Frequency:** annual. **Remuneration:** $10,000 fellowship. **Guidelines:** U.S. citizen or permanent resident; translator who, since 1 Jan 1981, has published English translation of novel or volume of fiction or poetry at least 50 pages long, or booklength translation of work of literary merit, or has had total of 50 pages of English translations of creative literature published in literary magazines, anthologies or books, or has had an English translation of at least 1 full-length play produced or published; creative translation from any language into English of published literary material of value and quality; priority given to translation of works not previously translated into English; applicant must be able to obtain permission to translate proposed work; program subject to change; write for guidelines. **Application procedure:** 9 copies of completed application with supporting materials, including sample, 10-15 pages long, of proposed translation. **Deadline:** Jan 1996; exact date TBA. **Notification:** Oct 1996. **Dates:** period of up to 2 years beginning between Dec 1996 and Dec 1997.

## NATIONAL ENDOWMENT FOR THE ARTS MEDIA ARTS: FILM/RADIO/TELEVISION PROGRAM

1100 Pennsylvania Ave NW, Room 720; Washington, DC 20506;
    (202) 682-5452
Brian O'Doherty, *Director*

Writers involved in media projects may benefit from grants to support film, video and radio production. Film and video producers should contact the Film/Video Art Section and radio producers the Radio/Audio Art Section for guidelines and application.

## NATIONAL ENDOWMENT FOR THE ARTS MUSIC PROGRAM

1100 Pennsylvania Ave NW, Room 702; Washington, DC 20506;
    (202) 682-5445
Omus Hirshbein, *Director*

**Composers Program**

*Collaborative Fellowships*

**Open to:** composers (and their collaborators). **Frequency:** annual. **Remuneration:** up to $35,000. **Guidelines:** money to be used for the creation or completion of collaborative works; may be used to pay for individual's time, copying and reproduction costs, studio expenses (use of established electronic or experimental facilities only) and other expenses directly related to proposed project; only composer applies, 1 or more partners may be in collaboration. **Application procedure:** completed application, supporting materials and work sample of each member of collaboration. **Deadline:** TBA (write for information after 1 Nov 1995).

*Fellowships*

**Open to:** composers. **Frequency:** annual. **Remuneration:** up to $25,000. **Guidelines:** money to be used for creation or completion of musical works; may be used to pay for composer's time, copying and reproduction costs, studio expenses (use of established electronic or experimental facilities only) and other expenses directly related to composer's proposed project. **Application procedure:** completed application, supporting materials and work sample. **Deadline:** TBA (write for information after 1 Nov 1995).

## NATIONAL ENDOWMENT FOR THE ARTS
## OPERA-MUSICAL THEATER PROGRAM

1100 Pennyslvania Ave NW, Room 703; Washington, DC 20506;
(202) 682-5447
Omus Hirshbein, *Director*

### New American Works: Project Support

**Open to:** individuals, including composers, librettists and lyricists, and not-for-profit professional producing organizations. **Frequency:** annual. **Remuneration:** matching grant to organization or individual (grants to individuals under creation phase nonmatching). **Guidelines:** individual must be U.S. citizen or permanent resident; money to be used for creation, development or production of new American opera-musical theatre works; seldom-produced American works of major significance also considered. **Application procedure:** completed application and supporting materials. **Deadline:** 1 Sep 1995 for letter of intent (first-time applicants only); 22 Sep 1995 for formal application. **Notification:** 1 Jun 1996.

## NATIONAL ENDOWMENT FOR THE ARTS
## PRESENTING PROGRAM

1100 Pennsylvania Ave NW, Room 726; Washington, DC 20506;
(202) 682-5444
Court Burns, *Program Administrator*

**Open to:** presenting organizations. **Frequency:** annual. **Remuneration:** grants of $5000–150,000. **Guidelines:** funds support performing arts presenters who provide programming of excellence; money may be used to commission new works; organizations call or write for guidelines. **Application procedure:** individual may not apply; organization submits completed application and supporting materials. **Deadline:** May 1996 (exact date TBA). **Notification:** Dec 1996.

## NATIONAL ENDOWMENT FOR THE ARTS
## THEATER PROGRAM

1100 Pennsylvania Ave NW; Washington, DC 20506; (202) 682-5425
Gigi Bolt, *Director*

### Fellowships for Playwrights

**Open to:** playwrights. **Frequency:** biennial (contingent on funding). **Remuneration:** 2-year fellowship (amount TBA); grantee may also receive additional sum of $2500 to defray costs of residency at theatre of playwright's choice. **Guidelines:** U.S. citizen or permanent resident; applicant must have had play produced within last 5 years by professional theatre under any AEA contract or by theatre that was NEA Theater Program grantee at time of production. **Application procedure:** completed application and supporting materials; write for guidelines after 30 Sep 1996. **Deadline:** 31 May 1996.

## NATIONAL ENDOWMENT FOR THE HUMANITIES
## PUBLIC PROGRAMS
1100 Pennsylvania Ave NW; Washington, DC 20506; (202) 606-8267
Donald Gibson, *Director*

### Humanities Projects in Media
James J. Dougherty, *Assistant Director* (202) 606-8278

**Open to:** independent producers, radio and television writers. **Frequency:** biannual. **Remuneration:** varies. **Guidelines:** support for planning, writing and/or production of television and radio projects focused on subjects and issues central to the humanities, and aimed at an adult national or broad regional audience; eligible projects include dramatizations; no adaptations of literary works; write for guidelines. **Application procedure:** submit draft proposal before making formal application. **Deadline:** 16 Sep 1995 for projects beginning on or after 1 Apr 1996; 17 Mar 1996 for projects beginning on or after 1 Oct 1996.

## NATIONAL ENDOWMENT FOR THE HUMANITIES
## RESEARCH PROGRAMS
1100 Pennsylvania Ave NW; Washington, DC 20506; (202) 606-8200
Guinevere L. Griest, *Director*

### Translations Program
Kathryn Hansen (202) 606-8207: E-mail: khansen@neh.fed.us

**Open to:** translators. **Frequency:** annual. **Remuneration:** grant; amount varies according to project. **Guidelines:** U.S. citizen or resident for 3 years; money to support individual or collaborative projects to translate into English works that provide insight into the history, literature, philosophy and artistic achievements of other cultures and that make available to scholars, students, teachers and the public the thought and learning of those civilizations. **Application procedure:** completed application and supporting materials; write for guidelines. **Deadline:** 1 Jul 1996. **Notification:** Apr 1997.

## NEW PLAY COMMISSIONS IN JEWISH THEATRE
National Foundation for Jewish Culture; 330 Seventh Ave, 21st Floor;
    New York, NY 10021; (212) 629-0500
Matt Price, *Grants Administrator*

**Open to:** North American nonprofit theatres. **Frequency:** annual. **Remuneration:** grant of $1000–5000. **Guidelines:** 1 award a year to theatre that has completed at least 2 seasons of public performances and is commissioning new full-length play, adaptation, work for young audiences, musical or opera dealing substantively with issues of Jewish history, tradition, values or contemporary life; theatre must commit to presenting at least a public workshop production and/or staged reading of work, followed by discussion with audience; funds may be applied to commissioning fee, playwright's residency expenses or workshop costs; write for guidelines. **Application procedure:** completed proposal cover sheet and supporting materials, submitted by theatre. **Deadline:** 26 Jan 1996. **Notification:** late April 1996.

## NEW YORK FOUNDATION FOR THE ARTS
## ARTISTS' FELLOWSHIPS

155 Ave of the Americas, 14th Floor; New York, NY 10013-1507;
   (212) 366-6900
Penelope Dannenberg, *Director, Artists' Programs and Services*

**Open to:** playwrights, composers, screenwriters. **Frequency:** awards alternate biennially among disciplines. **Remuneration:** $7000 fellowship. **Guidelines:** NY State resident for 2 years prior to deadline; students ineligible. **Application procedure:** completed application and supporting materials; application seminars held each Sep. **Deadline:** next deadline for playwrights, composers and screenwriters Oct 1995; exact date TBA.

## NLAPW SCHOLARSHIPS FOR MATURE WOMEN

National League of American Pen Women; 1300 17th St NW;
   Washington, DC 20036-1973; (202) 785-1997
Shirley Holden Helberg, *National Scholarship Chairman*

**Open to:** playwrights, composers, librettists, lyricists. **Frequency:** biennial. **Remuneration:** grant; amount TBA ($1000 in 1994). **Guidelines:** American woman aged over 35; 3 awards (1 in art, 1 in music, 1 in letters) to further creative goals of women at age when encouragement can lead to realization of long-term purposes; NLAPW members ineligible; to obtain guidelines, available after 1 Aug 1995, call (717) 225-3023 or (410) 522-2557 or send SASE. **Application procedure:** work sample; statement of purpose for which money will be used; statement that applicant is over age 35 and is not a member of NLAPW; and fee ($8 in 1994). **Deadline:** 15 Jan 1996. **Notification:** Jun 1996.

## PILGRIM PROJECT

156 Fifth Ave, Suite 400; New York, NY 10010; (212) 627-2288
Davida Goldman, *Secretary*

**Open to:** playwrights, individual producers and theatre companies. **Frequency:** ongoing. **Remuneration:** grant of $1000–7000. **Guidelines:** grant towards cost of reading, workshop production or full production of play that deals with questions of moral significance; write for further information. **Application procedure:** script only. **Deadline:** ongoing.

## THE PLAYWRIGHTS' CENTER GRANT PROGRAMS

2301 Franklin Ave East; Minneapolis, MN 55406-1099; (612) 332-7481
David Moore, Jr., *Executive Director*

### Jerome Playwright-in-Residence Fellowships

**Open to:** playwrights. **Frequency:** annual. **Remuneration:** 5 1-year fellowships of

$7000. **Guidelines:** U.S. citizen or permanent resident; emerging playwright whose work has not received more than 2 professional full productions; fellow must spend year in residence at Center, where fellow has access to developmental workshops, readings and other services; send SASE for guidelines. **Application procedure:** completed application and supporting materials. **Deadline:** 15 Sep 1995. **Notification:** 15 Jan 1996. **Dates:** 1 Jul 1996–30 Jun 1997.

## Many Voices Multicultural Collaboration Grants

**Open to:** playwrights, translators, composers, librettists, screenwriters. **Frequency:** annual, contingent on funding. **Remuneration:** $200–2000 grant to each of 2–4 teams. **Guidelines:** team of 2 or more artists of differing cultural backgrounds with commitment from MN organization to produce proposed collaborative work; team's lead artist must be MN playwright of color. **Application procedure:** send SASE for guidelines. **Deadline:** 15 Sep 1995. **Notification:** 16 Nov 1995. **Dates:** 1 Dec 1995–1 Dec 1996.

## Many Voices Playwriting Residency Awards

**Open to:** playwrights. **Frequency:** annual, contingent on funding. **Remuneration:** 8 awards: $750 stipend, playwriting-class scholarship, 1-year Playwrights' Center membership, opportunity to participate in culturally focused playwriting roundtables, dramaturgical assistance, workshop and public reading. **Guidelines:** MN resident of color. **Application procedure:** send SASE for guidelines. **Deadline:** 15 Sep 1995. **Notification:** 1 Dec 1995. **Dates:** 1 Dec 1995–1 Dec 1996.

## McKnight Advancement Grants

**Open to:** playwrights. **Frequency:** annual. **Remuneration:** 3 grants of $8500; up to $1500 per fellow for workshops and staged readings using center's developmental program or for allocation to partner organization for joint development and/or production. **Guidelines:** U.S. citizen or permanent resident and legal MN resident since 1 May 1995; playwright of exceptional merit and potential who has had at least 2 plays fully produced by professional theatres; funds intended to significantly advance fellow's art and/or career and may be used to cover a variety of expenses, including writing time, residency at theatre or other arts organization, travel/study, production or presentation; fellow must participate actively in Center's outreach or educational programming (at least 20 hours), and must designate 2 months of grant year during which he or she plans to participate actively in Center's programs, including weekly attendance at and critical participation in readings and workshops of other members' work; send SASE for guidelines after 1 Dec 1995. **Application procedure:** completed application and supporting materials. **Deadline:** 1 Feb 1996. **Notification:** 1 May 1996. **Dates:** 1 Jul 1996–30 Jun 1997.

## McKnight Fellowships

**Open to:** playwrights. **Frequency:** annual. **Remuneration:** 2 fellowships of $10,000; up to $2000 program allocation to cover reading/workshop expenses; possible partial travel and living expenses for fellows living outside 150-mile radius of Twin Cities. **Guidelines:** U.S. citizen or permanent resident whose work has made significant impact on contemporary theatre and who has had at least 2 plays fully produced by professional theatres; fellow must spend 1 month in residence at Center, where fellow has access to developmental workshops, readings and other services; send SASE for guidelines after 15 Nov 1995. **Application procedure:** completed application and supporting materials. **Deadline:** 16 Jan 1996. **Notification:** 15 Apr 1996. **Dates:** 1 Jul 1996–30 Jun 1997.

## PRINCESS GRACE AWARDS: PLAYWRIGHT FELLOWSHIP

Princess Grace Foundation–USA; 725 Park Ave; New York, NY 10021;
(212) 744-3221
Jennifer B. Reis, *Director of Grants Program*

**Open to:** playwrights. **Frequency:** annual. **Remuneration:** $7500 grant; 10-week residency with travel at New Dramatists, New York City (see entry in Membership and Service Organizations); inclusion of submitted script in New Dramatists' lending library and in its ScriptShare national script-distribution program for 1 year. **Guidelines:** U.S. citizen or permanent resident; under ordinary circumstances, playwright not more than 30 years of age at time of application; award based primarily on artistic quality of submitted play and potential of fellowship to assist writer's growth; original, unproduced, unpublished play (no adaptations); eligibility requirements and application procedures currently under review; write for guidelines. **Application procedures:** see guidelines. **Deadline:** 31 Mar 1996.

## TCG GRANT PROGRAMS

Theatre Communications Group; 355 Lexington Ave; New York, NY 10017-0217;
(212) 697-5230
Fran Kumin, *Director of Artistic Programs*

### Extended Collaboration Grants

**Open to:** nonprofit theatres, in collaboration with playwrights. **Frequency:** annual, contingent on funding. **Remuneration:** grant of $3000–6000 (3 awarded in 1994–95). **Guidelines:** augments normal development resources of TCG Constituent theatre by enabling playwright to develop work over an extended period of time in collaboration with director, designer, choreographer, composer and/or artist from another discipline; period of collaboration must exceed that which theatre would normally support; funds cover inter-city transportation within the U.S. and Canada and other expenses related to research and meetings among the collaborators. **Application procedure:** playwright may not apply; completed application submitted by artistic director of theatre. **Deadline:** 30 Nov 1995 (contingent on funding).

### National Theatre Artist Residency Program

*Category I: Residency Grants*

**Open to:** playwrights, translators, composers, librettists, lyricists and other theatre artists in association with nonprofit professional theatres. **Frequency:** annual, contingent on funding. **Remuneration:** approximately 10–14 grants of $50,000 or

$100,000; supplemental travel funds, not to exceed 10% of principal request are available to first-time residency-grant recipients only. **Guidelines:** experienced theatre artists who have created significant body of work and theatres with high artistic standards and organizational capacity to provide substantial support services to artists; funds cover compensation and residency expenses of 1 or 2 resident artists, working singly or in collaboration, during discrete periods used exclusively for residency-related activities that total at least 6 full months over 2-year period; proposals must be developed jointly by artists and institutions; theatres applying for $100,000 grant must have minimum operating budget of $500,000 in most recently completed fiscal year; theatres applying for $50,000 grant must have minimum operating budget of $250,000 in most recently completed fiscal year; write for guidelines. **Application procedure:** 2 copies of completed application and supporting materials. **Deadline:** write for 1996 deadlines.

### Category II: Matching Grants to Continue Existing Residencies

**Open to:** previous Category I grant recipients. **Frequency:** annual, contingent on funding. **Remuneration:** up to $50,000 in matching funds. **Guidelines:** matching funds to support the continuation of particularly fruitful partnerships; to be considered, applicants must meet Category I eligibility requirements. **Application procedure:** 2 copies of completed application and supporting materials. **Deadline:** write for 1996 deadlines.

## TRAVEL AND STUDY GRANT PROGRAM

c/o Jerome Foundation; West 1050, First National Bank Bldg; 332 Minnesota St;
    St. Paul, MN 55101-1312; (612) 224-9431
Cynthia Gehrig, *President*

**Open to:** theatre artists and administrators, including playwrights, composers, librettists and lyricists. **Frequency:** annual. **Remuneration:** grant of up to $5000 for foreign or domestic travel. **Guidelines:** resident of Twin Cities metropolitan area; program funded by Dayton-Hudson, General Mills and Jerome Foundation to support short-term travel or period of significant professional development through travel and study for independent professional artist or staff member of nonprofit organization; write for guidelines. **Application procedure:** completed application, work sample and resume. **Deadline:** 2 Oct 1995.

## U.S.-MEXICO FUND FOR CULTURE

Londres 16 P.B.; Col. Juárez México, DF; Mexico 06600; 52-5-592-5386
Beatriz Nava, *Assistant to the Coordinator*

**Open to:** playwrights, translators, composers, librettists, lyricists, screenwriters, TV and radio writers, and producing organizations. **Frequency:** annual. **Remuneration:** grants of $2000-25,000. **Guidelines:** Mexican and American artists and cultural institutions; program sponsored by Bancomer Cultural Foundation, the Rockefeller Foundation and Mexico's National Fund for Culture and the Arts to fund performing arts projects of excellence that reflect artistic and cultural diversity of Mexico and U.S. and encourage mutual collaboration between specialists of both countries; in media arts, script translation and adaptation of fiction, drama and poetry also considered; for brochure and application materials, send 78¢-postage SASE to U.S. Mexico Fund for Culture, c/o Benjamin Franklin Library, Laredo, TX 78044-3087. **Application procedure:** original and 3 copies of: completed financial support application; full project description in Spanish or English; summary project description in Spanish or English (whichever language not used in full description); detailed project budget; letters from participating institutions; resumes of all project participants; completed sample material specifications and checklist form; application acknowledgment card; sample materials of earlier work, if available (materials will not be returned); for institutional applications, letter designating project coordinator. **Notification:** Aug 1996.

## THE WALT DISNEY STUDIOS FELLOWSHIP PROGRAM

500 South Buena Vista St; Burbank, CA 91521-0880; (818) 560-6894
Brenda Vangsness, *Program Administrator*

**Open to:** playwrights, screenwriters, television writers. **Frequency:** annual. **Remuneration:** 1-year salary of $30,000 for 10–15 writers; travel and 1 month's housing for fellows from outside Los Angeles area. **Guidelines:** to enable writers to work full-time at developing their craft in Disney Studios features or television division; focus on hiring African Americans, Latinos, Asian Americans, Native Americans and women; no previous film or TV writing experience necessary; writer with Writers Guild of America credits eligible but should apply through the Guild's Employment Access at (310) 205-2548; call or write for guidelines. **Application procedure:** completed application and notarized standard letter agreement with resume and writing sample (for feature division: screenplay approximately 120 pages long or full-length play; for TV division: 30-minute TV script approximately 45 pages long, full-length play, or one-act more than 24 pages long). **Deadline:** TBA (7 Apr in 1995 with no submission before 13 Mar 1995); call for exact date. **Notification:** summer 1996. **Dates:** fellowship year begins Oct 1996.

# Emergency Funds

**How do emergency funds differ from other sources of financial aid?**

Emergency funds are for writers in severe *temporary* financial difficulties. Some funds give outright grants, others make interest-free loans. For support for anything other than a genuine emergency, turn to Fellowships and Grants.

## THE AUTHORS LEAGUE FUND AND
## THE DRAMATISTS GUILD FUND
330 West 42nd St, 29th Floor; New York, NY 10036; (212) 268-1208
Susan Drury, *Administrator*

**Open to:** playwrights, composers, librettists, lyricists. **Type of assistance:** interest-free loan; no restriction on amount but request should be limited to immediate needs. **Guidelines:** published or produced working professional; must demonstrate real need. **Application procedure:** completed application and supporting materials. **Notification:** 2–4 weeks.

## CARNEGIE FUND FOR AUTHORS
1 Old Country Rd, Suite 113; Carle Place, NY 11514

**Open to:** playwrights. **Type of assistance:** emergency grant. **Guidelines:** playwright who has had at least 1 play or collection of plays published commercially in book form (anthologies excluded); emergency which has placed applicant in substantial verifiable financial need. **Application procedure:** write for application form.

## CHANGE
Box 705, Cooper Station; New York, NY 10276; (212) 473-3742

**Open to:** playwrights, composers, librettists, lyricists. **Type of assistance:** grant of up to $1000. **Guidelines:** to assist in emergency financial situation such as overdue medical bills, utility turnoffs, eviction or fire damage; applicant must verify professional status and financial need; students ineligible; write or call for fact sheet. **Application procedure:** apply by letter only, detailing financial emergency and explaining its causes; enclose copies of outstanding bills or eviction notices, resume, reviews, production announcements and at least 2 letters from theatre professionals verifying applicant's professional status.

## PEN FUND FOR WRITERS & EDITORS WITH AIDS
PEN American Center; 568 Broadway; New York, NY 10012; (212) 334-1660
India Amos, *Program Coordinator*

**Open to:** playwrights, translators. **Type of assistance:** grant or interest-free loan of up to $1000. **Guidelines:** emergency assistance for published or produced writer in financial difficulties due to HIV or AIDS-related illness. **Application procedure:** completed application, work sample and supporting materials. **Notification:** within 6–8 weeks.

## PEN WRITERS FUND
PEN American Center; 568 Broadway; New York, NY 10012; (212) 334-1660
India Amos, *Program Coordinator*

**Open to:** playwrights, translators. **Type of assistance:** grant or interest-free loan of up to $500. **Guidelines:** emergency assistance for published or produced writer in financial difficulties. **Application procedure:** completed application, work sample and supporting materials. **Notification:** within 6–8 weeks.

# State Arts Agencies

**What can my state arts agency do for me?**

Possibly quite a bit—the only way to find out is to ask your agency for guidelines and study them carefully. State programs vary greatly and change frequently. Most have some sort of residency requirement, but eligibility is not always restricted to current residents, and may include people who were born in, raised in, attended school in or had some other association with the state in question.

**What if my state doesn't give grants to individual artists?**

A number of state arts agencies are restricted in this way. However, those with such restrictions, by and large, are eager to help artists locate nonprofit organizations that channel funds to individuals; you should ask specifically about this.

The New York State Council on the Arts, for example, is prohibited from funding individuals directly, and must contract with a sponsoring nonprofit organization when it awards grants to individual artists. Yet NYSCA has a number of ways of supporting the work of theatre writers. The Literature Program funds, in alternate years, translations, and writers' residencies in communities. The Individual Artists Program assists nonprofit organizations in commissioning works, including plays, music-theatre pieces; theatre and composers' commissions are also granted in alternate years. Moreover, NYSCA subgrants funds to the New York Foundation for the Arts, which in turn provides project development assistance for individual artists and creative teams (see NYFA Artists' New Works in Development) and funds fellowships (see Fellowships and Grants). NYFA also assists residencies (see Artists in Residence Program in Colonies and Residencies).

At the least, every state has some kind of Artist-in-Education program; if you are able and willing to function in an educational setting you should certainly investigate this possibility.

### ALABAMA STATE COUNCIL ON THE ARTS
1 Dexter Ave; Montgomery, AL 36130-1800; (334) 242-4076
Al Head, *Executive Director*

### ALASKA STATE COUNCIL ON THE ARTS
411 West 4th Ave, Suite 1E; Anchorage, AK 99501-2343; (907) 269-6610
Timothy Wilson, *Executive Director*

### AMERICAN SAMOA COUNCIL ON CULTURE, ARTS AND HUMANITIES
Box 1540; Office of the Governor; Pago Pago, AS 96799; 684-633-4347
(Mrs.) Fa'ailoilo Lauvao, *Executive Director*

### ARIZONA COMMISSION ON THE ARTS
417 West Roosevelt St; Phoenix, AZ 85003; (602) 255-5882
Shelley Cohn, *Executive Director*

### ARKANSAS ARTS COUNCIL
1500 Tower Bldg; 323 Center St; Little Rock, AR 72201; (501) 324-9766
Mona Hughes, *Acting Executive Director*

### CALIFORNIA ARTS COUNCIL
2411 Alhambra Blvd; Sacramento, CA 95817; (916) 227-2550
Barbara Pieper, *Executive Director*

### COLORADO COUNCIL ON THE ARTS
750 Pennsylvania St; Denver, CO 80203; (303) 894-2617
Fran Holden, *Executive Director*

### CONNECTICUT COMMISSION ON THE ARTS
227 Lawrence St; Hartford, CT 06106; (203) 566-4770
John Ostrout, *Executive Director*

### DELAWARE DIVISION OF THE ARTS
820 North French St; Wilmington, DE 19801; (302) 577-3540
Peggy Amsterdam, *Director*

## District of Columbia (DC) Commission on the Arts and Humanities
410 8th St NW, 5th Floor; Washington, DC 20004; (202) 724-5613
Pamela Holt, *Executive Director*

## Florida Division of Cultural Affairs
Department of State, The Capitol; Tallahassee, FL 32399-0250; (904) 487-2980
(Ms.) Peyton C. Fearington, *Executive Director*

## Georgia Council for the Arts
530 Means St NW, Suite 115; Atlanta, GA 30318; (404) 651-7920
Caroline Ballard Leake, *Executive Director*

## Guam Council on the Arts & Humanities Agency
Office of the Governor; Box 2950; Agana, GU 96910; 671-647-2242
Deborah Bordallo, *Executive Director*

## State Foundation on Culture and the Arts (Hawaii)
44 Merchant St; Honolulu, HI 96813; (808) 586-0306
Wendell Silva, *Executive Director*

## Idaho Commission on the Arts
Box 83720; Boise, ID 83720-0008; (208) 334-2119
Margot H. Knight, *Executive Director*

## Illinois Arts Council
State of Illinois Center; 100 West Randolph St, Suite 10-500; Chicago, IL 60601;
(312) 814-6750
Lori Spears Montana, *Executive Director*

## Indiana Arts Commission
402 West Washington St, Room 072; Indianapolis, IN 46204; (317) 232-1268
Dorothy Ilgen, *Executive Director*

## Iowa Arts Council
Capitol Complex; 600 East Locust; Des Moines, IA 50319; (515) 281-4451
William H. Jackson, *Executive Director*

## Kansas Arts Commission
Jayhawk Tower; 700 Southwest Jackson, Suite 1004; Topeka, KS 66603;
(913) 296-3335
Joan Wingerson, *Interim Director*

## KENTUCKY ARTS COUNCIL
31 Fountain Pl; Frankfort, KY 40601; (502) 564-3757
Lou DeLuca, *Executive Director*

## LOUISIANA DIVISION OF THE ARTS
Box 44247; Baton Rouge, LA 70804; (504) 342-8180
James Borders, *Executive Director*

## MAINE ARTS COMMISSION
55 Capitol St; State House Station 25; Augusta, ME 04333; (207) 287-2724
Alden C. Wilson, *Executive Director*

## MARYLAND STATE ARTS COUNCIL
601 North Howard St, 1st Floor; Baltimore, MD 21201; (410) 333-8232
Jim Backas, *Executive Director*

## MASSACHUSETTS CULTURAL COUNCIL
120 Boylston St, 2nd Floor; Boston, MA 02116-4600; (617) 727-3668
Rose Austin, *Executive Director*

## MICHIGAN COUNCIL FOR THE ARTS & CULTURAL AFFAIRS
1200 6th Ave, Executive Plaza; Detroit, MI 48226-2461; (313) 256-3731
Betty Boone, *Executive Director*

## MINNESOTA STATE ARTS BOARD
432 Summit Ave; St. Paul, MN 55102; (612) 297-2603
Sam Grabarski, *Executive Director*

## MISSISSIPPI ARTS COMMISSION
239 North Lamar St, 2nd Floor; Jackson, MS 39201; (601) 359-6030, -6040
Jane Hiatt, *Executive Director*

## MISSOURI ARTS COUNCIL
111 North 7th St, Suite 105; St. Louis, MO 63101; (314) 340-6845
Anthony Radich, *Executive Director*

## MONTANA ARTS COUNCIL
316 North Park Ave, Room 252; Box 202201; Helena, MT 59620-2201;
(406) 444-6430
Arlynn Fishbaugh, *Executive Director*

## NEBRASKA ARTS COUNCIL
Joslyn Castle Carriage House; 3838 Davenport; Omaha, NE 68131-2329;
(402) 595-2122
Jennifer Severin Clark, *Executive Director*

## NEVADA STATE COUNCIL ON THE ARTS
Capitol Complex; 602 North Curry St; Carson City, NV 89710; (702) 687-6680
Susan Boskoff, *Executive Director*

## NEW HAMPSHIRE STATE COUNCIL ON THE ARTS
40 North Main St, Phenix Hall; Concord, NH 03301; (603) 271-2789
Sue Bonaiuto, *Executive Director*

## NEW JERSEY STATE COUNCIL ON THE ARTS
20 West State St, 3rd Floor, CN 306; Trenton, NJ 08625-0306; (609) 292-6130
Barbara Russo, *Executive Director*

## NEW MEXICO ARTS DIVISION
228 East Palace Ave; Santa Fe, NM 87501; (505) 827-6490
Lara Morrow, *Director*

## NEW YORK STATE COUNCIL ON THE ARTS
915 Broadway; New York, NY 10010; (212) 387-7000
Al Berr, *Acting Executive Director*

## NORTH CAROLINA ARTS COUNCIL
Department of Cultural Resources; Raleigh, NC 27611; (919) 733-2821
Mary Regan, *Executive Director*

## NORTH DAKOTA COUNCIL ON THE ARTS
418 East Broadway, Suite 70; Bismarck, ND 58501-4086; (701) 328-3954
Patsy Thompson, *Executive Director*

## COMMONWEALTH COUNCIL FOR ARTS AND CULTURE (NORTHERN MARIANAS ISLANDS)
Box 5553, CHRB; Saipan, MP 96950; 670-322-9982, -9983
Margarita De Leon Guerrero Wonenberg, *Executive Director*

## OHIO ARTS COUNCIL
727 East Main St; Columbus, OH 43205; (614) 466-2613
Wayne Lawson, *Executive Director*

## STATE ARTS COUNCIL OF OKLAHOMA
Jim Thorpe Bldg; Box 52001-2001;
Oklahoma City, OK 73152-2001; (405) 521-2931
Betty Price, *Executive Director*

## OREGON ARTS COMMISSION
775 Summer St, NE; Salem, OR 97310; (503) 986-0082
Christine D'Arcy, *Executive Director*

## PENNSYLVANIA COUNCIL ON THE ARTS
216 Finance Bldg; Harrisburg, PA 17120; (717) 787-6883
Philip Horn, *Executive Director*

## INSTITUTE OF PUERTO RICAN CULTURE
Box 4184; San Juan, PR 00902-4184; (809) 723-2115
Awilda Palau Suarez, *Executive Director*

## RHODE ISLAND STATE COUNCIL ON THE ARTS
95 Cedar St, Suite 103; Providence, RI 02903-1034; (401) 277-3880
Randall Rosenbaum, *Executive Director*

## SOUTH CAROLINA ARTS COMMISSION
1800 Gervais St; Columbia, SC 29201; (803) 734-8696
Suzette Surkamer, *Executive Director*

## SOUTH DAKOTA ARTS COUNCIL
230 South Phillips Ave, Suite 204; Sioux Falls, SD 57102-0720; (605) 367-5678
Dennis Holub, *Executive Director*

## TENNESSEE ARTS COMMISSION
404 James Robertson Pkwy; Parkway Towers, Suite 160;
Nashville, TN 37243-0780; (615) 741-1701
Bennett Tarleton, *Executive Director*

## TEXAS COMMISSION ON THE ARTS
Box 13406, Capitol Station; Austin, TX 78711; (512) 463-5535
John Paul Batiste, *Executive Director*

## UTAH ARTS COUNCIL
617 East South Temple St; Salt Lake City, UT 84102; (801) 533-5895
Bonnie Stephens, *Executive Director*

## VERMONT COUNCIL ON THE ARTS
136 State St, Drawer 33; Montpelier, VT 05633-6001; (802) 828-3291
Nicolette Clarke, *Executive Director*

## VIRGIN ISLANDS COUNCIL ON THE ARTS
41-42 Norre Gade; Box 103; St. Thomas, VI 00804; (809) 774-5984
John Jowers, *Executive Director*

## VIRGINIA COMMISSION FOR THE ARTS
223 Governor St; Richmond VA 23219; (804) 225-3132
Peggy Baggett, *Executive Director*

## WASHINGTON STATE ARTS COMMISSION
Box 42675; Olympia, WA 98504-2675; (360) 753-3860
Karen Kamara Gose, *Executive Director*

## ARTS & HUMANITIES SECTION
## WEST VIRGINIA DIVISION OF CULTURE & HISTORY
1900 Kanawha Blvd E; Cultural Center; Charleston, WV 25305; (304) 558-0240
Lakin Ray Cook, *Executive Director*

## WISCONSIN ARTS BOARD
101 East Wilson St, 1st Floor; Madison, WI 53702; (608) 266-0190
Dean Amhaus, *Executive Director*

## WYOMING ARTS COUNCIL
2320 Capitol Ave; Cheyenne, WY 82002; (307) 777-7742
John G. Coe, *Executive Director*

# Colonies and Residencies

**What entries make up this section?**

Though artist colonies that admit theatre writers constitute the majority of the listings, there are other kinds of residencies, such as artist-in-residence positions at universities, listed here as well. You can also find listings in the Development and Fellowships and Grants sections that could be considered residencies. Finally, we have included several "writers' rooms" where playwrights in need of a quiet place for uninterrupted work are welcome.

Note: you should assume that each deadline listed in this section is the date application materials must be *received*, unless you have ascertained that it is the postmark date.

## THE ADAMANT PROGRAM
Box 73; Adamant, VT 05640-0073; (802) 223-2324, -3347
Patricia Hutchinson, *Resident Manager*

**Open to:** playwrights, composers, screenwriters. **Description:** residencies of 4–8 weeks for artists, including writers, composers and visual artists, at retreat in small VT village of Adamant, near Montpelier; small individual studio in woods and private bedroom in 1 of 2 main houses; experimental theatre for the use of playwrights, grand pianos available for composers; lunch and dinner provided, residents make own breakfast and share light housekeeping chores. **Financial**

**arrangement:** resident pays $25 a day towards cost of room, board and studio; very limited number of fellowships available for those who show genuine need. **Guidelines:** creative artist with professional standing in field; less established artists of recognized ability also considered; write for guidelines. **Application procedure:** completed application, work sample, 3 references and $10 fee. **Deadline:** 30 Apr 1996. **Dates:** Sep–Oct.


## ALDEN B. DOW CREATIVITY CENTER

Northwood University; Midland, MI 48640-2398; (517) 837-4478
Carol B. Coppage, *Executive Director*

**Open to:** playwrights, translators, composers, librettists, lyricists, screenwriters. **Description:** 4 "Creativity Fellowships" each year for individuals working in any field, including the arts; 8-week summer residency at Northwood University, which provides environment for intense independent study; program includes interaction among fellows and formal presentation of work in Aug. **Financial arrangement:** travel, room, board, $750 for personal expenses and project materials. **Guidelines:** projects that are creative, original and have potential for impact on applicant's field; prefers 1 applicant per project; no accommodation for spouses or children. **Application procedure:** completed application, brief project description, budget, work sample and resume. **Deadline:** 31 Dec 1995. **Notification:** 1 Apr 1996. **Dates:** Jun–Aug 1996.


## ALTOS DE CHAVON

c/o Parsons School of Design; 2 West 13th St, Room 707; New York, NY 10011;
    (212) 229-5370
Stephen D. Kaplan, *Arts/Education Director*

**Open to:** playwrights, composers, screenwriters. **Description:** residencies of 3½ months for 15 artists a year, 1–2 of whom may be writers or composers, at nonprofit arts center located in tropical Caribbean surroundings 8 miles from town of La Romana in the Dominican Republic; efficiency studios or apartments with kitchenettes; small individual studios nearby; small visual-arts–oriented library; no typewriters for writers. **Financial arrangement:** $100 nonreturnable reservation fee; resident pays rent of $300 a month and provides own meals (estimated cost $20 a day). **Guidelines:** prefers Spanish-speaking artists who can use talents to benefit community, and whose work relates to Dominican or Latin American context; residents may teach workshops and are expected to contribute to group exhibition/performance at end of stay; write for further information. **Application procedure:** letter explaining applicant's interest in program, work sample and resume. **Deadline:** 1 Jul 1996. **Notification:** 15 Aug 1996. **Dates:** residencies start 1 Feb 1997, 1 Jun 1997, 1 Sep 1997.

## ATLANTIC CENTER FOR THE ARTS

1414 Art Center Ave; New Smyrna Beach, FL 32168; (904) 427-6975;
(800) 393-6975
Suzanne Fetscher, *Executive Director*
Nicholas Conroy, *Program Director*

**Open to:** playwrights, composers. **Description:** 6 1–3-week workshops each year offering writers and visual and performing artists opportunity of concentrated study with internationally known Master Artists-in-Residence. **Financial arrangement:** resident pays $100 a week for tuition, $25 a day for private room with bath. **Application procedure:** Master Artist specifies submission materials and selects participants; write or call for brochure. **Deadline:** 4 months before residency. **Notification:** 3 months before residency. **Dates:** TBA; see brochure.

## BLUE MOUNTAIN CENTER

Blue Mountain Lake, NY 12812; (518) 352-7391
Harriet Barlow, *Director*

**Open to:** playwrights, composers, librettists, lyricists. **Description:** 4-week residency at center in Adirondack Mountains. **Financial arrangement:** free room and board; voluntary contribution requested. **Guidelines:** artist whose work is aimed at a general audience and reflects social concerns. **Application procedure:** statement of plan for work at center, including preference for early or late summer or fall residency; work sample, bio and reviews; $20 fee. **Deadline:** 1 Feb 1996. **Notification:** early Apr 1996. **Dates:** mid-Jun–mid-Oct 1996.

## BYRDCLIFFE ART COLONY

The Woodstock Guild; 34 Tinker St; Woodstock, NY 12498; (914) 679-2079
*Artists Residency Program*

**Open to:** playwrights, translators, librettists, lyricists, screenwriters. **Description:** 10 concurrent summer residencies of 1–4 4-week sessions (6 Jun–3 Jul, 4–31 Jul, 1–28 Aug, 29 Aug–25 Sep) for artists in all disciplines at historic 600-acre colony in the Catskill Mountains, 1½ miles from Woodstock village center, 90 miles north of New York City; private room and separate individual studio space in Villetta Inn, spacious turn-of-the-century mountain lodge; common dining room and living room; residents provide own meals, using community kitchen. **Financial arrangement:** resident pays fee of $400 for 6 Jun session, $500 for 4 Jul session, $500 for 1 Aug session, $400 for 29 Aug session; reductions offered to residents staying more than 1 session; limited scholarships available to eligible applicants. **Guidelines:** proof of serious commitment to field of endeavor is major criterion for acceptance; professional recognition helpful but not essential; send SASE for further information. **Application procedure:** completed application, work sample, project description, resume, reviews and articles if available, contact information for 2 references and $10 fee. **Deadline:** 15 Apr (applications received after deadline considered for any space still available). **Dates:** Jun–Sep.

## CAMARGO FOUNDATION
B.P. 75; 13260 Cassis; France; 33-42-01-1157, -1311
Michael Pretina, *Director*
*U.S. Office:*
W1050 First National Bank Bldg; 332 Minnesota St; St. Paul, MN 55101

**Open to:** playwrights, translators, composers. **Description:** 11 concurrent residencies, most for scholars and teachers pursuing projects relative to France, but also including 1 for writer, 1 for composer and 1 for visual artist, at estate in ancient Mediterranean fishing port 30 minutes from Marseilles; furnished apartments; music studio available for composer. **Financial arrangement:** free housing; residents provide own meals. **Guidelines:** resident outlines project to fellow colony members during stay and writes final report; families welcome when space available; write to U.S. office for guidelines. **Application procedure:** completed application, project description, bio and 3 letters of recommendation. **Deadline:** 1 Mar 1996. **Notification:** 15 Apr 1996. **Dates:** Sep–Dec; Jan–May.

## CHATEAU DE LESVAULT
58370 Onlay; Villapourçon; France; 33-86-843291, FAX -843578
Bibbi Lee, *Director*

**Open to:** playwrights, translators, librettists. **Description:** 5 concurrent winter residencies at 19th-century French château located in "le Morvan," a national park in western Burgundy 3½ hours from Paris, 3 hours from Geneva; large bedroom/studio with private bath; use of salon, library and grounds. **Financial arrangement:** resident pays Fr. 4500 (about $900) a month or Fr. 2500 (about $500) for 2 weeks, which covers room, utilities, and meals 7 days a week. **Application procedure:** brief description of project, maximum 3-page work sample, list of publications (if any) and 2 references; 50% deposit required 30 days before start of residency. **Deadline:** 90 days before proposed residency. **Dates:** Oct–Apr.

## DJERASSI RESIDENT ARTISTS PROGRAM
2325 Bear Gulch Rd; Woodside, CA 94062-4405; (415) 747-1250
Charles Amirkhanian, *Executive Director*
Carol Law, *General Manager*

**Open to:** playwrights, translators, composers, librettists, lyricists. **Description:** residencies of 1-month for 10 writers; choreographers; composers; media, visual and interdisciplinary artists and performers concurrently at 600-acre ranch in Santa Cruz mountains 1 hour south of San Francisco; interdisciplinary projects encouraged; collaborative projects considered. **Financial arrangement:** free room and board. **Guidelines:** emerging or established artist whose work has clear direction; write for brochure. **Application procedure:** completed application with sample of published work or work-in-progress, resume and $20 fee. **Deadline:** 15 Feb 1996 for 1997 residencies. **Notification:** 3 months. **Dates:** Apr–Oct.

## DORLAND MOUNTAIN ARTS COLONY
Box 6; Temecula, CA 92593; (909) 676-5039
*Admissions*

**Open to:** playwrights, composers, lyricists. **Description:** 1-month residencies for 6 writers, composers and visual artists concurrently in individual studios on 300-acre nature preserve 50 miles northeast of San Diego; no electricity. **Financial arrangement:** $50 processing fee on acceptance; resident pays rent of $150 a month. **Guidelines:** artist must demonstrate clear direction and accomplishment in field. **Application procedure:** send SASE for application and information. **Deadline:** 1 Sep 1995; 1 Mar 1996. **Notification:** 2 months.

## DORSET COLONY FOR WRITERS
Box 519; Dorset, VT 05251; (802) 867-2223
John Nassivera, *Director*

**Open to:** playwrights, composers, librettists, lyricists and collaborative teams. **Description:** residencies of 1 week–1 month at house located in historic village in southern VT. **Financial arrangement:** resident pays fee for housing according to means (suggested fee $90 a week); meals not provided; large, fully equipped kitchen. **Guidelines:** artist must demonstrate seriousness of purpose and have record of professional achievement (readings or productions of works); work sample may be requested from less established artist. **Application procedure:** letter of inquiry with description of proposed project and desired length and dates of stay; resume. **Deadline:** open. **Dates:** Sep–Nov; Mar–May.

## THE HAMBIDGE CENTER FOR CREATIVE ARTS AND SCIENCES
Box 339; Rabun Gap, GA 30568; (706) 746-5718
Judith Barber, *Executive Director*

**Open to:** playwrights, translators, composers, librettists, lyricists. **Description:** residencies of 2 weeks–2 months for professionals in all areas of arts and humanities on 600 acres in northeast GA mountains; 7 private cottages with bedroom, kitchen, bathroom and studio/work area; evening meal provided Mon–Fri, May–Oct only; send SASE for guidelines. **Financial arrangement:** resident pays $125 a week toward total cost. **Application procedure:** completed application, work sample, resume, reviews and 3 letters of recommendation from professionals in applicant's field. **Deadline:** 31 Jan 1996. **Notification:** 2–3 months. **Dates:** year-round; most residencies May–Oct.

## HAWTHORNDEN CASTLE INTERNATIONAL
## RETREAT FOR WRITERS
Lasswade, Midlothian; Scotland EH18 1EG; 441-31-440-2180
*Administrator*

**Open to:** playwrights. **Description:** spring, summer and fall residencies of 4 weeks at medieval castle on secluded crag overlooking valley of the River Esk 8 miles south of Edinburgh; 5 writers in residence at any one time; fully furnished study-bedroom; communal breakfast and dinner, lunch brought to writer's room; typewriter rental and use of excellent libraries in Edinburgh can be arranged. **Financial arrangement:** free room and board. **Guidelines:** author of at least 1 published work. **Application procedure:** write for application and further information. **Deadline:** 30 Sep 1995. **Notification:** Jan 1996. **Dates:** Feb–Dec 1996.

## HEADLANDS CENTER FOR THE ARTS
944 Fort Barry; Sausalito, CA 94965; (415) 331-2787
Jennifer Dowley, *Director*

**Open to:** playwrights, composers, librettists, lyricists, screenwriters, television writers. **Description:** residencies of 1–3 months for artists in all disciplines at center in national park on 13,000 acres of coastal wilderness across the bay from San Francisco; accommodation in 4-bedroom house with communal kitchen; evening meal provided in mess hall Sun–Thur; 11-month "live-out" residencies available for Bay Area artists only, providing studio space, 2 meals a week and access to center's facilities but no housing; all residents encouraged to interact with fellow artists in other media and with the environment. **Financial arrangement:** stipend of $500 a month, travel and free housing for artist from outside Bay Area; $2500 stipend and studio space for Bay Area artist. **Guidelines:** professional artist. **Application procedure:** non-Bay Area artist write for information; completed application from Bay Area artist (applications available Apr 1996). **Deadline:** Jun 1996 for Bay Area artists (exact date TBA). **Dates:** Feb–Dec 1997.

## HEDGEBROOK
(formerly Cottages at Hedgebrook)
2197 East Millman Rd; Langley, WA 98260; (360) 321-4786
Linda Bowers, *Director*

**Open to:** playwrights, librettists. **Description:** residencies of 1 week–3 months for women writers of diverse cultural backgrounds working in all literary genres; 6 individual cottages on 30 wooded acres on Whidbey Island, near Seattle; writer furnishes own typewriter or computer. **Financial arrangement:** free room and board. **Guidelines:** woman writer of any age, published or unpublished; women of color encouraged to apply. **Application procedure:** send SASE for application; submit completed application, project description and work sample. **Deadline:** 1 Oct 1995 for winter–spring 1996; 1 Apr 1996 for summer–fall 1996. **Notification:** 2 months.

## HELENE WURLITZER FOUNDATION OF NEW MEXICO
Box 545; Taos, NM 87571; (505) 758-2413
Henry A. Sauerwein, Jr., *Executive Director*

**Open to:** playwrights, composers, librettists, lyricists, screenwriters, television and radio writers. **Description:** 12 studio/apartments available to creative artists working in all media (performing artists ineligible); length of residency flexible, usually 3 months. **Financial arrangement:** free housing; resident provides own meals; no financial aid. **Application procedure:** completed application with project description, work sample and resume. **Deadline:** open. **Dates:** 1 Apr–30 Sep.

### THE JAMES THURBER WRITER-IN-RESIDENCE

The Thurber House; 77 Jefferson Ave; Columbus, OH 43215; (614) 464-1032
Michael J. Rosen, *Literary Director*

**Open to:** playwrights. **Description:** 4 residencies a year, each for 1 academic quarter (2 for journalists, 1 for playwright, 1 for poet or fiction writer); writer teaches course at Ohio State University. **Financial arrangement:** $5000 stipend; 2-bedroom apartment provided. **Guidelines:** playwright who has had at least 1 play produced by a major theatre; teaching experience helpful; write or call for further information. **Application procedure:** letter of interest and curriculum vita. **Deadline:** 15 Dec 1995. **Notification:** within 2 months. **Dates:** winter or spring 1997.

### JENNY MCKEAN MOORE VISITING WRITER IN WASHINGTON

Department of English; The George Washington University;
     Washington, DC 20052; (202) 994-6180
Christopher Sten, *English Department*

**Open to:** writers of poetic drama. **Description:** 1-year fellowship/teaching position for creative writers; fellow gives public reading of own work in fall and teaches a community writing workshop and 1 class for GWU students each semester. **Financial arrangement:** minimum salary of $40,000, benefits, moving allowance. **Guidelines:** practicing writer with experience of and commitment to teaching; conventional academic credentials not necessary; must reside in Washington area Sep–May of residency year. **Application procedure:** work sample, resume and letters of recommendation; write for details. **Deadline:** TBA (15 Nov in 1994).

### THE JOHN STEINBECK WRITER'S ROOM

Long Island University–Southampton Campus Library; Southampton, NY 11968;
     (516) 287-8382
Robert Gerbereux, *Library Director*

**Open to:** playwrights. **Description:** small room, space for 4 writers; carrel, storage space, access to reference material in room and to library. **Financial arrangement:** free. **Guidelines:** writer working under contract or with specific commitment. **Application procedure:** completed application.

### LEIGHTON STUDIOS

The Banff Centre for the Arts; Box 1020, Station 28; 107 Tunnel Mountain Dr;
     Banff, Alberta; Canada T0L 0C0; (403) 762-6180 or (800) 565-9989,
     FAX (403) 762-6345
*Office of the Registrar*

**Open to:** playwrights, composers. **Description:** residencies of 1 week–3 months for writers, composers, musicians and visual artists at colony situated in mountains of Banff National Park; 8 specially designed studios, each with washroom and kitchenette; living accommodation (single room with bath) on Centre's main campus; nearby access to all amenities of Centre, including communal cafeteria, library and recreation complex. **Financial arrangement:** resident pays for studio, room and meals; discount on studio cost only available for those who demonstrate need. **Guidelines:** artist who can demonstrate sustained contribution to own field and show evidence of significant achievement. **Application procedure:** write for application and further information. **Deadline:** open; apply at least 6 months before desired residency. **Dates:** year-round.

## THE MACDOWELL COLONY

100 High St; Peterborough, NH 03458; (603) 924-3886 or (212) 535-9690
Mary Carswell, *Executive Director*

**Open to:** playwrights, composers, film and video writers. **Description:** residencies of up to 2 months for writers, visual artists, video/filmmakers, architects and interdisciplinary artists at 450-acre estate; studios and common areas accessible for those with mobility impairments. **Financial arrangement:** voluntary contributions appreciated; fellowships and travel grants available. **Guidelines:** admission based on talent. **Application procedure:** send SASE or call for application; submit completed application, work samples, names of 2 professional references and $20 fee; collaborating artists must apply separately. **Deadline:** 15 Sep 1995 for Jan–Apr 1996; 15 Jan 1996 for May–Aug 1996; 15 Apr 1996 for Sep–Dec 1996. **Notification:** 2 months.

## MARY ANDERSON CENTER FOR THE ARTS

101 St. Francis Dr; Mount St. Francis, IN 47146; (812) 923-8602
Sarah Roberson Yates, *Executive Director*

**Open to:** playwrights, translators, composers, librettists, lyricists. **Description:** residencies of 1 week–3 months for 6 writers and visual artists concurrently at center on beautiful 400-acre wooded site with lake, 15 minutes from Louisville, KY; private studio/bedroom, communal kitchen and dining room. **Financial arrangement:** resident pays suggested minimum fee of $175 a week and provides own meals; possibility of funded residencies; write for information. **Guidelines:** formal education and production credits are not requirements but will be taken into consideration when applications are reviewed. **Application procedure:** completed application, project description, work sample, resume and 2 references. **Deadline:** open. **Dates:** year-round.

## THE MILLAY COLONY FOR THE ARTS

East Hill Rd; Box 3; Austerlitz, NY 12017-0003; (518) 392-3103
Gail Giles, *Assistant Director*

**Open to:** playwrights, composers, screenwriters. **Description:** 1-month residencies for up to 5 writers, composers and visual artists concurrently at 600-acre estate in upstate NY; studio space and separate bedroom. **Financial arrangement:** free room, board and studio space. **Application procedure:** send SASE for application; submit completed application and supporting materials. **Deadline:** 1 Sep for Feb–May; 1 Feb for Jun–Sep; 1 May for Oct–Jan. **Notification:** 10–12 weeks after deadline.

## NANTUCKET PLAYWRIGHTS RETREAT
Box 2177; Nantucket MA 02584; (508) 228-5002
Jim Patrick, *Director*

**Open to:** playwrights. **Description:** new project of Nantucket Theatrical Productions (see also Nantucket Short Play Festival in Prizes) to start in winter of 1995–96; residencies of 1 week or longer will probably be offered with opportunity to have work-in-progress read and discussed with directors, actors and peers during stay; accommodation in guest house with kitchen privileges. **Financial arrangement:** TBA; playwright will probably pay $100 workshop fee plus $200 a week for housing. **Application procedure:** write for information. **Deadline:** open. **Dates:** probably Jan–Mar.

## NEW YORK FOUNDATION FOR THE ARTS—ARTISTS IN RESIDENCE PROGRAM
155 Ave of the Americas, 14th Floor; New York, NY 10013-1507;
    (212) 366-6900, ext 222
Greg McCaslin, *Director, Education and Information*

**Open to:** schools and cultural organizations. **Description:** matching grants to assist schools and organizations bring in artists, including playwrights, composers, librettists and lyricists, for residencies of 12 days–10 months; residency activities include artist-conducted student or teacher workshops, lecture-demonstrations, readings and performances. **Financial arrangement:** artist is paid by school or organization; recommended minimum fee of $250 a day. **Guidelines:** artist must be NY State resident. **Application procedure:** completed application from school or organization; individual artists may not apply but are encouraged to write for guidelines and to collaborate with eligible sponsors to set up residencies; artists may also contact program for information and for help in finding sponsors. **Deadline:** 2 Apr 1996; subsidiary deadlines for smaller grants in Oct, Nov, Feb and Jun each year. **Dates:** Sep 1996–Jun 1997.

## NORCROFT
Box 300105; Minneapolis, MN 55403; (612) 377-8431
Marilyn Crawford, *Administrator*

**Open to:** playwrights. **Description:** four concurrent residencies of 1–4 weeks for writers of drama, fiction and poetry at remote lodge on shores of Lake Superior; private bedroom and separate individual "writing shed." **Financial arrangement:** free housing; groceries provided, resident does own cooking. **Guidelines:** women only; artist whose work demonstrates an understanding of and commitment to feminist change. **Application procedure:** completed application, five-page writing sample and description of project to be pursued at colony. **Deadline:** Nov or Dec 1995; exact date TBA. **Dates:** May–Oct.

## RAGDALE FOUNDATION

1260 North Green Bay Rd; Lake Forest, IL 60045; (708) 234-1063
Michael Wilkerson, *Director*

**Open to:** playwrights, composers, librettists, lyricists. **Description:** residencies of 2 weeks–2 months for writers and visual artists from all over the U.S. and abroad at estate situated on edge of prairie, 1 mile from center of town. **Financial arrangement:** resident pays $105 a week for room and board; partial or full fee waivers awarded on basis of financial need. **Guidelines:** admission based on quality of work submitted. **Application procedure:** send SASE for application; submit completed application, description of work-in-progress, work sample, resume, 3 references and $20 fee. **Deadline:** 15 Jan for Jun–Dec; 1 Jun for Jan–May. **Dates:** year-round except for 2 weeks in summer and 2 weeks in Dec.

## SAMUEL BECKETT PLAYWRITING INTERNSHIP

Gloucester Stage Company; 267 East Main St; Gloucester, MA 01930;
(508) 281-4099
Israel Horovitz, *Artistic Director*

**Open to:** playwrights. **Description:** 10-week residency for 1–2 playwrights at Gloucester Stage Company, a nonprofit professional theatre located in small working-class seaport on the Atlantic coast; intern, who is expected to start and complete new play under artistic director's guidance during residency, works on own writing each morning (word processor not provided), assists artistic director in afternoon and works as crew member on theatre's current production at night. **Financial arrangement:** $1000 stipend; free housing. **Guidelines:** early-career playwright. **Application procedure:** 20-page writing sample; detailed cover letter describing playwright's goals; resume and references; program contingent on funding (call before submitting). **Deadline:** 1 Mar 1996. **Notification:** May 1996. **Dates:** summer 1996.

## SHENANDOAH PLAYWRIGHT RESIDENCIES

ShenanArts; Rt 5, Box 167-F; Staunton, VA 24401; (703) 248-1868
Robert Graham Small, *Director of Playwriting and Screenwriting Programs*
Kathleen Tosco, *Managing Director*

**Open to:** playwrights, screenwriters. **Description:** residencies of 1 weekend–3 weeks at spacious rural home in Staunton, VA; private bedroom, shared common rooms, kitchen privileges; access to Staunton & Augusta County Library and to libraries at ShenanArts and Mary Baldwin College; writer may arrange for dramaturgical support from staff of Shenandoah Playwrights Retreat (see Development). **Financial arrangement:** resident pays $60 a weekend (Fri–Sun) or $100 a week. **Guidelines:** writer with substantial accomplishment in field who is working on specific project. **Application procedure:** 2 copies of draft of project with brief bio. **Deadline:** open. **Notification:** 2 months. **Dates:** year-round.

## Snug Harbor Cultural Center

1000 Richmond Terr; Staten Island, NY 10301-9926; (718) 448-2500
*Rental Coordinator*

**Open to:** playwrights, composers. **Description:** studio workspace in performing and visual arts center with theatre, art galleries, shops, museum, meeting rooms and banquet hall, located in 80-acre historic park. **Financial arrangement:** current monthly rental approximately $10 per sq. ft.; renewable 1-year lease; tenant must carry own insurance. **Guidelines:** professional artist. **Application procedure:** work sample with resume.

## The Tyrone Guthrie Centre

Annaghmakerrig; Newbliss; County Monaghan; Ireland; 353-47-54003,
    FAX -54380
Bernard Loughlin, *Resident Director*

**Open to:** playwrights, composers, librettists, lyricists, screenwriters, television writers. **Description:** residencies of 3 weeks–3 months for artists in all disciplines from Ireland and abroad at former country home of Tyrone Guthrie, set amid 400 acres of forested estate overlooking large lake; private apartments; music room, rehearsal/performance space and extensive library. **Financial arrangement:** non-Irish artists pay about Irish £1600 (about $2600) a month May–Aug, £1200 (about $1950) a month the rest of the year for housing and meals; self-catering houses also available at reasonable rents. **Guidelines:** artist must show evidence of sustained dedication and a significant level of achievement; prefers artists with clearly defined projects; artist teams (e.g. writer/director, composer/librettist) welcome; several weeks reserved each year for development of projects. **Application procedure:** write for application and further information.

## Ucross Foundation Residency Program

2836 U.S. Hwy 14-16 East; Clearmont, WY 82835; (307) 737-2291
Elizabeth Guheen, *Executive Director*

**Open to:** playwrights, translators, composers, librettists, lyricists. **Description:** residency of 2 weeks–2 months at "Big Red," restored historic site in the foothills of the Big Horn Mountains; 8 concurrent residencies for writers, composers and visual artists; opportunity to concentrate on own work without distraction and to present work to local communities, if desired. **Financial arrangement:** free room, board and studio space. **Guidelines:** criteria are quality of work and commitment. **Admission procedure:** completed application, project description and work sample; send SASE for application and further information. **Deadline:** 1 Oct for Jan–May; 1 Mar for Aug–Dec. **Notification:** 8 weeks.

## Vermont Studio Center

Box 613NW; Johnson, VT 05656; (802) 635-2727

**Open to:** playwrights, translators, screenwriters. **Description:** residencies of 2 or 4 weeks for up to 25 writers and visual artists "who, together with the year-round

VSC staff artists, form a dynamic working community" in Green Mountains of northern VT; opportunity for as much solitude or interchange and support as each resident wishes; private workspace and housing for writers in village residencies within walking distance of Red Mill complex containing dining room, lounge, offices and galleries; Johnson State College also within walking distance. **Financial arrangement:** resident pays $1400 for room and board for 4 weeks, $750 for 2 weeks; work-exchange fellowships awarded, based on financial need, to cover up to 50% of costs; write for information. **Guidelines:** established writer or one who shows promise. **Application procedure:** completed application, project description, 3 copies of script, resume, names of 3 references and $25 fee. **Deadline:** open. **Notification:** 2–3 weeks. **Dates:** year-round.

## VILLA MONTALVO ARTIST RESIDENCY PROGRAM
Box 158; Saratoga, CA 95071-0158; (408) 741-3421
Lori A. Wood, *Artist Residency Program Director*

**Open to:** playwrights, composers, screenwriters. **Description:** residencies of 1–3 months for 5 writers, musicians and visual artists concurrently at Mediterranean-style villa on 175 acres; rural setting close to major urban center. **Financial arrangement:** free housing; resident provides own meals, transportation; 4 fellowships available. **Guidelines:** spouses welcome; no children or pets. **Application procedure:** send SASE for application and guidelines. **Deadline:** 1 Sep for Apr–Sep; 1 Mar for Oct–Mar.

## VIRGINIA CENTER FOR THE CREATIVE ARTS
Box VCCA, Mt. San Angelo; Sweet Briar, VA 24595; (804) 946-7236
William Smart, *Director*

**Open to:** playwrights, translators, composers, librettists, lyricists, screenwriters. **Description:** residencies of 2 weeks–2 months for writers, composers, and visual and performance artists at 450-acre estate in Blue Ridge Mountains; separate studios and bedrooms; all meals provided. **Financial arrangement:** resident pays suggested minimum of $30 a day for room and board or as means allow; financial status not a factor in selection process. **Guidelines:** admission based on achievement or promise of achievement. **Application procedure:** completed application with work sample, resume and 2 recommendations. **Deadline:** 15 Sep for Jan–Apr; 15 Jan for May–Aug; 15 May for Sep–Dec. **Notification:** 2 months. **Dates:** year-round.

## WALDEN RESIDENCY PROGRAM
Northwest Writing Institute; Box 100, Lewis and Clark College;
    Portland, OR 97219; (503) 768-7745
Kim Stafford, *Director*

**Open to:** playwrights. **Description:** 3 6-week residencies for writers of drama, fiction, poetry and creative nonfiction at farm near Ashland, OR; 1 writer at a time housed in cabin with kitchen facilities, which opens onto meadow surrounded by forest. **Financial arrangement:** free; no meals provided. **Guidelines:**

OR resident only; write for brochure in fall. **Application procedure:** completed application, project description, work sample and list of publications or productions. **Deadline:** 30 Nov 1995. **Notification:** mid-Dec 1995. **Dates:** Mar–Sep 1996.

## WILLIAM FLANAGAN MEMORIAL CREATIVE PERSONS CENTER

Edward F. Albee Foundation; 14 Harrison St; New York, NY 10013;
(212) 226-2020

**Open to:** playwrights, translators, composers, librettists, screenwriters. **Description:** 1-month residencies for up to 6 writers, composers and visual artists concurrently at "The Barn" in Montauk, Long Island. **Financial arrangement:** free housing. **Guidelines:** admission based on talent and need. **Application procedure:** completed application, script (recording for composers) and supporting materials; write for information. **Deadline:** 1 Apr 1996; no submission before 1 Jan 1996. **Notification:** May 1996. **Dates:** Jun–Sep 1996.

## THE WRITERS ROOM

10 Astor Pl, 6th Floor; New York, NY 10003
Donna Brodie, *Executive Director*

**Open to:** playwrights, translators, composers, librettists, lyricists. **Description:** large room with 36 desks separated by partitions, space for 200 writers; open 24 hours a day year-round; kitchen, lounge and bathrooms, storage for files and typewriters, small reference library; monthly readings. **Financial arrangement:** $50 initiation fee; fee for 3-month period: $350 for permanent desk, $165 for "floater" desk. **Guidelines:** writer with specific project for 3-month period, renewal possible for up to 2 years or for duration of project. **Application procedure:** completed application and references; all inquiries by mail (no visits without appointment).

## THE WRITERS' STUDIO

The Mercantile Library Association; 17 East 47th St; New York, NY 10017;
(212) 755-6710
Harold Augenbraum, *Director*

**Open to:** playwrights, composers. **Description:** carrel space for 17 writers (3 reserved for writers of children's literature) in nonprofit, private lending library of 175,000 volumes; storage for personal computers or typewriters, library membership, access to special reference collection and rare collection of 19th-century American and British literature. **Financial arrangement:** $200 fee for 3 months, renewal possible for up to 1 year. **Guidelines:** open to all writers; unpublished writer must submit evidence of serious intent. **Application procedure:** completed application and work sample or project outline.

# YADDO

Box 395; Saratoga Springs, NY 12866-0395; (518) 584-0746
*Admissions Committee*

**Open to:** playwrights, composers, screenwriters. **Description:** residencies of 2 weeks–2 months for artists in all genres, working individually or as collaborative teams of up to 3 persons, at 19th-century estate on 400 acres; approximate total of 200 residents a year (15 concurrently Sep–May, 35 concurrently May–Labor Day). **Financial arrangement:** free room, board and studio space; contribution suggested to help underwrite cost of program. **Guidelines:** admission based on review by judging panels composed of artists in each genre; quality of work submitted is major criterion; send SASE for application and further information. **Application procedure:** completed application with work sample, resume, 2 letters of support, $20 fee and SASP for acknowledgment of receipt. **Deadline:** 15 Jan 1996 for 15 May 1996–28 Feb 1997; 1 Aug 1996 for 1 Nov 1996–mid-May 1997. **Notification:** 1 Apr 1996 for Jan deadline; 1 Oct 1996 for Aug deadline. **Dates:** year-round except early Sep.

# Membership and
# Service Organizations

**What's included here?**

A number of organizations that exist to serve either the American playwright or a wider constituency of writers, composers and arts professionals. Some have a particular regional or special-interest orientation; some provide links to theatres in other countries. Taken together, these organizations represent an enormous range of services available to those who write for the theatre, and it is worth getting to know them.


## THE ALLIANCE OF LOS ANGELES PLAYWRIGHTS
7510 Sunset Blvd, Suite 1050; Los Angeles, CA 90046-3418;
   (213) 957-4752
Hollis Evans, Monique Friedman and Michael Van Duzer, *Co-Chairs*

Founded in 1993, ALAP is a support and service organization dedicated to addressing the professional needs of the diverse Los Angeles playwriting community by facilitating creative programs nurturing the critical analysis of the theory and craft of playwriting, administering grants and fellowships, documenting and publishing the work of L.A. playwrights, creating an archive, and providing continuing advocacy for the playwright's voice in society. ALAP's programs and activities include general membership meetings; a voice-mail service which announces members' play readings, productions and other projects and provides information and referrals; a database of plays by L.A. playwrights to be made available to theatres and producers; a lab series; a community outreach program; and a quarterly newsletter. Dues are $29.95 a year (this sum is a donation and no playwright is turned away for lack of funds).

## THE ALLIANCE OF RESIDENT THEATRES/NEW YORK

131 Varick St, Room 904; New York, NY 10013-1410; (212) 989-5257
Virginia P. Louloudes, *Executive Director*
Mary Harpster, *Deputy Director*

A.R.T./New York is the trade and service organization for the New York City nonprofit professional theatre, serving more than 250 New York theatre companies and professional affiliates (theatres outside NY, colleges and universities, and organizations providing services to the theatre field). Publications of interest to playwrights include *Hot Seats*, which lists current productions in NYC, *Theatre Member Directory* ($5), and NYC Rehearsal and Performance Space Lists ($15 each), which provide information on spaces currently available for rent.

## ALTERNATE ROOTS

1083 Austin Ave; Atlanta, GA 30307; (404) 577-1079
Kathie deNobriga, *Executive Director*

Alternate ROOTS is a service organization run by and for southeastern artists. Its mission is to support the creation and presentation of original performing art that is rooted in a particular community of place, tradition or spirit. It is committed to social and economic justice and the protection of the natural world and addresses these concerns through its programs and services. Founded in 1976, ROOTS now has more than 260 individual members across the 13 states of the Southeast, including playwrights, directors, choreographers, musicians, storytellers, clowns and new vaudevillians—both solo artists and representatives of 60 performing and presenting organizations. ROOTS aims to make artistic resources available to its members through workshops; to create appropriate distribution networks for the new work being generated in the region via touring, publications and liaison activity; and to provide opportunities for enhanced visibility and financial stability via publications and periodic performance festivals. Opportunities for member playwrights include readings and peer critiques of works-in-progress at the organization's annual meeting. Artists who are residents of the Southeast and whose work is consistent with the goals of ROOTS are accepted as new members after a year's provisional status. Annual membership dues are $50. The organization's meetings and workshops are open to the public and its quarterly newsletter is available free to the public.

## THE AMERICAN ALLIANCE FOR THEATRE & EDUCATION (AATE)

c/o Department of Theatre; Arizona State University; Box 873411;
    Tempe, AZ 85287-3411; (602) 965-6064 (Mon–Fri, 8:30–2:30)
Barbara Salisbury Wills, *Executive Director*
Julie DeChurch, *Administrative Director*

AATE is a membership organization created in 1987 with the merger of the American Association of Theatre for Youth and the American Association for Theatre in Secondary Education. AATE provides a variety of services to support the work of theatre artists and educators who work with young people and to promote theatre and drama/theatre education in elementary and secondary schools. To encourage the development and production of plays for young audiences the AATE Unpublished Play Reading Project annually selects and publicizes promising new plays in this field. AATE also sponsors annual awards for the best play for young people and the outstanding book relating to any aspect of the field published in the past calendar year; only the play or book's publisher may nominate a candidate for these awards. AATE's publications, which are free to members, include a quarterly newsletter with a Playwright's Page; the quarterly *Youth Theatre Journal;* and the quarterly *STAGE of the Art.* Membership is open to all and costs $100 for organizations, $75 for individuals, $48 for retirees and $38 for students; please add $20 (U.S. funds) for foreign members (outside the U.S. and Canada).

## The American Film Institute

2021 North Western Ave; Box 27999; Los Angeles, CA 90027; (213) 856-7600
Jean Picker Firstenberg, *Director*
James Hindman, *Deputy Director*

*East Coast Offices:*
The John F. Kennedy Center for the Performing Arts; Washington, DC 20566; (202) 828-4000
1180 Ave of the Americas, 10th Floor; New York, NY 10036; (212) 398-6890

The American Film Institute is an independent nonprofit organization established by the National Endowment for the Arts in 1967 to advance and preserve the arts of film and television and to encourage and develop new talent in the field. In pursuit of these goals, the AFI runs the Center for Advanced Film and Television Studies at its L.A. campus, coordinates the preservation of the nation's moving-image heritage through its National Center for Film and Video Preservation, and maintains the American Film Institute Theater at the Kennedy Center. AFI also sponsors festivals and touring programs and conducts workshops such as the Directing Workshop for Women. Of special interest to writers is AFI's annual Television Writers Summer Workshop, held in L.A., which provides 2–4 weeks of intensive advanced training for 10 competitively selected writers, preferably new writers with media or theatre backgrounds who have no major commercial television writing credits; participants pay a fee of $475 and some scholarship assistance is available; interested writers should call (213) 856-7721 for guidelines and application information.

## American Indian Community House

404 Lafayette St; New York, NY 10003; (212) 598-0100
Rosemary Richmond, *Executive Director*
Jim Cyrus, *Director of Theatre*

American Indian Community House was founded in 1969 to encourage the interest of all U.S. ethnic groups in the cultural contributions of the American Indian, as well as to foster intercultural exchanges. The organization now serves the Native American population of the New York City region through a variety of social, economic and educational programs, and through cultural programs which include theatre events, an art gallery and a newsletter. Native Americans in the Arts, the performing arts component of the Community House, is committed to the development and production of works by Indian authors, and presents staged readings, workshop productions and full productions. The Community House also sponsors several other performing groups, including Spiderwoman Theatre Workshop, Coatlicue las Colorado, the actors' group Off the Beaten Path, the Thunderbird American Indian Dancers, and the jazz-fusion and traditional singing group Ulali (formerly known as Pura Fe). A showcase for Native American artists is presented to agents and casting directors once or twice a year.

## AMERICAN MUSIC CENTER

30 West 26th St, Suite 1001; New York, NY 10010-2011; (212) 366-5260
Nancy S. Clarke, *Executive Director*
Stacie W. Johnston, *Director of Information Services*

The American Music Center provides numerous programs and services for composers, performers and others interested in contemporary American music. The Jory Copying Assistance Program helps composers pay for copying music and extracting performance materials. The center's library contains more than 50,000 scores and recordings available for perusal by interested performers. The AMC provides information on competitions, publishers, performing ensembles, composers and other areas of interest in new music, and its publication *Opportunities for Composers* is updated annually. Membership is open to any person or organization wishing to support the center's promotion of the creation, performance and appreciation of American music. Annual dues are $45 for individuals ($25 for junior members). Members receive discounts on AMC publications, monthly "Opportunity Updates" and the option of participating in group health insurance. New members receive a free packet of information and articles of interest to the American composer. All members may vote in the annual board elections and attend the annual meeting.

## AMERICAN TRANSLATORS ASSOCIATION (ATA)

1800 Diagonal Rd, Suite 220; Alexandria, VA 22314-2840;
    (703) 683-6100, FAX (703) 683-6122
Walter W. Bacak, Jr., *Executive Director*

Founded in 1959, the ATA is a national not-for-profit association which seeks to promote recognition of the translation profession; disseminate information for the benefit of translators and those who use their services; define and maintain professional standards; foster and support the training of translators and interpreters; and provide a medium of cooperation with persons in allied professions. Active membership is open to U.S. citizens and permanent residents who have professionally engaged in translating or closely related work and have passed an ATA accreditation examination or demonstrated professional attainment by other prescribed means. Those who meet these professional standards but are not U.S. citizens or residents may hold Corresponding membership; other interested persons may be Associate members. All members receive the monthly *ATA Chronicle* and a membership directory. Other publications include a *Translation Services Directory* containing professional profiles of Active members. ATA holds an annual conference and sponsors several honors and awards (see American Translators Association Awards in Prizes). Interested persons should write for a membership application. Annual dues are $75 for Active, Corresponding and Associate members; $40 for Associate-Students; $100 for institutions; and $150 for corporations.

## ASCAP (AMERICAN SOCIETY OF COMPOSERS, AUTHORS AND PUBLISHERS)

1 Lincoln Plaza; New York, NY 10023; (212) 621-6234
Michael A. Kerker, *Director of Musical Theatre*

ASCAP is a nonprofit organization whose members are writers and publishers of musical works. It operates as a clearinghouse for performing rights, offering licenses that authorize the public performance of all the music of its composer, lyricist and music publishing members, and collecting license fees for these members. ASCAP also sponsors workshops for member and nonmember theatre writers (see ASCAP Musical Theatre Workshop in Development). Membership in ASCAP is open to any composer or lyricist who has been commercially recorded or "regularly published." Annual dues are $10 for individuals.

## ASIAN AMERICAN ARTS ALLIANCE

339 Lafayette St; New York, NY 10012-2725;
        (212) 979-6734, FAX (212) 979-8472
June Choi, *Executive Director*

Formed in 1983, Asian American Arts Alliance is a nonprofit organization dedicated to increasing the support, recognition and appreciation of Asian-American arts. Alliance activities focus on relaying information, networking, providing advocacy services and pursuing related special projects. Ongoing services include information referrals; a resource library of books, journals, periodicals, files and other unique information on Asian-American culture and arts; and publications such as a directory of *Asian American Arts Organizations in New York & New Jersey* and *Beyond Boundaries National Resource Book.* Current initiatives include a 3-year Technical Assistance and Regrant Initiative (TARI) to help New York City Asian-American arts groups strengthen and grow; a 2-year Presenting Opportunities Pilot (POP) to cultivate presenting opportunities for Asian-American artists; and a national research project culminating in a report on the state of Asian Pacific American arts. Interested individuals may call to be included on the mailing list. There are 6 membership levels: artist/student/senior, $20; individual, $35; nonprofit organization, $50; patron, $100; benefactor, $250 and corporate, $500. Contributing members receive free library borrowing privileges, and are sent the monthlies *Asian American Arts Calendar* and *Asian American Arts Resources and Opportunities* as well as the quarterly magazine *Dialogue.* Members also receive discounts on advertising, special publications and events;

additional services and savings are provided to patron, benefactor and corporate members.

## ASSITEJ/USA (INTERNATIONAL ASSOCIATION OF THEATRE FOR CHILDREN AND YOUNG PEOPLE)

2707 East Union St; Seattle, WA 98122; (206) 860-9212, FAX (206) 323-4611
Jolly Sue Baker, *Executive Director*

ASSITEJ/USA is a nonprofit theatre agency which advocates the development of professional theatre for young audiences in the USA and facilitates interchange among theatre artists and scholars of the 60 member countries of ASSITEJ. ASSITEJ/USA sponsors festivals and seminars, operates an international playscript exchange and, with ASSITEJ/Japan, is founder of the Pacific-Asia Exchange program. Members are theatres, institutions and individuals concerned for the theatre, young audiences and international goodwill. Members receive *Theatre for Young Audiences Today* and priority consideration for participation in national and international events. Membership costs $50 a year for individuals, $25 for students and retirees, $100–300 for organizations, depending on size of budget, and $30 for libraries. Write for membership application.

## THE ASSOCIATED WRITING PROGRAMS

Tallwood House, Mail Stop 1E3; George Mason University; Fairfax, VA 22030;
    (703) 993-4301
Markham Johnson, *Executive Director*

Founded in 1967, AWP serves the needs of writers, college and university writing programs, and students of writing by providing information services, job placement assistance, publishing opportunities, literary arts advocacy, and forums on all aspects of writing and its instruction. Writers not affiliated with colleges and universities but who support collective efforts to improve opportunities are also represented by AWP. The *AWP Chronicle*, published 6 times annually and available for $18 a year, includes listings of publishing opportunities, grants, awards and fellowships; interviews with writers; and essays on teaching creative writing. *The AWP Official Guide to Writing Programs* (7th edition, $23.95 postpaid) offers a comprehensive listing of writing programs and an expanded section on writing conferences, colonies and centers. Write or call AWP for information on membership requirements.

## THE ASSOCIATION OF HISPANIC ARTS

173 East 116th St; New York, NY 10029; (212) 860-5445
Sandra Perez, *Director of Programs*

A nonprofit organization founded in 1975, AHA promotes the Latin American arts as an integral part of this country's cultural life. It acts as a clearinghouse for information on all the arts, including theatre, and 9 times a year publishes a newsletter, *Hispanic Arts News*, that provides information on playwriting contests, workshops, forums and other items of interest to Latin American writers. AHA also provides technical assistance to Latin American writers seeking funding.

## ASSOCIATION OF INDEPENDENT VIDEO AND FILMMAKERS
625 Broadway, 9th Floor; New York, NY 10012;
    (212) 473-3400, FAX (212) 677-8732
Ruby Lerner, *Executive Director*

The association is a national trade organization of 5000 independent film and video makers. The independent producer's advocate in Washington and within the entertainment industry, AIVF offers members a subscription to *The Independent Film & Video Monthly* magazine; group insurance for health, disability, production liability and equipment; and other benefits. AIVF's educational arm, the Foundation for Independent Video and Film (FIVF), publishes *The Independent* as well as books related to the field, runs a festival bureau and conducts public events on independent production issues.

## THE AUDREY SKIRBALL-KENIS THEATRE
9478 West Olympic Blvd, Suite 304; Beverly Hills, CA 90212; (310) 284-8965
Mead Hunter, *Director of Literary Programs*

Since 1989, the Audrey Skirball-Kenis Theatre has been an arts service organization dedicated to playwrights and new playwriting. Each year A.S.K. presents 15–20 rehearsed readings, out of which 2–3 plays are selected for workshop productions (see the theatre's entry in Development). Allied programs supported by A.S.K. include: the A.S.K. Unpublished Plays Project, a repository of plays that premiered in southern California, housed in the L.A. Central Library; the international playwriting program at London's Royal Court Theatre; 2 playwright exchange programs, one with the Playwrights' Center of Minneapolis and another with the Royal Court; the Audrey Skirball-Kenis Playwrights Program at Lincoln Center; the Mark Taper Forum's New Work Festival; the UCLA Playwriting Award and the UCLA Playwriting Fellowship; the Los Angeles Drama Critics Circle Ted Schmitt Award; the playscript publication in TCG's *American Theatre* magazine; the *L.A. Weekly* Playwriting Award; and the commissioning of original work for the Los Angeles Festival. A.S.K. sponsors symposiums, caucuses and playwriting labs, which serve to create ongoing forums wherein issues may be explored or practical approaches to writing shared. In addition, the theatre offers playwrights various services, the latest of which is the Electronic Library, a computer bulletin-board system that enables potential producers to search on-line for plays meeting specific criteria, and that provides writers with interactive opportunities for information-sharing and networking. A.S.K.'s publications include summary booklets of the symposium series entitled *Inventing the Future*, the *Directory of Los Angeles Playwright Groups*; the texts of plays given workshop productions; *Plays for Consideration*, an annual publication that documents the plays presented by A.S.K.; and a news magazine featuring interviews with and essays by leading theatre professionals. For additional information about A.S.K.'s programs and publications, contact the theatre.

## AUSTRALIAN NATIONAL PLAYWRIGHTS' CENTRE
Box 1566 Rozelle; Sydney, New South Wales, Australia 2039; 61-2-555-9377, FAX 61-2-555-9370
Kate Riedl, *General Manager*

Founded in 1972, the Australian National Playwrights' Center (ANPC) is a developmental organization formed to aid Australian playwrights and promote and nurture high-quality stage writing in Australia. The ANPC holds staged readings and workshops; provides a year-round script assessment service (for a fee), through which 16–18 plays are selected for development; holds the annual 2-week Australian National Playwrights' Conference, which provides full workshops for 8–10 scripts; and hosts Young Playwrights' Weekends in 5 Australian states. Together with New Dramatists in New York City, ANPC sponsors the ANPC New Dramatists Award, a playwright exchange program that provides workshop development and a public presentation of a play by an Australian playwright at the New Dramatists facilities; *deadline:* Jul 1996. To become a member of the ANPC, writers pay $30 to join and a $30 annual subscriber's fee. Members receive *Dialogue,* a quarterly journal, and reduced fees for the script assessment service and playwriting courses.

## BLACK THEATRE NETWORK
Box 11502, Fisher Bldg Station; Detroit, MI 48211; (313) 577-7906
Lundeana Thomas, *President*
Addell Austin Anderson, *Membership Services*

Black Theatre Network (BTN) is a national network of professional artists, scholars and community groups founded in 1986 to provide an opportunity for the interchange of ideas; to collect and disseminate through its publications information regarding black theatre activity; to provide an annual national forum for the viewing and discussing of black theatre; and to encourage and promote black dramatists and the production of plays about the black experience. BTN members attend national conferences and workshops and receive complimentary copies of all BTN publications, which include the quarterly *BTN News,* listing conferences, contests, employment opportunities, BTN business matters and other items of interest from across the country; *Black Theatre Directory,* which contains over 800 listings of black theatre artists, scholars, companies, higher education programs and service organizations; *Dissertations Concerning Black Theatre: 1900–1994,* a listing of Ph.D. theses on black theatre; and *Minority Job Bulletin,* a quarterly listing of jobs in educational and professional theatre. *Black Voices,* a catalogue of works by black playwrights, is available from BTN for $15. Annual dues are $95 for organizations, $60 for individuals, $25 for retirees and students.

## BMI (BROADCAST MUSIC INCORPORATED)
320 West 57th St; New York, NY 10019; (212) 586-2000
Jean Banks, *Senior Director, Musical Theater and Jazz*

BMI, founded in 1940, is a performing rights organization which acts as steward for the public performance of the music of its writers and publishers, offering licenses to music users. BMI monitors music performances and distributes royalties to those whose music has been used. Any writer whose songs have been published and are likely to be performed can join BMI at no cost. BMI also sponsors a musical theatre workshop (see BMI-Lehman Engel Musical Theatre Workshop in Development).

The BMI Foundation (President, Theodora Zavin) was established in 1984 to provide support for individuals in furthering their musical education and to assist organizations involved in the performance of music and music training.

## BRITISH AMERICAN ARTS ASSOCIATION

116 Commercial St; London E1 6NF; England; 441-71-247-5385
Jennifer Williams, *Executive Director*

British American Arts Association acts as an information service and clearing-house for exchange between British and American cultural activities in all the arts fields. It provides information, advice, advocacy and technical assistance to professional artists, administrators and sponsors working in all arts disciplines, as well as in arts-and-education programs, throughout both countries.

## BROADWAY ON SUNSET

c/o Songwriters Guild of America; 6430 Sunset Blvd; Hollywood, CA 90028;
    (818) 508-9270
Libbe S. HaLevy, *Artistic Director*

Broadway on Sunset, established in 1981, has been sponsored by the Songwriters Guild of America since 1992 (see entry in this section). Broadway on Sunset provides developmental programs that emphasize a full understanding of the principles and standards of Broadway-level craft, and that provide musical theatre writers (composers, lyricists, librettists) with the opportunity to test their material at each level of development in front of an audience. In 1994, 18 new musicals received a first reading for an audience of music-theatre professionals. Except for the Musical Theater Referral Service, which draws from a national population, writers and composers must have access to the Los Angeles area to benefit from the programs. There are no membership dues; participants pay nominal fees for classes, readings and workshops. Scholarships are available. After 1 Oct 1995, writers may submit book and cassette tape containing no more than 4 songs for consideration. .

## CAROLINA PLAYWRIGHTS CENTER

(formerly North Carolina Playwrights Center)
Box 1705; Pinehurst, NC 28374; (910) 295-6896
Carolyn Cole Montgomery, *Artistic Director*

Founded in 1989, CPC is a service organization for member playwrights, providing developmental opportunities up to and including full production and marketing support. Member playwrights receive script mailing and duplicating services; newsletter; library privileges; and a 10% discount on all Center events and items. The Center selects playwrights from its membership to participate in Playwrights-at-Work, a play-development program and prerequisite for participation in all developmental programs and productions, such as Carolina Playwrights Festival and Tour Network. Playwrights must be dues-paying members or invited guests to participate in the Center's programs. Member playwrights must be native or current residents of North or South Carolina. To become a member or to be considered as a guest artist, submit a letter of introduction and resume. Playwrights eligible for membership will receive a contract to be signed and returned along with annual dues payment of $100. Guest artist inquiries will be placed on file.

## Chicago Alliance for Playwrights (CAP)

Theatre Building; 1225 West Belmont; Chicago, IL 60657; (312) 929-7367
Allan Chambers, *Board Member*

The Chicago Alliance for Playwrights is a service organization founded in 1990 to establish a network for Chicago-area playwrights and others committed to the development of new work for the stage. Members of the coalition include Bailiwick Repertory (see Production), Columbia College New Musicals Project, Music/Theatre Workshop, New Tuners Theatre Workshop, Studio Z, Voices, Women's Theatre Alliance (see this section), Writers Bloc and Zebra Crossing. The alliance sponsors forums of interest to writers and publishes an annual directory of Chicago-area playwrights and their principal works. Write or call for membership details; annual dues are $15 for individuals and $75 for groups.

## Chicago Dramatists Workshop

1105 West Chicago Ave; Chicago, IL 60622; (312) 633-0630
Russ Tutterow, *Artistic Director*

Founded in 1980, Chicago Dramatists Workshop is dedicated to the development and advancement of playwriting and new plays. It employs a variety of programs to nurture the artistic and career development of both established and emerging playwrights. These programs include play readings, classes, workshops, symposiums, discussions, panels, productions, festivals, talent coordination, marketing services, collaborative projects with other theatres, national playwright exchanges and referrals to producers.

   The Resident Playwright program seeks to nurture and promote the work and careers of dramatists who will make potentially significant contributions to the national theatre repertory. At no charge, Resident Playwrights benefit from the Workshop's fullest and longest-term support (a 3-year, renewable term), with full access to all of the Workshop's programs and services. Admittance to the program is selective, with emphasis on artistic and professional accomplishment or potential. While most Resident Playwrights are from the Chicago area, dramatists from around the country who are able to spend substantial time in Chicago may also apply. Interested playwrights should contact the Workshop for full information and details of the application procedure, which includes the submission of 2 plays, a resume and letters of recommendation and intent. *Deadline:* 1 Jun each year (no submission before 1 Apr).

   The Playwrights' Network provides any U.S. playwright the opportunity to form an association with the Workshop. For an annual fee of $95, Network

Playwrights receive written script critiques, consideration for all Workshop programs (including the annual New Voices Festival), class discounts and free admittance to Workshop events.

Classes, Script Consultancies, the bimonthly 10-Minute Workshop and the triannual Deadline Workshop are open to all playwrights. A quarterly newsletter announces the Workshop's events and programs and includes application procedures.

### COLORADO DRAMATISTS
Box 101405; Denver, CO 80250; (303) 595-5600
Wesley Webb, *President*

Founded in 1981, Colorado Dramatists, with chapters in Denver and Boulder, is a service organization for playwrights at all levels of development. In addition to bimonthly public readings, the organization sponsors private developmental readings, workshops and group nights at the theatre. Members receive a monthly newsletter, *The Colorado Theatre Guide*, and access to rehearsal space, and make photocopies at a discount. Annual membership dues are $30 a year.

### CONMOCIÓN'S LATINA LESBIAN WRITERS' TELARAÑA
1521 Alton Rd, #336; Miami Beach, FL 33139;
    (305) 751-8385, FAX (305) 642-8522
tatiana de la tierra, *Director*

Conmoción's latina lesbian writers' telaraña supports Latina lesbian writers by providing information, access to resources and a connection to each other through publications, such as *telaraña alert*, a quarterly newsletter that includes current news and information on contests, conferences, courses, calls for writing submission and retreats; a networking/support list of members for members; and *conmoción*, a 3 issue-per-year Latina lesbian magazine. Members pay $27 per year and receive all publications.

### CORPORATION FOR PUBLIC BROADCASTING
901 E St NW; Washington, DC 20004; (202) 879-9600
Rick Madden, *Director, Radio Program Fund*
Don Marbury, *Director, Television Program Fund*

The Corporation for Public Broadcasting, a private nonprofit organization funded by Congress and by private sources, promotes and helps finance public television and radio. CPB provides grants to local public television and radio stations; conducts research in audience development, new broadcasting technologies and other areas. The corporation helped establish the Public Broadcasting Service and National Public Radio (see entries in this section). It supports public radio programming through programming grants to stations and other producers, and television programming by funding proposals made by stations and independent producers.

## THE DRAMATISTS GUILD

234 West 44th St, Penthouse; New York, NY 10036-3909; (212) 398-9366
Peter Stone, *President*
Richard Garmise, *Executive Director*

Founded over 70 years ago, the Dramatists Guild is the professional association of playwrights, composers and lyricists, with more than 6000 members worldwide. All theatre writers are eligible to apply for 1 of the following 7 membership levels. 1. Associate ($75 a year): any interested theatre writer, whether produced or not, is eligible. 2. Active ($125 a year): writers who have been produced on Broadway, Off-Broadway or on the main stage of a regional theatre. 3. Estate ($125 a year): representatives of the estates of deceased Active members. 4. Institutional Subscriber ($100 a year): colleges, universities, libraries and educational theatres. 5. Subscriber ($50 a year): non-playwrights engaged in a drama-related field. 6. Professional Subscriber ($200 a year): agents and attorneys. 7. Student ($35 a year): students enrolled in a college or university writing degree program. For most categories of membership the Guild offers the following activities and services: use of the Guild's contracts, including the Approved Production Contract for Broadway musicals and plays, the regional theatre contract, a collaboration agreement for both musicals and dramas, the 99 Seat Theatre Plan contract (Los Angeles), the showcase contract (New York) and the Small Theatre contract; advice on all theatrical contracts including Broadway, Off-Broadway, regional, showcase, Equity-waiver, dinner-theatre, collaboration agreements, underlying rights agreements and dramatic publishing contracts; a nationwide toll-free number for all members with business or contract questions or problems; advice and information on a wide spectrum of issues affecting writers; free and/or discounted ticket service; symposiums led by experienced professionals in major cities nationwide; access to 2 health insurance programs and a group term life insurance plan; a reference library; a spacious and elegant meeting room which can accommodate up to 50 people for readings and auditions and which is available to members on a rental basis; and a Committee for Women.

The Guild publishes *The Dramatists Guild Quarterly*, a journal which contains articles on all aspects of theatre; *The Dramatists Guild Resource Directory*, published annually with up-to-date information on agents, attorneys, grants, producers, playwriting contests, conferences and workshops; and *The Dramatists Guild Newsletter*, issued 8 times a year to Active, Associate, Estate, Professional Subscriber and Student members only, with announcements of all Guild activities, and news and information of more immediate interest to dramatists.

## THE FIELD

161 Sixth Ave; New York, NY 10013; (212) 691-6969
Steve Gross, *Executive Director*

The Field is a not-for-profit organization dedicated to helping independent performing artists and groups develop artistically and professionally through a variety of performance opportunities, workshops, services and publications. The Field does not engage in curatorial activity; all artists are eligible to participate in its programs. Of special interest to New York metropolitan area playwrights wishing to produce their own work are programs such as the 90 Plays in 9 Days festival; marathon performances of 12-minute works; and Fieldwork, 10-week group developmental workshops for works-in-progress, culminating in performances. The Field assists artists with all aspects of producing their work, including grant writing, fund raising, project management, securing performance and rehearsal space, and cooperative promotional efforts. Publications include *Self-Production Guide*; *Funding Guide for Independent Artists*; *Space Chase*, a listing of performance opportunities in New York City as well as out-of-town festivals, residencies and artist colonies; and *Dealing with Healing*, a listing of healing practitioners who have artists' budgets in mind. All programs are available to members and non-members; members receive publications free, discounts on programs and may use the Field as an umbrella organization, falling under its nonprofit status. Annual membership costs $75; individual programs range in cost from $15–65. Striving to bring its programs to locations outside New York, the Field has initiated project sites in Atlanta, Chicago, Houston, Miami, Philadelphia, Seattle and Washington D.C.

## First Stage
Box 38280; Los Angeles, CA 90038; (213) 850-6271
Dennis Safren, *Literary Manager*

Founded in 1983, First Stage is a service organization for playwrights that holds staged readings, which are videotaped for the author's archival purposes; conducts workshops; provides referral services for playwrights; and publishes *First Stage Newsletter*. Services are free to nonmembers, except for workshops, which are available to members only. Membership dues are $35 per quarter or $115 per year.

## The Foundation Center
*National Libraries:*
1001 Connecticut Ave NW; Washington, DC 20036; (202) 331-1400
79 Fifth Ave; New York, NY 10003; (212) 620-4230
Judith Margolin, *Director of Public Services, New York Library*

*Field Offices:*
312 Sutter St; San Francisco, CA 94108; (415) 397-0902
Hurt Bldg, Suite 150, Grand Lobby; 50 Hurt Plaza; Atlanta, GA 30303;
    (404) 880-0094
1422 Euclid, Suite 1356; Cleveland, OH 44115; (216) 861-1934

The Foundation Center is a nationwide service organization established and supported by foundations to provide a single authoritative source of information on foundation giving. It disseminates information on foundations through a public service program and through such publications as *The Foundation Directory* and *The Foundation Grants Index*. Of special interest is *Foundation Grants to Individuals*, which lists scholarships, fellowships, residencies, internships, grants, loans, awards, prizes and other forms of assistance available to individuals from approximately 2600 grantmakers (1995 edition $65). The center maintains 5 libraries and a national network of more than 190 cooperating collections. For the name of the collection nearest you or for more information about the center's programs, call toll free (800) 424-9836.

## THE GOLDEN WEST PLAYWRIGHTS AT THE ROAD THEATRE

Box 2149; Los Angeles, CA 90078-2149
Jon Bastian, *Co-Director*

Founded in 1985, the Golden West Playwrights at the Road Theatre is a playwright-run developmental workshop and professional support group, which holds cold readings and closed and public staged readings performed by its resident acting company; and provides a reference and script library. The theatre also holds occasional one-act festivals, off-night workshop productions and mainstage productions. Services are provided to members only, who must be South California residents. Membership is free and obtained by submission or through member referral. The theatre is especially interested in women and minority playwrights.

## HATCH-BILLOPS COLLECTION

491 Broadway, 7th Floor; New York, NY 10012; (212) 966-3231
James V. Hatch, *Executive Secretary*

The Hatch-Billops Collection is a nonprofit research library specializing in black American art and theatre history. It was founded in 1975 to collect and preserve primary and secondary resource materials in the black cultural arts; to provide tools and access to these materials for artists and scholars, as well as the general public; and to develop programs in the arts which use the collection's resources. The library's holdings include 1800 oral-history tapes; theatre programs; approximately 300 unpublished plays by black American writers from 1858 to the present; files of clippings, letters, announcements and brochures on theatre, art and film; slides, photographs and posters; and more than 4000 books and 400 periodicals. The collection also presents a number of salon interviews and films, which are open to the public; and publishes transcriptions of its annual "Artist and Influence" series of salon interviews, many of which are with playwrights. The collection is open to artists, scholars and the public by appointment only.

## HISPANIC ORGANIZATION OF LATIN ACTORS (HOLA)

250 West 65th St; New York, NY 10023; (212) 595-8286
Manuel Alfaro, *Executive Director*

Founded in 1975, HOLA is an arts service organization for Hispanic performers and related artists. HOLA provides information, casting referral services, professional seminars and workshops. The organization publishes a biennial *Directory of Hispanic Talent* and a newsletter, *La Nueva Ola,* that lists job opportunities, grants and contests of interest to Hispanic artists. Members pay annual dues of $45.

## INDEPENDENT FEATURE PROJECT
104 West 29th St, 12th Floor; New York, NY 10001-5310;
(212) 465-8200, FAX (212) 465-8525
Catherine Tait, *Executive Director*

The Independent Feature Project (IFP), a nonprofit membership-supported organization, was founded in 1979 to encourage creativity and diversity in films produced outside the established studio system. The IFP produces the Independent Feature Film Market (IFFM), the premiere film event for independent cinema from both U.S. and international producers. The IFFM features over 350 independent features, shorts, and works-in-progress and feature scripts. The IFP and IFP/West publish *Filmmaker,* a quarterly magazine. IFP also sponsors a series of screenings, professional seminars and industry showcases, including a conference on screenplay development. Group health insurance, a production insurance package, a Resource Program, publications, and a series of audiotapes of previous seminars and workshops are available to members. Membership dues start at $100 a year ($65 for students).

## INSTITUTE FOR CONTEMPORARY EAST EUROPEAN AND SLAVIC DRAMA AND THEATRE
Graduate Center of the City University of New York; Box 355; 33 West 42nd St;
New York, NY 10036-8099; (212) 642-2231, -2235
Daniel C. Gerould and Alma H. Law, *Co-Directors*

The Institute for Contemporary East European and Slavic Drama and Theatre, under the auspices of the Center for Advanced Study in Theatre Arts (CASTA), publishes annotated bibliographies of translations of East European plays written since 1945. Two bibliographies are currently available at $5 each ($6 foreign): *Soviet Plays in Translation* and *Polish Plays in Translation.* The institute is interested in hearing of published or unpublished translations for possible listing in updated editions of these bibliographies; translators may submit descriptive letters or scripts. A triquarterly journal published by the institute/CASTA, *Slavic and East European Performance: Drama, Theatre, Film,* is available by subscription ($10 a year, $15 foreign) and includes articles about current events in the East European and Slavic theatre, as well as reviews of productions and interviews with playwrights, directors and other theatre artists.

## INSTITUTE OF OUTDOOR DRAMA
CB #3240; Nations Bank Plaza; University of North Carolina;
Chapel Hill, NC 27599-3240; (919) 962-1328
Scott J. Parker, *Director*

The Institute of Outdoor Drama, founded in 1963, is a research and advisory agency of the University of North Carolina. It serves as a communications link between producers of existing outdoor dramas and is a resource for groups, agencies or individuals who wish to create new outdoor dramas or who are seeking information on the field. The institute provides professional consultation and conducts feasibility studies; holds annual auditions for summer employment in outdoor drama; sponsors conferences, lectures and symposiums; and publishes a quarterly newsletter, as well as information bulletins. Writers should note that the institute maintains a roster of available artists and production personnel, including playwrights and composers. It seeks to interest established playwrights and composers in participating in the creation of new outdoor dramas, and to encourage and advise new playwrights who wish to write for this specialized form of theatre. On occasion the institute will read scripts by produced playwrights, who should send a letter of inquiry before submitting their work.

## INTERNATIONAL CENTER FOR WOMEN PLAYWRIGHTS
819 Forest Ave; Buffalo, NY 14209; (716) 882-9238, FAX (716) 883-6300
Deborah Kane, Carolyn Kawecka and Camille Kazmierczak, *Co-Directors*

The ICWP supports women playwrights around the world, continuing the work begun with the First International Women Playwrights Conference, held in Buffalo in 1988. The center solicits new work at intervals, presents readings and channels work to production venues; it welcomes contact with theatre organizations seeking new plays by women. The center also publishes a periodical and newsletter which provide information about upcoming International Women Playwrights Conferences, and it handles communications for the International Advisory Committee, which determines sites and policies for these conferences. Basic membership dues are $20 (larger contributions are welcome); checks should be made out to the U.B. Foundation-ICWP.

## INTERNATIONAL THEATRE INSTITUTE
## OF THE UNITED STATES (ITI/US)
47 Great Jones St; New York, NY 10012; (212) 254-4141, FAX (212) 254-6814
Martha W. Coigney, *Director*
Lynn Gross, *Associate Director*
Louis A. Rachow, *Library Director*

Now operating centers in 90 countries, ITI was founded in 1948 by UNESCO "to promote the exchange of knowledge and practice in the theatre arts." ITI assists foreign theatre visitors in the U.S. and American theatre representatives traveling abroad. The ITI International Theatre Collection is a reference library which documents theatrical activity in 146 countries and houses over 12,700 plays from 97 countries. American playwrights, as well as other theatre professionals, frequently use the collection to make international connections; to consult foreign theatre directories for names of producers, directors or companies with a view to submitting plays abroad; and to research the programs and policies of theatres or managements. ITI answers numerous requests from abroad about American plays and also provides information on rights to foreign plays to American producers, directors and literary managers. Building upon its commitment to theatre professionals, ITI recently began the University and Theatre Partner Programs in order to work more closely with institutions interested in international exchange.

## THE INTERNATIONAL WOMEN'S WRITING GUILD

Box 810, Gracie Station; New York, NY 10028-0082; (212) 737-7536
Hannelore Hahn, *Executive Director*

The International Women's Writing Guild, founded in 1976, is a network of women writers in the U.S., Canada and abroad. Playwrights, television and film writers, songwriters, producers and other women involved in the performing arts are included in its membership. Workshops are offered at 13 events throughout the U.S. and annually at a week-long writing conference/retreat at Skidmore College in Saratoga Springs, NY. Members may also submit playscripts to theatres who have offered to read, critique and possibly produce IWWG members' works. *Network*, a 32-page newsletter published 6 times a year, provides a forum for members to share views and to learn about playwriting contests and awards, and theatre- and TV-related opportunities. The guild offers contacts with literary agents, group health and life insurance and other services to its members. Annual dues are $35 ($45 for foreign membership).

## LATIN AMERICAN THEATER ARTISTS

30 Grant Ave; San Francisco, CA 94108; (415) 834-3225
Luis Oropeza, *Artistic Director*

Latin American Theater Artists is a performing and support organization. As a theatre, LATA "embraces Latino theatre from its indigenous roots in Spain and the Americas through its classical development and its contemporary expression." LATA annually produces one full production, a reading series and a children's show. As an organization, LATA offers a casting and referral service to its dues-paying members, training workshops and a newsletter. LATA primarily serves Bay Area Latinos and Latinas, but is open for membership nationally. Annual dues are $25; checks should be made out to LATA.

## LEAGUE OF CHICAGO THEATRES/
## LEAGUE OF CHICAGO THEATRES FOUNDATION

67 East Madison, Suite 2116; Chicago, IL 60603-3013; (312) 977-1730
Tony Sertich, *Executive Director*

Founded in 1979, the League of Chicago Theatres/League of Chicago Theatres Foundation is a trade and service organization for Chicago theatre companies, theatre personnel and freelance artists. It provides marketing, advocacy and membership services; and acts as an information clearinghouse, maintains resource files, conducts seminars and publishes a bimonthly newsletter. The League's HOTTIX program sells full-price theatre, concert and sports-related tickets as well as half-price day-of-performance theatre tickets.

## LEAGUE OF PROFESSIONAL THEATRE WOMEN/NEW YORK

c/o Shari Upbin; 45 East 89th St, 19F; New York, NY 10128; (212) 534-7983
Shari Upbin, *President*

Founded in 1979, the league is a not-for-profit organization of theatre professionals providing programs and services which promote women in all areas of professional theatre, create industry-related opportunities for women, and highlight contributions of theatre women, past and present. Through its seminars, educational programs, social events, awards and festivals, the league links professional, university and community theatres with theatre women nationally and internationally and provides an ongoing forum for ideas, methods and issues of concern to the theatrical community and its audiences. Programs include the Lee Reynolds Award, given annually to a woman or women whose work for, in, about or through the medium of theatre has helped to illuminate the possibilities for social, cultural or political change; the League Scholarship, given to a girl of high school age to study theatre in a professional setting during the summer; the annual Short Plays festival; the Oral History Project, which seeks to chronicle and document the contribution of significant theatre women; a Careers Committee; a membership directory; and panels discussing topics of interest to women theatre professionals with well-known experts in the field. Regular monthly meetings enable members to network, initiate programs and serve on committees. To be eligible for membership in the league, playwrights, composers, librettists and lyricists must have had a work presented in a First Class production in the U.S. or Canada; or in a New York City theatre under Equity's Basic Minimum Contract, excluding showcases; or at least 2 productions presented in a resident theatre, as defined under Equity's Minimum Basic Contract for Resident Theatres. Annual dues are $75. For further details of membership eligibility and application procedure, write or call for Membership Information brochure.

## LEND (LESBIAN EXCHANGE OF NEW DRAMA)
559 Third St; Brooklyn, NY 11215
Anne Harris, *Artistic Director*

LEND is a play development organization and support group for lesbian playwrights and directors. The organization produces the year-round Sunday Morning Reads of New Lesbian Plays, workshops and rehearsed readings of new plays for an audience of theatre professionals on the last Sunday of each month. In addition, LEND publishes a quarterly newsletter and circulates scripts through its LENDlist program. The group also sponsors the annual Lesbian Play Award for a previously produced or unproduced play by a lesbian writer which focuses on issues relevant to lesbian life. The award carries a $200 cash prize and possible production in a festival of staged readings; playwrights must be from the New York City area or able to travel to rehearsals and the reading at their own expense; *deadline:* 1 Apr 1996; *notification:* 1 Jun 1996; *dates:* Jun 1996.

## LITERARY MANAGERS AND DRAMATURGS
## OF THE AMERICAS
Box 355–CASTA; CUNY Graduate Center; 33 West 42nd St;
New York, NY 10036; (212) 642-2657

LMDA is the professional service organization for American and Canadian literary managers and dramaturgs, founded in 1985 to affirm, examine and encourage these professions. Among the programs and services it offers are a free 800-

number telephone job line; insurance coverage; the quarterly *LMDA Review*, the LMDA Script Exchange; the Production Diaries project; New Dramaturgs, which identifies and encourages new members of the profession and works to establish them in productive professional affiliations; the University Program, which provides a liaison between training programs and the profession; and the National Theater Translation Fund. Activities include public panels, symposiums and workshops, as well as membership-only meetings and an annual conference. Associate membership is open to playwrights, artistic directors, literary agents and other theatre professionals interested in dramaturgy. Dues are $45 for voting members, $35 for associates, $20 for students and $100 for institutional memberships.

## LUMINOUS VISIONS

267 West 89th St; New York, NY 10024; (212) 581-7455
Carla Pinza, *Founder and Artistic Director*

Founded in 1976, Luminous Visions is a multicultural, nonprofit organization dedicated to developing the creative skills and culture of writers, directors and actors seeking employment within the English-speaking television and film mainstream. The organization sponsors a weekly workshop for writers, an annual Writers Forum and a spring Stage Reading Festival.

## MARY ANDERSON CENTER FOR THE ARTS

101 St. Francis Dr; Mount Saint Francis, IN 47146; (812) 923-8602
Sarah Roberson Yates, *Executive Director*

The Mary Anderson Center, founded in 1989, is a nonprofit organization dedicated to cultivating multidisciplinary exchange between artists and those who celebrate the artistic experience. Named after the 19th-century actress from Louisville who rose to become an international celebrity, the center is located on 400 acres in southern Indiana. The center's goal is to provide retreats and residencies for artists in many disciplines (see the organization's entry in Colonies and Residencies). As part of its outreach effort to the Midwest and the nation, the center sponsors symposiums, conferences and other gatherings which explore, in a multidisciplinary mode, topics of major interest to society and to artists. Contributors to the center receive a quarterly newsletter featuring center activities and news of area artists.

## MEET THE COMPOSER

2112 Broadway, Suite 505; New York, NY 10023; (212) 787-3601
John Duffy, *Director*

Meet The Composer, a national composer service organization, was founded in 1974 to foster the creation, performance and recording of music by American composers and to broaden audiences for music of our time. A nonprofit organization, Meet The Composer raises money from foundations, corporations, individual patrons and government sources, and designs programs that support all styles and genres of music—from folk, ethnic, jazz, electronic, symphonic and chamber to choral, music theatre, opera and dance. MTC awards grants for composer fees to nonprofit organizations that perform, present or commission original works. Its programs include the Meet the Composer Fund and Affiliate Network, Education Program, Composer/Choreographer Project, and Meet the Composer/Reader's Digest Commissioning Program and New Residencies (see Meet The Composer Grant Programs in Fellowships and Grants).

## MIDWEST RADIO THEATRE WORKSHOP
KOPN; 915 East Broadway; Columbia, MO 65201;
    (314) 874-5676, FAX (314) 499-1662
Steve Donofrio, *Director*

MRTW is a national resource center for radio theatre in the areas of writing, directing, acting and sound design. Founded in 1979, it is a project of KOPN Radio/New Wave Corporation, a nonprofit community radio station serving central Missouri. MRTW holds an annual script contest (see MRTW Script Contest in Prizes) to identify and promote emerging and established radio writers. Winning scripts may be produced during one of a series of radio-theatre workshops held each year (see the organization's entry in Development). MRTW provides information and referral services and technical assistance to interested individuals and groups, distributes educational tapes and publishes an annual Scriptbook. MRTW is also developing a radio-theatre talent bank to enable it to make referrals and identify potential new trainers and directors for its own and other organizations.

## MISSOURI ASSOCIATION OF PLAYWRIGHTS
830 Spoede Rd; St. Louis, MO 63141; (314) 567-6341
Jo Lovins, *President*

Missouri Association of Playwrights (M.A.P.) was founded in 1976 to help playwrights develop their skills. The association's activities include monthly meetings at which members' scripts are presented as staging readings, periodic workshops, visits from guest speakers from the theatrical arena, seminars on writing for the theatre and full production of one-act plays. Through its affiliation with the Theatre Guild of Webster Groves, M.A.P. submits one-act plays by its members to the theatre to be included in a program of one-acts that opens its season each year. Membership in M.A.P. is open to playrights living in the greater St. Louis area (including southwest IL). Annual dues are $20.

## NATIONAL ACADEMY OF SONGWRITERS
6381 Hollywood Blvd, Suite 780; Hollywood, CA 90028;
    (213) 463-7178 (in CA), (800) 826-7287 (outside CA)
Brett W. Perkins, *Executive Director*

Founded in 1973, NAS is a nonprofit organization dedicated to educating, assisting and protecting songwriters. Members may call a toll-free number for answers to questions about the music business, have songs evaluated by industry professionals and, as proof of authorship, deposit songs in the academy's

SongBank. NAS sponsors seminars and workshops. Members receive the newspaper *SongTalk* and a listing of publishers and producers looking for new songs. Annual dues are $125 for Pro Membership (for those who have had at least one song commercially released and distributed) and $75 for General Membership.

## NATIONAL ALLIANCE FOR MUSICAL THEATRE

330 West 45th St, Lobby B; New York, NY 10036-3854; (212) 265-5376
Jim Thesing, *Executive Director*

The National Alliance for Musical Theatre is a service organization dedicated to supporting professional companies in their efforts to preserve and extend the American musical theatre as an art form. As part of its services, the Alliance annually publishes a Membership Directory with profiles of each member company, including details on those companies which develop and produce new works. The Alliance also produces an annual Festival of New Musicals in New York City, which aims to encourage further productions of the showcased works. Works to be considered for the festival should be submitted to member theatres, not to the Alliance.

## THE NATIONAL FOUNDATION FOR JEWISH CULTURE

330 Seventh Ave, 21st Floor; New York, NY 10001; (212) 629-0500
Richard A. Siegel, *Executive Director*

The National Foundation for Jewish Culture (NFJC) is the central cultural agency of the American Jewish community. Founded in 1960, the NFJC has been dedicated to the enhancement of Jewish life in America through the support and promotion of the arts and humanities. Rooted in the principle that memory, knowledge and creativity are essential to Jewish continuity, the NFJC encourages innovation and excellence in artistic, scholarly and communal expression of Jewish culture. For the past 30 years, the NFJC has been a leader in advancing Jewish scholarship and preserving the Jewish cultural heritage in America. In recent years, the NFJC's program has expanded to include supporting new creativity in the arts, as well as bringing Jewish culture to local communities throughout North America.

The NFJC provides programs and services to cultural institutions, local communities and individual artists and scholars in every region of the country. It serves as: advocate and coordinator for the fields of Jewish culture through its Council of American Jewish Museums, Council of Jewish Theatres, and Council of Archives and Research Libraries in Jewish Studies; sponsor of grants and awards to artists, scholars and major cultural institutions such as YIVO, Leo Baeck Institute, American Jewish Historical Society and the Jewish Publication Society of America; cultural innovator through conferences, symposia, publications, media productions, traveling exhibitions, residencies and performances which promote an understanding and appreciation of contemporary Jewish life and culture; and presenter of the annual Jewish Cultural Achievement Awards recognizing outstanding contributions to Jewish life in America through the arts and scholarship.

## NATIONAL LEAGUE OF AMERICAN PEN WOMEN
1300 17th St NW; Washington, DC 20036-1973; (202) 785-1997
Mary Latka, *Secretary*

Founded in 1897, NLAPW is a national membership organization for professional women writers, composers and visual artists. Its local branches meet monthly. It holds annual State Association meetings, a National Biennial Convention and a National Art Show, and sponsors the biennial NLAPW Scholarships for Mature Women (see Fellowships and Grants). Members, who receive a bimonthly magazine, *The Pen Woman*, and a National Roster, pay dues of $30 a year.

## NATIONAL PUBLIC RADIO
635 Massachusetts Ave NW; Washington, DC 20001-3753; (202) 414-2399
Andy Trudeau, *Director, Program Acquisition and Production*

National Public Radio is a private nonprofit membership organization which provides a national program service to its over 400 member noncommercial radio stations. It is funded by its member stations, the Corporation for Public Broadcasting and corporate grants. Among the programs available to member stations is *NPR Playhouse*, which presents 29-minute dramatic programs, series and serials. Writers should note that NPR does not itself read or produce plays. It acquires broadcast rights to produced packages. It will consider fully produced programs or works-in-progress on tape only.

## NATIONAL THEATRE WORKSHOP OF THE HANDICAPPED
354 Broome St, Loft 5-F; New York, NY 10013; (212) 941-9511
Rick Curry, *Founder and Artistic Director*

Founded in 1977, the National Theatre Workshop of the Handicapped (NTWH) is a training, production and advocacy organization serving physically disabled adults who are talented in the performing arts. It is one of the very few places in the country where new dramatic literature on themes of disability is regularly tested and produced. In addition to offering professional instruction in acting, music, voice and movement, and playwriting, NTWH maintains a professional repertory theatre company which showcases the talents of its students. To help serve the interests of the 43 million disabled Americans, NTWH solicits the participation of both playwrights with disabilities and the playwriting community at large in its annual Festival of Short Works. Playwrights wishing to submit scripts to the festival should write for guidelines; submissions are accepted throughout the year. Artists with disabilities who are interested in participating in NTWH's training programs should contact the workshop for information.

## NEW DRAMATISTS
424 West 44th St; New York, NY 10036; (212) 757-6960
Elana Greenfield, *Director of Artistic Programs*

New Dramatists is a service organization for member playwrights, which is designed to meet the varying needs of a large number of writers of diverse styles.

Rather than producing plays, New Dramatists serves as a laboratory where writers can develop their craft through a comprehensive program which includes script-in-hand readings followed by panel discussions; a loan fund; a library; free tickets to Broadway and Off-Broadway productions; a monthly bulletin for members detailing grants, contests and opportunities; a biannual newsletter, *The New Dramatist*, whose subscribers include 5000 theatre professionals; exchanges with theatres in other countries; a national script distribution service, ScriptShare; and the Composer/Librettist Studio, a workshop exploring the composer/librettist relationship. Annual New Dramatists awards for which members are eligible include the Joe A. Callaway Award, the Frederick Loewe Award in Music Theatre, the Mary Lea Johnson Richards Playwright Scholarship and the Clara Rotter Fellowship.

Membership is open to all playwrights living in the greater New York area, and to those living elsewhere who are able to spend sufficient time in the city to use membership to their advantage. To apply for membership submit 2 copies of 2 full-length plays (no screenplays or adaptations), 2 large SASEs, a resume, a bio and a statement outlining what you wish to accomplish over the next few years and how New Dramatists would serve that purpose; inclusion of letters of recommendation and reviews is optional. If admitted, a playwright is eligible for all the organization's services for 7 years. *Deadline:* 15 Sep 1995; *notification:* May 1996.

Members of New Dramatists regularly offer classes to other playwrights; the fee for a 10-week session is currently $225. The organization also rents workspace with typewriters to writers. Write or call for further information.

New Dramatists administers the L. Arnold Weissberger Playwriting Competition (see Prizes); and selects, and hosts a residency for, the winner of the Princess Grace Awards: Playwright Fellowship (see Fellowships and Grants).

## NEW GEORGES

550 West 43rd St; New York, NY 10036; (212) 967-2718
Susan Bernfield, *Artistic Director*

New Georges is a professional theatre organization that produces and develops new works by women and supports the creative efforts of emerging women theatre artists. The group's programs include The Conversation, a network of affiliated artists which holds informal readings of works-in-progress; and Next Georges, a play development program designed to respond to the needs of the individual playwright, with emphasis on bringing her into collaboration with a director and a consistent group of designers and actors. In addition to producing an annual season of new plays by women and Georges Noir, a late-night comedy cabaret/one-act festival, New Georges occasionally presents solo performances and already existing productions of pieces by artists affiliated with the company. Women playwrights interested in working with New Georges may submit a completed script or work-in-progress, together with a resume and cover letter.

## NEW PLAYWRIGHTS FOUNDATION

c/o 608 San Vicente Blvd, #18; Santa Monica, CA 90402; (310) 393-3682
Jeffrey Lee Bergquist, *Artistic Director*

Founded in 1968, New Playwrights Foundation is a service organization for writers working in theatre, film, television and video. The foundation runs developmental workshops, holds readings, coproduces video and film projects and assists members in furthering their careers. The foundation is occasionally able to obtain commissions for playwrights and to mount productions of their work. Membership in NPF is limited to a maximum of 15 writers who must be able to attend meetings in Santa Monica every other Monday. Applicants for membership attend meetings before submitting materials to be reviewed by the group.

## NEW VOICES

44 Washington St, #513; Brookline, MA 02146; (617) 731-1103
Stanley Richardson, *Artistic Director*

Founded in 1984, New Voices is a writers' theatre committed to developing new venues for dramatic writing. For the past four years, New Voices has produced (with the Public Media Foundation) *The Radio Play*, a weekly series currently broadcast via National Public Radio's *NPR Playhouse*. Current projects include consultation with the BBC's Radio Four on the U.S. New Writer's Initiative and ongoing stage work. Writers are encouraged to send queries, bios and suggestions for programs.

## THE NEW YORK PUBLIC LIBRARY
## FOR THE PERFORMING ARTS

40 Lincoln Center Plaza; New York, NY 10023-7498; (212) 870-1639
Bob Taylor, *Curator, The Billy Rose Theatre Collection*

The Billy Rose Theatre Collection, a division of the Library for the Performing Arts, is open to the public (aged 18 and over) and contains material on all aspects of theatrical art and the entertainment world, including stage, film, radio, television, circus, vaudeville and burlesque. The Theatre on Film and Tape Project (TOFT) is a special collection of films and videotapes of theatrical productions recorded during performance, as well as informal dialogues with important theatrical personalities. Tapes are available for viewing by appointment (call 870-1641) to students, theatre professionals and researchers.

## NON-TRADITIONAL CASTING PROJECT

1560 Broadway, Suite 1600; New York, NY 10036;
(212) 730-4750 (voice), -4913 (TDD)
Sharon Jensen, *Executive Director*

Founded in 1986, the Non-Traditional Casting Project is a nonprofit organization which exists to address and seek solutions to the problems of racism and exclusion in the theatre and related media, particularly as they relate to creative personnel: including, but not limited to, actors, directors, writers, designers and producers. The project works to advance the creative participation of artists of color and artists with disabilities through both advocacy and specific projects. Key NTCP programs include Artist Files/Artist Files Online, a national talent bank; roundtable discussions with industry leaders; a national Information and Consulting Service; and the publications: *New Traditions*, a quarterly newsletter; and *Beyond Tradition*, transcripts of the first national symposium on Non-Traditional Casting. In development is a 3-part series called *Resource Guides on Actors with Disabilities*. Writers of color and/or with disabilities, who are citizens or residents of the U.S. or Canada and have had at least one play given a professional production or staged reading should send a resume for inclusion in Artist Files/Artist Files Online, indicating their cultural identification and, in the case of disabled artists, any accommodation they may use; those interested in contacting listed artists will call them or their agents directly.

## NORTHWEST PLAYWRIGHTS GUILD
1819 Northwest Everett, Suite 104; Portland, OR 97209; (503) 222-7010
Bill Johnson, *Office Manager*

Northwest Playwrights Guild is an information clearinghouse and support group for playwrights. The guild sponsors public readings, holds workshops and produces regional conferences on theatre that include the full production of original scripts. The guild publishes a quarterly, *Script*, that contains articles on theatre in the Northwest, as well as update newsletters that provide information on current script opportunities. Membership dues are $25 a year.

## OLLANTAY CENTER FOR THE ARTS
Box 720636; Jackson Heights, NY 11372-0636;
   (718) 565-6499, FAX (718) 446-7806
Pedro R. Monge-Rafuls, *Executive and Artistic Director*

Founded as a multidisciplinary Hispanic arts center in 1977, OLLANTAY has developed a Hispanic Heritage Center for the arts in America with a view to providing the knowledge and resources needed to pursue research and develop new programs and initiatives in the field. The center maintains a resource bank of video and audio tapes, slides, books, plays and articles, which may be consulted by writing for an appointment. OLLANTAY's Traveling Theater Program tours plays by local writers. Its unique Playwriting Workshop, an annual intensive course of 3–6 weeks, provides an opportunity for playwrights wishing to write in Spanish to work under the direction of major Latin American playwrights who reside outside the U.S. *OLLANTAY Theater Magazine* is a biannual journal in English and Spanish which gives local playwrights, critics and scholars the opportunity to share their knowledge and experience of Hispanic theatre within the framework of American and world drama. The magazine, which publishes at least one play in each issue, is available to subscribers. Annual subscription is $18 for individuals, $25 for organizations.

## OPERA America

1156 15th St NW, Suite 810; Washington, DC 20005-3287; (202) 347-9262;
E-mail: 72420.2256@compuserve.com (also through Arts Wire)
Marianne Harding, *Project Manager, Lila Wallace–Reader's Digest Opera for a New America*

Founded in 1970, OPERA America is the not-for-profit service organization for the professional opera field in North America with allied international members. OPERA America, which also has affiliate, individual, library and business members, provides a variety of informational, technical and financial services to its membership, and serves as a resource to the media, funders, government agencies and the general public.

The goal of *Lila Wallace–Reader's Digest Opera for a New America*, a project of OPERA America and the Lila Wallace–Reader's Digest Fund, is to help opera companies build lasting relationships with current and potential audiences through the production of new works and the implementation of audience development projects complementing these works. The project provides information and financial support to OPERA America's Professional Company Members and their producing partners.

Application for grants awarded through the project are accepted only from Professional Company Members of OPERA America. Individual artists and other organizations may request information about the program. (This program will end in 1996.)

## PEN American Center

568 Broadway; New York, NY 10012; (212) 334-1660
Karen Kennerly, *Executive Director*

PEN is an international association of writers. The American Center is the largest of the 106 centers which comprise International PEN. The 2800 members of PEN American Center are established North American writers and translators, and literary editors. PEN activities include the Freedom-to-Write program; monthly symposiums, readings and other public events; a prison writing program; and a translator-publisher clearinghouse. PEN's publications include *Grants and Awards Available to American Writers*, a biennially updated directory of prizes, grants, fellowships and awards (1994–95 edition $10 postpaid); and *The PEN Prison Writing Information Bulletin*. Among PEN's annual prizes and awards are the Gregory Kolovakos Award, PEN–Book-of-the-Month Club Translation Prize and the Renato Poggioli Award (see Prizes); and Writing Awards for Prisoners, awarded to the authors of the best fiction, nonfiction, drama and poetry received from prisoner-writers in the U.S. The PEN Writers Fund assists writers (see Emergency Funds).

## Playmarket

Box 9767; Wellington; New Zealand; 64-4382-8462, FAX 64-4382-8461
John McDavitt, *Executive Officer*
Susan Wilson, *Script Advisor*

Playmarket is a service organization for playwrights, established in 1973 as a result of a growing interest in plays by New Zealand writers and a need to find new writers. The organization runs a script advisory and critiquing service, arranges workshop productions of promising scripts, and serves as the country's principal playwrights' agency, preparing and distributing copies of scripts and negotiating and collecting royalties. Playmarket's publications include *The Playmarket Directory of New Zealand Plays and Playwrights*, and a script series *New Zealand Theatrescripts*.

## THE PLAYWRIGHTS' CENTER

2301 Franklin Ave East; Minneapolis, MN 55406-1099; (612) 332-7481
David Moore, Jr., *Executive Director*

The Playwrights' Center is a service organization for playwrights. Its programs include: developmental services (cold readings and workshops using an Equity acting company); fellowships; exchanges with theatres and other developmental programs; a newsletter; the Jones one-act commissioning program; PlayLabs (see Development); Playworks, a professional touring company performing for schools and community organizations; playwriting classes; year-round programs for young writers; and the Many Voices program, designed to provide awards, education and lab services to new and emerging Minnesota playwrights of color. The center awards annually 5 Jerome Playwright-in-Residence Fellowships and 2 McKnight Fellowships, for which competition is open nationally; McKnight Advancement Grants open to Minnesota playwrights; and 3 Many Voices Multicultural Collaboration Grants (see The Playwrights' Center Grant Programs in Fellowships and Grants). The annual Young Playwrights Summer Conference, open to playwrights grades 8–12, offers 2 weeks of workshops and classes for 40 young writers, with daily workshops and readings of students' work; participants, who are selected on the basis of writing samples and recommendations, receive college credit; scholarships are available; applications are available 31 Jan 1996; *deadline:* 22 Apr 1996; *dates:* 16–28 Jun 1996.

A broad-based center membership is available to any playwright or interested person. Benefits of general membership for playwrights include discounts on classes, applications for all center programs, eligibility to apply for one-act commissions and script-development readings, and the center's newsletter. Core (must be MN resident) and Associate Member Playwrights are selected by a review panel each spring, based on script submission. They have primary access to all center programs and services, including developmental workshops and public readings. Write for Membership brochure. Membership applications are available 1 Feb 1996, *deadline:* 1 Apr 1996; *notification:* 1 Jul 1996.

## THE PLAYWRIGHTS FOUNDATION

Box 460357; San Francisco, CA 94114; (415) 777-2996
Dyke Garrison, *President*

The Playwrights Foundation provides developmental support to playwrights throughout the U.S., with emphasis on the northern California region. It produces the annual Bay Area Playwrights Festival (see Development). The foundation also sponsors a 10-minute play contest for members only and presents readings of the winning pieces at an annual benefit. Playwrights interested in becoming members should write for an application form. Annual dues are $25.

## PLAYWRIGHTS HARBOR

160 West 71st St; New York, NY 10023; (212) 787-1945 (c/o M&C Productions)
Stuart Warmflash, *Artistic Director*

Founded in 1994, Playwrights Harbor provides developmental workshops for 10 member theatre writers. Membership is available to playwrights, composers and librettists who have a body of work; are committed to rewrites and developing one project for an entire season; and who seek supportive criticism. The workshop meets every Monday in New York City for 3 hours and provides cold and/or rehearsed readings, followed by a short critique by a professional acting company. Dues for the 1994–1995 season were $250. The organization is especially, but not exclusively, seeking minority playwrights.

## THE PLAYWRIGHTS' PROJECT

Sammons Center for the Arts, #12; 3630 Harry Hines Blvd; Dallas, TX 75219;
   (214) 497-1752
Elizabeth Clark, *Executive Director*

The Playwrights' Project was founded in 1990 as a service organization for playwrights from the north Texas area. The project holds biweekly group labs and in-house and public readings, organizes workshops and lecture series, publishes a newsletter and sponsors the annual Robert Bone Memorial Playwriting Award (see Prizes). While the group's resident playwrights pay annual dues of $50, no qualified playwright is excluded for lack of funds. New resident playwrights, who must be from the Dallas area or able to travel to meetings and events in Dallas, are selected annually; applicants should submit 1 full-length play, or 2 one-acts totaling a minimum of 60 minutes, a cover letter containing a brief synopsis of the play(s), a bio and an optional SASE for acknowledgment of receipt; *deadline:* 1 Jun 1996 for residencies starting in the fall of 1996.

## PLAYWRIGHTS THEATRE OF NEW JERSEY

33 Green Village Rd; Madison, NJ 07940; (201) 514-1787
John Pietrowski, *Producing Artistic Director*

Founded in 1986, the Playwrights Theatre of New Jersey is both a service organization for playwrights of all ages and a developmental theatre. In addition to its New Play Development Program (see Playwrights Theatre of New Jersey in Development), PTNJ sponsors a state-wide playwriting-in-the-schools program; a playwriting-for-teachers project; adult playwriting classes; children's creative dramatics classes; acting classes; and "special needs" playwriting projects which include work in housing projects and with senior citizens, teenage substance abusers, persons with physical disabilities and court-appointed youth, as well as a playwriting-in-prisons initiative. Young playwrights festivals are held in Madison and Newark, in addition to a statewide festival which is part of the New Jersey Young Playwrights Program. Gifted and talented playwriting symposiums, hosted by well-known playwrights, provide intensive 2-day experiences for up to 60 students from various school districts. With the New Jersey State Council on the Arts, PTNJ cosponsors the Writers-in-the-Schools Program, which teaches poetry and prose in schools and community centers statewide.

## PLAYWRIGHTS UNION OF CANADA

54 Wolseley St; Toronto, Ontario; Canada M5T 1A5; (416) 703-0201
Tony Hamill, *Managing Editor, Canadian Plays Abroad Director*

Founded in 1972, Playwrights Union of Canada is a service organization and information clearinghouse for Canadian playwrights who have had a professional production at a Canadian Actors' Equity Theatre, or who are members of the Professional Association of Canadian Theatre or equivalent. The organization publishes books under the imprint Playwrights Canada Press; prepares and makes members' copyscripts available for sale; negotiates contracts with the Professional Association of Canadian Theatres; administers amateur productions; and publishes a bimonthly newsletter *CanPlay* at a nonmember rate of $26 per year and $45 for 2 years. Annual membership dues are $135 plus 7% tax; membership includes a subscription to *CanPlay*.

## PLAZA DE LA RAZA

3540 North Mission Rd; Los Angeles, CA 90031; (213) 223-2475
Rose Cano, *Interim Executive Director*

Founded in 1970, Plaza de la Raza is a cultural center for the arts and education, primarily serving the Chicano community of East Los Angeles. Of special interest to playwrights is the center's Nuevo L.A. Chicano TheatreWorks project, designed to discover, develop and present the work of Chicano playwrights. Initiated in 1989 and recurring approximately every 4 years, depending on funding, as part of the Nuevo L.A. Chicano Art Series cycle (Visual Arts, Music, Dance and Theatre), the project develops new one-acts through a 2-week workshop with director and actors, culminating in public readings; some plays are selected for subsequent full production. Latino playwrights who are California residents should contact the center for information on when and how to apply for the next round of the program. In addition to its playwrights' project, Plaza de la Raza conducts classes in drama, dance, music and the visual arts; provides resources for teachers in the community; and sponsors special events, exhibits and performances. Membership in Plaza de la Raza is open to all.

## PROFESSIONAL ASSOCIATION OF CANADIAN THEATRES/ PACT COMMUNICATIONS CENTRE

64 Charles St East, 2nd Floor; Toronto, Ontario; Canada; M4Y 1T1;
    (416) 968-3033, FAX (416) 968-3035
Pat Bradley, *Executive Director*
Tracy Sigurdson, *Membership and Communications Coordinator*

PACT is the national service and trade association representing professional English-language theatres in Canada. PACT was incorporated in 1976 to work on behalf of its member theatres in the areas of advocacy, labor relations, professional development and communications. The members' newsletter *impact!* is published quarterly. PACT Communications Centre (PCC) was established in 1985 as the charitable wing of PACT in order to improve and expand communications and information services. PCC publishes *The Theatre Listing*, an annual directory of English-language Canadian theatres which also includes valuable information on rehearsal and performance spaces, government agencies and arts service organizations; *Artsboard*, the monthly bulletin of employment opportunities in the arts in Canada; and *Canada on Stage*, an illustrated, fully indexed series of volumes documenting professional productions across the country.

## PUBLIC BROADCASTING SERVICE
1320 Braddock Pl; Alexandria, VA 22314-1698; (703) 739-5000
*Corporate Information*

The Public Broadcasting Service is a private nonprofit corporation that acquires and distributes programs to its 345 member stations. The PBS Programming Department can advise independent producers about the development of specific projects. Information about the preparation, presentation and funding of projects can be obtained from PBS. Printed materials such as the *PBS Packaging & Technical Guidelines* are also available.

## THE PURPLE CIRCUIT
2025 Griffith Park Blvd, Suite 4; Los Angeles, CA 90039; (213) 661-1982
Bill Kaiser, *Coordinator*

The Purple Circuit is a network of gay, lesbian, queer, bisexual and transsexual theatres, producers and performers, and "Kindred Spirits" (theatres which are not exclusively gay or lesbian in orientation but are interested in producing gay or lesbian material on a regular basis). The Purple Circuit publishes news, information and articles of interest to its constituency in its quarterly newsletter, *On the Purple Circuit. The Purple Circuit Directory* lists theatres and producers around the world, including "Kindred Spirits," that are interested in presenting gay, lesbian, bisexual and transsexual works. The Purple Circuit Hotline (213) 666-0693 provides information on gay and lesbian shows currently playing in southern California and elsewhere, as well as information for playwrights and for journalists and others interested in promoting gay and lesbian theatre and performance art.

## THE SCRIPTWRITERS NETWORK
11684 Ventura Blvd, #508; Studio City, CA 91604; (213) 848-9477
Bettina Moss, *Chair*

Though the Scriptwriters Network, founded in 1989, is predominantly an affiliation of film, television and corporate/industrial writers, playwrights are welcome. Meetings feature guest speakers, developmental feedback on scripts is available, and staged readings may be arranged in conjunction with other groups. The network sponsors members-only contests and publishes a newsletter. Prospective members submit a professionally formatted script and a completed application; membership is not based on the quality of the script. There is a $10 initiation fee, and dues are $60 a year.

## THE SONGWRITERS GUILD OF AMERICA

1560 Broadway, Room 1306; New York, NY 10036; (212) 768-7902
George Wurzbach, *National Projects Director*

*Head Office:*
1500 Harbor Blvd; Weehawken, NJ 07087-6732; (201) 867-7603
*Los Angeles Office:*
6430 Sunset Blvd; Hollywood, CA 90028; (213) 462-1108
*Nashville Office:*
1222 16th Ave; Nashville, TN 37212; (615) 329-1782

The Songwriters Guild is a voluntary national association run by and for songwriters; all officers and directors are unpaid. Among its many services to composers and lyricists, the guild provides a standard songwriter's contract and reviews this and other contracts on request; collects writers' royalties from music publishers; maintains a copyright renewal service; conducts songwriting workshops and critique sessions with special rates for members; provides a songwriter collaboration service; issues news bulletins with essential information for writers; and offers a group medical and life insurance plan. Full members of the guild must be published songwriters and pay dues on a graduated scale from $70–400. Unpublished songwriters may become associate members and pay dues of $55 a year. Write for membership application.

## SOUTHEAST PLAYWRIGHTS PROJECT

1085 Bellevue Dr NE, #1; Atlanta, GA 30306; (404) 727-1801
(Ms.) Russel Faulk, *Executive Director*

Southeast Playwrights Project (SEPP) is a service organization for playwrights who live, or have lived, in the Southeast. Its programs fall into two general areas: script development (cold readings, rehearsed readings, staged readings and nonperformance workshops) and career development (dramaturgical advice, free theatre tickets, a mentor program, retreats and networking). Members of SEPP, who pay dues of $50 a year, receive the SEPP newsletter, are eligible for all career development services and for discounts on workshops, and can have their plays listed in a nationally distributed play catalogue. They can also participate in the Writers' Lab, which meets twice a month to read and discuss scenes from members' works-in-progress. For full information send an SASE for the SEPP membership brochure.

## S.T.A.G.E. (SOCIETY FOR THEATRICAL ARTISTS' GUIDANCE AND ENHANCEMENT)

Box 214820; 4633 Insurance; Dallas, TX 75221; (214) 559-3917
Merri Brewer, *Executive Director*

Founded in 1981, S.T.A.G.E. acts as an information clearinghouse for theatre artists and theatre organizations in the north Texas region. The society maintains a library of plays, theatre texts and resource information; offers counseling on agents, unions, personal marketing and other career-related matters; posts listings of miscellaneous job opportunities; and maintains an audition callboard for regional opportunities in theatre and film; sponsors an actor's showcase, Noon Preview; and produces Stages Festival of New Plays, the longest running new play festival in Dallas. Any playwright may submit to the festival, which seeks unproduced one-acts, not more than 20 minutes long, with minimal sets and props and preferably 8 or fewer characters; winning playwrights receive an honorarium and production; *deadline:* 15 Apr 1996. Members of S.T.A.G.E., who pay annual dues starting at $45, receive a monthly publication, *CENTERSTAGE.*

## THEATRE ASSOCIATION OF PENNSYLVANIA (TAP)

1919 North Front St, 3rd Floor; Harrisburg, PA 17102-2284;
(717) 232-9752, FAX (717) 232-9756
Al Franklin, *Executive Director*

Founded in 1968, TAP is Pennsylvania's theatre service organization. Its membership includes theatres of every type, academic institutions, theatre training programs, and artists, educators and other individuals committed to the continuing development of quality theatre and the vital role that theatre plays in the life of the Commonwealth. TAP serves as the central information agency for its membership; sponsors festivals, conferences, workshops and auditions; administers granting programs; acts as a liaison with state and national organizations; and produces a variety of publications, including *TAPLINE, Seasons-at-a-Glance* and *Pennsylvania Theatre Directory.* Membership in TAP is open to all. Annual dues are $25 for individuals, $10 for students, and $35–250 for organizations.

## THEATRE BAY AREA

657 Mission St, Suite 402; San Francisco, CA 94105; (415) 957-1557

TBA is a resource organization for San Francisco theatre workers whose members include 3200 individuals and more than 240 theatre companies. Its programs include TIX Bay Area, San Francisco's half-price ticket booth; workshops; conferences; and office referral services. Annual dues of $35 (out-of-state residents add $12 for 1st-class postage) include a subscription to *Callboard,* a monthly magazine featuring articles, interviews and essays by critics and playwrights from the Bay Area and elsewhere, as well as information on play contests and festivals, and listings of production activity, workshops, classes, auditions, jobs and services. TBA also biennially publishes *Theatre Directory of the Bay Area* (1993–94 edition $18/member, $24/nonmember, postpaid), which includes entries on organizations serving playwrights; profiles of local theatre companies; listings of rehearsal and performance spaces, classes, workshops, schools, agents and unions; and sources for commercial supplies and technical services.

## THEATRE COMMUNICATIONS GROUP
355 Lexington Ave; New York, NY 10017-0217;
(212) 697-5230, FAX (212) 983-4847; E-mail: tcg@tmn.com
John Sullivan, *Executive Director*

Founded in 1961, TCG is the national organization for the American theatre. Its mission is to celebrate and inspire excellence in the artistry of theatre in America. To carry out this mission, TCG serves theatre artists and nonprofit professional theatre organizations by recognizing and encouraging artistic diversity; providing a forum for open and critical examination of issues, standards and values; fostering interaction among theatre professionals; collecting, analyzing and disseminating information regarding the profession; and serving as the principal advocate for America's nonprofit professional theatre. With a constituency of more than 300 theatres across America that reach a combined audience of more than 20 million each year, TCG provides centralized services to aid the work of thousands in the field. Its chief programs include grants, fellowships and awards to theatre artists and institutions; conferences, workshops and roundtables; government affairs; surveys and research; and publications. (For more information, see American Theatre and PlaySource in Publication, and TCG Grant Programs in Fellowships and Grants.)

In addition to *American Theatre* magazine and *PlaySource*, TCG publications of interest to theatre writers include *Theatre Profiles*, a biennial reference guide offering comprehensive statistical, historical and production information on more than 200 nonprofit theatres; *Theatre Directory*, which provides complete contact information for more than 350 theatres and related arts organizations across the U.S.; and *ArtSEARCH*, a biweekly bulletin of job opportunities in the arts. The "Opportunities" column of *American Theatre* supplements information provided in this *Sourcebook*. TCG also publishes plays, translations and anthologies in book form, play texts in *American Theatre*, and books dealing with all aspects of theatre. (For further information, see Useful Publications, and Publications from TCG in the back of this book, or contact TCG for the current Publications catalogue.)

Individual Members receive a free subscription to *American Theatre*, discounts on tickets to performances at more than 150 theatres nationwide, cost-savings on TCG resource materials, and discounts on all books from TCG and other select theatre publishers. Members are also eligible to apply for the TCG credit card, a no-annual fee MasterCard, and receive discounts from Budget Rent A Car, Airborne Express and the Hotel Reservation Network. Individual memberships are available to all theatre professionals, as well as to theatre enthusiasts, for $35 a year. (See membership application in the back of this book.)

## THE THEATRE MUSEUM
1E Tavistock St; London WC2E 7PA; England; 441-71-836-7891

The Theatre Museum, a branch of the Victoria & Albert Museum, is Britain's national museum of the performing arts. In addition to its regular displays, which feature 400 years of the history, technology, art and craft of theatre, and its special exhibitions, the museum houses the U.K.'s largest archive of performing arts materials, including play texts, photographic and biographical files, theatre programs and reviews, and books about the theatre. The archive and study room is available by appointment (call during office hours) Tuesday to Friday, 10:30–1:00 p.m. and 2:00–4:30 p.m. The museum's innovative education department runs workshops and study days on theatre practice and set texts for children, students and teachers. The museum also runs a program of celebrity play readings, seminars and events to give visitors insight into current theatre production.

## UBU REPERTORY THEATER
15 West 28th St; New York, NY 10001; (212) 679-7540
Françoise Kourilsky, *Artistic Director*

Ubu Repertory Theater, founded in 1982, is a nonprofit theatre center dedicated to introducing translations of contemporary French-language plays to the English-speaking audience (see theatre's entry in Production). In addition to producing several plays a year, Ubu commissions translations and schedules reading programs, photography exhibits, panel discussions and workshops. Ubu publishes a series of contemporary plays by French-speaking playwrights in English translation, distributed nationally by TCG, and houses a French-English reference library of published plays and manuscripts.

## VOLUNTEER LAWYERS FOR THE ARTS
1 East 53rd St, 6th Floor; New York, NY 10022;
    (212) 319-2787 (administrative office), 319-2910 (Art Law Hotline)
Daniel Y. Mayer, *Executive Director*

Volunteer Lawyers for the Arts arranges free legal representation and legal education in the arts community. Individual artists and nonprofit arts organizations unable to afford private counsel are eligible for VLA's services; VLA can be especially useful to playwrights with copyright or contract problems. There is an administrative fee per referral of $30–50 for individuals, $50–100 for nonprofit organizations and $250 for nonprofit incorporation and tax exemption. VLA's education program offers biweekly seminars on nonprofit incorporation and evening seminars held regularly to educate attorneys and artists in specific areas of art law. Publications include the *VLA-Columbia Journal of Law & the Arts*, containing articles on legal aspects of the arts (annual subscription $35); and the *VLA Guide to Copyright for the Performing Arts* ($5.95 plus $2 postage and handling). For more information about VLA's publications and the 40 VLA affiliates across the country, contact the New York office; referrals can be made to volunteer lawyer organizations nationwide.

## WOMEN'S THEATRE ALLIANCE
Box 64446; Chicago, IL 60664-0446; (312) 907-1110
Jennifer Yeo, *President*

W.T.A. is a networking and resource organization for Chicago-area theatre artists including actors, directors, playwrights, producers, stage managers, technicians, designers and educators. Its mission is to advocate women's leadership in the Chicago-area theatre community; to create an empowering resource for women theatre artists to ensure that their voices are heard within that community; and to provide a support network for women theatre artists that will enable them to share their artistic diversity and learn from one another. In pursuit of these goals, W.T.A. holds quarterly meetings; sponsors informal readings, staged readings, play development workshops and an annual actors' showcase and new plays festival; and publishes a monthly newsletter. To join W.T.A., write or call for a Membership/Information Request Form. Membership dues are $30 a year.

## The WOW Cafe
59 East 4th St; New York, NY 10003; (212) 460-8067 (service)

The WOW (Women's One World) Cafe is a women's theatre collective whose membership is primarily but not exclusively lesbian. WOW produces the work of women playwrights and performers. It has no permanent staff and its members are encouraged to participate in all aspects of the group's operations. In lieu of dues, members volunteer their services backstage on fellow members' productions in exchange for the opportunity to present their own work. Each show is produced by the member who initiates it. Women interested in becoming members of the WOW Cafe may attend one of the collective's regular meetings, which are scheduled every Tuesday at 6:30 PM.

## Writers Guild of America, East (WGAE)
555 West 57th St; New York, NY 10019-2967; (212) 767-7800
Mona Mangan, *Executive Director*

WGAE is the union for freelance writers in the fields of motion pictures, television and radio who reside east of the Mississippi River. The union negotiates collective bargaining agreements for its members and represents them in grievances and arbitrations under those agreements. It also makes credit determinations for the writing of its members. The guild gives annual awards, and sponsors a foundation which currently teaches film writing to disadvantaged high school students. WGAE participates in reciprocal arrangements with the International Affiliation of Writers Guilds and with its sister union, Writers Guild of America, west. The guild publishes a monthly newsletter, which is available to nonmembers by subscription; and a quarterly journal, *On Writing*. Write for information on WGAE's registration service for registering literary material, or call (212) 757-4360.

## Writers Guild of America, west (WGAw)
8955 Beverly Blvd; West Hollywood, CA 90048-2456; (310) 550-1000
After 1 Dec 1995: 7000 West 3rd St; Los Angeles, CA 90048
Brian Walton, *Executive Director*

WGAw is the union for writers in the fields of motion pictures, television, radio and new media who reside west of the Mississippi. It represents its members in collective bargaining and other labor matters. It publishes a monthly magazine, *The Journal*. The Guild registers material, including screen- and teleplays, books, plays, poetry and songs. The library is open to the public Mon, Wed and Fri.

# YOUNG PLAYWRIGHTS INC.
321 West 44th St, #906; New York, NY 10036; (212) 307-1140
Sheri M. Goldhirsch, *Artistic Director*

Young Playwrights Inc. (YPI) was founded in 1981 by Stephen Sondheim and members of the Dramatists Guild to introduce young people to the theatre and to encourage self-expression through the art of playwriting. In the past 13 years, YPI strives to identify, develop and encourage playwrights aged 18 years and younger; to develop new works for the theatre and to aid in the creation of the next generation of professional playwrights through the Young Playwrights Festival (see Prizes) and the Young Playwrights Spring Conference; to expose young people to theatre and playwriting through WRITING ON YOUR FEET! in-school playwriting workshops; to train teachers through the TEACHING ON YOUR FEET! Teacher Training Institute; to develop and serve audiences that reflect the complex makeup of our society and to create the next generation of theatregoers through the TAKE A GROWNUP TO THE THEATER! ticket subsidy program, student matinees and a discount voucher program; to bring the vital experience of professional theatre free of charge to neglected inner-city public schools, community organizations and youth centers through the Young Playwrights School Tour; to serve as an advocate for young writers regardless of ethnicity, physical ability, sexual orientation or economic status, and to ensure that their voices are heard and acknowledged by a diverse community of artists and theatregoers.

# Epilogue

- **Useful Publications**
- **Submission Calendar**
- **Special Interests**
- **Index**

# Useful Publications

This is a highly selective listing of the publications that we think most usefully supplement the information given in the *Sourcebook*. Note that publications of interest to theatre writers are also described throughout this book, particularly in introductions to sections, in Membership and Service Organizations listings, and on the Publications from TCG pages in the back. Before ordering you would be wise to find out if the prices given in all listings still pertain.

We have purposely left out any "how to" books on the art of playwriting because we do not want to promote the concept of "writing-by-recipe." However, we do recommend David Savran's *In Their Own Words: Contemporary American Playwrights* and *The Production Notebooks: Theatre in Process, Volume One*, edited by Mark Bly (see Publications from TCG).

*American Theatre;* Theatre Communications Group; 355 Lexington Ave; New York, NY 10017-0217; (212) 697-5230. 1-year subscription/TCG membership $35, 2 years $70; single issue $3.95. This monthly magazine includes an "Opportunities" column which updates *Sourcebook* information between editions, announcing new grants and contests. A special Season Preview issue each October lists schedules for some 200 theatres nationwide and monthly schedules are published in each issue. As part of its comprehensive coverage of all aspects of theatre, *American Theatre* regularly features articles and interviews dealing with theatre writers and their works, and publishes the complete texts of 6 new plays a year.

*Back Stage;* 1515 Broadway, 14th Floor; New York, NY 10036; (212) 764-7300. 1-year subscription $69, 2 years $119; single issue $2.25, $3.25 by mail. This performing arts weekly includes industry news; reports from cities across the country; reviews; and columns, including "Playwrights' Corner." Though the primary focus is on casting, theatres and other producers sometimes run ads soliciting scripts; workshops and classes for playwrights are also likely to be advertised here.

*A Handbook for Literary Translators;* PEN American Center; 568 Broadway; New York, NY 10012; (212) 334-1660. 3rd edition, 1995. 35 pp, $2.50 (includes postage and handling) paper. Contents include "A Translator's Model Contract," "Negotiating a Contract," "Selected Resources" and "The Responsibilities of Translation."

*Hollywood Scriptwriter;* 1626 North Wilcox, #385; Hollywood, CA 90028; (805) 495-5447. 1-year subscription (12 issues) $44, 6 months $25; discount on renewals. This 12-page newsletter contains a "MARKETS for Your Work" section that includes "Plays Wanted" listings, as well as interviews and articles giving advice that is sometimes useful to playwrights as well as screenwriters. A list of back issues with a summary of the contents of each issue is available; call for information and a free sample.

*The Individual's Guide to Grants* by Judith B. Margolin; Plenum Press; 233 Spring St; New York, NY 10013; (212) 620-8051 or toll-free 1-800-221-9369. 1983. 276 pp, $19.95 cloth. This comprehensive guide to individual grantseeking, written by a former director of the New York library of the Foundation Center, offers detailed advice on each step of the process.

*Into Print: A Guide to the Writing Life;* Quality Paperback Book Club, in conjunction with Poets & Writers; 72 Spring St; New York, NY 10012; (212) 226-3586. $12.95 paper. Based on practical articles on the business of writing published in *Poets & Writers Magazine* (see below), this book has an all-new introduction and is completely revised and updated. Topics covered include "Contracts and Royalties: Negotiating Your Own," "Cutting the High Cost of Health Care" and "On Cloud Nine: Writers' Colonies, Retreats, Ranches, Residencies and Sanctuaries."

*Literary Agents: A Writer's Guide* by Adam Begley; Poets & Writers; 72 Spring St; New York, NY 10012; (212) 226-3586. 1993. 196 pp, $10 (plus $3.90 postage and handling plus sales tax where applicable) paper. This book contains several chapters exploring the functions of literary agents and the agent-writer relationship, and includes listings of 196 agencies which will consider unsolicited *queries* plus 37 more agencies which charge fees.

*Literary Agents of North America;* Author Aid/Research Associates International; 340 East 52nd St; New York, NY 10022; orders to Box 7263, FDR Station; New York, NY 10150; (212) 758-4213 or 980-9179. 5th edition, 1994. 315 pp, $33 (plus $3.50 postage and handling, $7.50 for priority mail, plus sales tax on NYS orders) paper. Profiles of more than 1000 U.S. and Canadian literary agencies include their areas of interest and policies regarding new writers and unsolicited manuscripts.

*Literary Market Place 1995;* R.R. Bowker; 121 Chanlon Rd; New Providence, NJ 07974; toll-free 1-800-521-8110, (908) 464-6800 in New Providence (may call collect). 1995. 1942 pp, $165 (plus 7% shipping and handling plus sales tax where applicable) paper. The "phone book" of American book publishing gives contact information for book publishers and those in related fields, and includes a "Names & Numbers" index over 450 pages long. The 1996 *LMP* is due out in September 1995.

*Market Insight...for Playwrights;* Box 4863; Englewood, CO 80155; 1-800-895-4720. 1-year subscription $40 (12 issues), 6 months $25. This monthly newsletter for playwrights provides submission guidelines for theatres, residencies, publishers and contests, as well as updates on personnel changes at theatres, special programs for women writers, and more; call for a free sample.

*Music, Dance & Theater Scholarships;* Conway Greene Publishing Company; 11000 Cedar Ave; Cleveland, OH 44106; (216) 721-0077 or toll-free 1-800-977-2665. 1995. 512 pp, $20.95 (plus $5.00 shipping and handling) paper. This guide provides information on more than 1800 theatre, music and dance conservatory and undergraduate programs, as well as more than 5000 professional and educational scholarship opportunities. It also includes detailed information on audition requirements, decision processes at individual schools, special scholarship stipulations and student profiles.

*The National Playwrights Directory;* Phyllis Johnson Kaye, ed; O'Neill Theater Center; 305 Great Neck Rd; Waterford, CT 06385; (203) 443-5378. 1986. 507 pp, $20 (plus $3.50 postage and handling) cloth. With entries on 495 writers and an index of over 4000 plays, this book is still a useful source of information. A new edition is planned, but will not be out in the near future.

*Playhouse America!;* Feedback Theatrebooks; 305 Madison Ave, Suite 1146; New York, NY 10165; (212) 687-4185. 1991. 300 pp, $16.95 (plus $3.00 postage and handling) paper. This directory contains the addresses and phone numbers of more than 3500 theatres across the country; it includes a cross-reference to specialty theatres (e.g., Dinner Theatres & Showboats, Military Theatres).

*The Playwright's Companion;* Mollie Ann Meserve, ed; Feedback Theatrebooks; 305 Madison Ave, Suite 1146; New York, NY 10165; (212) 687-4185. 1995. 416 pp, $20.95 (plus $3.00 postage and handling) paper. This annual guide for playwrights publishes submission guidelines for more than 1400 theatres, contests, publishers and special programs. The *Companion* includes useful tips on query letters, synopses, resumes and submission etiquette. The 1996 edition is due out in December 1995.

*Poets & Writers Magazine;* Poets & Writers; 72 Spring St; New York, NY 10012; (212) 226-3586. 1-year subscription (6 issues) $19.95, single issue $3.95. Though primarily aimed at writers of poetry and fiction, this newsletter does include some announcements of grants and awards as well as other opportunities open to theatre writers.

*Professional Playscript Format Guidelines and Sample;* Feedback Theatrebooks; 305 Madison Ave, Suite 1146; New York, NY 10165; (212) 687-4185. 1991. 28 pp, $4.95 (plus $1.75 postage and handling) paper. This booklet provides detailed instructions for laying out a script in a professional manner.

*Songwriter's Market;* Cindy Laufenberg, ed; Writer's Digest Books; 1507 Dana Ave; Cincinnati, OH 45207; (513) 531-2690. 1995. 523 pp, $21.99 (plus $3 shipping and handling) cloth. This annually updated directory, which lists contact information for more than 2000 song markets, includes a section on musical theatre. It also lists clubs, associations, contests and workshops of interest to songwriters. The 1996 edition is due out in September 1995.

*Stage Directions;* SMW Communications; Box 41202; Raleigh, NC 27629; (919) 872-7888. 1-year subscription $26 (10 issues), 2 years $48; single issue $3.50. This magazine provides information on royalty issues, play publishing, new play festivals and workshops/seminars for playwrights. A special Season Planner issue each November/December contains a directory of royalty houses.

*Theatre Directory 1995-96;* Theatre Communications Group; 355 Lexington Ave; New York, NY 10017-0217; (212) 697-5230. 1995. 96 pp, $5.95 (plus $3 postage and handling) paper. TCG's annually updated directory provides complete contact information for more than 300 nonprofit professional theatres—including new TCG Constituent and Associate theatres that join after this *Sourcebook* is published—and more than 50 arts resource organizations.

*Theatre Profiles 11;* Theatre Communications Group; 355 Lexington Ave; New York, NY 10017-0217; (212) 697-5230. 1994. 256 pp, $21.95 (plus $3 postage and handling) paper. Useful for finding out about this country's nonprofit professional theatres, the 11th volume of this biennial series contains artistic profiles, production photographs, 1992–93 financial information and repertoire information for the 1991–93 seasons of 238 theatres. *Theatre Profiles 12* is due out January 1996, covering 1993–95 seasons.

U.S. Copyright Office publications; Register of Copyrights; Library of Congress; Washington, DC 20559; (202) 707-9100 for orders only (machine); 707-3000 for questions and advice. Call and ask for available free circulars, which include No. 1, "Copyright Basics." If you write for information instead, expect to wait a long time for a response.

*The Writer;* 120 Boylston St; Boston, MA 02116-4615; (617) 423-3157. 1-year subscription (12 issues) $28, 2 years $52, 3 years $75. This monthly magazine announces contests in a "Prize Offers" column, and publishes a special "Where to Sell Manuscripts" section, which includes lists of play publishers, in the September issue.

*A Writer's Guide to Copyright;* Poets & Writers; 72 Spring St; New York, NY 10012; (212) 226-3586. 1990. 63 pp, $10 (plus $3.90 postage and handling plus sales tax where applicable) paper. This guide contains simply and clearly written information on copyright laws, authors' rights and the functions of the Copyright Office; it is illustrated with sample forms.

*Writer's Market;* Mark Garvey, ed; Writer's Digest Books; 1507 Dana Ave; Cincinnati, OH 45207; (513) 531-2690. 1995. 1008 pp, $26.99 (plus $3 postage and handling plus sales tax where applicable) cloth. This annually updated directory lists 4000 places to sell what you write. It includes many opportunities for playwrights and screenwriters. The 1996 edition is due out in September 1995.

*Writers' Resources;* Poets & Writers; 72 Spring St; New York, NY 10012; (212) 226-3586. Series of guides. Each $8 (plus $3.90 postage and handling) paper. These 9 "literary address books" covering the entire U.S. list resources available to the writer in different areas of the country (Deep South, Mid-Atlantic, Mid-South, Midwest, New England, Northwest, Southwest, Pacific and Northwest, and Great Plains). Included are arts councils, bookstores, conferences, grants, literary agencies, magazines, readings, support groups, typists, workshops and more. For complete information, call or write for Poets & Writers' catalogue.

# Submission Calendar

## September 1995–August 1996

Included here are all *specified* deadlines contained in Production, Prizes, Publication, Development, Fellowships and Grants, Colonies and Residencies, and Membership and Service Organizations. Please note that suggested submission dates for theatres listed in Production are not included. There are always important deadlines that are not available at press time and so cannot be included here. The "Opportunities" column of *American Theatre* is one place to look for these.

## September 1995 ———————————————————

| | | |
|---|---|---|
| 1 | ASCAP Musical Theatre Workshop | *131* |
| 1 | Cleveland Public Theatre New Plays Festival | *18* |
| 1 | Dorland Mountain Arts Colony (1st deadline) | *196* |
| 1 | Harold Prince Musical Theatre Program | *137* |
| 1 | Katherine and Lee Chilcote Award | *85* |
| 1 | Maxim Mazumdar Competition | *90* |
| 1 | Midwest Theatre Workshop (scholarships) | *141* |
| 1 | Millay Colony for the Arts (1st deadline) | *199* |
| 1 | National Hispanic Playwriting Contest | *94* |

1   NEA Opera-Musical Theater Program (letter of intent)   *176*
1   Playwrights Forum (1st deadline)   *147*
1   Sam Edwards Deaf Playwrights Competition   *101*
1   Villa Montalvo Residency Program (1st deadline)   *203*
1   Waldo and Grace Bonderman Competition for Young
      Audiences   *108*
1   White-Willis Contest   *109*
8   Douglass Center Workshops (1st deadline)   *136*
15   Jerome Fellowships   *178*
15   MacDowell Colony (1st deadline)   *199*
15   Many Voices Multicultural Collaboration Grants   *179*
15   Many Voices Residency Awards   *179*
15   New Dramatists membership   *227*
15   New Women Playwright's Contest   *96*
15   Virginia Center residencies (1st deadline)   *203*
16   NEH Humanities Projects in Media (1st deadline)   *177*
20   Susan Smith Blackburn Prize   *103*
22   NEA Opera-Musical Theater Program (application)   *176*
30   Dayton Playhouse FutureFest   *76*
30   Hawthornden Castle Retreat for Writers   *196*
30   Lamia Ink! (1st deadline)   *121*
30   Love Creek Annual Short Play Festival   *89*
30   Paul Green Playwrights Prize   *98*
30   Puerto Rican Traveling Theatre Workshop   *149*
30   Theater at Lime Kiln Playwriting Contest   *105*

*Contact for exact deadline during this month:*
NEA/Fund for U.S. Artists at International Festivals   *173*
New City Theater Festival   *96*

# October 1995 ——————————————

1   Hedgebrook (1st deadline)   *197*
1   John Guggenheim fellowships   *170*
1   Southern Appalachian Playwrights' Conference   *151*
1   Ucross Foundation Residency Program (1st deadline)   *202*
1   Vermont Playwrights Award   *108*
2   Travel and Study Grant Program   *181*
12   Letras de Oro Competition   *88*
13   NYFA Artists' New Works (1st deadline)   *144*
15   Bunting Fellowship Program   *167*

**15**    Ferndale New Works Competition    *78*
**15**    Love Creek Gay and Lesbian Festival    *89*
**15**    Playwrights First Plays-in-Progress Award    *99*
**15**    Year-End-Series Festival    *110*
**15**    Young Playwrights Festival    *111*
**23**    Institute of International Education    *170*
**30**    New Voices Play Development Program    *144*

*Contact for exact deadline during this month:*
Bush Artist Fellowships    *167*
Meet The Composer New Residencies (letter of intent)    *172*
NEA International Projects Initiative    *173*
NYFA Fellowships    *178*

# November 1995 ━━━━━━━━━━

**1**    American-Scandinavian Foundation grants    *165*
**1**    Beverly Hills Theatre Guild Award    *73*
**1**    Live Oak Theatre Harvest Festival awards    *88*
**1**    Richard Rodgers Awards    *150*
**15**    MRTW Script Contest    *93*
**15**    New Harmony Project Conference/Laboratory    *143*
**17**    Panowski Award    *92*
**18**    Midwest Theatre Network/Rochester Playwright Festival    *91*
**30**    Francesca Primus Southern Playwriting Competition    *80*
**30**    Pacific Rim Play Festival    *135*
**30**    TCG Extended Collaboration Grants    *180*
**30**    Walden Residency Program    *203*

*Contact for exact deadline during this month:*
Atlanta Artists Project    *166*
Meet The Composer New Residencies (application)    *172*
Sundance Institute Film Program (1st deadline)    *152*

# December 1995 ━━━━━━━━━━

**1**    Carnegie-Mellon Showcase of New Plays    *133*
**1**    Cunningham Prize    *75*
**1**    Drury College One-Act Competition    *78*
**1**    George Bennett Fellowship    *170*

1    Gregory Kolovakos Award   *82*
1    Japan Foundation grants   *170*
1    KC/ACTF Michael Kanin Awards   *85*
1    National Children's Theatre Festival   *94*
1    National Playwrights Conference   *142*
1    National Ten-Minute Play Contest   *94*
1    Playwrights Week   *148*
1    Red Octopus Theatre Workshop   *149*
15   Dorothy Silver Competition   *77*
15   James Thurber residency   *198*
15   PlayLabs   *146*
15   Playwrights' Theater of Denton Competition   *99*
15   Sundance Playwrights Laboratory   *152*
15   Thurber Writer-in-Residence   *198*
20   PEN Translation Prize   *98*
20   Renato Poggioli Award   *100*
30   Lamia Ink! (2nd deadline)   *121*
31   Alcazar Scripts in Progress   *131*
31   Alden B. Dow Creativity Center   *193*
31   Artists-in-Berlin Programme   *165*
31   Biennial Promising Playwright Award   *73*
31   Goshen College Contest   *81*
31   Harold Morton Landon Translation Award   *82*
31   New American Comedy Festival   *95*
31   PEN Center USA West Awards   *98*
31   Robert J. Pickering Award   *100*
31   Tennessee Williams One-Act Competition   *104*
31   Warehouse Theatre One-Act Competition   *108*
31   West Coast Ensemble Full-Length Play Competition   *109*

*Contact for exact deadline during this month:*
Morton R. Sarett Award   *93*

# January 1996

1    Dale Wasserman Drama Award   *75*
1    Kumu Kahua Contest   *86*
1    Lee Korf Awards   *87*
1    Mill Mountain Theatre Competition   *92*
1    Oglebay Institute Towngate Theatre Contest   *97*
1    Playwrights Forum (2nd deadline)   *147*

1   Towngate Theatre Playwriting Contest   *106*
5   Douglass Center Workshops (2nd deadline)   *136*
15   Jewel Box Theatre Playwrighting Award   *84*
15   MacDowell Colony (2nd deadline)   *199*
15   New York Comedy Competition   *97*
15   NLAPW Scholarships for Mature Women   *178*
15   Poems & Plays' Tennessee Chapbook Prize   *125*
15   Ragdale Foundation residencies (1st deadline)   *201*
15   Reva Shiner Contest   *100*
15   Society of Midland Authors Award   *102*
15   Source Theatre Competition   *102*
15   Summerfield G. Roberts Award   *103*
15   Three Genres Short Play Competition   *106*
15   Tomorrow's Playwrights   *57*
15   Virginia Center residencies (2nd deadline)   *203*
15   Voice and Vision Retreat for Women   *154*
15   Washington Theatre Festival   *56*
15   Yaddo residencies (1st deadline)   *205*
16   McKnight Fellowships   *179*
26   Dobie-Paisano Fellowship   *168*
26   New Play Commissions in Jewish Theatre   *177*
29   University of Louisville Award for Music Competition   *107*
30   Perishable Theatre Women's Playwriting Festival   *99*
31   Baker's Plays High School Contest   *73*
31   David James Ellis Award   *76*
31   Dubuque Fine Arts Players One-Act Contest   *78*
31   Hambidge Center residencies   *196*
31   James D. Phelan Award   *83*
31   Margaret Bartle Playwriting Award   *90*
31   McLaren Comedy Playwriting Competition   *91*
31   PlayWorks Festival   *147*
31   Texas Playwrights Festival   *153*

*Contact for exact deadline during this month:*
NEA Fellowships for Translators   *174*
NEA Fund for U.S. Artists at International Festivals   *173*
NYFA Artists' New Works (2nd deadline)   *144*
Scholastic Writing Awards   *101*

# February 1996 ─────────────────────

1   Asian Cultural Council grants   *166*
1   Blue Mountain Center   *194*
1   HBO New Writers Project   *137*
1   Lois and Richard Rosenthal Prize   *88*
1   McKnight Advancement Grants   *179*
1   Millay Colony for the Arts (2nd deadline)   *199*
1   Mount Sequoyah New Play Retreat   *141*
1   National Music Theater Conference   *142*
1   TADA! Staged Reading Series   *104*
1   TheatreVirginia New Voices for the Theatre   *63*
15   Center Theater Contest   *74*
15   Djerassi Resident Artists Program   *195*
15   Jane Chambers Playwriting Award   *84*
15   NEA ArtsLink Collaborative Projects   *173*
15   Southern Playwrights Competition   *103*
15   Ventana Publications Award   *129*
15   White Bird Contest   *109*
15   Wichita State University Contest   *110*
28   Artist Trust Grants for Artist Projects   *166*
28   FEAT Competition   *79*

*Contact for exact deadline during this month:*
Atlanta Mayor's Fellowships   *166*
Marilyn Bianchi Kids' Playwriting Festival   *21*
NEA U.S./Canada/Mexico fellowships   *174*
NEA U.S./Japan fellowships   *174*
Owen Kelly Adopt-a-Playwright Program   *21*

# March 1996 ──────────────────────

1   Bay Area Playwrights Festival   *132*
1   Camargo Foundation residencies   *195*
1   Cintas Fellowship Program   *168*
1   Dorland Mountain Arts Colony (2nd deadline)   *196*
1   George Houston Bass Festival and Award   *80*
1   Nantucket Short Play Competition   *93*
1   New Musical Writers Competition and Festival   *95*
1   Plays-in-Progress April Festival   *146*
1   Samuel Beckett Playwriting Internship   *201*

1    Shenandoah Playwrights Retreat   *151*
1    Shubert Fendrich Memorial Playwriting Contest   *101*
1    South Carolina Playwrights' Festival   *102*
1    Ucross Foundation Residency Program (2nd deadline)   *202*
1    Villa Montalvo Residency Program (2nd deadline)   *203*
15   Dramarama   *77*
15   Electronic Arts Grant Program Finishing Funds   *168*
15   Florida Studio Theatre Young Playwrights Festival   *24*
15   Fund for New American Plays   *169*
15   Isidora Aguirre Playwrighting Lab   *138*
15   Lamia Ink! One Page Play Competition   *87*
15   Mixed Blood Versus America   *92*
15   Pacific Northwest Writers Conference Contest   *98*
17   NEH Humanities Projects in Media (2nd deadline)   *177*
20   Alaska Native Plays Contest   *71*
20   George Hawkins Contest   *80*
29   Hispanic Playwrights Project   *137*
30   Border Playwrights Project   *133*
30   Lamia Ink! (3rd deadline)   *121*
31   Lawrence S. Epstein Award   *87*
31   Little Theatre of Alexandria One-Act Competition   *88*
31   New Christian Plays Award   *95*
31   Princess Grace Fellowship   *180*
31   SWTA New Play Contest   *104*
31   U.S.-Mexico Fund for Culture grants   *181*

*Contact for exact deadline during this month:*
Brody Art Fund Fellowship (music-theatre writers)   *167*

# April 1996 _____

1    California Young Playwrights Contest   *73*
1    Connections   *75*
1    Great Platte River Playwrights' Festival   *81*
1    Hedgebrook (2nd deadline)   *197*
1    LEND Lesbian Play Award   *223*
1    Playhouse on the Square Competition   *99*
1    Playwrights' Center membership   *232*
1    Remembrance New Play Development   *149*
1    Threshold Theater Metaphysical Play Contest   *106*
1    William Flanagan Memorial Center   *204*

2    NYFA—Artists in Residence Program    *200*
5    Douglass Center Workshops (3rd deadline)    *136*
15   Byrdcliffe Art Colony    *194*
15   John Gassner Award    *84*
15   MacDowell Colony (3rd deadline)    *199*
15   Meet the Composer Commissioning Program    *172*
15   Stages Festival of New Plays    *236*
18   Annual Blank Theatre Company Young Playwrights
       Festival    *72*
22   Playwrights' Center Young Playwrights Conference    *232*
30   Adamant Program residencies    *192*
30   Loft Fest '96—Festival of Shorts    *139*

*Contact for exact deadline during this month:*

NYFA Artists' New Works (3rd deadline)    *144*
Very Special Arts Young Playwrights Program    *108*

# May 1996 ——————————————————

1    BMI Musical Theatre Workshop (librettists)    *132*
1    Don and Gee Nicholl Fellowships in Screenwriting    *168*
1    Midwestern Playwrights Festival    *91*
1    Millay Colony for the Arts (3rd deadline)    *199*
1    Playwrights Forum (3rd deadline)    *147*
1    Robert Bone Memorial Award    *100*
15   Amelia Magazine's Frank McClure One-Act Award    *113*
15   Lewis Galantiere Translation Prize    *71*
15   Marc A. Klein Award    *90*
15   Towson State University Prize    *106*
15   Utah Playfest    *107*
15   Virginia Center residencies (3rd deadline)    *203*
20   Padua Hills student workshop    *145*
30   Jackie White Children's Playwriting Contest    *83*
31   L. Arnold Weissberger Competition    *87*
31   NEA Theater Program fellowships    *176*
31   Writer's Digest Writing Competition    *110*

*Contact for exact deadline during this month:*

Chesterfield Film Company Project    *134*
NEA Fund for U.S. Artists at International Festivals    *173*

# June 1996

1   ASF Translation Prize   *72*
1   Chicago Dramatists Workshop Resident Playwrights
       Program   *215*
1   George R. Kernodle Contest   *80*
1   HRC's Annual Contest   *83*
1   New England New Play Competition   *96*
1   NPT Screenplay/Playwriting Festival   *97*
1   Playwrights' Project membership   *233*
1   Ragdale Foundation residencies (2nd deadline)   *201*
1   SETC New Play Project   *103*
2   Headlands Center for the Arts   *197*
3   Western Great Lakes Competition   *109*
7   Douglass Center Workshops (4th deadline)   *136*
15  Urban Stages Award   *107*
30  National Play Award   *94*
30  Siena College Competition   *102*
30  West Coast Ensemble Musical Stairs   *109*

*Contact for exact deadline during this month:*
Coe College Competition   *75*
Sundance Institute Film Program (2nd deadline)   *152*

# July 1996

1   Altos de Chavon residencies   *193*
1   Bailiwick Repertory Director's Festival   *11*
1   FMCT Competition   *79*
1   Henrico Theatre Company Playwriting Competitions   *82*
1   National Playwright Residencies   *154*
1   NEH Research Programs   *177*
1   Theatre Memphis Competition   *105*
15  Deep South Writers Conference Awards   *77*
15  James H. Wilson Award   *76*
15  Paul T. Nolan Award   *76*
22  Inner City Cultural Center Competition   *83*

*Contact for exact deadline during this month:*
ANPC New Dramatists Award   *213*
NYFA Artists' New Works (4th deadline)   *144*

# August 1996 ———————————————

1   BMI Musical Theatre Workshop (composers, lyricists)   *132*
1   Fulbright Scholar Awards   *169*
1   Lehman Engel Musical Theatre Workshop   *138*
1   Plays-in-Progress Oct Festival   *146*
1   Theodore Ward Prize   *105*
1   Yaddo residencies (2nd deadline)   *205*
31   Broadway Tomorrow   *133*
31   Festival of Firsts Competition   *79*
31   Marvin Taylor Award   *90*
31   Ten-Minute Musicals Project   *152*

# Special Interests

Here is a guide to entries which indicate a particular or exclusive interest in certain types of material, or which contain an element of special interest to writers in certain categories. Under Young Audiences and Media, we try to list every entry of interest to writers in these fields. In the case of adaptations, musicals, one-acts and translations, there are numerous theatres willing to consider these types of material; we list here only those theatres and other organizations that give major focus to them. Under African-American, Asian-American, Hispanic/Latin-American and Native American Theatre, we have opted to include not only programs that specifically seek "works by minority writers," but also those that indicate an interest in, for example, "a multiethnic world view" or "works that reflect a multicultural society."

## Adaptation

American Conservatory Theater  8
Arden Theatre Company  9
Bailiwick Repertory  11
Classic Stage Company (CSC)  17
Cornerstone Theater
  Company  19
The Coterie Theatre  19
El Teatro Campesino  22
Germinal Stage Denver  25
Honolulu Theatre for Youth  28
Indiana Repertory Theatre  30
INTAR Hispanic American Arts
  Center  30
Jomandi Productions  32
L. A. Theatre Works  32
New Jersey Shakespeare
  Festival  40
Northlight Theatre  42
Omaha Theater Company for
  Young People  43

Remains Theatre   50
Shakespeare & Company   55
Shakespeare Santa Cruz   55
The Shakespeare Theatre   55
StageWest (MA)   58
Theatreworks/USA   63, 105
West Coast Ensemble   66, 109
The Wilma Theater   67
Wisdom Bridge Theatre Chicago
   Company   67

## African-American Theatre

The Actor's Express   6
Alabama Shakespeare Festival   7
Alice B. Theatre   7
Alliance Theatre Company   7
American Music Theater
   Festival   8
American Playwright Program   131
Arena Stage   9, 143
Black Theatre Network   213
Border Playwrights Project   133
Borderlands Theater   13, 133
Brody Arts Fund   167
Callaloo   116
Cleveland Public Theatre   18, 85
Company One Theater   18
Connections   75
Cornerstone Dramaturgy and
   Development Project   134
The Coterie Theatre   19
Crossroads Theatre Company   19
Dallas Theater Center   20
Dobama Theatre   21
El Teatro Campesino   22
Emerging Playwright Award   78
The Ensemble Theatre   23
The Frank Silvera Writers'
   Workshop   136
Free Street Programs   24
George Hawkins Playwriting
   Contest   80
George Houston Bass Play-Rites
   Festival and Memorial
   Award   80

The Golden West Playwrights at
   the Road Theatre   219
The Group: Seattle's Multicultural
   Theatre   27, 141
Hatch-Billops Collection   219
The HBO New Writers
   Project   137
Hedgebrook   197
Indiana Repertory Theatre   30
Jane Chambers Playwriting
   Award   84
Jomandi Productions   32
L. A. Black Playwrights   138
La MaMa Experimental Theater
   Club   33
The Lee Korf Playwriting
   Awards   87
The Lorraine Hansberry
   Playwriting Award   85
Luminous Visions   224
Manhattan Theatre Club
   Playwriting Fellowships   171
Many Voices Multicultural
   Collaboration Grants   179
Merrimack Repertory Theatre   36
Midwest Radio Theatre
   Workshop   93, 141, 225
Mill Mountain Theatre   37, 92
MRTW Script Contest   93
MultiCultural Theatre Works   141
Nantucket Short Play Festival and
   Competition   93
National Children's Theatre
   Festival   94
National Theatre of the Deaf   39
NEA International Program   173
Nebraska Repertory Theatre   40
New Federal Theatre   40
New Repertory Theatre   41
New Voices for a New
   America   143
New Voices Play Development
   Program   144
New York Theatre Workshop   41
Non-Traditional Casting
   Project   229

NPT Screenplay/Playwriting
Festival  *97*
Odyssey Theatre Ensemble  *42*
The Open Eye Theater  *43*
Oregon Shakespeare Festival  *44*
Organic Theater Company  *44*
The Penumbra Theatre
Company  *45, 134*
Perseverance Theatre  *46*
The Philadelphia Theatre
Company  *46*
Pillsbury House Theatre  *47*
The Playwrights' Center  *146, 178,
232*
Playwrights Harbor  *233*
Playwrights Horizons  *48*
Puerto Rican Traveling Theatre
Playwrights' Workshop  *149*
San Diego Repertory Theatre  *52*
Second Stage Theatre  *54*
7 Stages  *54*
St. Louis Black Repertory
Company  *57*
Studio Arena Theatre  *59*
The Studio Theatre  *59*
Syracuse Stage  *59*
Theatre Gael  *61*
TheatreWorks  *63*
Theodore Ward Prize for African-
American Playwrights  *105*
Utah Shakespearean Festival  *65*
Venture's Playwright
Connection  *154*
Victory Gardens Theater  *65*
Voice and Vision Retreat for
Women Theatre Artists  *154*
The Walt Disney Studios
Fellowship Program  *182*
Young Playwrights Festival  *111*
Young Playwrights Inc.  *111, 241*

**Asian-American Theatre**

The Actor's Express  *6*
Alice B. Theatre  *7*
Alliance Theatre Company  *7*

American Music Theater
Festival  *8*
American Playwright Program  *131*
Arena Stage  *9, 143*
Asian American Arts Alliance  *210*
Asian American Theater Company
New Plays & Playwrights
Development Program  *132*
Asian Cultural Council  *166*
Asian Pacific American
Journal  *115*
Asian-Pacific American Friends of
the Center Theater Group
(APAF-CTG) Reading
Series  *140*
ASSITEJ/USA  *211*
Border Playwrights Project  *133*
Borderlands Theater  *13, 133*
Brody Arts Fund  *167*
Cleveland Public Theatre  *18, 85*
Company One Theater  *18*
Connections  *75*
The Coterie Theatre  *19*
Dobama Theatre  *21*
East West Players  *22*
El Teatro Campesino  *22*
Emerging Playwright Award  *78*
The Frank Silvera Writers'
Workshop  *136*
Free Street Programs  *24*
The Golden West Playwrights at
the Road Theatre  *219*
The Group: Seattle's Multicultural
Theatre  *27, 141*
The HBO New Writers
Project  *137*
Hedgebrook  *197*
Honolulu Theatre for Youth  *28*
Indiana Repertory Theatre  *30*
Jane Chambers Playwriting
Award  *84*
The Japan Foundation  *170*
Key West Theatre Festival  *138*
Kumu Kahua Playwriting
Contest  *86*
La MaMa Experimental Theater
Club  *33*

Lamia Ink! *87, 121*
The Lee Korf Playwriting
  Awards *87*
Luminous Visions *224*
Manhattan Theatre Club
  Playwriting Fellowships *171*
Many Voices Multicultural
  Collaboration Grants *179*
Merrimack Repertory Theatre *36*
Midwest Radio Theatre
  Workshop *93, 141, 225*
Mill Mountain Theatre *37, 92*
MRTW Script Contest *93*
MultiCultural Theatre Works *141*
Nantucket Short Play Festival and
  Competition *93*
National Children's Theatre
  Festival *94*
National Theatre of the Deaf *39*
NEA International Program *173*
Nebraska Repertory Theatre *40*
New Federal Theatre *40*
New Repertory Theatre *41*
New Voices for a New
  America *143*
New York Theatre Workshop *41*
Non-Traditional Casting
  Project *229*
NPT Screenwriting/Playwriting
  Festival *97*
Odyssey Theatre Ensemble *42*
The Open Eye Theater *43*
Oregon Shakespeare Festival *44*
Organic Theater Company *44*
Pan Asian Repertory Theatre *44*
Perseverance Theatre *46*
The Philadelphia Theatre
  Company *46*
Pillsbury House Theatre *47*
The Playwrights' Center *146, 178,*
  *232*
Playwrights Harbor *233*
Playwrights Horizons *48*
Puerto Rican Traveling Theatre
  Playwrights' Workshop *149*
San Diego Repertory Theatre *52*
Second Stage Theatre *54*

St. Louis Black Repertory
  Company *57*
Studio Arena Theatre *59*
The Studio Theatre *59*
Syracuse Stage *59*
Theatre Gael *61*
TheatreWorks *63*
Urban Stages Award *107*
Utah Shakespearean Festival *65*
Venture's Playwright
  Connection *154*
Victory Gardens Theater *65*
The Walt Disney Studios
  Fellowship Program *182*
Young Playwrights Festival *111*
Young Playwrights Inc. *111, 241*

## Disabilities: Theatre for, by and about People with Disabilities

Jane Chambers Playwriting
  Award *84*
Milwaukee Public Theatre *38*
National Theatre of the Deaf *39*
National Theatre Workshop of the
  Handicapped *227*
Non-Traditional Casting
  Project *229*
Perseverance Theatre *46*
Pillsbury House Theatre *47*
Playwrights Theatre of New
  Jersey *233*
Sam Edwards Deaf Playwrights
  Competition *101*
Very Special Arts Young Playwrights
  Program *108*
Young Playwrights Inc. *111, 241*

## Experimental Theatre

American Music Theater
  Festival *8*
American Writing: A
  Magazine *113*
Barter Theatre *11*
Cleveland Public Theatre *18, 85*
Collages & Bricolages *117*

Coney Island, USA   *18*
The Cream City Review   *117*
Crossroads Theatre Company   *19*
Djerassi Resident Artists
    Program   *195*
En Garde Arts   *23*
Jane Chambers Playwriting
    Award   *84*
La MaMa Experimental Theater
    Club   *33*
Lamia Ink!   *87, 121*
Magic Theatre   *35, 132*
Midwest Theatre Network Original
    Play Competition/Rochester
    Playwright Festival   *91*
Music-Theatre Group   *39*
The Richard Rodgers Awards   *150*
The Road Company   *51*
Round House Theatre   *52*
Scripts and Scribbles   *127*
7 Stages   *54*
Stages   *58*
Stet Magazine   *127*
Theater   *128*
Theater for the New City   *61*
Theatre X   *63*
United Arts   *129*

## Gay and Lesbian Theatre

The Actor's Express   *6*
Alice B. Theatre   *7*
Cleveland Public Theatre   *18, 85*
conmoción's latina lesbian writers'
    telaraña   *216*
Jane Chambers Playwriting
    Award   *84*
LEND   *223*
Love Creek One-Act Mini-
    Festivals   *89*
MRTW Script Contest   *93*
PEN Fund for Writers & Editors
    with AIDS   *184*
Perseverance Theatre   *46*
Pillsbury House Theatre   *47*
The Purple Circuit   *235*
Sinister Wisdom   *127*

The WOW Cafe   *240*
Young Playwrights Inc.   *111, 241*

## Hispanic/Latin-American Theatre

The Actor's Express   *6*
Alice B. Theatre   *7*
Alliance Theatre Company   *7*
Altos de Chavon   *193*
American Music Theater
    Festival   *8*
American Playwright Program   *131*
The Americas Review   *114*
Arena Stage   *9, 143*
Arte Público Press   *114*
The Association of Hispanic
    Arts   *211*
Bilingual Foundation of the
    Arts   *12*
Border Playwrights Project   *133*
Borderlands Theater   *13, 133*
Brody Arts Fund   *167*
Chicano/Latino Literary
    Contest   *74*
Cintas Fellowship Program   *168*
Cleveland Public Theatre   *18, 85*
Company One Theater   *18*
conmoción's latina lesbian writers'
    telaraña   *216*
Connections   *75*
The Coterie Theatre   *19*
Dallas Theater Center   *20*
Dobama Theatre   *21*
El Teatro Campesino   *22*
Emerging Playwright Award   *78*
The Frank Silvera Writers'
    Workshop   *136*
Free Street Programs   *24*
GALA Hispanic Theatre   *25*
The Golden West Playwrights at
    the Road Theatre   *219*
The Gregory Kolovakos Award   *82*
The Group: Seattle's Multicultural
    Theatre   *27, 141*
The HBO New Writers
    Project   *137*

Hedgebrook   197
Hispanic Organization of Latin
   Actors (HOLA)   219
Hispanic Playwrights Project   137
Indiana Repertory Theatre   30
INTAR Hispanic American Arts
   Center   30
The Isidora Aguirre Playwrighting
   Lab   138
Jane Chambers Playwriting
   Award   84
La MaMa Experimental Theater
   Club   33
Latin American Theater
   Artists   222
The Lee Korf Playwriting
   Awards   87
Letras de Oro Spanish Literary
   Prize Competition   88
Libreto/as   122
Luminous Visions   224
Manhattan Theatre Club
   Playwriting Fellowships   171
Many Voices Multicultural
   Collaboration Grants   179
Merrimack Repertory Theatre   36
Midwest Radio Theatre
   Workshop   93, 141, 225
Mill Mountain Theatre   37, 92
MRTW Script Contest   93
MultiCultural Theatre Works   141
Nantucket Short Play Festival and
   Competition   93
National Children's Theatre
   Festival   94
National Hispanic Playwriting
   Contest   94
National Theatre of the Deaf   39
NEA International Program   173
Nebraska Repertory Theatre   40
New Federal Theatre   40
New Repertory Theatre   41
New Voices for a New
   America   143
New York Theatre Workshop   41
Non-Traditional Casting
   Project   229

NPT Screenplay/Playwriting
   Festival   97
Odyssey Theatre Ensemble   42
OLLANTAY Center for the
   Arts   230
Omaha Theater Company for
   Young People   43
The Open Eye Theater   43
Oregon Shakespeare Festival   44
Organic Theater Company   44
Perseverance Theatre   46
The Philadelphia Theatre
   Company   46
Pillsbury House Theatre   47
PlayWorks Festival   147
The Playwrights' Center   146, 178,
   232
Playwrights Harbor   233
Playwrights Horizons   48
Plaza de la Raza   234
Puerto Rican Traveling Theatre
   Playwrights' Workshop   149
Repertorio Español   50
San Diego Repertory Theatre   52
Second Stage Theatre   54
St. Louis Black Repertory
   Company   57
Studio Arena Theatre   59
The Studio Theatre   59
Syracuse Stage   59
Thalia Spanish Theatre   60
Theatre Gael   61
TheatreWorks   63
Urban Stages Award   107
U.S.-Mexico Fund for Culture   181
Utah Shakespearean Festival   65
Venture's Playwright
   Connection   154
Victory Gardens Theater   65
Voice and Vision Retreat for
   Women Theatre Artists   154
The Walt Disney Studios
   Fellowship Program   182
Young Playwrights Festival   111
Young Playwrights Inc.   111, 241

## Jewish Theatre

Dorothy Silver Playwriting
  Competition   77
Jewish Ensemble Theatre   31
Jewish Repertory Theatre   32
The National Foundation for
  Jewish Culture   226
National Jewish Theater   39
New Play Commissions in Jewish
  Theatre   177
Studio Arena Theatre   59
The Studio Theatre   59

## Media (Film, Radio and Television)

Alcazar Scripts in Progress   131
Alden B. Dow Creativity
  Center   193
Altos de Chavon   193
The American Film Institute   208
Artist Trust   165
Association of Independent Video
  and Filmmakers   212
Brody Arts Fund   167
Bush Artist Fellowships   167
Byrdcliffe Art Colony   194
The Chesterfield Film
  Company/Writer's Film
  Project   134
Christopher Columbus Screenplay
  Discovery Awards   74
Corporation for Public
  Broadcasting   216
Djerassi Resident Artists
  Program   195
The Don and Gee Nicholl
  Fellowships in
  Screenwriting   168
Electronic Arts Grant
  Program   168
Fairchester Playwrights   135
First Stage   136, 218
Frederick Douglass Creative Arts
  Center Writing Workshops   136

Harold Prince Musical Theatre
  Program   137
Hatch-Billops Collection   219
The HBO New Writers
  Project   137
Headlands Center for the
  Arts   197
Helen Wurlitzer Foundation of
  New Mexico   197
Hollywood Scriptwriter   246
Independent Feature Project   220
Inner City Cultural Center
  Competition   83
The International Women's
  Writing Guild   222
The Japan Foundation   170
L. A. Theatre Works   32
Luminous Visions   224
MacDowell Colony   199
Manhattan Playwrights Unit   139
Many Voices Multicultural
  Collaboration Grants   179
Midwest Radio Theatre
  Workshop   93, 141, 225
Millay Colony for the Arts   199
MRTW Script Contest   93
National Playwrights
  Conference   142
National Public Radio   227
NEA Media Arts: Film/Radio/
  Television Program   175
NEH Humanities Projects in
  Media   177
The New Harmony Project
  Conference/Laboratory   143
New Playwrights Foundation   229
New Voices   229
The New York Public Library for
  the Performing Arts   229
NPT Screenplay/Playwriting
  Festival   97
NYFA Artists' Fellowships   178
NYFA Artists' New Works   144
PEN Center USA West Literary
  Awards   98
PKE Theatre   146
Players Press   124

Playwrights Forum   147
Public Broadcasting Service   235
Scholastic Writing Awards   101
The Scripteasers   150
The Scriptwriters Network   235
Shenandoah International
   Playwrights Retreat   151
Shenandoah Playwright
   Residencies   201
The Sundance Institute
   Independent Feature Film
   Program   152
The Tyrone Guthrie Centre   202
U.S.-Mexico Fund for Culture   181
Vermont Studio Center   202
Villa Montalvo Artist Residency
   Program   203
Virginia Center for the Creative
   Arts   203
The Walt Disney Studios
   Fellowship Program   182
William Flanagan Memorial
   Creative Persons Center   204
Writer's Digest Writing
   Competition   110
Writers Guild of America, East
   (WGAE)   240
Writers Guild of America, west
   (WGAw)   240
Writer's Market   110, 249
Yaddo   205

## Musical Theatre

Alliance Theatre Company   7
American Music Center   209
American Music Theater
   Festival   8
ASCAP   131, 210
ASCAP Musical Theatre
   Workshop   131
BMI (Broadcast Music
   Incorporated)   132, 213
BMI-Lehman Engel Musical
   Theatre Workshop   132
Brave New Workshop & Instant
   Theatre Company   14

Broadway on Sunset   214
Broadway Tomorrow   133
CitiArts Theatre   16
The Coterie Theatre   19
Freelance Press   120
Gilman and Gonzalez-Falla Theatre
   Foundation Musical Theatre
   Award   81
Goodspeed Opera House   26
The Group: Seattle's Multicultural
   Theatre   27, 141
Harold Prince Musical Theatre
   Program   137
The KC/ACTF Musical Theater
   Award   85
The Kleban Award   171
La MaMa Experimental Theater
   Club   33
Manhattan Theatre Club   35, 171
Mary Flagler Cary Charitable Trust
   Commissioning Program   171
Meet The Composer   172, 224
Meet The Composer Grant
   Programs   172
Metro Theater Company   37
Music, Dance & Theater
   Scholarships   247
Music-Theatre Group   39
Musical Theatre Works   142
National Academy of
   Songwriters   225
National Alliance for Musical
   Theatre   226
National Music Theater
   Conference   142
National Music Theater
   Network   142
NEA Music Program: Composers
   Program   175
NEA Opera-Musical Theater
   Program   176
New American Musical Writers
   Competition and Festival   95
New Dramatists   87, 227
NEW STAGES Musical Workshop
   Program   95, 143
The Open Eye Theater   43

OPERA America  *231*
The Richard Rodgers Awards  *150*
San Diego Repertory Theatre  *52*
San Jose Repertory Theatre  *53*
Seacoast Repertory Theatre  *53*
Seaside Music Theater  *53*
Society Hill Playhouse  *56*
The Songwriters Guild of
  America  *236*
Songwriter's Market  *248*
The Ten-Minute Musicals
  Project  *152*
Tennessee Repertory Theatre  *60*
Theatreworks/USA  *63, 105*
Theatreworks/USA Commissioning
  Program  *105*
Theatrical Outfit  *64*
University of Louisville
  Grawemeyer Award for Music
  Composition  *107*
Vineyard Theatre  *65*
The Walnut Street Theatre
  Company  *66*
West Coast Ensemble  *66, 109*
West Coast Ensemble Musical
  Stairs  *109*
The Wilma Theater  *67*
Wisdom Bridge Theatre Chicago
  Company  *67*

**Native American Theatre**

The Actor's Express  *6*
Alaska Native Plays Contest  *71*
Alice B. Theatre  *7*
Alliance Theatre Company  *7*
American Indian Community
  House  *208*
American Music Theater
  Festival  *8*
American Playwright Program  *131*
Arena Stage  *9, 143*
Border Playwrights Project  *133*
Borderlands Theater  *13, 133*
Brody Arts Fund  *167*
Cleveland Public Theatre  *18, 85*
Company One Theater  *18*

Connections  *75*
The Coterie Theatre  *19*
Dobama Theatre  *21*
El Teatro Campesino  *22*
Emerging Playwright Award  *78*
The Four Directions American
  Indian Literary Quarterly  *119*
The Frank Silvera Writers'
  Workshop  *136*
The Golden West Playwrights at
  the Road Theatre  *219*
The Group: Seattle's Multicultural
  Theatre  *27, 141*
The HBO New Writers
  Project  *137*
Hedgebrook  *197*
Indiana Repertory Theatre  *30*
Jane Chambers Playwriting
  Award  *84*
La MaMa Experimental Theater
  Club  *33*
Lamia Ink!  *87, 121*
The Lee Korf Playwriting
  Awards  *87*
Luminous Visions  *224*
Manhattan Theatre Club
  Playwriting Fellowships  *171*
Many Voices Multicultural
  Collaboration Grants  *179*
Merrimack Repertory Theatre  *36*
Midwest Radio Theatre
  Workshop  *93, 141, 225*
Mill Mountain Theatre  *37, 92*
The Montana Repertory
  Theatre  *39*
MRTW Script Contest  *93*
MultiCultural Theatre Works  *141*
Nantucket Short Play Festival and
  Competition  *93*
National Children's Theatre
  Festival  *94*
National Theatre of the Deaf  *39*
Nebraska Repertory Theatre  *40*
New Repertory Theatre  *41*
New Voices for a New
  America  *143*
New York Theatre Workshop  *41*

Non-Traditional Casting
    Project  229
NPT Screenplay/Playwriting
    Festival  97
Odyssey Theatre Ensemble  42
Omaha Theater Company for
    Young People  43
The Open Eye Theater  43
Oregon Shakespeare Festival  44
Organic Theater Company  44
Perseverance Theatre  46
The Philadelphia Theatre
    Company  46
Pillsbury House Theatre  47
PlayWorks Festival  147
The Playwrights' Center  146, 178,
    232
Playwrights Harbor  233
Playwrights Horizons  48
Puerto Rican Traveling Theatre
    Playwrights' Workshop  149
San Diego Repertory Theatre  52
Second Stage Theatre  54
St. Louis Black Repertory
    Company  57
Studio Arena Theatre  59
The Studio Theatre  59
Syracuse Stage  59
Theatre Gael  61
TheatreWorks  63
Urban Stages Award  107
Utah Shakespearean Festival  65
Venture's Playwright
    Connection  154
Victory Gardens Theater  65
Voice and Vision Retreat for
    Women Theatre Artists  154
The Walt Disney Studios
    Fellowship Program  182
Young Playwrights Festival  111
Young Playwrights Inc.  111, 241

## One-Acts and Short Plays

Alabama Literary Review  113
Amelia Magazine  113
American Shorts Contest  71
The Bellingham Review  115
Callaloo  116
Collages & Bricolages  117
Confrontation  117
CrazyQuilt Quarterly  117
The Cream City Review  117
Deep South Writers
    Conference  76
Drury College One-Act Play
    Competition  78
Dubuque Fine Arts Players
    National One-Act Playwriting
    Contest  78
The Festival of Emerging American
    Theatre (FEAT)
    Competition  79
First Stage  136, 218
The Four Directions American
    Indian Literary Quarterly  119
George Houston Bass Play-Rites
    Festival and Memorial
    Award  80
George R. Kernodle Playwriting
    Contest  80
Goshen College Peace Playwriting
    Contest  81
Henrico Theatre Company One-
    Act Playwriting Competition  82
Horizon Theatre Company  28
Inner City Cultural Center
    Competition  83
Kalliope, A Journal of Women's
    Art  121
The Kenyon Review  121
Lamia Ink!  87, 121
Lamia Ink! International One-Page
    Play Competition  87
The Little Theatre of Alexandria
    National One-Act Playwriting
    Competition  88
The Loft Fest '96—Festival of
    Shorts  139
Love Creek One-Act Festivals  89
Mill Mountain Theatre  37, 92
Missouri Association of
    Playwrights  225

Nantucket Short Play Festival and
Competition  93
National Ten-Minute Play
Contest  94
National Theatre Workshop of the
Handicapped  227
New City Theater and Art Center
Playwright's Festival  96
Off-Off Broadway Original Short
Play Festival  97
Pacific Review  123
Passaic Review  123
Performing Arts Journal  123
Perishable Theatre Women's
Playwriting Festival  99
The Playwrights Foundation  132,
232
Poems & Plays  125
Portland Review  125
Prism International  125
Rag Mag  126
Red Octopus Theatre Company
Original Scripts Workshop  149
Resource Publications  126
Rockford Review  126
The Short Play Awards
Program  86
Sinister Wisdom  127
S.T.A.G.E.  236
Tennessee Williams/New Orleans
Literary Festival One-Act Play
Competition  104
This Month ON STAGE  128
The Three-Genres Short Play
Competition  106
Tomorrow Magazine  128
Warehouse Theatre Company One-
Act Competition  108

## Performance Art/Multimedia
(see also Experimental Theatre)

Alice B. Theatre  7
American Writing: A
Magazine  113
Coney Island, USA  18
Descant  118

Djerassi Resident Artists
Program  195
The Emelin Theatre for the
Performing Arts  22
En Garde Arts  23
The Field  217
Free Street Programs  24
Hip Pocket Theatre  27
Jane Chambers Playwriting
Award  84
La MaMa Experimental Theater
Club  33
Lamia Ink!  87, 121
Live Bait Theatrical Company  33
Mark Taper Forum  36, 140
Milwaukee Public Theatre  38
New City Theater and Art Center
Playwright's Festival  96
New York Theatre Workshop  41
NYFA Artists' New Works  144
The Phoenix Theatre
Company  47
Pillsbury House Theatre  47
PlayLabs  146
Provincetown Arts/Provincetown
Arts Press  125
The Purple Circuit  235
San Diego Repertory Theatre  52
Scripts and Scribbles  127
7 Stages  54
Stet Magazine  127
Theatre X  63
Tomorrow Magazine  128
United Arts  129
Voice and Vision Retreat for
Women Theatre Artists  154

## Religious/Spiritual Theatre

A. D. Players  5
Alliance Theatre Company  7
Baker's Plays  73, 115
The Cunningham Prize for
Playwriting  75
Eldridge Publishing
Company  119

Encore Performance
  Publishing  119
Henrico Theatre Company Full-
  Length Play Competition  82
Lillenas Drama Resources  122
Love Creek One-Act Festivals  89
New Christian Plays Award  95
The New Harmony Project
  Conference/Laboratory  143
Pioneer Drama Service  101, 123
Resource Publications  126
7 Stages  54
Threshold Theater Metaphysical
  Play Contest  106

## Social-Political Theatre

A Contemporary Theatre  5
ACTheater  5
The Actor's Express  6
Alabama Shakespeare Festival  7
Alice B. Theatre  7
Alternate ROOTS  207
ArtReach Touring Theatre  10
Bailiwick Repertory  11
Barter Theatre  11
Blue Mountain Center  194
BoarsHead: Michigan Public
  Theater  13
Borderlands Theater  13, 133
Brave New Workshop & Instant
  Theatre Company  14
Cleveland Public Theatre  18, 85
Collages & Bricolages  117
Connections  75
Contemporary American Theater
  Festival  19
The Coterie Theatre  19
Crossroads Theatre Company  19
Dell'Arte Players Company  20
The Dennis McIntyre Playwriting
  Award  77
Detroit Repertory Theatre  21
Dobama Theatre  21
El Teatro Campesino  22
Ensemble Theatre of
  Cincinnati  23

Eureka Theatre Company  23
The Festival of Emerging American
  Theatre (FEAT)
  Competition  79
The Fourth Freedom Forum
  Playwriting Award  85
Free Street Programs  24
Freelance Press  120
George Street Playhouse  25
Goodman Theatre  26
Goshen College Peace Playwriting
  Contest  81
Great American History
  Theatre  26
The Group: Seattle's Multicultural
  Theatre  27, 141
Horizon Theatre Company  28
Indiana Repertory Theatre  30
InterAct Theatre Company  30
Invisible Theatre  31
Irondale Ensemble Project  31
Katherine and Lee Chilcote
  Award  85
Long Wharf Theatre  34, 139
Mabou Mines  34
Magic Theatre  35, 132
Milwaukee Public Theatre  38
MRTW Script Contest  93
MultiCultural Theatre Works  141
National Children's Theatre
  Festival  94
New Federal Theatre  40
New York Theatre Workshop  41
Northlight Theatre  42
Odyssey Theatre Ensemble  42
Omaha Theater Company for
  Young People  43
Philadelphia Festival Theatre for
  New Plays at Annenberg
  Center  46
The Philadelphia Theatre
  Company  46
Pilgrim Project  178
Pillsbury House Theatre  47
Pope Theatre Company  49
Remains Theatre  50

Remembrance Through the
   Performing Arts New Play
   Development  *149*
The Repertory Theatre of St.
   Louis  *50*
Round House Theatre  *52*
Sacramento Theatre Company  *52*
San Diego Repertory Theatre  *52*
Second Stage Theatre  *54*
7 Stages  *54*
Signature Theatre  *56*
Stage West (TX)  *58*
Stamford Theatre Works  *58*
Theater for the New City  *61*
Theater of the First
   Amendment  *62*
Theatreworks/USA  *63, 105*
Unicorn Theatre National
   Playwrights' Award  *107*
Virginia Stage Company  *65*
The Walnut Street Theatre
   Company  *66*
White Bird Annual Playwriting
   Contest  *109*
The Wilma Theater  *67*

## Translation

American Translators Association
   (ATA)  *71, 209*
American Translators Association
   Awards  *71*
The American-Scandinavian
   Foundation  *72, 165*
ASF Translation Prize  *72*
Bailiwick Repertory  *11*
Bloomsburg Theatre Ensemble  *13*
Camargo Foundation  *195*
Classic Stage Company (CSC)  *17*
GALA Hispanic Theatre  *25*
German Literary Translation
   Prize  *71*
The Gregory Kolovakos Award  *82*
A Handbook for Literary
   Translators  *246*
Harold Morton Landon
   Translation Award  *82*

Institute for Contemporary East
   European and Slavic Drama and
   Theatre  *220*
Institute of International
   Education  *170*
INTAR Hispanic American Arts
   Center  *30*
International Theatre Institute of
   the United States (ITI/US)  *221*
Lewis Galantiere Literary
   Translation Prize  *71*
Modern International Drama  *122*
NEA International Program  *173*
NEA Literature Program  *174*
NEH Research Programs:
   Translations Program  *177*
New Jersey Shakespeare
   Festival  *40*
Northlight Theatre  *42*
PAJ Books  *123*
PEN American Center  *82, 98,*
   *100, 184, 231, 246*
PEN–Book-of-the-Month Club
   Translation Prize  *98*
Performing Arts Journal  *123*
Renato Poggioli Award  *100*
Round House Theatre  *52*
The Shakespeare Theatre  *55*
Stages  *58*
StageWest (MA)  *58*
The Studio Theatre  *59*
Ubu Repertory Theater  *64, 239*
West Coast Ensemble  *66, 109*
The Wilma Theater  *67*
Yale Repertory Theatre  *68*

## Women's Theatre

Arena Stage  *9, 143*
Bailiwick Repertory  *11*
Borderlands Theater  *13, 133*
Bunting Fellowship Program  *167*
Cleveland Public Theatre  *18, 85*
Collages & Bricolages  *117*
Company One Theater  *18*
conmoción's latina lesbian writers'
   telaraña  *216*

The Dramatists Guild   *217*
Earth's Daughters   *119*
The Golden West Playwrights at the Road Theatre   *219*
Hedgebrook   *197*
Horizon Theatre Company   *28*
International Center for Women Playwrights   *221*
The International Women's Writing Guild   *222*
Invisible Theatre   *31*
Jane Chambers Playwriting Award   *84*
Kalliope, A Journal of Women's Art   *121*
League of Professional Theater Women/New York   *222*
LEND   *223*
Love Creek One-Act Festivals   *89*
Midwest Radio Theatre Workshop   *93, 141, 225*
MRTW Script Contest   *93*
National League of American Pen Women   *178, 227*
New Georges   *228*
New Women Playwright's Contest   *96*
NLAPW Scholarships for Mature Women   *178*
Norcroft   *200*
NPT Screenplay/Playwriting Festival   *97*
Oregon Shakespeare Festival   *44*
Organic Theater Company   *44*
Perishable Theatre Women's Playwriting Festival   *99*
Perseverance Theatre   *46*
Pillsbury House Theatre   *47*
San Diego Repertory Theatre   *52*
Second Stage Theatre   *54*
7 Stages   *54*
Shubert Fendrich Memorial Playwriting Contest   *101*
Sinister Wisdom   *127*
The Susan Smith Blackburn Prize   *103*
Syracuse Stage   *59*

Victory Gardens Theater   *65*
Voice and Vision Retreat for Women Theatre Artists   *154*
The Walt Disney Studios Fellowship Program   *182*
Warehouse Theatre Company One-Act Competition   *108*
Women's Project & Productions   *67*
Women's Theatre Alliance   *239*
The WOW Cafe   *240*

## Young Audiences

A. D. Players   *5*
Alabama Shakespeare Festival   *7*
Alaska Native Plays Contest   *71*
The American Alliance for Theatre and Education (AATE)   *207*
American Theatre   *113, 238, 245*
The Americas Review   *114*
Anchorage Press   *114*
Anna Zornio Memorial Children's Theatre Playwriting Award   *72*
The Annual Blank Theatre Company Young Playwrights Festival   *72*
Apple Tree Theatre   *9*
Arte Público Press   *114*
ArtReach Touring Theatre   *10*
ASSITEJ/USA   *211*
Baker's Plays   *73, 115*
Baker's Plays High School Playwriting Contest   *73*
Barksdale Theatre   *11*
Barter Theatre   *11*
Bilingual Foundation of the Arts   *12*
Birmingham Children's Theatre   *13*
Blizzard Publishing   *116*
BoarsHead: Michigan Public Theater   *13*
California Theatre Center   *14*
Chicago Plays   *116*
The Children's Theatre Company   *15*

Childsplay  16

Coe College New Works for the
  Stage Competition  75

Contemporary Drama Service  117

The Coterie Theatre  19

Cumberland County Playhouse  20

The Cunningham Prize for
  Playwriting  75

Dale Wasserman Drama Award  75

Dell'Arte Players Company  20

Dramafest '98  77

The Dramatic Publishing
  Company  118, 161

Dramatics Magazine  118

Dramatists Play Service  118

Earth's Daughters  119

East West Players  22

El Teatro Campesino  22

Eldridge Publishing
  Company  119

Encore Performance
  Publishing  119

The Ensemble Theatre  23

Ensemble Theatre of
  Cincinnati  23

First Stage Milwaukee  124

The Foothill Theatre
  Company  24

The Four Directions American
  Indian Literary Quarterly  119

Free Street Programs  24

George Hawkins Playwriting
  Contest  80

George Street Playhouse  25

Gilmore Creek Playwriting
  Competition  81

Great Platte River Playwrights'
  Festival  81

Gretna Theatre  27

The Group: Seattle's Multicultural
  Theatre  27, 141

Heuer Publishing Company  120

Holvoe Books  120

Honolulu Theatre for Youth  28

Horizon Theatre Company  28

The Human Race Theatre
  Company  29

I. E. Clark  121

Indiana Repertory Theatre  30

Inner City Cultural Center
  Competition  83

Irondale Ensemble Project  31

Jackie White Memorial National
  Children's Playwriting
  Contest  83

James D. Phelan Award in
  Literature  83

Jewish Ensemble Theatre  31

Jomandi Productions  32

Key West Theatre Festival  138

Laguna Playhouse  33

Libreto/as  122

Los Angeles Designers' Theatre
  Commissions  89

Margaret Bartle Playwriting
  Award  90

Marin Theatre Company  35

Mark Taper Forum  36, 140

McLaren Memorial Comedy
  Playwriting Competition  91

Merrimack Repertory Theatre  36

Merry-Go-Round Playhouse  36

Metro Theater Company  37

MetroStage  37

Milwaukee Public Theatre  38

MultiCultural Theatre Works  141

National Children's Theatre
  Festival  94

National Theatre of the Deaf  39

Nebraska Theatre Caravan  40

New Play Commissions in Jewish
  Theatre  177

New Plays  122

Novel Stages  42

Omaha Theater Company for
  Young People  43

Passaic Review  123

Penobscot Theatre Company  45

The Penumbra Theatre
  Company  45, 134

The Phoenix Theatre
  Company  47

Pillsbury House Theatre  47

Pioneer Drama Service  101, 123

Pirate Playhouse—Island
  Theatre  *47*
Players Press  *124*
Plays, The Drama Magazine for
  Young People  *124*
PlaySource  *124, 238*
Pope Theatre Company  *49*
Repertorio Español  *50*
Resource Publications  *126*
Riverside Theatre (FL)  *51*
Robert J. Pickering Award for
  Playwriting Excellence  *100*
Round House Theatre  *52*
Samuel French  *126, 162*
Santa Monica Playhouse  *53*
Seacoast Repertory Theatre  *53*
Seaside Music Theater  *53*
Seattle Children's Theatre  *54*
Shakespeare Santa Cruz  *55*
Shubert Fendrich Memorial
  Playwriting Contest  *101*
Smith and Kraus  *127*
St. Louis Black Repertory
  Company  *57*
Stage One: The Louisville
  Children's Theatre  *57*
The Sundance Playwrights
  Laboratory  *152*
TADA! Spring Staged Reading
  Series  *104*
The Theater at Monmouth  *60*
Theatre IV  *61*
Theatre Gael  *61*
Theatre West  *62*
Theatreworks/USA  *63, 105*
Theatreworks/USA Commissioning
  Program  *105*
Waldo M. and Grace C.
  Bonderman IUPUI Playwriting
  Competition for Young
  Audiences  *108*
West Coast Ensemble  *66, 109*
The Writers' Studio  *204*
Young Playwrights Inc.  *111, 241*
Zachary Scott Theatre Center
  (ZACH)  *68*

## Young Playwright Programs

The Annual Blank Theatre
  Company Young Playwrights
  Festival  *72*
Baker's Plays  *73, 115*
Baker's Plays High School
  Playwriting Contest  *73*
California Young Playwrights
  Contest  *73*
Dobama Theatre  *21*
Florida Studio Theatre  *24, 71*
Pegasus Players  *44*
The Playwrights' Center  *146, 178, 232*
Playwrights Theatre of New
  Jersey  *233*
Scholastic Writing Awards  *101*
Stage One: The Louisville
  Children's Theatre  *57*
TheatreVirginia  *63*
Very Special Arts Young Playwrights
  Program  *108*
Young Playwrights Festival  *111*
Young Playwrights Inc.  *111, 241*

# Index

Remember the two alphabetizing principles used throughout the book: First, entries beginning with a person's name are alphabetized by the first name rather than the surname. However, this year, you can find these entries indexed by both names. Hence you will find the Robert Bone Memorial Playwriting Award under R and B, the Jenny McKean Moore Visiting Writer in Washington under J and M and the Helene Wurlitzer Foundation of New Mexico under H and W. Second, regardless of which way "theatre" is spelled in an organization's title, it is alphabetized as if it were spelled "re," not "er."

## A

A Contemporary Theatre  5
A. D. Players  5
Abe Newborn Associates  160
Academy Theatre  5
Academy Theatre New Play Development Program  131
ACME Originals  70
ACTheater  5
Acting Company, The  6
Actor's Express, The  6
Actors Theatre of Louisville  6, 94
Adamant Program, The  192
Adams Ltd., Bret  160

AFI Television Writers Summer Workshop  208
Agency, The  160
Agency for the Performing Arts  160
Aguirre Playwrighting Lab, The Isidora  138
Alabama Literary Review  113
Alabama Shakespeare Festival  7
Alabama State Council on the Arts  186
Alaska Native Plays Contest  71
Alaska State Council on the Arts  186
Alcazar Scripts in Progress  131
Alden B. Dow Creativity Center  193
Alfred Hodder Fellowship, The  165
Alice B. Theatre  7
Alley Theatre  7

Alliance of Los Angeles Playwrights, The 206

Alliance of Resident Theatres/New York, The 207

Alliance Theatre Company 7

Alternate ROOTS 207

Altos de Chavon 193

Amelia Magazine 113

American Alliance for Theatre & Education (AATE), The 207

American Conservatory Theater 8

American Film Institute, The 208

American Indian Community House 208

American Music Center 209

American Music Theater Festival 8

American Playwright Program 131

American Repertory Theatre 8

American Samoa Council on Culture, Arts and Humanities 186

American Shorts Contest 71

American Stage Festival 8

American Theatre 113, 238, 245

American Theater and Literature Program Contest 128

American Translators Association (ATA) 71, 209

American Translators Association Awards 71

American Writing: A Magazine 113

American-Scandinavian Foundation, The 72, 165

Americas Review, The 114

Anchorage Press 114

Anderson Center for the Arts, Mary 199, 224

Anderson Playwrights Series (MAPS), The Maxwell 140

Ann Elmo Agency 160

Anna Zornio Memorial Children's Theatre Playwriting Award 72

Annual Blank Theatre Company Young Playwrights Festival, The 72

Annual Short Play Festival 89

Apple Tree Theatre 9

Aran Press 114

Arden Theatre Company 9

Arena Stage 9, 143

Arizona Commission on the Arts 186

Arizona Theatre Company 9, 94

Arkansas Arts Council 186

Arkansas Repertory Theatre 10

Arrow Rock Lyceum Theatre 10

Art Craft Publishing Company 114

A.R.T./New York 207

Arte Público Press 114

Artist Trust 165

Artists Repertory Theatre 10

Artists-in-Berlin Programme 165

ArtReach Touring Theatre 10

Arts & Humanities Section, West Virginia Division of Culture & History 191

Arts International 168, 173

Artsboard 234

ArtSEARCH 238

ASCAP (American Society of Composers, Authors and Publishers) 131, 210

ASCAP Musical Theatre Workshop 131

ASF Translation Prize 72

Asian American Arts Alliance 210

Asian American Arts Calendar 210

Asian American Arts Organizations in New York & New Jersey 210

Asian American Arts Resources and Opportunities 210

Asian American Theater Company New Plays & Playwrights Development Program 132

Asian Cultural Council 166

Asian Pacific American Journal 115

Asian-Pacific American Friends of the Center Theater Group (APAF-CTG) Reading Series 140

Asolo Theatre Company 11

ASSITEJ/USA (International Association of Theatre for Children and Young People) 211

Associated Writing Programs, The 211

Association of Authors' Representatives, The 159

Association of Hispanic Arts, The 211

Association of Independent Video and Filmmakers 212

ATA Chronicle 210

Atlanta Bureau of Cultural Affairs 166

Atlantic Center for the Arts 194

Audrey Skirball-Kenis Theatre, The 132, 212

Australian National Playwrights' Centre 213

Authors League Fund, The 183

AWP Chronicle 211

AWP Official Guide to Writing Programs, The 211

**B**

Back Stage 246

Bailiwick Repertory 11

Baker's Plays 73, 115

Baker's Plays High School Playwriting
  Contest 73
Barbara Hogenson Agency, Inc., The 160
Barksdale Theatre 11
Barter Theatre 11
Bartle Playwriting Award, Margaret 90
Bass Play-Rites Festival and Memorial,
  George Houston 80
Bay Area Playwrights Festival 132
Bay Street Theatre 12
Beckett Playwriting Internship, Samuel 201
Bellingham Review, The 115
Bellowing Ark 115
Bennett Fellowship, George 170
Berkeley Repertory Theatre 12
Berkshire Theatre Festival 12
Berman, Boals & Flynn 160
Bernice Cohen Musical Theatre Fund
  Award 131
Bertha Klausner International Literary
  Agency 160
Bethel Agency, The 160
Beverly Hills Theatre Guild-Julie Harris
  Playwright Award 73
Beyond Boundaries National Resource
  Book 210
Beyond Tradition 230
Bianchi Kids' Playwriting Festival, Marilyn
  21
Biennial Promising Playwright Award 73
Bilingual Foundation of the Arts 12
Billy Rose Theatre Collection, The 229
Birmingham Children's Theatre 13
Black Theatre Directory 213
Black Theatre Network 213
Black Voices 213
Blackburn Prize, The Susan Smith 103
Blizzard Publishing 116
Bloomsburg Theatre Ensemble 13
Blue Mountain Center 194
BMI (Broadcast Music Incorporated) 132,
  213
BMI-Lehman Engel Musical Theatre
  Workshop 132
BoarsHead: Michigan Public Theater 13
Bonderman IUPUI Playwriting
  Competition for Young Audiences 108
Bone Memorial Playwriting Award, Robert
  100
Border Playwrights Project 133
Borderlands Theater 13, 133
Brave New Workshop & Instant Theatre
  Company 14
Bret Adams Ltd. 160
British American Arts Association 214

Broadway on Sunset 214
Broadway Play Publishing 116
Broadway Tomorrow 133
Brody Arts Fund 167
Brown Theatre Company, Clarence 17
BTN News 213
Buchwald & Associates, Don 161
Bunting Fellowship Program 167
Bush Artist Fellowships 167
Byrdcliffe Art Colony 194

C

CAC Playwright's Unit 133
California Arts Council 186
California Theatre Center 14
California Young Playwrights Contest 73
Callaloo 116
Callboard 237
Camargo Foundation 195
Canada on Stage 235
CanPlay 234
Capital Repertory Company 14
Carnegie Fund for Authors 184
Carnegie-Mellon Showcase of New Plays
  133
Carolina Playwrights Center 214
Cary Charitable Trust Commissioning
  Program, Mary Flagler 171
Center for Advanced Study in Theatre Arts
  (CASTA) 220
Center Stage 14
Center Theater 15, 74
Center Theater International Playwrighting
  Contest 74
CENTERSTAGE 237
Chambers Playwriting Award, Jane 84
Change 184
Chapbook 76
Charlotte Festival/New Plays in America
  134
Chateau de Lesvault 195
Cheltenham Center for the Arts 15
Chesterfield Film Company/Writer's Film
  Project, The 134
Chicago Alliance for Playwrights (CAP)
  215
Chicago Dramatists Workshop 215
Chicago Plays 116
Chicago Young Playwrights Festival 44
Chicano/Latino Literary Contest 74
Chilcote Award, Katherine and Lee 85
Children's Theatre Company, The 15
Childsplay 16

Christian Drama Magazine  95
Christopher Columbus Screenplay
    Discovery Awards  74
Cincinnati Playhouse in the Park  16, 88
Cintas Fellowship Program  168
Circle Repertory Company  16
CitiArts Theatre  16
City Theatre Company  17
Clarence Brown Theatre Company  17
Clark, I. E.  121
Classic Stage Company (CSC)  17
Clauder Competition for Excellence in
    Playwriting  74
Cleveland Play House, The  17, 145
Cleveland Public Theatre  18, 85
Coe College New Works for the Stage
    Competition  75
Cohen Musical Theatre Fund Award,
    Bernice  131
Collages & Bricolages  117
Colony Studio Theatre, The  18
Colorado Council on the Arts  186
Colorado Dramatists  216
Colorado Theatre Guide, The  216
Columbus Screenplay Discovery Awards,
    Christopher  74
Commonwealth Council for Arts and
    Culture (Northern Marianas Islands)
    189
Company One Theater  18
Coney Island, USA  18
Confrontation  117
conmoción's latina lesbian writers' telaraña
    216
Connecticut Commission on the Arts  186
Connections  75
Contemporary American Theater Festival
    19
Contemporary Arts Center  133
Contemporary Drama Service  117
Contemporary Theatre, A  5
Cornerstone Dramaturgy and Development
    Project  134
Cornerstone Theater Company  19
Corporation for Public Broadcasting  216
Coterie Theatre, The  19
Cottages at Hedgebrook  197
Council for International Exchange of
    Scholars (CIES)  169
Council of Literary Magazines and Presses
    112
CrazyQuilt Quarterly  117
Cream City Review, The  117
Crossroads Theatre Company  19

Cumberland County Playhouse  20
Cunningham Prize for Playwriting, The  75


D

Dale Wasserman Drama Award  75
Dallas Theater Center  20
David James Ellis Memorial Award  76
Dayton Playhouse FutureFest  76
Dealing with Healing  218
Deep South Writers Conference  76
Delaware Division of the Arts  186
Delaware Theatre Company  20, 75
Dell'Arte Players Company  20
Dennis McIntyre Playwriting Award, The
    77
Denver Center Theatre Company  21, 134
Denver Center Theatre Company U S
    WEST Workshops  134
Descant  118
Detroit Repertory Theatre  21
Dialogue  210, 213
Diamond Head Theatre Developmental
    Programs  135
Directors Company, The  137
Directory of Hispanic Talent  219
Directory of Literary Magazines  112
Directory of Los Angeles Playwright Groups
    212
Disney Studios Fellowship Program, The
    Walt  182
Dissertations Concerning Black Theatre:
    1900–1994  213
District of Columbia (DC) Commission on
    the Arts and Humanities  187
Djerassi Resident Artists Program  195
Dobama Theatre  21
Dobie-Paisano Fellowship  168
Don and Gee Nicholl Fellowships in
    Screenwriting, The  168
Don Buchwald & Associates  161
Dorese Agency Ltd.  161
Dorland Mountain Arts Colony  196
Dorothy Silver Playwriting Competition  77
Dorset Colony for Writers  196
Douglass Creative Arts Center Writing
    Workshops, Frederick  136
Dow Creativity Center, Alden B.  193
Drama League Developing Artists Series
    135
Drama League of New York, The  135
Dramafest '98  77
Dramarama  77

Dramatic Publishing Company, The  *118,*
*161*
Dramatics Magazine  *118*
Dramatists Guild, The  *217*
Dramatists Guild Fund, The  *183*
Dramatists Guild Newsletter, The  *217*
Dramatists Guild Quarterly, The  *217*
Dramatists Guild Resource Directory, The
*217*
Dramatists Play Service  *118*
Drury College One-Act Play Competition
*78*
Dubuque Fine Arts Players National
One-Act Playwriting Contest  *78*

# E

Earth's Daughters  *119*
East West Players  *22*
Edwards Deaf Playwrights Competition,
Sam  *101*
El Teatro Campesino  *22*
Eldridge Publishing Company  *119*
Electronic Arts Grant Program  *168*
Elisabeth Marton Agency  *161*
Ellis Memorial Award, David James  *76*
Elmo Agency, Ann  *160*
Emelin Theatre for the Performing Arts,
The  *22*
Emerging Playwright Award  *78*
Emmy Gifford Children's Theater, The  *43*
Empty Space Theatre, The  *22*
En Garde Arts  *23*
Encore Performance  *95*
Encore Performance Publishing  *119*
Engel Musical Theatre Workshop, The
Lehman  *138*
Ensemble Theatre, The  *23*
Ensemble Theatre of Cincinnati  *23*
Epstein Playwriting Award, Lawrence S.  *87*
Eureka Theatre Company  *23*
Extended Collaboration Grants  *180*

# F

Fairchester Playwrights  *135*
Feedback Theatrebooks  *247, 248*
Fendrich Memorial Playwriting Contest,
Shubert  *101*
Ferndale Repertory Theatre New Works
Competition  *78*
Festival of Emerging American Theatre
(FEAT) Competition, The  *79*

Festival of Firsts Playwriting Competition
*79*
Festival of Southern Theatre Playwriting
Competition  *80*
Field, The  *217*
Fifi Oscard Associates  *161*
Filmmaker  *220*
First Stage  *136, 218*
First Stage Milwaukee  *24*
First Stage Newsletter  *218*
Fishbein Ltd., Freida  *161*
Flanagan Memorial Creative Persons
Center, William  *204*
Flora Roberts  *161*
Florida Division of Cultural Affairs  *187*
Florida Studio Theatre  *24, 71*
FMCT National Playwrights Competition
*79*
Foothill Theatre Company, The  *24*
Foundation Center, The  *218*
Foundation Directory, The  *218*
Foundation Grants Index, The  *218*
Foundation Grants to Individuals  *218*
Four Directions American Indian Literary
Quarterly, The  *119*
Fourth Freedom Forum Playwriting Award,
The  *85*
Francesca Primus Southern Playwriting
Competition  *80*
Frank McClure One-Act Play Award  *113*
Frank Silvera Writers' Workshop, The  *136*
Frederick Douglass Creative Arts Center
Writing Workshops  *136*
Free Street Programs  *24*
Freedman Dramatic Agency, Robert A.
*162*
Freelance Press  *120*
Freida Fishbein, Ltd.  *161*
French Guidelines Samuel  *127*
French, Samuel  *126, 162*
Fulbright Scholar Awards  *169*
Full Moon Playwright's Exchange  *136*
Fulton Theatre Company  *25*
Fund for New American Plays  *169*
Funding Guide for Independent Artists
*218*

# G

GALA Hispanic Theatre  *25*
Galantiere Literary Translation Prize, Lewis
*71*
GAP (Grants for Artist Projects)  *166*

Gassner Memorial Playwriting Award, John 84

George Bennett Fellowship *170*

George Hawkins Playwriting Contest *80*

George Houston Bass Play-Rites Festival and Memorial Award *80*

George R. Kernodle Playwriting Contest *80*

George Street Playhouse *25*

Georgia Council for the Arts *187*

German Academic Exchange Service (DAAD) *165*

German Literary Translation Prize *71*

Germinal Stage Denver *25*

Gersh Agency, The *161*

GeVa Theatre *26*

Gifford Children's Theater, The Emmy *43*

Gilman and Gonzalez-Falla Theatre Foundation Musical Theatre Award *81*

Gilmore Creek Playwriting Competition *81*

Gloucester Stage Company *201*

Golden West Playwrights at the Road Theatre, The *219*

Goodman Theatre *26*

Goodspeed Opera House *26*

Goshen College Peace Playwriting Contest *81*

Graham Agency *161*

Grants and Awards Available to American Writers *231*

Great American History Theatre *26*

Great Platte River Playwrights' Festival *81*

Green Playwrights Prize, Paul *98*

Gregory Kolovakos Award, The *82*

Gretna Theatre *27*

Group: Seattle's Multicultural Theatre, The *27, 141*

Guam Council on the Arts & Humanities Agency *187*

Guggenheim Memorial Foundation, John Simon *170*

Gurman Agency, The Susan *163*

Guthrie Centre, The Tyrone *202*

Guthrie Theater, The *27*


**H**

Hambidge Center for Creative Arts and Sciences, The *196*

Handbook for Literary Translators, A *246*

Hansberry Playwriting Award, The Lorraine *85*

Harold Morton Landon Translation Award *82*

Harold Prince Musical Theatre Program *137*

Hartford Stage Company *27*

Hatch-Billops Collection *219*

Hawai'i Review *120*

Hawkins Playwriting Contest, George *80*

Hawthornden Castle International Retreat for Writers *196*

HBO New Writers Project, The *137*

Headlands Center for the Arts *197*

Hedgebrook *197*

Heideman Award *94*

Helen Merrill *161*

Helene Wurlitzer Foundation of New Mexico *197*

Henrico Theatre Company Playwriting Competitions *82*

Heuer Publishing Company *120*

Hip Pocket Theatre *27*

Hippodrome State Theatre, The *28*

Hispanic Arts News *211*

Hispanic Organization of Latin Actors (HOLA) *219*

Hispanic Playwrights Project *137*

Hodder Fellowship, The Alfred *165*

Hogenson Agency, Inc., The Barbara *160*

Hollywood Scriptwriter *246*

Holvoe Books *120*

Honolulu Theatre for Youth *28*

Horizon Theatre Company *28*

Horse Cave Theatre *29*

Hot Seats *207*

HRC's Annual Playwriting Contest *83*

Human Race Theatre Company, The *29*

Huntington Theatre Company *29*


**I**

I. E. Clark *121*

Idaho Commission on the Arts *187*

Illinois Arts Council *187*

Illinois Theatre Center *29*

Illusion Theater *29*

Imison Playwrights, Michael *162*

impact! *234, 235*

In Their Own Words: Contemporary American Playwrights *245*

Independent Feature Project *220*

Independent Film & Video Monthly, The *212*

Indiana Arts Commission *187*

Indiana Repertory Theatre *30*

Individual's Guide to Grants, The *246*

Inner City Cultural Center Competition *83*

Institute for Contemporary East European and Slavic Drama and Theatre  220
Institute of International Education  170
Institute of Outdoor Drama  220
Institute of Puerto Rican Culture  190
INTAR Hispanic American Arts Center  30
InterAct Theatre Company  30
International Center for Women Playwrights  221
International Creative Management  161
International Directory of Little Magazines and Small Presses  112
International Theatre Institute of the United States (ITI/US)  221
International Women Playwrights Conference  221
International Women's Writing Guild, The  222
Intiman Theatre Company  31
Into Print: A Guide to the Writing Life  246
Inventing the Future  212
Invisible Theatre  31
Iowa Arts Council  187
Irondale Ensemble Project  31
Isidora Aguirre Playwrighting Lab, The  138
ITI/US  221

**J**

Jackie White Memorial National Children's Playwriting Contest  83
James D. Phelan Award in Literature  83
James H. Wilson Full-Length Play Award  76
James Thurber Writer-in-Residence, The  198
Jane Chambers Playwriting Award  84
Japan Foundation, The  170
Jenny McKean Moore Visiting Writer in Washington  198
Jerome Playwright-in-Residence Fellowships  178
Jewel Box Theatre Playwrighting Award  84
Jewish Ensemble Theatre  31
Jewish Repertory Theatre  32
John Gassner Memorial Playwriting Award  84
John Simon Guggenheim Memorial Foundation  170
John Steinbeck Writer's Room, The  198
Jomandi Productions  32
Jory Copying Assistance Program, The  209

Journal, The  240
Joyce Ketay Agency, The  162

**K**

Kalliope, A Journal of Women's Art  121
Kansas Arts Commission  187
Katherine and Lee Chilcote Award  85
KC/ACTF Musical Theater Award, The  85
Kelly Adopt-a-Playwright Program, Owen  21
Kennedy Center American College Theater Festival: Michael Kanin Playwriting Awards Program  85
Kentucky Arts Council  188
Kenyon Review, The  121
Kernodle Playwriting Contest, George R.  80
Ketay Agency, The Joyce  162
Key West Theatre Festival  138
Klausner International Literary Agency, Bertha  160
Kleban Award, The  171
Klein Playwriting Award, The Marc A.  90
Kolovakos Award, The Gregory  82
Kopaloff Company, The  162
Korf Playwriting Awards, The Lee  87
Kumu Kahua Playwriting Contest  86

**L**

L. A. Black Playwrights  138
L. A. Theatre Works  32
L. Arnold Weissberger Playwriting Competition  87
La Jolla Playhouse  32
La MaMa Experimental Theater Club  33
La Nueva Ola  219
Laguna Playhouse  33
Lamia Ink!  87, 121
Lamia Ink! International One-Page Play Competition  87
Landon Translation Award, Harold Morton  82
Lantz-Harris Literary Agency  162
Latin American Theater Artists  222
Lawrence S. Epstein Playwriting Award  87
League of Chicago Theatres/ League of Chicago Theatres Foundation  222
League of Professional Theatre Women/New York  222
Lee Korf Playwriting Awards, The  87

Lehman Engel Musical Theatre Workshop, The *138*
Leighton Studios *198*
LEND (Lesbian Exchange of New Drama) *223*
Letras de Oro Spanish Literary Prize Competition *88*
Lewis Galantiere Literary Translation Prize *71*
Libreto/as *122*
Lila Wallace—Reader's Digest Opera for a New America, The *231*
Lillenas Drama Resources *122*
Lincoln Center Theater *33*
Literary Agents: A Writer's Guide *246*
Literary Agents of North America *247*
Literary Managers and Dramaturgs of the Americas *223*
Literary Market Place *247*
Little Theatre of Alexandria National One-Act Playwriting Competition, The *88*
Live Bait Theatrical Company *33*
Live Oak Theatre *34, 88*
Live Oak Theatre's Harvest Festival of New American Plays *88*
LMDA Review *224*
Loft Fest '96—Festival of Shorts, The *139*
Lois and Richard Rosenthal New Play Prize *88*
Long Wharf Theatre *34, 139*
Long Wharf Theatre Stage II Workshops *139*
Lorraine Hansberry Playwriting Award, The *85*
Los Angeles Designers' Theatre Commissions *89*
Louisiana Division of the Arts *188*
Love Creek One-Act Festivals *89*
Love Creek Productions *89, 97*
Luminous Visions *224*

**M**

Mabou Mines *34*
MacDowell Colony, The *199*
Mad River Theater Works *34*
Madison Repertory Theatre *35*
Magic Theatre *35, 132*
Maine Arts Commission *188*
Manhattan Playwrights Unit *139*
Manhattan Theatre Club *35, 171*
Manhattan Theatre Club Playwriting Fellowships *171*

Many Voices Multicultural Collaboration Grants *179*
Many Voices Playwriting Residency Awards *179*
Marc A. Klein Playwriting Award, The *90*
Margaret Bartle Playwriting Award *90*
Marilyn Bianchi Kids' Playwriting Festival *21*
Marin Theatre Company *35*
Mark Taper Forum *36, 140*
Mark Taper Forum Developmental Programs *140*
Market Insight...for Playwrights *247*
Marton Agency, Elisabeth *161*
Marvin Taylor Playwriting Award *90*
Mary Anderson Center for the Arts *199, 224*
Mary Flagler Cary Charitable Trust Commissioning Program *171*
Mary Roberts Rinehart Awards, The *172*
Maryland State Arts Council *188*
Massachusetts Cultural Council *188*
Maxim Mazumdar New Play Competition *90*
Maxwell Anderson Playwrights Series (MAPS), The *140*
Mazumdar New Play Competition, Maxim *90*
McCarter Theatre Center for the Performing Arts *36*
McClure One-Act Play Award, Frank *113*
McIntyre Playwriting Award, The Dennis *77*
McKnight Advancement Grants *179*
McKnight Fellowships *179*
McLaren Memorial Comedy Playwriting Competition *91*
Meet The Composer *172, 224*
Meet The Composer Grant Programs *172*
Meet the Composer/Reader's Digest Commissioning Program *172*
Merely Players *140*
Merrill, Helen *161*
Merrimack Repertory Theatre *36*
Merry-Go-Round Playhouse *36*
Metro Theater Company *37*
MetroStage *37*
Michael Imison Playwrights *162*
Michigan Council for the Arts & Cultural Affairs *188*
Midwest Radio Theatre Workshop *93, 141, 225*
Midwest Theatre Network Original Play Competition/Rochester Playwright Festival *91*

Midwestern Playwrights Festival  91
Mildred and Albert Panowski Playwriting Award  92
Mill Mountain Theatre  37, 92
Mill Mountain Theatre New Play Competition: The Norfolk Southern Festival of New Works  92
Millay Colony for the Arts, The  199
Miller Award  76
Milwaukee Chamber Theatre  37
Milwaukee Public Theatre  38
Milwaukee Repertory Theater  38
Minnesota State Arts Board  188
Minority Job Bulletin  213
Mississippi Arts Commission  188
Missouri Arts Council  188
Missouri Association of Playwrights  225
Missouri Repertory Theatre  38
Mixed Blood Theatre Company  38, 92
Mixed Blood Versus America  92
Mobil Playwriting Competition  92
Modern International Drama  122
Montana Arts Council  188
Montana Repertory Theatre, The  39
Moore Visiting Writer in Washington, Jenny McKean  198
Morris Agency, William  163
Morton R. Sarett Memorial Award  93
Mount Sequoyah New Play Retreat  141
MRTW Script Contest  93
MultiCultural Theatre Works  141
Music, Dance & Theater Scholarships  247
Music-Theatre Group  39
Musical Theatre Works  142

N

Nantucket Playwrights Retreat  200
Nantucket Short Play Festival and Competition  93
National Academy of Songwriters  225
National Alliance for Musical Theatre  226
National Children's Theatre Festival  94
National Endowment for the Arts
    International Program  173
    Literature Program  174
    Media Arts: Film/Radio/Television Program  175
    Music Program: Composers Program  175
    Opera-Musical Theater Program  176
    Presenting Program  176
    Theater Program  176

National Endowment for the Humanities
    Public Programs: Humanities Projects in Media  177
    Research Programs: Translations Program  177
National Foundation for Jewish Culture, The  226
National Hispanic Playwriting Contest  94
National Jewish Theater  39
National League of American Pen Women  178, 227
National Music Theater Conference  142
National Music Theater Network  142
National Play Award  94
National Playwrights Conference  142
National Playwrights Directory, The  247
National Public Radio  227
National Student Playwriting Award, The  86
National Ten-Minute Play Contest  94
National Theatre Artist Residency Program  180
National Theatre of the Deaf  39
National Theatre Workshop of the Handicapped  227
Native Americans in the Arts  209
Nebraska Arts Council  188
Nebraska Repertory Theatre  40
Nebraska Theatre Caravan  40
Network  222
Nevada State Council on the Arts  189
New American Comedy (NAC) Festival  95
New American Musical Writers Competition and Festival  95
New Christian Plays Award  95
New City Theater and Art Center Playwright's Festival  96
New Dramatist, The  228
New Dramatists  87, 227
New England New Play Competition and Showcase  96
New Federal Theatre  40
New Georges  228
New Hampshire State Council on the Arts  189
New Harmony Project Conference/Laboratory, The  143
New Jersey Shakespeare Festival  40
New Jersey State Council on the Arts  189
New Mexico Arts Division  189
New Play Commissions in Jewish Theatre  177
New Plays  122
New Playwrights Foundation  229
New Repertory Theatre  41

New Residencies *172*
New Stage Theatre *41*
NEW STAGES Musical Workshop Program *95, 143*
New Traditions *230*
New Voices *229*
New Voices for a New America *143*
New Voices Play Development Program *144*
New Women Playwright's Contest *96*
New Work Festival *140*
New York Comedy Playwriting Competition *97*
New York Foundation for the Arts *144, 178, 185*
New York Foundation for the Arts Artists' Fellowships *178*
New York Foundation for the Arts—Artists in Residence Program *200*
New York Foundation for the Arts Artists' New Works *144*
New York Public Library for the Performing Arts, The *229*
New York State Council on the Arts *185, 189*
New York State Theatre Institute *41*
New York Theatre Workshop *41*
New Zealand Theatrescripts *232*
Newborn Associates, Abe *160*
NewGate Theatre New Play Development *144*
Next Stage, The *145*
Nicholl Fellowships in Screenwriting, The Don and Gee *168*
NLAPW Scholarships for Mature Women *178*
Nolan One-Act Play Award, Paul T. *76*
Non-Traditional Casting Project *229*
Norcroft *200*
North Carolina Arts Council *189*
North Carolina Playwrights Center *214*
North Dakota Council on the Arts *189*
Northlight Theatre *42*
Northwest Playwrights Guild *230*
Novel Stages *42*
NPR Playhouse *227, 229*
NPT Screenplay/Playwriting Festival *97*
Nueva Ola, La *219*
Nuevo L. A. Chicano TheatreWorks *234*
NYC Performance Space List *207*
NYC Rehearsal Space List *207*
NYSCA *185*

**O**

Odyssey Theatre Ensemble *42*
Off-Off Broadway Original Short Play Festival *97*
Oglebay Institute Towngate Theatre Playwriting Contest *97*
Ohio Arts Council *189*
Old Globe Theatre *42*
OLLANTAY Center for the Arts *230*
OLLANTAY Theater Magazine *230*
Olney Theatre Center for the Arts *43*
Omaha Theater Company for Young People *43*
On the Purple Circuit *235*
On Writing *240*
O'Neill Theater Center *142, 247*
Ontological-Hysteric Theater *43*
Open Eye Theater, The *43*
OPERA America *231*
Opportunities for Composers *209*
Oregon Arts Commission *189*
Oregon Shakespeare Festival *44*
Organic Theater Company *44*
Originals *135*
Oscard Associates, Fifi *161*
Owen Kelly Adopt-a-Playwright Program *21*

**P**

Pacific Northwest Writers Conference Literary Contest *98*
Pacific Review *123*
Pacific Rim Play Festival *135*
Padua Hills Playwrights' Workshop/Festival *145*
PAJ Books *123*
Pan Asian Repertory Theatre *44*
Panowski Playwriting Award, Mildred and Albert *92*
Paramuse Artists Associates *162*
Parness Agency, The *162*
Passaic Review *123*
Paul Green Playwrights Prize *98*
Paul T. Nolan One-Act Play Award *76*
PBS Packaging & Technical Guidelines *235*
Pegasus Players *44*
PEN American Center *82, 98, 100, 184, 231, 246*
PEN Center USA West Literary Awards *98*
PEN Fund for Writers & Editors with AIDS *184*

PEN Prison Writing Information Bulletin, The *231*
Pen Woman, The *227*
PEN Writers Fund *184*
PEN–Book-of-the-Month Club Translation Prize *98*
Pennsylvania Council on the Arts *190*
Pennsylvania Stage Company *45*
Pennsylvania Theatre Directory *237*
Penobscot Theatre Company *45*
Penumbra Theatre Company, The *45, 134*
People's Light and Theatre Company, The *45*
Peregrine Whittlesey Agency *162*
Performing Arts Journal *123*
Perishable Theatre Women's Playwriting Festival *99*
Perseverance Theatre *46*
Peterborough Players *46*
Pevner, Inc., Stephen *163*
Phelan Award in Literature, James D. *83*
Philadelphia Festival Theatre for New Plays *77*
Philadelphia Festival Theatre for New Plays at Annenberg Center *46*
Philadelphia Theatre Company, The *46*
Phoenix Theatre, The *79*
Phoenix Theatre Company, The *47*
Pickering Award for Playwriting, Robert J. *100*
Pilgrim Project *178*
Pillsbury House Theatre *47*
Pioneer Drama Service *101, 123*
Pioneer Theatre Company *47*
Pirate Playhouse—Island Theatre *47*
Pittsburgh Public Theater *48*
PKE Theatre *146*
Players Press *124*
Playformers *146*
Playhouse America! *247*
Playhouse on the Square *48, 99*
Playhouse on the Square New Play Competition *99*
PlayLabs *146*
PlayMakers Repertory Company *48*
Playmarket *231*
Playmarket Directory of New Zealand Plays and Playwrights, The *232*
Plays for Consideration *212*
Plays, The Drama Magazine for Young People *124*
Plays-in-Progress Festivals of New Works *146*
PlaySource *124, 238*
PlayWorks Festival *147*

Playwrights' Center, The *146, 178, 232*
Playwrights' Center Grant Programs, The *178*
Playwright's Companion, The *248*
Playwrights First Plays-in-Progress Award *99*
Playwrights Forum *147*
Playwrights Foundation, The *132, 232*
Playwrights Harbor *233*
Playwrights Horizons *48*
Playwrights' Platform *147*
Playwrights' Preview Productions *78, 148*
Playwrights' Project, The *100, 233*
Playwrights' Theater of Denton Playwriting Competition *99*
Playwrights Theatre of Los Angeles, The *148*
Playwrights Theatre of New Jersey *233*
Playwrights Theatre of New Jersey New Play Development Program *148*
Playwrights Union of Canada *234*
Playwrights Week *148*
Plaza de la Raza *234*
Poems & Plays *125*
Poets & Writers *246, 248, 249*
Poets & Writers Magazine *248*
Poggioli Award, Renato *100*
Polish Plays in Translation *220*
Pope Theatre Company *49*
Portland Repertory Theatre *49*
Portland Review *125*
Portland Stage Company *49*
Primary Stages Company *149*
Primus Southern Playwriting Competition, Francesca *80*
Prince Musical Theatre Program, Harold *137*
Princess Grace Awards: Playwright Fellowship *180*
Prism International *125*
Professional Association of Canadian Theatres/PACT Communications Centre *234*
Professional Playscript Format Guidelines and Sample *248*
Provincetown Arts/Provincetown Arts Press *125*
Public Broadcasting Service *235*
Public Theater/New York Shakespeare Festival, The *49*
Puerto Rican Traveling Theatre Playwrights' Workshop *149*
Purple Circuit, The *235*
Purple Circuit Directory, The *235*
Purple Rose Theatre Company, The *50*

# Q

QRL Poetry Series Awards  99

# R

Radio Play, The  229
Rag Mag  126
Ragdale Foundation  201
Red Octopus Theatre Company Original
    Scripts Workshop  149
Remains Theatre  50
Remembrance Through the Performing
    Arts New Play Development  149
Renato Poggioli Award  100
Repertorio Español  50
Repertory Theatre of St. Louis, The  50
Resource Guides on Actors with Disabilities
    230
Resource Publications  126
Reva Shiner Full-Length Play Contest  100
Rhode Island State Council on the Arts
    190
Richard Rodgers Awards, The  150
Rinehart Awards, The Mary Robert  172
Riverside Theatre (FL)  51
Riverside Theatre (IA)  51
Road Company, The  51
Roadside Theater  51
Robert A. Freedman Dramatic Agency  162
Robert Bone Memorial Playwriting Award
    100
Robert J. Pickering Award for Playwriting
    Excellence  100
Roberts Award, Summerfield G.  103
Roberts Company, The  162
Roberts, Flora  161
Rockford Review  126
Rodgers Awards, The Richard  150
Rose Theatre Collection, The Billy  229
Rosenstone/Wender  162
Rosenthal New Play Prize, Lois and
    Richard  88
Round House Theatre  52

# S

Sacramento Theatre Company  52
Salt Lake Acting Company, The  52
Sam Edwards Deaf Playwrights Competition
    101
Samuel Beckett Playwriting Internship  201
Samuel French  126, 162

Samuel French Guidelines  126
San Diego Repertory Theatre  52
San Jose Repertory Theatre  53
Santa Monica Playhouse  53
Sarasota Festival of New Plays  24
Sarett Memorial Award, Morton R.  93
Scandinavian Review  72
Scholastic Writing Awards  101
Schoolhouse, The  150
Schulman Literary Agency, Susan  163
Script  230
Scripteasers, The  150
Scripts and Scribbles  127
ScriptShare  228
Scriptwriters Network, The  235
Seacoast Repertory Theatre  53
Seaside Music Theater  53
Seasons-at-a-Glance  237
Seattle Children's Theatre  54
Seattle Repertory Theatre  54
Second Stage Theatre  54
Self-Production Guide  218
7 Stages  54
Shakespeare & Company  55
Shakespeare Santa Cruz  55
Shakespeare Theatre, The  55
Shenandoah International Playwrights
    Retreat  151
Shenandoah Playwright Residencies  201
Shenandoah Playwrights Retreat  201
Shiner Full-Length Play Contest, Reva  100
Short Play Awards Program, The  86
Shubert Fendrich Memorial Playwriting
    Contest  101
Shukat Company, Ltd.  162
Siena College International Playwrights
    Competition  102
Signature Theatre  56
Silver Playwriting Competition, Dorothy  77
Silvera Writers' Workshop, The Frank  136
Sinister Wisdom  127
Skirball-Kenis Theatre, The Audrey  132,
    212
Slavic and East European Performance:
    Drama, Theatre, Film  220
Smith and Kraus  127
Snug Harbor Cultural Center  202
Society Hill Playhouse  56
Society of Midland Authors Drama Award,
    The  102
SongTalk  226
Songwriters Guild of America, The  236
Songwriter's Market  248
Source Theatre Company  56, 102

Source Theatre Company National Playwriting Competition  102
South Carolina Arts Commission  190
South Carolina Playwrights' Festival  102
South Coast Repertory  56, 137
South Dakota Arts Council  190
Southeast Playwrights Project  236
Southeastern Theatre Conference New Play Project  103
Southern Appalachian Playwrights' Conference  151
Southern Playwrights Competition  103
Southern Writers' Project  7
Soviet Plays in Translation  220
Space Chase  218
Spokane Interplayers Ensemble  57
St. Louis Black Repertory Company  57
S.T.A.G.E. (Society for Theatrical Artists' Guidance and Enhancement)  236
Stage Directions  248
STAGE of the Art  208
Stage One: The Louisville Children's Theatre  57
Stage West (TX)  58
Stages  58
StageWest (MA)  58
Stamford Theatre Works  58
State Arts Council of Oklahoma  189
State Foundation on Culture and the Arts (Hawaii)  187
Steinbeck Writer's Room, The John  198
Stephen Pevner, Inc.  163
Steppenwolf Theatre Company  59
Stet Magazine  127
Studio Arena Theatre  59
Studio Theatre, The  59
Summerfield G. Roberts Award  103
SummerNITE, New Play Studio  151
Sun & Moon Press  128
Sundance Institute Independent Feature Film Program, The  152
Sundance Playwrights Laboratory, The  152
Susan Gurman Agency, The  163
Susan Schulman Literary Agency  163
Susan Smith Blackburn Prize, The  103
SWTA Annual New Play Contest  104
Syracuse Stage  59

T

Tacoma Actors Guild  59
TADA! Spring Staged Reading Series  104
Tantleff Office, The  163

Taper Forum Developmental Programs, Mark  140
Taper Forum, Mark  36, 140
TAPLINE  237
Taylor Playwriting Award, Marvin  90
TCG  113, 124, 180, 238, 245, 248
TCG Grant Programs  180
Teatro Campesino, El  22
telaraña alert  216
Television Writers Summer Workshop  208
Ten-Minute Musicals Project, The  152
Tennessee Arts Commission  190
Tennessee Chapbook Prize  125
Tennessee Repertory Theatre  60
Tennessee Williams/New Orleans Literary Festival One-Act Plat Competition  104
Texas Commission on the Arts  190
Texas Playwrights Festival  153
Thalia Spanish Theatre  60
Theater  128
Theatre Artists Workshop of Westport  153
Theatre Association of Pennsylvania (TAP)  237
Theater at Lime Kiln  60, 105
Theater at Lime Kiln Regional Playwriting Contest  105
Theater at Monmouth, The  60
Theatre Bay Area  237
Theatre Communications Group  113, 124, 180, 238, 245, 248
Theatre de la Jeune Lune  61
Theatre Directory  238, 248
Theatre Directory of the Bay Area  237
Theatre for a New Audience  61
Theater for the New City  61
Theatre for Young Audiences Today  211
Theatre IV  61
Theatre Gael  61
Theatre in the Square  62
Theatre Listing, The  235
Theatre Member Directory  207
Theatre Memphis New Play Competition  105
Theatre Museum, The  238
Theater of the First Amendment  62
Theatre on Film and Tape (TOFT), The  229
Theatre Profiles  238, 248
Theatre Southwest  104
Theatre West  62
Theatre X  63
TheatreForum  128
TheatreVirginia  63
TheatreWorks  63
Theatreworks/USA  63, 105

Theatreworks/USA Commissioning Program 105
Theatrical Outfit 64
Theodore Ward Prize for African-American Playwrights 105
This Month ON STAGE 128
Three-Genres Short Play Competition, The 106
Threshold Theater Metaphysical Play Contest 106
Thurber Writer-in-Residence, The James 198
Tomorrow Magazine 128
Touchstone Theatre 64
Towngate Theatre Playwriting Contest 106
Towson State University Prize for Literature 106
Translation Services Directory 210
Travel and Study Grant Program 181
Trinity Repertory Company 64
Trustus Theatre 102
Tyrone Guthrie Centre, The 202

## U

Ubu Repertory Theater 64, 239
Ucross Foundation Residency Program 202
Unicorn Theatre National Playwrights' Award 107
United Arts 129
University of Alabama New Playwrights' Program 153
University of Louisville Grawemeyer Award for Music Composition 107
Urban Stages Award 107
U.S. Copyright Office publications 249
U.S.-Mexico Fund for Culture 181
Utah Arts Council 190
Utah Playfest 107
Utah Shakespearean Festival 65

## V

Ventana Productions/Publications 129
Ventana Publications Play Award 129
Venture Theatre 154
Venture to Write 154
Venture's National Playwright Residencies 154
Venture's Playwright Connection 154
Vermont Council on the Arts 190
Vermont Playwrights Award 108

Vermont Studio Center 202
Very Special Arts Young Playwrights Program 108
Victory Gardens Theater 65
Villa Montalvo Artist Residency Program 203
Vineyard Theatre 65
Virgin Islands Council on the Arts 190
Virginia Center for the Creative Arts 203
Virginia Commission for the Arts 190
Virginia Stage Company 65
VLA Guide to Copyright for the Performing Arts 239
VLA-Columbia Journal of Law & the Arts 239
Voice and Vision Retreat for Women Theatre Artists 154
Volunteer Lawyers for the Arts 239

## W

Walden Residency Program 203
Waldo M. and Grace C. Bonderman IUPUI Playwriting Competition for Young Audiences 108
Wallace—Reader's Digest Opera for a New America, The Lila 231
Walnut Street Theatre Company, The 66
Walt Disney Studios Fellowship Program, The 182
Ward Prize for African-American Playwrights, Theodore 105
Warehouse Theatre Company One-Act Competition 108
Washington State Arts Commission 191
Washington Theatre Festival 56, 102
Wasserman Drama Award, Dale 75
Waterfront Ensemble, The 155
Weissberger Playwriting Competition, L. Arnold 87
West Coast Ensemble 66, 109
West Coast Ensemble Contests 109
West Virginia Division of Culture & History 191
Western Great Lakes Playwriting Competition 109
Whetstone Theatre Company Playwrights Program 155
White Bird Annual Playwriting Contest 109
White Memorial National Children's Playwriting Contest, Jackie 83
White-Willis New Playwrights Contest, The 109

Whittlesey Agency, Peregrine *162*
Wichita State University Playwriting Contest *110*
William Flanagan Memorial Creative Persons Center *204*
William Morris Agency *163*
Williams/New Orleans Literary Festival One-Act Play Competition, Tennessee *104*
Williamstown Theatre Festival *66*
Wilma Theater, The *67*
Wilson Full-Length Play Award, James H. *76*
Wisconsin Arts Board *191*
Wisdom Bridge Theatre Chicago Company *67*
Women's Project & Productions *67*
Women's Theatre Alliance *239*
Woolly Mammoth Theatre Company *67*
Worcester Foothills Theatre Company *68*
Wordsmiths *155*
WOW Cafe, The *240*
Writer, The *249*
Writers & Artists Agency *163*
Writer's Digest *110*
Writer's Digest Books *248, 249*
Writer's Digest Writing Competition *110*
Writer's Guide to Copyright, A *249*
Writers Guild of America, East (WGAE) *240*
Writers Guild of America, west (WGAw) *240*
Writer's Market *110, 249*
Writers' Resources *249*
Writers Room, The *204*
Writers' Studio, The *204*
Wurlitzer Foundation of New Mexico, The Helene *197*
Wyoming Arts Council *191*

**Y**

Yaddo *205*
Yale Repertory Theatre *68*
Year-End-Series (Y.E.S.) New Play Festival *110*
Young Playwrights Festival *111*
Young Playwrights Inc. *111, 241*
Young Playwrights Summer Conference *232*
Youth Theatre Journal *208*

**Z**

Zachary Scott Theatre Center (ZACH) *68*
Zornio Memorial Children's Theatre Playwriting Award, Anna *72*

# About Theatre Communications Group

Theatre Communications Group is the national organization for the American theatre. Since its founding in 1961, TCG has provided a national forum and communications network for a field that is as aesthetically diverse as it is geographically widespread, developing a unique and comprehensive support system that addresses the concerns of the theatre companies and individual artists that collectively represent our "national theatre."

TCG's mission is to celebrate and inspire excellence in the artistry of theatre in America. To carry out this mission, TCG serves theatre artists and nonprofit professional theatre organizations by: recognizing and encouraging artistic diversity; providing a forum for the open and critical examination of issues, standards and values; fostering interaction among theatre professionals; collecting, analyzing and disseminating information within the profession and to others interested in, and influential to, the health of the field; and serving as the principal advocate for America's nonprofit professional theatre.

TCG's centralized services facilitate the work of thousands of actors, artistic and managing directors, playwrights, literary managers, directors, designers, trustees and administrative personnel, as well as a constituency of more than 300 theatre institutions across the country that present performances to a combined annual attendance of over 20 million people.

# Related TCG Publications

**American Theatre**
The national monthly theatre magazine containing news, features and opinion; includes complete texts of 6 plays a year.

**Theatre Profiles**
The biennial illustrated reference guide to America's nonprofit professional theatres.

**Theatre Directory**
The annual pocket-sized contact resource of theatres and related organizations.

**Between Worlds: Contemporary Asian-American Plays**
Edited by Misha Berson, this volume includes works by Ping Chong, Philip Kan Gotanda, Jessica Hagedorn, David Henry Hwang, Wakako Yamauchi and Laurence Yep.

**Coming to Terms: American Plays & the Vietnam War**
Includes works by David Rabe, Terrence McNally, Amlin Gray, Tom Cole, Michael Weller, Emily Mann and Stephen Metcalfe. Introduction by James Reston, Jr.

**In Their Own Words: Contemporary American Playwrights** *interviews by David Savran*

**Moon Marked and Touched by Sun: Plays by African-American Women**
Edited by Sydné Mahone, this volume includes works by Laurie Carlos, Kia Corthron, Thulani Davis, Judith Alexa Jackson, Adrienne Kennedy, Robbie McCauley, Suzan-Lori Parks, Aishah Rahman, Ntozake Shange, Anna Deavere Smith and Danitra Vance.

**On New Ground: Contemporary Hispanic-American Plays**
Edited by M. Elizabeth Osborn, this volume includes works by Lynne Alvarez, Maria Irene Fornes, John Jesurun, Eduardo Machado, José Rivera and Milcha Sanchez-Scott.

**Out from Under: Texts by Women Performance Artists**
Edited by Lenora Champagne, this volume includes works by Laurie Anderson, Laurie Carlos, Lenora Champagne, Karen Finley, Jessica Hagedorn, Holly Hughes, Robbie McCauley, Rachel Rosenthal, Beatrice Roth, Leeny Sack and Fiona Templeton.

**Plays of the Holocaust: An International Anthology**
Edited by Elinor Fuchs, this volume includes works by Nelly Sachs, Peter Barnes, Liliane Atlan, Joshua Sobol, James Schevill and Józef Szajna.

**The Way We Live Now: American Plays and the AIDS Crisis**
Edited by M. Elizabeth Osborn, this volume includes works by William M. Hoffman, Harry Kondoleon, Harvey Fierstein, Susan Sontag, Terrence McNally, Lanford Wilson, David Greenspan, Tony Kushner, Christopher Durang and Paula Vogel. Introduction by Michael Feingold.

**The Substance of Fire and Other Plays** *by Jon Robin Baitz*

**Three Hotels: Plays and Monologues** *by Jon Robin Baitz*

**The Essential Bogosian: Talk Radio, Drinking in America, FunHouse and Men Inside** *by Eric Bogosian*

Pounding Nails in the Floor with My Forehead *by Eric Bogosian*

subUrbia *by Eric Bogosian*

The Gospel at Colonus *adapted by Lee Breuer*

Sister Suzie Cinema: Collected Poems and Performances 1976–1986 *by Lee Breuer*

Three Sisters *by Anton Chekhov, translated by Paul Schmidt*

Cloud Nine *by Caryl Churchill*

The Skriker *by Caryl Churchill*

Tales of the Lost Formicans and Other Plays *by Constance Congdon*

The Illusion *by Pierre Corneille, freely adapted by Tony Kushner*

Love & Science: Selected Music-Theatre Texts *by Richard Foreman*

Unbalancing Acts *by Richard Foreman*

A Lesson from Aloes *by Athol Fugard*

Blood Knot and Other Plays *by Athol Fugard*

My Children! My Africa! *by Athol Fugard*

Playland and A Place with the Pigs *by Athol Fugard*

The Road to Mecca *by Athol Fugard*

Statements: Three Plays *by Athol Fugard with John Kani and Winston Ntshona*

Blood Wedding and Yerma *by Federico García Lorca, translations by Langston Hughes and W. S. Merwin*

Swimming to Cambodia *by Spalding Gray*

Approaching Zanzibar and Other Plays *by Tina Howe*

Coastal Disturbances: Four Plays *by Tina Howe*

Peer Gynt *by Henrik Ibsen, translated by Gerry Bamman and Irene B. Berman*

Self Torture and Strenuous Exercise: Selected Plays *by Harry Kondoleon*

Through the Leaves and Other Plays *by Franz Xaver Kroetz, translated by Roger Downey*

Angels in America, Part One: Millenium Approaches *by Tony Kushner*

Angels in America, Part Two: Perestroika *by Tony Kushner*

A Bright Room Called Day *by Tony Kushner*

Six Plays *by Romulus Linney*

**Reckless and Blue Window: Two Plays** *by Craig Lucas*

**The Floating Island Plays** *by Eduardo Machado*

**Fantasio and Other Plays** *by Alfred de Musset*
Translations by Michael Feingold, Richard Howard, Nagle Jackson and Paul Schmidt.

**Four Plays** *by Marsha Norman*

**The Secret Garden** *book and lyrics by Marsha Norman*

**Shimmer & Other Texts** *by John O'Keefe*

**The America Play and Other Works** *by Suzan-Lori Parks*

**Full Moon and Other Plays** *by Reynolds Price*

**New Music: A Trilogy** *by Reynolds Price*

**The Rug Merchants of Chaos and Other Plays** *by Ronald Ribman*

**Assassins** *by Stephen Sondheim and John Weidman*

**Gypsy** *by Stephen Sondheim and Arthur Laurents*

**Into the Woods** *by Stephen Sondheim and James Lapine*

**Pacific Overtures** *by Stephen Sondheim and John Weidman*

**Passion** *by Stephen Sondheim and James Lapine*

**Driving Miss Daisy** *by Alfred Uhry*

**Jelly's Last Jam,** *book by George C. Wolfe, lyrics by Susan Birkenhead*

**Spunk: Three Tales by Zora Neale Hurston** *adapted by George C. Wolfe*

*Catalogue available upon request*

# TCG Individual Membership

$A$s a *Sourcebook* user, you're invited to become an Individual Member of **Theatre Communications Group**— the national organization for the American Theatre and the publisher of *American Theatre* magazine.

As an Individual Member of TCG, you'll get inside information about theatre performances around the country, as well as substantial discounts on tickets to performances and publications about the theatre. Plus, as the primary advocate for nonprofit professional theatre in America, TCG will ensure that your voice is heard in Washington. We invite you to join us today and receive all TCG's benefits!

## Members Receive These Special Benefits

- A FREE subscription to *American Theatre*—10 issues…complete playscripts…artist profiles…in-depth coverage of contemporary, classical and avant-garde performances…4 special issues—including *Season Preview* (October), *Summer Festival Preview* (May) and *Theatre Facts* (April).
- Discounts on tickets to performances at more than 180 participating theatres nationwide.
- 15% discount on resource materials including *Theatre Profiles, Theatre Directory, ArtSEARCH, PlaySource* and *Dramatists Sourcebook*—all musts for the theatre professional or the serious theatregoer.
- A FREE catalogue of publications.
- 10% discount on all books from TCG and other select theatre publishers.
- Your personalized Individual Membership card.
- Customized TCG Credit Card
- Special discount for Budget Rent-A-Car and Airborne Express
- Up to 60% off regular hotel rate from Hotel Reservations Network

# TCG Individual Membership

## Members get a FREE Subscription to *American Theatre*...

## ...That's a $39.50 Savings on What You Would Pay at the Newsstand...

*American Theatre* magazine, available 10 issues a year, provides up-to-the-minute coverage of the trends, artists and topics shaping American theatre today. In addition to all the hot articles, you'll also receive six full-length plays—the newest works by prominent playwrights like Edward Albee, Tony Kushner, David Henry Hwang, David Mamet, Maria Irene Fornes and George C. Wolfe. Plus four special issues including "Season Preview" in October, listing the complete performance schedules for more than 200 theatres across the U.S.; "Summer Festival Preview" in May, listing theatre festivals worldwide; "Theatre Facts" in April, providing an invaluable overview of the economic state of the American theatre; and "Approaches to Theatre Training" in January, reporting on the opinions, evolution and theory of theatre education in America.

# *Join Now and Save*

## *Receive 15% Savings Off TCG Resources...*

- *Theatre Profiles* provides a historical record of the national theatre movement. Contains comprehensive information on more than 200 theatres nationwide, including production histories.

- *ArtSEARCH,* TCG's twice-monthly national employment bulletin, with more than 6,000 listings of available jobs for the entire spectrum of the arts each year.
- *Dramatists Sourcebook,* the essential annual guide for playwrights, translators, composers, lyricists and librettists, listing hundreds of fellowships, grants and awards, and submission requirements for almost 300 theatres.
- *Theatre Directory,* a handy pocket-sized annual directory providing contact information for more than 300 nonprofit professional theatres and dozens of related organizations.
- *PlaySource,* the national bulletin for new American plays, is published four times a year and contains concise, comprehensive descriptions of hundreds of new plays each year.

## *...and 10% Off Other Publications*

- Save 10% on all TCG publications as well as theatre books published by Nick Hern, Absolute Classics and Ubu Repertory Theater.

## Take Advantage Now and Save!
## Become a TCG Individual Member and Receive
## Extraordinary Benefits

☐ **YES**, I would like a one-year Individual Membership to TCG

    ☐ Individual Membership $35.00 $30.00.

    ☐ Student Membership (enclose copy of ID) $20.

☐ I prefer a two-year membership.

    ☐ Individual Membership $70.00 $55.00.

### Not only would I like to become a member,
### but I would like to take advantage of my discounts right now!
(Discount prices are only good if you are a member. If you are not a member,
please use the full price for your order.)

☐ Please begin my subscription to *ArtSEARCH*.

    ☐ Individual $54.00 $45.90    ☐ Institutional.$75.00 $63.75

☐ Please begin my subscription to *PlaySource*.

    ☐ Individual $20.00 $17.00

### I would like the following resource materials:

☐ *Theatre Profiles 11* $21.95 $18.65

☐ *Theatre Directory* $5.95 $5.00

    (For the first book purchase, add $3.00 for postage and handling. For every book thereafter, add $1.00.)

☐ **TOTAL ORDER** _____

**To order : Send this form to: TCG Order Dept., 355 Lexington Ave., N.Y, N.Y 10017-0217 or Call TCG's Order Dept. (212) 697 - 5230**

☐ **Please charge my credit card.** ☐ VISA  ☐ MC  ☐ AMEX

☐ **Check is enclosed.**

| NAME |
| --- |
| ADDRESS |

| CITY | STATE | ZIP |
| --- | --- | --- |

| PHONE/FAX/E-MAIL |
| --- |

| CARD # | EXP. DATE: |
| --- | --- |

| SIGNATURE |
| --- |
| OCCUPATION/TITLE |

Outside the U.S. add $12 per year (U.S. currency only). Allow 6-8 weeks from receipt of order.